Cursed with a poor sense of direction and a propensity to read, **Annie Claydon** spent much of her childhood lost in books. A degree in English Literature followed by a career in computing didn't lead directly to her perfect job—writing romance for Mills & Boon—but she has no regrets in taking the scenic route. She lives in London: a city where getting lost can be a joy.

Karin Baine lives in Northern Ireland with her husband, two sons and her out-of-control notebook collection. Her mother and her grandmother's vast collection of books inspired her love of reading and her dream of becoming a Mills & Boon author. Now she can tell people she has a *proper* job! You can follow Karin on Twitter, @karinbaine1, or visit her website for the latest news—karinbaine.com.

CHILDREN'S DOC TO HEAL HER HEART

ANNIE CLAYDON

FALLING AGAIN FOR THE SURGEON

KARIN BAINE

MILLS & BOON

First published in Great Britain 2023
by Mills & Boon, an imprint of HarperCollins*Publishers* Ltd,
1 London Bridge Street, London, SE1 9GF

www.harpercollins.co.uk

HarperCollins*Publishers*, Macken House, 39/40 Mayor Street Upper, Dublin 1, D01 C9W8, Ireland

Children's Doc to Heal Her Heart © 2023 by Annie Claydon

Falling Again for the Surgeon © 2023 by Karin Baine

ISBN: 978-0-263-30603-3

04/23

MIX
Paper | Supporting responsible forestry
FSC
www.fsc.org
FSC™ C007454

This book is produced from independently certified FSC™ paper to ensure responsible forest management.
For more information visit: www.harpercollins.co.uk/green.

Printed and Bound in the UK using 100% Renewable Electricity at CPI Group (UK) Ltd, Croydon, CR0 4YY

CHILDREN'S DOC
TO HEAL HER HEART

ANNIE CLAYDON

MILLS & BOON

CHAPTER ONE

REBA RUSHES IN where angels fear to tread... Rebekah Sloane's friends made the joke on a relatively regular basis, and usually she laughed and agreed with them. But right now she wasn't laughing.

She had rushed in, wanting this job because she knew that it would be challenging. When the position of music therapist in the paediatric department of the London and Surrey hospital had become vacant, it had been decided to expand the role from one day a week to two. Reba had sent off her CV, along with a hastily prepared document outlining some ideas for how she might make use of the extra time. She'd been interviewed by the head of rehabilitation services at the hospital and offered the post almost immediately, which Reba reckoned was not so much an indication that her skills were so much better than any other music therapist, but that there were precious few applicants who were willing to put their heads into a lion's mouth for a living.

But if she didn't take on the most difficult jobs, and her interview had left her in no doubt that this *would* be difficult, then how would she ever know what she was capable of doing? Her father had drummed that piece of wisdom into Reba from a very early age, although medicine wasn't quite what he'd had in mind as a career for his only child.

Working with children was always challenging, and that was one of the reasons why Reba loved it so much. Filling the shoes of the previous music therapist, who'd been highly respected and attached to the ward for the last twenty years, made things even harder. The tragic circumstances in which her predecessor had died meant that Reba was going to have to be sensitive and respectful in what she did. She'd been fully prepared for that, by the hospital's grassroots network and her new boss when he'd called her in for a chat before he'd put the final paperwork through the system.

But nobody—not one single person—had thought to prepare her for Dr John Thornton. He rose from his seat, grabbing a pile of papers from the chair opposite his desk so that she could sit down, and suddenly all that Reba could think of was that she'd omitted a very important entry on her list of challenges and solutions.

She could accept gorgeous and move on. Work had taught her how to face challenges, think outside the box and find ways forward. Life hadn't prepared her for someone who made all of the hairs stand up on the back of her neck and her fingers tingle.

He introduced himself, mentioning almost in passing that he was head of department here. And then he retreated behind his desk, taking his heady scent, his spectacular body and that gorgeous kissable mouth with him. Beyond reach. That was actually something of a relief.

'I'm sorry we haven't had a chance to meet up before now. Welcome to the department.'

'Thank you.' Reba smiled, and then decided she was probably smiling too much and straightened her face. 'I'm really looking forward to being here.'

'And that'll be Tuesdays and Fridays.'

'Yes, that's right. I work with private patients for the rest of the time. I gather that your previous music therapist was here for one day a week.'

'Yes, we've only recently received funding to increase that to two. We're all looking forward to working with you in expanding the role of music therapy in the department.'

Yeah. He was saying all of the right things but there wasn't any sincerity in his tone. He looked down at the copy of her CV that he'd plucked from one of the piles of files and papers on his desk, suddenly freeing Reba of the dilemma of deciding whether his eyes were grey or blue. Whatever colour, they were entrancing, and she'd noticed the dark rings beneath them as well. She'd bet they'd taken more than one sleepless night to form.

'Rebekah Sloane. No relation to Hans Sloane, the pianist?'

Good. A much-asked question that had a very simple answer, as long as no one thought too deeply about the realities of the situation. Most people worked that out from the blurb about her education, which skimmed as tactfully as possible over her chaotic childhood, travelling between the world's greatest cities, immersed in the all-encompassing belief that music was the key to almost everything.

'Actually, he's my father.'

He was still scanning the paper in front of him. 'And you play the piano yourself, I see.'

'Yes, I do, but when I'm working I find that sitting behind a keyboard sometimes separates me a little from the people I'm playing for. The violin's my first love, and it's much more portable as well.'

'This isn't a second interview but… I'm just interested…' He seemed to want permission to ask questions. That was fine with Reba, she had any number of answers.

'Yes?' She smiled encouragingly.

'What you do seems very different from a concert hall,

where you're shushed if you don't keep quiet. You're looking for reactions.'

That was generally one of her answers. Dr John Thornton was perceptive, and she should concentrate on what he said, rather than letting those beautiful lips claim her attention.

'That's right. It's one of the reasons why I love playing sea shanties and folk songs, along with popular songs, because it's really hard not to join in and tap your feet. Although I know a little boy who loves Bach and has a whole robotic dance routine worked out to the *Ode to Joy*.'

That made him smile. 'That's not what music therapy is really about though, is it? Entertaining.'

'No, but it's my way in. Music reaches people, and who better to reach than a seven-year-old in hospital?' Hans would disagree with her there. Maybe if she'd grown up calling him *Daddy* then there would be some distinction between the father and the pianist, but Hans had always seemed like a much-loved mentor. She'd worked with what she had, trying to ignore the hurt over his obvious disappointment at her career choice.

It wasn't like Reba to allow her mind to wander during a business meeting, and she swallowed down the temptation to meet his gaze and tell him everything about herself. 'Isn't a connection what every medical professional seeks to establish? It doesn't really matter how someone does it, just that they do.'

There was something about the wry smile he gave in reply, which emphasised the gaunt lines on his face, and told Reba that John Thornton had been reaching out a little too much recently. That he was exhausted and too hurt to maintain his engagement with the people around him. She wondered if anyone had suggested he take a break and find a quiet place to let the sounds of the world flow past him, instead of blowing through him like a hurricane.

'Yes, you're right. Cathy had a very different way of working but…that's not really relevant, is it? No one wants to be told how their predecessor did things differently on their first day in a job.'

That she had an answer for. 'I still have plenty to learn. When I find that I can't take anything from the way that other people do things then I'll reckon I need to give this job up. And I'm very conscious of the need for continuity.'

He smiled suddenly. The first real smile she'd seen from him.

'Cathy may have used slightly different techniques from the ones you're outlining, but her approach was essentially the same as yours. She used who she was to connect with her patients.'

He was fiddling with one of the pens on his desk, and there was more he wanted to say. Reba waited. One of the things that Hans had taught her was that it was best to get your emotions off your chest. It was a good principle, although Hans' habit of shouting at the top of his voice wasn't always the best way to do it.

'I'm sure you already know what happened with Cathy…'

Reba didn't nod. Everyone had their own story to tell about any given situation, and it was clear that John was no exception to that.

'She'd been here for many years, and was very well liked. Cathy had a massive cardiac event in the staff break room here and even though there were doctors on hand, myself included, we couldn't save her. It's been difficult for everyone here.'

'I can only imagine.'

'But that's something *we* need to deal with, and we're

doing so. The recent amendment in structure means that I'm not your line manager and you report direct to the head of rehabilitation, but the staff on the ward here are my responsibility. I'd like to work with you to make sure everything goes smoothly.'

It was nice of him to address the elephant in the room and just come out and say what everyone had gone around the houses in an effort to say tactfully. It would make broaching the subject much easier if she ever needed to. But still his gaunt face and embattled air was ringing alarm bells at the back of Reba's mind.

'I'm sure there'll be no problems…' She'd fallen into the habit of papering over the cracks and that wasn't true. Reba had been told outright that there might be problems, and she'd prepared herself for that. The flash of his grey-blue eyes told her that he wasn't buying it either.

Reba shrugged. 'Actually, I'm sure there may be one or two. But I'm determined to make this work, for me and for you. I think one of the ways I can do that is to accept that everyone would rather not be in the situation of needing a new music therapist, and not take that too personally. Maybe let them get to know me a bit and go from there.'

'Sounds like a constructive start.' His guarded smile crashed against her defences. 'I may be able to contribute something to that. Joanne's our trainee administrator, and when she steps fully into the job she'll be the one to greet new staff and take them on a tour. I asked her to write something up for me as an exercise and she's made a good job of it…'

He was obviously waiting for her reaction, and it occurred to Reba that this might be her first test. 'I'm used to being shown the way to the therapy room and left to get on with things. If Joanne would give me her tour I'd really appreciate it.'

Right answer. John nodded, reaching for the phone and then pausing. 'If you have any clinical questions, or want to know how things are supposed to work, then my door's always open. If you want to know how things *actually* work then Joanne's probably the one to ask.'

'Thanks, that'll save me some time. It usually takes me at least a couple of days to find the person in any department who knows how everything works.'

He nodded. 'Is there anything else you'd like to raise with me, Rebekah?'

'Nothing else. Apart from saying that most people call me Reba.' Rebekah always sounded as if she was in trouble about something, because generally when Hans called her that she was.

He nodded, picking up the phone and dialling an extension number. 'Joanne, Rebekah's here and I'm wondering whether you'll be able to give her the grand tour...'

What's in a name? It was probably just a slip of the tongue, but there was something in the way that John had called her Rebekah that said he was being careful to keep his distance. Maybe he was putting an emphasis on the idea that he wasn't her line manager, by maintaining a degree of formality. Or maybe something behind those beautiful, haunted eyes was telling her that she shouldn't get too close. He'd delivered the perfect welcome chat, and Reba was suddenly conscious that it had been all about how she felt, and he had never once betrayed his own feelings.

Rebekah. It was a lovely name, the old-fashioned spelling making it delightfully hers. But he should remember to call her Reba in future, since that was her preference. John swung his office chair back and forth, staring out of the window. Anyone who passed her in the street might say that she was beautiful, but that wouldn't be doing her justice. She was striking, with bright blue eyes and hair that was almost black, tied up at the back of her head in a slightly spiky arrangement that seemed to defy the laws of gravity. Her jaw was a little too broad and decisive and her gaze a little too frank for conventional beauty, but the effect was electrifying. And the way she moved had a rhythm about it all of its own, as if Reba was dancing to a melody that ordinary mortals weren't able to hear.

Reba. As he mouthed the name silently it almost felt like a kiss. That was going to be the biggest difficulty of all, because John had no time for this. He had a child to look after and a job to do, and both of them required every last drop of his emotional energy.

He had no spare capacity for grief either. Cathy had been a good friend, the mother of two grown-up daughters who'd applied a great deal of common sense to the situation when his sister had died and John had found that being the sole guardian of a four-year-old was a great deal more complicated than being a favourite uncle. Rosalie was five now, and beginning to settle after the upheaval of losing her mother, which was in no small part the result of Cathy's good advice and the good humour with which it had been given.

'You reckon pink?' He could practically see her now, standing in the sunny room that he was decorating as a bedroom for Rosalie. 'You're sure about that, John?'

He'd shrugged. 'Little girls like pink, don't they?'

Cathy had rolled her eyes. 'Sure they do. And they're made of sugar and spice as well...'

'All right. So what colour do you think, then?'

'You could always ask her. Only don't just give her a paint chart and tell her to pick something out. If she's anything like my eldest she'll decide she likes crimson and it'll give her nightmares.' Cathy had smirked at him. 'I made all these mistakes, so you don't have to.'

'How did you do it, then? When you were deciding what colour to paint the crimson over with?'

'Choose a few different colours that you think might be suitable. Then get some tester pots and paint squares on the wall. See if you can get Rosalie to help you with that, and then ask her to choose the one she likes the best.'

It had been good advice. Rosalie had selected a pale apple green, which wouldn't have been John's first choice but actually looked very nice when he'd finished. They'd kept going like that and by the end of it Rosalie had a bedroom that she loved, which incorporated all of the things that he'd brought from her room at home, along with a few new things to delight a child, which Cathy had helped him choose.

And now Cathy was gone, leaving behind a devastated husband and two daughters. John had known he couldn't save her, but tried anyway. And all of his own medical training and the quiet assurance of the cardiac specialist who had arrived and made the call that John had been unable to make…none of that was enough to assuage the guilt he'd felt when Cathy's husband had somehow found it in himself to shake John's hand at the funeral, thanking him for doing his best for her.

But he couldn't stop and feel that grief. Just as he'd been unable to stop and feel the grief when his sister had died. As a single mother, his sister Cara had relied on him to help take care of Rosalie and he'd agreed that he would always be there to look after her if anything should happen to Cara. All that mattered to John now was Rosalie's welfare, and falling apart wasn't going to do anyone any good.

Neither would feeling what he imagined he could very easily feel for Reba. He'd learned that lesson when his partner, Elaine, had made him choose between her and adopting Rosalie, throwing in the warning that coping with a child would be impossible while he was settling in to a new promotion at work and grieving for his sister. He had to kiss a sweet goodbye to thoughts of any relationship because even if a partner did accept that he was a single father, it presented a whole new set of possibilities for loss.

His phone rang, and he jumped. The department secretary reminded him that he was late for ward rounds, and John got to his feet. This was what he did best, pushing everything else aside and getting on with the job in hand.

CHAPTER TWO

JOANNE WAS A bright-eyed, energetic young woman, who clearly spent a bit more time than Reba did deciding what to wear every morning. She shook Reba's hand enthusiastically and started off along the corridor at a jaunty pace.

'This is our therapy room. It's all yours for the two days a week that you're here, which are Tuesdays and Fridays, and the other occupational therapists use it at other times.' Joanne opened the door of a large, bright room.

'What happens if someone else wants the room during my two days?' Reba had fallen foul of room allocation systems in various hospitals before now.

Joanne shook her head. 'They can't have it. It's yours. The department secretary's in charge of the rota for all of the therapy rooms, and she sorts out who can have what if someone's sick or on holiday. I heard that there used to be a very complicated system that relied on a mixture of bribery and seniority, but when Dr Thornton took over the department a year ago it was one of the first things he changed.'

'Thanks, that's a relief. And what about the garden outside? Can I use that when I'm working in here?' There was a pair of doors at the far end of the room, leading out into a paved space, shaded by trees and decorated with tubs of flowers. A low brick wall around the perimeter separated the garden from the rest of the hospital grounds.

Joanne grinned suddenly. 'Yes, this area is for the therapists' use. Cathy held sessions out there all the time when the weather was nice. It's away from the wards so you can make some noise without disturbing anyone.'

'That's great, thank you.'

'Over there is your pinboard.' Joanne gestured towards a large, empty pinboard on the wall. 'And here's your cupboard…'

There was something about the way that Joanne ran her hand across one of the two bright posters that decorated the cupboard doors. Reba hesitated.

'These are Cathy's posters?' Even mentioning the previous music therapist's name seemed a little presumptuous, but Joanne had already done so and Reba reckoned it would be all right.

'Yeah. I should have taken them down when I got everything ready for you, but I left it until later… But this cupboard's yours now.' Joanne began to pick half-heartedly at the sticky tape in the corner of one of the posters.

'Wait… Couldn't we put them somewhere else, maybe on the pinboard?' Reba was new here and she wanted to make her own mark, but sweeping everything of Cathy's away really wasn't the way to go.

'That's a really good idea, but…aren't you going to need all of the space for your notices?'

'I can manage. Do you think it would be nice to keep them?'

'Yes, it would.' Joanne nodded, frowning as she started to peel the sticky tape carefully from the cupboard door. 'This is *your* job though…'

Reba grinned. 'Dr Thornton told me that as well. I appreciate the thought, but I know you're all still thinking of Cathy and my turning up here to replace her can't be easy.'

'He was the one who tried to save Cathy, you know.'

'He did?' Something prickled at the back of Reba's neck.

'Yes, she was sitting in the staff common room, obviously having a cup of tea because it was spilled all over the floor. She had a sudden cardiac arrest. I found her, when I went in to fetch something from my locker...' Joanne's eyes misted suddenly with tears. This couldn't have been the first time that Joanne had spoken about this, but grief required that she repeat it until it hurt a little less.

'I'm so sorry that you had to experience that, Joanne.'

'I ran to find Dr Thornton, but...they said afterwards that she was already gone. He tried CPR anyway... I think we all wanted him to because we couldn't take in what was happening...' Joanne straightened suddenly, wiping her eyes with her hand. 'You don't want to hear about this. Not on your first day.'

The points to note on Reba's list had suddenly become personal. Real people, who cried real tears. Hans would have thrown his arms up in despair at her, but Reba should remember Joanne whenever she was tempted to fall into her father's habit of categorising everything and feeling only the music.

'Thank you for telling me. I can see that this has affected you very deeply.'

Joanne nodded. 'When the cardiac consultant arrived and took over and said...'

'He said that Cathy was gone?' Joanne obviously wanted to talk about this and Reba supplied the words that she seemed unable to say.

'Everyone was really quiet and Dr Thornton was as white as a sheet. I thought he was going to pass out. But suddenly he was organising everything, telling everyone what to do. He took me to his office and gave me a cup of tea, and then called my boyfriend and asked if he could come and take me home.'

'That was kind of him.'

'Yeah. I heard afterwards that he went with the hospital social worker to tell Cathy's family. And he spoke to everyone here as well, telling them what had happened. Most people knew anyway, but he said that he had to speak with everyone so that they got the proper story.'

'Yes, that would have been very important.' And it seemed that none of this had come without a cost, which was written in the creases in John's brow. 'Will you help me with this, Joanne?'

Reba carefully peeled the sticky tape from the cupboard door, carrying the first poster over to the noticeboard that had been assigned to her. When they'd pinned both of the posters up, Joanne smoothing them carefully into place, they took up less than a third of her allotted space.

'There are some things in the cupboard… Tambourines, mostly. Is there anything you've brought with you that you want to put in there?' Joanne fished in her pocket and handed over the key.

'I've got a couple of boxes in my car boot. I'll bring them up later.'

'That's okay, I'll give you a hand carrying them. Then we can go to the wards and I'll introduce you, and then I'll show you the things you really need to know about.' Joanne grinned. 'Ladies' restrooms, and the canteen…'

Joanne's tour had been both thorough and helpful. She'd made a beeline for the people she'd clearly identified as the most helpful on each of the wards, and made introductions. Reba wasn't sure that she'd remember all of the names, but being on smiling terms was a good start. They sat down for lunch together in the canteen, and Reba had decided to ask Joanne one of the questions she'd been saving for John.

'One of the things I like to do if I can is to make music a part of the everyday culture of a department. That's not a part of the therapy that I do but I think it's important.'

Joanne's gaze was animated. 'Because music makes you feel better? That's never a bad thing around here.'

'Yes, exactly. And since today's Friday I thought that I might stay late after work and just play something. It's not a structured thing, more a way of seeing if anyone's interested and comes along.'

'On the violin? What will you play?'

'Anything that anyone wants. Do you have any requests?'

Joanne was obviously thinking about it. 'Dr Thornton would have to give the go-ahead for something like that…'

'That's where I was hoping you might come in. I was wondering if you might ask him and spread the word a bit. Give me some guidance on how to do it without stepping on anyone's toes. If you have time, that is. I don't want to keep you if there's something else you should be doing.'

Joanne grinned. 'No! Nothing else. Dr Thornton said I should help you settle in.' She picked up her phone from the table. 'I'll see what he says right now…'

First-night nerves. Hans specialised in those, and his process was to hurt feelings and fling anything breakable that came to hand against the wall. Reba preferred the more silent approach, her stomach twisting into knots.

Joanne had been a marvel. She'd not only obtained permission from John, but brought some extra chairs into the therapy room and helped fold and stack the tables against the wall. The door from the corridor was closed so that the work of the hospital wasn't disturbed, and those to the small garden were opened so that people could enter that way. Everything was ready and a cool breeze curled around Reba's shoulders, making her shiver. Hopefully, a room full of people and even some dancing would warm things up.

Joanne appeared in the garden outside, gesturing to her to start playing. Reba raised her violin, feeling the comfort of its touch against her cheek, and sound began to stretch out and fill the empty room. A woman was ushered in from the garden and she beckoned to a man behind her, who was carrying a small boy wearing superhero pyjamas. The family sat down in the far corner of the room and Reba segued into the theme tune from the latest superhero film. The boy grinned, climbing down from his father's lap and inching forward towards her. More people started to arrive and Reba played for each of the children, moving amongst them so that those using wheelchairs weren't left out.

She was starting to enjoy herself now. She played music from cartoons and films, advertising jingles and the choruses of popular songs. Then some tunes to appeal to the adults. She saw Joanne leading a little girl with blonde curls into the room, sitting her down on a chair in the corner and then stopping to smile and listen to the music with her.

Now that people were here and engaged, Reba picked up the pace a little. She played a folk tune that was made for dancing, and feet started to tap. As she played, Reba strolled towards the doors that led out into the garden and Joanne got the message, following her out into the evening sunshine to dance.

Everyone was doing their own thing. A couple of the mums were outside now, dancing with the children, and a nurse was making sure that those who shouldn't be running around stayed sitting, fetching tambourines for those who wanted them. A porter who had brought a little girl seated in a wheelchair made sure that she was comfortable out in the garden space and then executed ballroom dance moves with an imaginary partner, which made everyone laugh.

The little blonde-haired girl was still sitting quietly in the corner, looking longingly out of the window at the people dancing in the garden. She was the only child here who wasn't obviously accompanied by a parent or under the watchful eye of one of the nurses, and Reba caught Joanne's eye and nodded towards the child. Joanne waved, beckoning the little girl to come outside into the garden.

She needed a little encouragement, and Reba walked over to where she was sitting. The music drew her from her chair and the little girl followed her outside and started to dance, her blonde curls bobbing in the sunshine.

'Uncle John!' Her shrill voice made Reba look around as she started to walk back to the group who were sitting inside. 'We're dancing!'

Dr John Thornton was standing in the shade of a tree that spread its branches across the entrance of the garden. He'd clearly come in disguise, because apart from his hair and his clothes nothing about him was the same as the sombre man she'd met.

His grin was all for the little girl, but still it sent a tingle down Reba's spine. He seemed relaxed, his shoulder leaning against the broad trunk of the tree as if he had nothing else to do with the next few minutes but to stay and enjoy. Reba poured all of her own joy into the music, wondering if he might be tempted to join the dancing…

No such luck. But when she moved on to a sea shanty, the rhythm of which reflected the movement of the waves and the *heave-ho* of the hoisting of sails, he started to clap his hands along with everyone else. Little victories.

Joanne caught sight of him and hurried across, clearly

worried about what he might think of all of this. A few words, and a smiled retort from John, sent her back to join in with the clapping and the dancing. Reba stationed herself in the doorway between the therapy room and the garden so that she could see everyone and gauge her performance from their reactions.

A quick look at the clock told her that she had time for another dance tune and she chose a pop song this time. Then it was time to slow things down, so that when the children who were on the wards went back they weren't hyped up from all the clapping and dancing. She saw that the little girl had run over to John, and he was sitting on the grass with her.

She should give her attention to everyone equally, even though the pair of them fascinated her. Reba strolled inside, playing as she went, feeling a quiver around her heart that couldn't entirely be put down to the melody she was playing. Even if John was out of sight now he could still hear the music.

At some point, after they'd lost Cathy, John had switched from music radio in the mornings to the sound of muted voices discussing news events that he hadn't bothered to read about in the paper. It was one more step into a world that was quieter and greyer.

He pretended it wasn't happening for Rosalie's sake. But that silent, featureless existence had become a place to retreat to when he was alone. Somewhere he wasn't torn by feelings of guilt and grief, and the endless questions about whether he could have noticed earlier that Cara or Cathy had been ill, and maybe saved either one of them.

He'd intended to just walk down here, make sure that everything was going well and check on Rosalie. But when he saw her, jumping up and down, dancing to the music, he couldn't leave. Rosalie called out to him excitedly and he waved back at her.

Uncle John. Maybe Rosalie did see a difference between the carefree man who'd been her uncle and the one who was now her father, because she didn't often call him *uncle* these days. John stayed beneath the branches of the tree that shadowed the entrance to the garden, watching.

And then he saw Reba. The way she moved, the music and the dancing, seemed to reach out and curl itself around him, leaving him defenceless against the vivid joy that emanated from her.

'Dr Thornton… *Dr Thornton!*' John had been unable to resist clapping along with the music and Joanne brought him back down to earth, a look of worried vigilance on her face. 'What do you think?'

He thought that he wanted to move closer to Reba and touch her. Feel the passion that she harnessed so skilfully. John tore his attention from the dancing and focused on a more acceptable answer.

'It all looks really good. Are you enjoying it?'

'Um…' Joanne shrugged. From the calls he'd received from her during the course of the afternoon, John suspected that Joanne had been so focused on practical preparations that she hadn't reckoned on enjoying this evening.

'All of the patients are supervised?'

Joanne nodded. 'Yes, Reba spoke to the ward manager this afternoon and there are nurses here to keep an eye on things.'

'Then you might like to think about relaxing and joining in now. You've done a really great job with organising this, thank you.' The advice came straight from the mouth of the old Dr John Thornton. The one who had learned how to do his best and then let go of the things he couldn't change.

Joanne grinned suddenly. 'Yes, okay. Thanks, Dr Thornton.'

He could go now. Joanne had walked back to the group of children and was dancing with them. Rosalie seemed to have forgotten he even existed in her excitement. John could go back to his office and finish reading the report he was halfway through...

Suddenly the black and white of print on the page could wait. He wanted this moment for himself. Walking through the gate that led into the garden, John sat down on the grass, watching Reba as she stood in the doorway between the therapy room and the garden. Feeling the glowing exhilaration that he saw on her face. And then the gathering calm as the music began to slow and she segued effortlessly into a slower melody.

Rosalie ran over to him, sitting down on his outstretched legs, her hand tapping his arm in time to the music.

'Enjoying yourself?'

Rosalie nodded. 'Do you like it, Dad?'

'Yes, I do. You want to go home now, or stay until it's finished?'

'Stay!'

Rosalie flung her arms around him as if to make sure he wouldn't move, and John laughed, hugging her back. 'Okay, we'll stay.'

Joanne had insisted on staying to help clear up, and they started to unfold the tables and put them back out, ready for Monday morning. Parents and children were drifting away now and when Reba looked outside John was gone, along with the little girl.

'I saw you talking to Dr Thornton. Was everything okay with him?'

'Yes, he said it all looked really good.'

'The little girl with him seemed to be enjoying herself. That's his niece?' Reba's curiosity got the better of her.

'Yes, Rosalie's his niece. But…' Joanne was interrupted as the last of the parents left the therapy room, calling out a goodbye.

'It was nice to see her joining in with the dancing.' Reba gently steered Joanne back to what she'd been saying.

'Yes, really nice, actually. I'm pretty sure Dr Thornton will give us the go-ahead to do it again.'

'And how about you? Are you okay with that?' It was nice that Joanne already felt involved enough to use the word *us*, and exactly what Reba had hoped to hear.

'Yes, count me in. If you don't mind…'

'Are you kidding? I did the easy bit. You sorted everything out and got everyone to come along.'

Joanne laughed. 'I suppose we make a good team then. I can't play the violin.'

'You've worked really hard to make this a success. Don't you have somewhere to go this evening?' Most people did on a Friday evening. Reba did too, but it was generally home to work out what she might have done better during the week, and how she could correct that next week.

'Everyone's going down to the wine bar for Lizzie's birthday. You should come, they won't mind if we turn up a bit late.'

'Did you introduce me to Lizzie today?' In the whirl of names and faces, Reba couldn't remember a Lizzie.

'No, but that doesn't matter. It'll give you a chance to get to know everyone.'

'Okay, thanks. Why don't you go now, though? There's

not much more to do here, and I'm really grateful for all your help today. I'd hate it if you missed out on some of your evening.'

Joanne paused and then nodded. 'If you don't mind. I'll see you down there then...'

Reba walked back to the hospital car park, deep in thought. One thing about driving home was that she'd been on soft drinks all evening, and sober enough to take in the gossip that had been running around the increasingly unruly birthday celebration.

Lizzie had been opening a stack of birthday cards, reading them all out as she went. There was one from John, and when someone had asked if he was here Reba had heard one of the nurses she'd met earlier bemoaning the fact that he never came to any of these after-work drinks.

'Such a shame. I wouldn't mind getting him drunk one night...'

'Probably why he doesn't come then.' The man sitting next to the nurse chuckled, digging her in the ribs. 'Give him a break, he's a good bloke. Looks after his staff, which is more than some of them do.'

Everyone around the table had nodded in agreement and Reba had stowed the information away for later. It seemed that her own impression, of John's self-contained reserve, was shared by others.

She flipped the remote to unlock her car, and the lights flashed in the darkness. Reba couldn't help being fascinated by John, even if her wish to connect with him, to see him smile, would only distract her from her main purpose. She was here to take on a challenging job, and to succeed. Generally speaking, personal attachments only got in the way of the kind of effort that success demanded.

And she *would* succeed. Hans had taught her that the pursuit of excellence involved single-mindedness, and he was the perfect role model. If he threw things it would be about the music. If he stayed up all night, unable to stop working because something had caught his imagination, it would be about the music. When Hans had shown her love, then that was all about the music that he and Reba shared too.

He'd reacted exactly as Reba had thought he might when he'd found out about her decision to become a music therapist, telling her that she was wasting her talent. They'd patched things up, but things between them had never been quite the same again, and Reba had channelled all of her energy and single-mindedness into proving him wrong. Maybe if he could have been a fly on the wall at the music evening tonight...

He still would have found her a disappointment. Not as worthy of his love as she had been. Reba had come to terms with that now, but couldn't help feeling that she needed to walk that extra mile to deserve the respect of people around her.

Respect was one thing. An understanding with John, a friendship even, was appropriate and it would help her build on the strong foundations that Cathy had laid. Anything more would be a distraction, which threatened to chip away at what Reba had managed to achieve.

She got into her car, feeling suddenly weary. She'd worked out the one thing that she could have done better this week. Getting through to John might have been her first thought when she'd arrived here, but she should be a little more careful with her emotions next week.

CHAPTER THREE

TUESDAY MORNING. TUESDAYS and Fridays were Reba's days, weren't they?

John frowned. Perhaps opening his laptop and taking another shot at the staff roster for next month was a suitable punishment for the thought. Tuesdays and Fridays were music therapy days for his young patients. He really didn't need to think about who was going to be providing the music therapy; all he needed to know was that it was someone who was suitably qualified, and who turned up on the right days.

He'd thought too much about Reba over the weekend, and John had had to remind himself of a few home truths. The days when meeting someone he liked was a simple matter of finding out tactfully whether they felt the same way were long gone. Reba was entrancing, but the life she represented was now lost to him. Just making it through the day, giving Rosalie what she needed and doing what needed to be done here at the hospital was more than enough.

He jumped as a knock sounded on the door of his office. *Now* he was feeling guilty for just thinking about Reba. John rolled his eyes at his own foolishness and waited, and the knock sounded again.

Maybe whoever was outside was carrying something and had their hands full. He got up from his seat, opening the door, and Reba jumped back from it, her eyes flaring in surprise. John realised that he too had started back and that they were now staring at each other.

'Sorry.' Reba was the first to compose herself. 'I didn't hear you call me in.'

'I didn't...' John twisted his lips in what he hoped looked like a suitable smile and not a surprised expression of joy at seeing her so soon after three very long days spent without her. 'Everyone generally just knocks and comes in. If I don't want to be interrupted I'll flip the light on the door, in which case they either come back later or speak to my secretary.'

'Got it... Thanks.' She inspected the small frosted glass panel on the door, which admittedly didn't look too much like an engaged sign when it was off. John walked over to his desk, flipping the remote to activate the panel.

'Oh! Yes, I see. What happens if you're out of your office?'

'The door's locked.'

'Of course it is.' Reba was hovering in the threshold, clearly waiting to be invited in.

'You wanted to speak with me?'

She smiled suddenly. 'Yes, if you have a moment.'

John waved her inside and took refuge behind his desk. Whatever Reba felt, be it joy or uncertainty, the emotion seemed to leak from her, filling the room, and he felt a little more comfortable with a solid barrier between them.

'What did you think of the session on Friday evening?' She didn't wait to get to the question that was obviously on her mind.

'I'd be happy to see it continue, if that's something you'd like to do. I think it will be of benefit.' John closed his mind to the thoughts that crowded in on him. He should forget about the deeply emotional experience of watching Reba play and concentrate on the quantifiable benefits it could bring to the department.

'Was it fun?' She seemed intent on coaxing something more from him.

'My daughter really enjoyed it.' John wondered if it was quite fair to bring Rosalie into it, but he didn't have what Reba seemed to want—couldn't dare to speak about his own reaction.

'The little girl I saw you with? I must have got the wrong idea. I thought someone said she was your niece.'

It would do no harm to explain; everyone here knew what had happened. And his own belief was that the sooner you answered questions honestly, the sooner a difficult subject would go away.

'Rosalie's my adopted daughter. Her mother—my sister—died a year ago.'

Reba's cheeks flushed suddenly, in obvious embarrassment.

'I'm sorry, I didn't mean to…' The look in her eyes said more about compassion than mere words ever could. 'I'm so sorry for your loss. Yours and Rosalie's.'

John nodded the appropriate acknowledgement, trying to distance himself from the feelings involved. 'It was really good to see Rosalie having fun and dancing with the other children. She's still very sad at times.'

'I'm sure she must be. I'm glad she had a good time. If Rosalie would like to come again, I'll make sure to ask her if there's something she'd like me to play…'

'Thank you, I'm sure she'd like that a lot.' John watched as Reba bent, her hair spilling across her shoulders, picking up a large leather handbag and hugging it to her chest. 'Was there something else?'

'Um…no, not really. I just wanted to find out what you thought and ask if it was okay to go ahead and organise another session this Friday evening.'

'Yes, please do.' The words were hardly out of his mouth before Reba got to her feet.

'That's great. Thank you, I'll let you get on.'

Some other emotion that John couldn't define seemed to be pushing Reba on to the next thing on her agenda. She whirled out of his office and John sighed, leaning back in his chair. It seemed that his fascination with Reba just wouldn't let him go, and he was going to have to concentrate a little harder on putting it out of his mind, getting their relationship onto a professional footing, and keeping it there.

Reba was trembling as she walked away from John's office, clutching her bag to her chest. She hadn't shown him the report she'd brought with her, or asked the questions she wanted to ask. She hadn't given the answers she'd prepared to every question he might possibly have asked either.

She walked quickly downstairs to the therapy room, still thinking through the implications of what John had said to her. She knew that he'd been in his current post for a year. And he'd lost his sister a year ago as well, and adopted little Rosalie. Any one of those things was a lot to take on, and all three together…

No wonder he'd retreated behind a wall of professionalism. And when Cathy had died, and John had vainly tried to save her, it must have seemed like the final blow in a whole succession of thunderbolts that had rocked his life.

He'd talked about his sister's death almost as if it had happened to someone else, and it was that disconnection that had shocked Reba the most. In many ways it was admirable that he'd devoted himself so selflessly to his niece and to the department, but he was living in denial and at some point he was going to break.

John Thornton was a man in trouble.

'Not your business, Reba. It's not even close to being your business...' She muttered the words to herself as she opened the music therapy cupboard, sliding the manila envelope that she'd meant to give to John onto one of the shelves. It had felt suddenly unimportant, and it could wait.

What seemed more important was the way that John had reacted to the music on Friday, seeming to relax and spend some time in the moment. Reba hadn't realised quite how precious that was, but she knew now. And she knew that she wasn't just responding to the attraction she felt for him, in wanting to help him.

It wouldn't be easy. Reba's brief conversations with him had given her the distinct impression that John didn't want anyone's help. But not being easy had never stopped her before.

Reba looked at her watch. She had an hour before she was due to see her first patient, and there was work to do.

Little Matthew was her last patient for the morning. He'd been in a car accident, and the resulting head trauma had left him with aphasia, which meant that he couldn't formulate his thoughts into words. Reba knew that she might not be able to help him, but she'd decided that it was worth a try.

'You're on your way to see Matthew? I'd like to join you if I may.' As she approached the four-person ward, John's voice behind her made her jump.

'Of course. Any particular reason?' Reba would actually rather he didn't. John had chosen the patient where she was the least sure of the outcome of her work.

'I'm interested in why you believe Matthew might benefit from music therapy. I thought I might learn something if I kept my eye on this case.'

Was that a nice way of saying that he didn't trust her, and was testing her out? Reba swallowed down her own defensiveness. He wasn't Hans, and he hadn't rejected her for making one decision. But all the same Reba cared what John thought of her and this was unsettling.

She took a breath, stopping and moving to one side in the corridor. It was probably best to have this conversation standing still. 'There's no guarantee of success with Matthew, but I noticed on Friday that he was trying to sing along with the tunes I was playing. I couldn't hear whether he was managing it, so I popped in to the hospital on Sunday, to spend a little time with him.'

'Okay. And what did you find, in this off-duty moment?' There was the trace of a challenge in his tone.

'Walking through the door here makes me on duty,' Reba couldn't help shooting back at him. 'There are documented cases where people with aphasia, who have lost the ability to formulate their thoughts into speech, can respond to music and sometimes even sing.'

'That's not the case for everyone though, is it.'

So this was his issue. It made sense that John might concentrate on numbers and probabilities, in a world where an improbable set of challenges had hit him all at the same time.

'No, but from my observations I think Matthew might. I've spoken to his speech therapist and she's happy for me to do this; she'll be teaching him to slow down and establish a rhythm to help him speak again. I also checked with Dr Curry and she said that it couldn't do any harm.' Matthew's doctor hadn't shown a great deal of enthusiasm for Reba's suggestion, but she hadn't said no either.

'Yes, I spoke with Anna Curry as well. I got the impression that she isn't holding out much hope of this succeeding.' John's expression gave no hint of his own thoughts.

'With all due respect, that's her opinion. If there's a chance I can help Matthew, then I'll take it. Shouldn't we all be taking every chance we have, for each child here…?' Reba pressed her lips together. She'd spoken with Anna Curry without feeling this rush of indignation at her diffidence. Why John?

He held up his hand, as if the feeling in her chest had somehow escaped and was attacking him. 'I agree with you. Anna's an exceptional doctor, but she relies a bit too much on the quantifiable. She'll learn—'

'Music therapy is *not* unquantifiable, John.' Maybe she shouldn't have interrupted him; a brief look of annoyance showed on his face. But somewhere, deep down, even this was welcome because it was an emotion. Any emotion was better than none.

'That's not what I meant. I'm interested in what you're doing with Matthew because I want you to succeed, and I want to learn from that.' He shot her a reproving look, and Reba frowned back at him. He might have said that a bit sooner.

'That's fine, then. You're always welcome at any of my sessions. You're the head of department, after all.' Reba couldn't resist the dig.

'You're not accountable to me. I dare say that the head of therapy will be on my case soon enough if I stand in your way.' John seemed to be intent on splitting hairs, and clearly didn't much mind if she shot back at him. Just as well, because somewhere deep down she wanted this quiet, reserved man to respond to her.

Reba gave a silent nod, ignoring the thought that maybe

she was just trying to annoy him now. That should be the end of it, but John seemed in no hurry to get to the ward to see Matthew, stepping out of the way as a porter approached, manoeuvring a bed along the corridor. They had a few more minutes before she was due to collect Matthew and clearly John was thinking of making use of them.

'Would you characterise yourself as ambitious?'

So now he was getting personal. Fair enough.

'I'm ambitious, and I'm not afraid of trying things out. Is there anything wrong with that?'

'No. As long as it works in our patients' favour then I'm all for a little moving and shaking.'

Right now she was moved to shake him. Hard.

'That's what I'd classify as ambition. Going the extra mile to get results for my patients.'

He nodded. 'I'm wondering—do you have anything else up your sleeve in that respect? I've already seen your Friday evening session working well for the children and their parents.'

It had worked well for John as well, although Reba didn't expect him to admit that.

'I have a few ideas. I'll be finished at six this evening; perhaps you have a moment?' Maybe she should have stayed in his office this morning and shown him the document that she'd wanted him to see.

He shook his head. 'Sorry, I'm picking Rosalie up this evening from the nursery. I'll be around on Friday though, and I'm in early most days.'

'No problem. I'll catch you then.' Reba looked at her watch again, in an indication that they'd be late for Matthew if they didn't go to the ward soon, and he nodded. As she started to walk, she thought she heard John murmur that he'd be looking forward to it.

* * *

Matthew's other injuries from the accident included a broken leg, and he was already in a wheelchair and waiting for his therapy session when they arrived in the four-bed ward. Beckoning to her, the senior nurse gave her a list made by Matthew's mother, noting down all his favourite songs. Reba stopped to ask a couple of questions about how Matthew had been since she'd last seen him, standing so that she could keep an eye on what John was up to.

He walked over to Matthew, squatting down on his heels in front of him. The boy grinned and gave him a wave, and John spoke to him quietly, waiting for Matthew's nod of agreement before he released the brakes on the wheelchair, bringing him over to where Reba was standing.

'Hey Matthew. Are you ready to come and do some work with me?' Reba waited. Giving Matthew time and showing that she was interested in his reactions, however he was able to express them, was important.

Matthew nodded, returning her smile.

'Right then. Shall we go?'

If the thought of working under John's watchful gaze was confronting, the reality wasn't so bad. He sat quietly in one corner of the therapy room, leaving her to start the process of singing the chorus of one of the songs on the list, to see how Matthew reacted. With a little practice and a great deal of encouragement, Matthew was able to reproduce the tune, and then a couple of indistinct words.

'That's really great, Matthew. Well done.' It took a great deal of effort on Matthew's part to do just this, and he needed all of the praise he could get.

'Nice one. Fantastic.' John added his own encouragement.

It was the first—no, the second time that Reba had seen

him really smile. Rosalie had brought that sudden grin to his face, and it had made Reba's knees go weak then too. Perhaps you had to be five years old, or in Matthew's case eight, to get the benefit of it.

It was just as well that he saved the tight-lipped, insincere looking ones for her. That way he could be classed as handsome but a little uptight. Goodness only knew how her already raging pheromones would react if she was the target of the encouragement that he was currently aiming at Matthew.

She was just contemplating the thought when John got to his feet. 'I'm looking forward to hearing what you have to say for yourself in the coming weeks, Matthew. Keep going, eh?'

Matthew nodded and gave him a thumbs-up. John nodded at her and walked quickly from the room, leaving her thumping heart a little time to return to something approaching normal.

'Okay. Shall we try that again, Matthew...?'

CHAPTER FOUR

REBA WAS GOOD at her job. She was patient and kind, giving Matthew exactly the kind of firm encouragement that he needed. When John had looked through the notes she'd written in preparation for joining the therapy team, it was clear that Reba was planning on involving herself in all aspects of the department's work. Comforting children and helping them to express their fears, through playing or songwriting. Making herself available to attend physical and speech therapy sessions, if the relevant therapists felt that she could help out there.

Cathy would have liked her. A lot. Even though Reba's approach was slightly different to hers, Cathy would have felt that the job she was so committed to was in good hands. And she would have admired Reba's passion...

And why would her passion be such a problem to you, John? He could practically see the twinkle in Cathy's eye as he imagined her asking the obvious question.

Because passion wasn't a part of his life any more. He'd taken on a new job that carried heavy responsibility soon after a bereavement and the adoption of a child. That was enough for anyone.

'You don't have anything to prove, John...'

Cathy had said that more than once to him, adding her gentle smile to the mix to soften the blow of truth. Because he *did* have something to prove. Elaine had left him because he couldn't turn away from Rosalie, telling him that he couldn't manage this along with a new job, and she wasn't going to watch him try.

In his own mind, John had questioned whether that was just Elaine's excuse—a reason to stop him from adopting a child—because she'd never questioned it when he'd accepted the new job. But all the same the suggestion had rankled. He knew he could be a good father to Rosalie, and that was what his sister had wanted. He knew that he could take this new job on, carefully ironing out all of the idiosyncrasies that had developed over the years, under a head of department who judged his staff in terms of their expressions of loyalty to him rather than their ability to do their jobs.

And he'd done it.

At a cost, John. If you can't give yourself time to grieve, then you can't move on. And if you don't move on then how can you feel passion...?

Enough! If he wanted to honour Cathy's memory, then stopping having imaginary conversations with her in his office would be an excellent first step. John snapped his laptop closed, tucking it under his arm and grabbing his jacket.

He needed to stop thinking about how Reba's passion had awakened a restless yearning in his own heart and get on with his life. Tonight was pizza night with Rosalie, and arranging smiley faces to eat with his daughter would fix everything.

Why wasn't he surprised to hear a knock on his office door at five past seven on Friday morning? Generally speaking, anyone who worked days and came in this early would be carving out some time to get on with something uninterrupted, and those who worked nights wouldn't be off shift yet. Obviously Reba didn't feel the need to conform to those expectations, and John couldn't help a quickly concealed smile as she burst into his office.

'You wanted to run something past me?'

'Yes. If you have a moment.'

He nodded, motioning her towards one of the chairs on the other side of his desk. Reba took possession of it, and John wondered whether she ever did anything as mundane as just sitting down. Whenever he found himself in her presence, Reba seemed to become the centre of everything. He watched her push her hair back, his gaze running along the curve of her cheek before he remembered not to stare. Reba pulled a manila envelope from her bag, sliding it across his desk.

'This document's just a draft. It's a few ideas, intended to open a conversation about how I might further develop music therapy services in the department. I was wondering if you might get a chance to look it over.'

'Yes, of course. I'd be very interested to see what your thoughts are.'

When he opened the envelope there were two bound copies of the report inside, their thickness telling him instantly that this was probably more than just a few ideas. It didn't look much like a draft either, on the front a vivid design, featuring line drawings of musical instruments and a wash of coloured shapes that curled and blended together like a melody. Reba had obviously put some work into the presentation, and John opened the top copy, scanning the contents page.

'There's a lot here. You're going to have to give me a chance to read this through carefully, but I'll give it my full attention and let you know what I think. Then perhaps we can set up a meeting with the head of therapy—I assume he'll have the last word on this.'

Reba scrunched up her face. John wondered if he'd innocently managed to put his finger on one of the hurdles that she had undoubtedly anticipated.

'The thing is… I gave him a copy of a document very much like this, which was a set of boilerplate ideas taken from my past experience and…he said he liked the look of some of them and I should update it with particular reference to *this* department once I'd got my feet under the table. Then give it to you…'

John was tempted to ask whether Reba really felt she'd got her feet under the table yet, when from what he'd seen she hardly ever even sat down. Even now she was shifting in her seat as if she'd rather be moving. But that would be a little too personal, and probably annoying.

'I see. You're in a position where neither of us will actually take responsibility for doing anything about your ideas.' He saw a flicker of something that looked like a frustrated *yes* on her face. 'In that case leave this with me. I'll take responsibility for it and come back to you with a solid response.'

She puffed out a breath. 'Thank you. I really appreciate that. And you're willing to put some of my ideas into practice?'

He hadn't even read her report yet, and until he had John should manage her expectations. 'Give me time to find out what they are first. And I'll tell you now that I don't intend to implement any changes without first discussing the implications with everyone involved in patient care here. And that's going to take time.'

'So…more red tape.' Reba shot him a look that suggested he was trying to strangle her with it. If he didn't know better John would have reckoned that Reba's ambition was making her forget what she was here for.

But he'd seen her with Matthew. And he'd heard the reports of doctors and ward managers that he trusted, and if Reba's approach was sometimes a little unorthodox it was always patient-centred and effective.

And he could feel a perverse, overpowering desire to see her stop looking so dejected and fight him. If he couldn't contemplate her passion in any other part of his life, it might be okay to allow himself a taste of it here, in the safety of his office.

'There's always red tape. Surely you know that.'

She frowned at him. 'But… John, my ideas are good. They're not just something I've plucked out of the air; they're backed up by my experience and other people's research.'

'And I have to make sure that we can implement them well.'

'I know that but…' Reba finally got to her feet, seeming suddenly to regain her rhythm as she paced back and forth. 'This isn't just about solid therapeutic principles, it's about delight. Making people smile and find a way to face what's coming next. We *all* need to do that, don't we?'

Was the smiling and facing what came next aimed solidly at him? Irrespective of Reba's intentions, John felt it like a blow to the chest.

'We need to do our jobs, Reba. You know full well that isn't all about delight.' He struck back unthinkingly now, hurt by the idea that Reba might think he wasn't coping.

'But you're happy for this evening to go ahead, at least?'

He'd already said yes. And he really didn't want to think any more about the feelings that last Friday night had engendered. The way he'd wanted to touch her, to feel the passion that she harnessed with such skill.

'I've given you my answer on that.'

'Thank you.'

Something about the way she marched back to the chair she'd been sitting in to fetch her handbag told him that her thanks were just another weapon in Reba's arsenal. John ignored the gesture, putting the reports into his in-tray with rather more of a flourish than he'd intended.

But Reba was clearly not finished with him yet. She got halfway to the door and then whirled round, her hair flying in synchronicity with the movement, in an expression of something that tore at his heart. A fluidity of emotion that he'd lost somewhere along the way.

She wasn't thinking any more, she was simply doing. A force of nature, seeming to bear down on him like a hurricane. This was the Reba he'd seen on Friday, who'd captured everyone's hearts with her music.

John moved back as she leaned over his desk. There was no arguing with a hurricane, it just went its own way and blew itself out when it was ready.

'I was taught never to walk away from a disagreement. Throw something, get it out of your system and move on.'

Ripping the blank sheet of paper from the pad in front of him, she screwed it up into a ball and threw it. It hit the wall and dropped into the wastepaper bin. Good shot.

'Am I supposed to take that as a peace offering?' John unsuccessfully tried to keep himself from smiling. If he engaged with this any more than he already had, who knew how else he might be tempted to engage with Reba?

'No. You can take it as a temporary respite. I'm not going to give up on this, John.' She jutted her chin towards him.

John met her gaze. 'Good. Looking forward to that.'

Her scent lingered for a moment as she left the room. Not *quite* slamming the door behind her, but John jumped anyway.

He stared at the door, wondering whether she'd be back with any last words for him. Hoping she might but wishing she wouldn't, all at the same time. His heart was pounding in his chest, and if the room seemed to have escaped any permanent disruption, he certainly hadn't.

John pinched the bridge of his nose, wondering whether he shouldn't have just taken the report, thanked her and left it at that. But something told him that none of this was about the things they'd acknowledged. It was about the clash of unacknowledged passion that seemed to hover in the air whenever they came within fifty feet of each other.

He was going to have to stop thinking with his heart and start using his head. Wanting to see Reba again, and indulge in throwing a few more things around with her, wasn't going to help in terms of getting things done today. And getting through the day, doing his job and keeping Rosalie safe and happy, was all that he could realistically expect at the moment.

Reba wanted to lock herself away in the therapy room and hide. What on earth had she been thinking? Throwing things, even if a balled-up piece of paper, couldn't do any damage. Practically declaring war on the head of department...

The answer was that she *hadn't* been thinking. She'd acted with her emotions, and that was never a good idea. She knew as well as John did that change took time, discussion and, most of all, a light touch. She'd never clashed with anyone, or pushed for her ideas to be heard like this. The report she'd written had been intended to support her application for this job and show that she did have ideas, and it had been the head of therapy who'd suggested that she pass it on to Dr Thornton when she felt the time was right.

But suddenly it had become important to her. She'd worked all weekend and a couple of evenings this week, updating and perfecting it. Reba really didn't want to think about what had driven her to do that, but she couldn't help it. Growing up with Hans, she'd learned that love was inextricably linked with achievement. And she'd found herself pushing to achieve something that really should have waited, in order to gain John's approval.

She wondered briefly whether John would raise her behaviour this morning with the head of therapy, and dismissed the thought. It hadn't taken long for her to find out that everyone in the department reckoned him to be an honest and fair boss. All the same, it would be best if she kept her head down for a little while. And maybe she could just hold on to a little of that warm, reassuring hope that John would like some of the ideas she'd presented…

It had been a busy day, and Reba was tired. Maybe that was why these second-night nerves felt more acute than the first-night ones had been. She'd seen John a couple of times as she'd moved around the department today and each time he'd acknowledged her with a smile, which Reba had quickly returned. It seemed that he'd taken her suggestion of moving on at face value, and she was grateful for that and didn't want anything to go wrong tonight.

It was a warm evening and Reba opened the doors into the garden, her stomach twisting into knots as she saw John walking towards her with Rosalie. The little girl was jumping up and down in excitement and John let go of her hand, letting her run ahead of him into the garden.

'Hi Rosalie. Are you coming for the music?'

Rosalie nodded, suddenly shy.

'I was hoping you'd be here. It wouldn't be the same without you. Would you like to choose a song for me to play?'

'Yes!'

Reba chuckled. 'Okay, you think about what you want and make sure to come and tell me.'

'Thank you.' John had caught up with his daughter, and when Reba looked up at him he was smiling.

'It's my pleasure.'

'Hey Rosalie.' Joanne appeared at the doors into the garden, holding a large carrier bag. After greeting Rosalie she beckoned to Reba, who left John and his daughter alone for a moment.

'What do you think? I went to my cousin's little girl's birthday party at the weekend and these were left over.'

Reba reached into the bag, drawing out a sparkly wand from the pile. 'They're brilliant!' She grinned, tapping Joanne on the head with it. Joanne laughed, mimicking a sudden transformation into a princess.

'And there are some fairy lights. They're the old ones from our tree, but I got them PAT tested and they work fine.'

'Joanne, you're a marvel. Thank you.' Reba felt a small body leaning against her leg and looked down to see Rosalie, her eyes fixed pleadingly on the sparkly wand she was holding. Joanne laughed, leading her away to choose her favourite from the bag.

When she'd started playing all of her fatigue and worry had disappeared. Reba had seen John on the outskirts of the group, circulating amongst the parents and children. Talking to everyone, joining in, but somehow still as separate from everyone as he always was.

The reserved smile gave it away. John was very definitely still at work.

Still buzzing from the music, she took the opportunity of John standing alone for a moment to approach him.

'What did you think?'

His smile faded suddenly, and that was something of a relief. Reba wanted his opinion, not pleasantries.

'I see you've been putting your own principles into practice. Letting people contribute and feel ownership, and allowing it to grow organically. When I spoke to Anya, she said she'd heard about this on the grapevine and decided to come along and see what it was all about.' He nodded towards the receptionist for the department, who'd collected her two-year-old from the hospital nursery and brought him along.

'You thought I'd been persuading people to come?'

John nodded. 'It had occurred to me. Clearly I was wrong, this seems to be gaining its own momentum.'

No smiles. If anything there was an undertone of hostility between them, but John had kept an open mind and was being honest with her. That seemed more intimate than anything else he'd done so far this evening.

'I stick to what my experience tells me will work. The same as you do.'

'What happens when you find you have more people than you can handle?'

'I don't think that'll be an issue for a while. I'm expecting fewer people once the novelty wears off. We'll deal with that if it happens. I'm sure you've gathered from my report that I advocate a very flexible and responsive approach to this kind of activity.' She let him know that she'd noticed he'd read at least some of the report that she'd given him this morning.

'Right, then. Well, have a good weekend…'

'You too. Thank you, John.'

His impassive nod was better than even the real smile that he gave when he looked around for Rosalie, calling to her that it was time to go now. Reba watched him walk away holding Rosalie's hand, his head bent towards his daughter's excited chatter.

John was a challenge. She'd always known he would be, but so far he'd managed to surpass even her wildest dreams. But she knew now that she could meet that challenge, although Reba wasn't sure what the cost might be.

CHAPTER FIVE

TUESDAY MORNING. TWO whole days at the weekend to think and prepare for the week ahead. She knocked on John's door at half past eight in the morning, and saw him look up from his laptop screen as she entered.

'You're late this morning.'

She reckoned he was referring to her presence in his office rather than what time she'd entered the building. Reba ignored the comment and laid the leaflets she'd printed at the weekend in front of him on his desk. John glanced at them and nodded.

'They look nice. Do I have anything to worry about?'

'Not if you don't mind orange.' The image on the front was an adaptation of the one that adorned the report she'd given him, and Reba had wondered on her way up here whether she'd overdone the bold orange splash of colour at the centre of the image.

'Nope. Orange is good.' He gestured towards the chair opposite him and opened the trifold leaflet. Reba watched him as he read the contents of it carefully.

'Looks good. I like your idea of making it a personal invitation to the Friday music evening. I assume you're intending to write each child's name inside.'

'Yes, that's the idea. Is it okay if I give some to each of

the ward managers, so they can distribute them as they see fit?'

John saw straight through the question. 'You're asking me? You're at liberty to spread the word about any of your agreed activities.'

'I know you're watching what I do, John.'

He leaned back in his seat, the flicker of a smile on his face. 'Fair enough. I think it's a good idea to have the ward managers decide whether a child or their parents should be given an invitation. They see everyone and not just the children who are referred to you. Is that okay?'

'It'll do.' Reba returned his look of amused confrontation, feeling a quiver of excitement in her stomach. It was good to see him after three days spent thinking about him. And *really* good that he'd liked what she'd done.

She took the leaflet from his grasp, writing his and Rosalie's names into the box intended for that purpose. Then she handed it back to him.

'Thanks. Anything else?'

'No, that's all for this morning.' Reba was going to quit while she was ahead this time.

'Okay. By the way, I finished reading your report over the weekend, and I'm just going through it again to add a few comments. You're free on Friday morning some time?'

Just when she was feeling in control of the situation. John really did know how to command the last word.

'Half seven?'

He nodded. 'Yep, I'll have my response ready by then. Look forward to discussing it with you.'

Reba had endured the pleasures of seeing John during the course of the day on Tuesday, telling herself that she could handle the way his grey-blue eyes always seemed a lot bluer when he smiled. The thrill she felt whenever she saw him, and the way she wanted to touch him.

She'd spent Thursday evening, and a large part of the following night, trying not to worry about John's reaction to her report and failing spectacularly. After four hours' sleep, she assessed the queue at the hospital coffee shop and decided that she didn't have time to order and get upstairs for seven-thirty.

'I suppose if we're both late then neither of us is.' She heard John's voice behind her.

'Hmm. Logical.' Reba joined the queue with him. He somehow managed to manoeuvre his way in front of her before they got to the cash desk, and paid for her coffee. Reba smiled a thank you, allowing herself to think of this as a kind gesture from a man she was beginning to like a lot. As long as she kept the lust out of it, that was appropriate.

They walked up to his office together, managing to keep the obligatory conversation about how the last few days had gone for each of them to the minimum, since it appeared they'd done much the same as they always did. Reba had worked, and John had got by. But they sat down on either side of his desk with a little more relaxed joviality than was usual between them.

'I was really impressed by your report.' He started off with a smile. 'I've made a few notes in the margins but they're really just points for discussion.'

John reached into his briefcase, taking out one of the copies of the report and leaning across to hand it to her. Reba took it and opened the front cover, leafing through.

His bold, clear handwriting was everywhere. Questions, points to consider…even a few remarks about passages that he particularly liked. John had been through everything she'd done with the same meticulous care that Hans took…

She should be pleased. She should thank him for the time he'd taken to do this. But all that Reba could think was that a man she cared about had applied his talent and knowledge to something she'd done. With that came the possibility of rejection and disappointment.

She blinked away the tears, making sure that John didn't see them. Took a sip of her coffee in the hope that it would steady her a bit, but it didn't.

'Thank you. I'm going to have to take some time to read all of this, but I really appreciate your having given it all such careful consideration.' She'd stopped to read some of the points that John had made, and they were good ones.

'My pleasure.' He seemed to have noticed her discomfiture. 'I hope you understand that my motives are to try and make this all happen, and not to throw a spanner into the works.'

That just made it worse. If he'd been a little more confrontational about it, Reba could have dealt with that. She knew how to stand up to John, and that he didn't react badly to her doing so. As a matter of fact, there seemed to be times when he enjoyed it as much as she did.

'Yeah… Yes, I understand. Thank you.' Reba gathered her bag and coat, getting ready to leave. An hour on her own, reading through his comments and convincing herself that this was all okay, and then things would seem a lot different.

'There was one other thing…that I wanted to raise with you personally.' The sudden crease in his brow told Reba that he was no more at home with the idea than she was.

'Of course…' She steeled herself for whatever was coming.

'I'm very happy for you to involve others in this but I have two concerns. Firstly that you're not asking people in the department to do more on top of their already considerable workload.'

Reba breathed a sigh of relief. She could answer that. 'That's not my intention at all. If anyone wants to come to something they're welcome. I'm going to be the one doing all the work.'

'It's a lot for just one person. From what I've seen already, you're spending a great deal of time on this.'

'It won't take any time away from my clinical work with patients.' Reba had learned all about commitment from Hans, and there was no such thing as skimping in one area to give time to another.

'That wasn't something that occurred to me. I'm just concerned that you're using too much of your own time on this.'

Pastoral care? Probably not. John knew exactly how things worked. These were questions he might ask his own staff, but if they were asked of her they'd be asked by the head of therapy. This was different, one friend caring about another. That was the part that really hurt.

Leave. Now. Give him some empty reassurance that this really didn't take as long as it sounded, which would get the message across that what she did with her time outside the hospital wasn't any of his concern.

Reba stayed in her seat. 'John, there's something I want to say.'

'Yes?'

'*You* need a break. Maybe music isn't your thing, but you need to let off a bit of steam.'

His face was suddenly blank, devoid of any emotion. This was exactly what she was talking about…

'I'll take that under advisement.'

'No, you won't.' Anger…passion…maybe a mix of the two began to rage in her chest. 'You're clearly tired and you've given so much that you don't have much more to give. What happens when there's nothing left?'

Something stirred in his face. The same kind of dangerous passion that she felt. They'd been playing with fire, allowing competitiveness and confrontation to shape their relationship. Reba had been using it as a barrier to contain her raging feelings, and she should have known that was never going to work, because it had slipped so easily into open confrontation.

'Thanks for the advice. But aren't you crossing a line here?'

That was the last straw. He'd started this.

'Yes, I'm crossing a line. One that you've drawn because you won't take anything from anyone here, because you're the boss and you're supposed to look after everyone else. Well, you're not *my* boss and so I'm going to tell you what everyone else can't.' The words came out in a mess of emotion.

'So now we're getting down to it, are we? You've decided to make a project out of me?' He got to his feet, raw power seeming to emanate from him. It sent shivers down Reba's spine. 'That's up to you, but I can tell you now that I'm not a willing participant, and frankly it's a bit of an insult.'

'There's no insult intended. I see what I see and I'm concerned. As a...'

Colleague? Not really. She wasn't strictly part of his department. Friend? She'd known him for two weeks. Someone who felt drawn into caring about him? Too embarrassing to admit.

'...as a musician.' Reba frowned. That wasn't it either.

Something seemed to break inside him, and he threw up his hands. His frustration washed over her like a great, exciting wave.

'Right. So you play a few well-chosen tunes, and everyone flocks to your bidding. Who are you, the Pied Piper of Hamlyn?'

'No! That's not what I mean at all.' She'd meant that she dealt in emotion. Not necessarily the kind of passion that seemed to be escaping from both of them now, hitting the walls with such force she could almost feel them shake. She didn't fully understand this desperate, glorious over-reaction. It came from a connection she felt with John that was far too complicated to name.

'Then what do you mean, Reba?' He planted his hands on his desk, leaning forward. 'Just tell me now so that I know what to expect and I can make arrangements to avoid it.'

As if she was going to back off now. The other side of his desk was a step away and she took it, staring him down. Staring at least because neither of them was going to give way and she would have been disappointed if John had.

'I mean that I'm a therapist. I'm trained to recognise the signs when someone's in emotional overload and I'm trained to offer help if I can.'

'Thanks for the offer, then. I'll decline…' He gritted the words out. 'And, by the way, I'm a doctor. I'm trained to recognise the signs when someone's in physical overload. You're excellent at your job, but sometimes you need to know when to let go of it and take some time for yourself. You want some help with that?'

Clearly that wasn't an offer. 'I work hard. I'm not ashamed of it. When did that hurt anyone?'

He rolled his eyes. 'You really want me to make a list of the kinds of things that happen when you don't get a break?'

They'd worked their way round in a circle. The only thing left to do was to forget their differences and channel that passion into something a little more intimate, or leave. Turning quickly, Reba grabbed her jacket and bag and headed for the door.

'Go ahead and make that list, John. You might see something there that strikes a chord and, who knows, you might even take the wild step of following your own advice, since you don't seem to want to listen to anyone else.'

She slammed the door behind her. Reba wasn't a big fan of slamming doors, she'd heard enough of that when she was a child, but sometimes it was just something you had to do.

Reba. Reba…

This had been inevitable from the first moment he'd seen her. Everything had been leading up to this sudden loss of control. John turned from his desk, pacing for a while like a caged animal. Then he took a couple of breaths.

The smile when he thought of her face, bright with anger and even more beautiful, wasn't appropriate. Nor was the way he'd wanted to follow her, catch her arm and make her see him. Make her understand the hurt he felt, in the hope that she might battle it on his behalf. She didn't need to be gentle with him—plenty of other people had tried gentle and failed. What he needed was a raging warrior, and he saw that in Reba's eyes.

He heard a knock on his door and jumped. John looked around his office to see if there were any signs of the battle that had taken place, before smiling at Joanne.

'Hey. You're early.'

'Yes, I decided to do eight until four today, so I'd have some time to help Reba with the music tonight. If that's okay…'

'Of course. As long as you're here during your core time that's entirely up to you.' The office staff were on flexihours and expected to work an eight-hour day and be in the office between ten and four. 'You seem to really enjoy it.'

Joanne smiled. 'Yes, I do. It's nice to let off a bit of steam at the end of the week, and I like seeing the children enjoy themselves.'

John nodded. Joanne very clearly wanted to do this, and felt under no pressure. 'What was it that you wanted?'

'Did you get a chance to sign those timesheets I passed over to you yesterday?'

They could have waited. Perhaps Joanne had really popped in to show him that she was here, so that he wouldn't question it if she wasn't at her desk after four o'clock. He grinned at her, feeling an inexplicable impulse to laugh. As regrettable as his shouting match with Reba had been, there was something about her passion that always made him feel alive.

'Sit down, I'll do it now.' John reached for the folder on his desk, flipping through the admin timesheets and signing them all, pausing when he got to Joanne's.

'This is a timesheet, Joanne. Not a work of fiction.'

Joanne's eyes widened in alarm. 'What's wrong with it?'

'You've put down nine till five for the Friday before last. You were at the admin meeting at eight in the morning, and you didn't leave until well after six-thirty that evening.'

'Oh.' Joanne was clearly pleased that he'd noticed. 'Well, yes, but that was Reba's first music session, and I was helping during the afternoon as well. So it kind of evens up, doesn't it?'

'No, it doesn't. I assigned you to helping Reba with whatever she needed that day, and when you came to me to get my go-ahead for the evening session I distinctly remember asking if you wouldn't mind keeping an eye on how it was all going.' He gave Joanne a kindly smile, to fix it clearly in her mind that this wasn't a telling-off.

'I have to put that down then?'

'For that day, yes. If you want to continue to go to the sessions, for your own enjoyment, then you can give it a miss on the timesheet. Does that sound fair?'

'Yes…' Joanne leaned over, grabbing the timesheet and carefully altering it, adding her initials to the amendments.

'Thank you.' John took the timesheet back and scribbled his signature at the bottom. 'Don't think I don't notice how conscientious you are about your work, Joanne.'

'Thanks…' Joanne was positively glowing with pleasure now. She seemed to be reacting far better than Reba had to the suggestion that she make more of a distinction between work and free time, although John had to admit that age, seniority and the fact that it was his business to look out for everyone in the department might have something to do with that.

'Is Rosalie coming along tonight? I can take her if you're busy. Unofficially, of course.'

John chuckled. 'That's really kind of you. I do have to work but my parents' regular Friday night dinner has been cancelled for this week, so my mother's going to bring her. I appreciate the offer though. Thank you for thinking of Rosalie.'

'Right then. Well, I'll look forward to seeing her and…' Joanne picked up the folder from his desk. 'Better get on.'

'Yep. Have a good day, Joanne.'

'Oh. Yes, you too…' Joanne bounced out of the room, grinning.

John leaned back in his seat, putting his hands behind his head. Maybe Reba did have a point about him needing to let off steam a bit from time to time. The whole episode had been frustrating, enraging and painful, and his first impulse was to try and forget all about it. But however challenging the truth was, it was still the truth.

CHAPTER SIX

REBA HADN'T SEEN John all day. Maybe she could just avoid him for a while, and pretend that what had happened this morning was all part of the only half-serious confrontations they'd had up till now. That didn't seem like a way forward. The sudden explosion had been waiting to happen, and neither of them could back away from it now.

Meanwhile she could concentrate on the here and now, and playing for whoever chose to attend the music hour. Reba closed her eyes, her fingers on the neck of her violin, going through the mental exercises she used to focus herself. They didn't seem to be working quite as well as they usually did.

A banging sounded on the doors that led out into the walled garden. Reba opened her eyes and saw Rosalie, pressing her nose against the glass. Sudden joy made her catch her breath. John had decided to come tonight.

Or…not. As she opened the door and Rosalie rushed inside she saw an older woman hurrying to catch up with her.

'Rosalie…' The woman gave Reba an apologetic smile. 'I'm sorry. Rosie and I were just looking for the music session. I suppose we must be in the right place.' She gestured towards Reba's violin.

'Yes, you are. You're the first to arrive.'

'Is it all right if we join in? I'm Babs Thornton, Rosalie's grandmother.'

She could see the resemblance now. Babs had the kind of ready smile that Reba reckoned John might have if he actually allowed himself to express any emotion without thinking about it first, and the same grey-blue eyes.

'Of course, everyone's welcome. I'm so pleased that you came.'

'Rosalie hasn't stopped talking about it and John tells me you've done a marvellous job...'

Had he, now? Reba felt her ears begin to redden. Interrogating his mother about what else he might have said was tempting but a very bad idea, and she made do with a smile and a thank you.

'This is Reba, Grandma.' Rosalie had come to rest beside her grandmother. 'I help her play the violin.'

Babs smiled, winking at Reba. 'Well, that's very good of you, Rosalie.' She held out her hand and Reba took it. Babs' handshake was surprisingly firm and businesslike.

'Now, we'd better give these to Reba, eh, Rosalie...' Babs reached into the bag she was carrying and produced two tins, giving the smaller one to Rosalie to hand over.

'Cakes! Thank you so much, they're beautiful!' The tin contained a dozen iced fairy cakes.

'There are more in here...' From the weight of the second tin, Babs had clearly made sure that there would be enough for everyone. 'The rather dodgy decorations are mine and the nice ones are Rosalie's.'

'I'll go and see if I can find a plate for them.'

'Oh, don't worry about that. I'm sure people can manage to take them out of the tins. I stopped off at the staff canteen and swiped some serviettes.' Babs produced a packet from her bag. 'I used to work here, so they know who I am.'

'What did you do?' This felt like going behind John's back and asking about his private life, but Babs had proffered the information and it seemed rude not to show some interest.

'I was a neurologist. John dallied with the idea of neurology when he was at medical school, but then he rotated to Paediatrics and after that it was all he ever wanted to do.' Babs' gaze focused over Reba's left shoulder and she turned to see Matthew and his mother in the doorway.

She whispered an, 'Excuse me,' to Babs, and went over to greet them.

'Are we too early?' Matthew's mother looked around the room.

'No, we'll be getting started very soon. Hello, Matthew...'

Matthew responded with a thumbs-up, and Reba smiled, shaking her head. Raising her violin, she played the chords that Matthew had been practising his hellos to.

Matthew replied with not just a hello but the words *music* and *mum* to indicate why he and his mother were here.

'That's brilliant, Matthew. Well done.' Reba grinned at his mother. One of the best things about helping a child to speak again was to see their parents' faces when they first started to say *Mum* and *Dad*.

'Wonderful!' Reba turned to see Babs' hand flying to her mouth. 'Sorry. Force of habit. Not interfering... Rosalie, shall we go and sit down now?'

Babs and John had survived the same tragedy but it appeared they'd done it in different ways. Reba decided not to ponder on that too much and saw Matthew's mother going over to the corner where Babs was now sitting, obviously introducing herself. Babs made room for Matthew's wheelchair and the two women sat chatting together as Rosalie ran over to Joanne, who was shepherding some of the unit's young patients into the room.

It was chillier this evening and the senior nurse had recommended they stay inside. Joanne helped give out the percussion instruments from the cupboard and Reba concentrated on getting the children to play this time. She knew some of her patients' favourite songs now, and when she played Matthew's she saw him nodding to the music, his lips moving as if he was trying to sing. Babs leaned towards him to listen, giving his mother an encouraging nod and a smile...

Everyone had gone home. It had been a good evening. The parents were getting to know each other and the children knew that they could request their favourite songs. Reba had finished off as usual by slowing down the pace, and after the children were back in their wards some of the parents stayed to chat together. This was one of the things that Reba had hoped would happen, that people would start making connections with each other.

She sat on the wall that divided the small therapy garden from the rest of the hospital grounds, wrapped in the large woollen jacket she kept in the car. Lights glimmered from the wards through bright patterned curtains, and on the top floor of the long three-storey building she could see the light in John's office, becoming brighter by the minute as dusk fell.

She saw him at the window, looking out and stretching his arms. The bright shadow of a man who seemed to haunt her every waking moment. Reba froze, hoping that she was hidden amongst the dark, anonymous shapes of the trees. John seemed to look down for a moment, but then turned away from the window.

Ten minutes later she was still there, still pondering the events of today. John's light flipped off and the slim connection that seemed to bind them, keeping her out here in the darkness, snapped. She should go home, pour herself a glass of wine, try to forget about the mistakes she'd made, which hadn't seemed like mistakes at all when she was making them…

That was probably the definition of a mistake. Something that seemed like a good idea at the time but turned out not to be. A cool breeze moved in the trees and she shivered, wrapping her jacket around her a little more tightly.

The door from the therapy room opened and closed behind her. John walked out into the garden, swinging his long legs over the wall and sitting down, a full two metres away from her.

'I should apologise. But—'

Reba shook her head. 'It's me that needs to apologise.'

John thought for a moment, staring into the darkness. 'Can either of us say that we're not planning on doing this again? An apology's no good without that.'

'No. I can't.'

Their mutual attraction—Reba knew that John felt it too—and their confrontational style. The passion of an argument was only ever the quickening of a heartbeat away.

'Are you free on Sunday?'

Reba stared wordlessly at him. Even now, with the light shining across his face, John was impossibly attractive. Magnetic even, because magnets had the power to attract and repel with equal force.

'You've booked brainwashing sessions for us both?' She ventured a joke and he smiled suddenly.

'I reckoned that might be the measure of last resort. I was

thinking lunch, at my place. Me and Rosalie. It's a little late to ask but if you don't have anything planned…'

Okay. Rosalie was the first thing to note about the invitation. Her presence would stop anything adult, such as a passionate argument. The second thing to note was that he'd included an excellent get-out clause for her. Most people had their Sundays planned by Friday evening.

'Sunday lunch?'

He shrugged. 'Yeah. Chicken probably, with roast potatoes and a few trimmings. Unless you're a vegetarian, in which case I'll think of something else…'

'I know what Sunday lunch is. I'm just not sure what I've done to earn the invitation.'

He shrugged. 'I reckon we have two options. Sit down somewhere neutral and get to know each other, or soundproof my office and wait for the next time. The first isn't quite as expensive or disruptive as the second.'

Or they could avoid each other completely. She was suddenly very grateful that John hadn't put that one on the table.

'Okay. I'd like to bring a dessert if that's okay. Just to show my commitment to the idea.'

'That's much appreciated. Maybe if we get to know each other a bit more, cut each other a bit of slack, then we can both apologise with a clear conscience.'

It was a good thought. They were trapped in a fascination with each other that wasn't going to go away, and making their peace wasn't just a good idea from a work point of view, it was something that Reba wanted. It seemed that John wanted it too.

'That would be nice, thank you for suggesting it. What time should I come?'

'Does any time between twelve and one suit you?'

'That's fine. I'll be there.'

John nodded. 'Thanks. I'll see you then.'

It was only after he'd got to his feet and was halfway back to the doors into the therapy room that it occurred to her.

'John. Where do you live?'

Reba thought she saw him smile in the darkness. They'd only met two weeks ago, but somehow it felt that they'd known each other for a long time, and she should already know where he lived.

'Eight Marvell Avenue. You turn left by the cinema on the High Street and then fourth right. Got your phone?'

Reba took her phone from her pocket and he rattled out his number. Then he turned, walking away.

This was practically a work lunch. There had been no need to spend fifteen minutes in the supermarket, sorting through the vegetables to find the best ones, and certainly no need to tidy up quite so thoroughly. Rosalie had decided to imitate his efforts and rearrange her toybox, and when the doorbell rang at exactly half past twelve, half its contents were still scattered across the floor.

His daughter crowded at his legs as he opened the door, jumping up and down with excitement. Reba was standing on the doorstep, looking wonderful in a boldly patterned wraparound skirt, secured at her waist with a wide leather belt, a black top and a thick knitted woollen jacket. She was always striking—her dark hair and strong features made sure of that. Beautiful—there was no doubt of that either. It occurred to John that she was probably the most interesting woman he'd ever met, and that seemed so much more than the sum of those parts.

'Come in.' Rosalie hadn't forgotten her manners, even if John was staring at her wordlessly. 'Everything's ready...'

So much for making this seem like a casual Sunday lunch. Reba ignored the suggestion, smiling and stepping into the hallway, bending down towards Rosalie.

'I brought something for us to eat.'

She held on to the glass bowl she was cradling, peeling back the silver paper that covered it. Rosalie leaned in, peering at the contents.

'Strawberries…!'

'You like strawberry trifle?'

Rosalie nodded. 'You have to give the food to Dad. You can give your coat to me.'

'Right you are.' Reba beamed at her, straightening up and thrusting the bowl into John's hands. Then she took her jacket off, handing it to Rosalie, who trailed it across the hall floor, climbing the bottom two stairs so that she could reach to hook it over the newel post.

He shot her an apologetic look, brushing a few specks of dust from the sleeve of her jacket as he made for the kitchen, and Reba laughed, telling him not to worry about that.

'Something smells nice…'

'It'll be ready in half an hour.' Opening the fridge to make space for the trifle, John pulled out a bottle. 'Would you like some wine?'

This all felt so strange. They weren't quite friends and yet they weren't enemies either. He'd known her for little more than two weeks, and yet he could almost see what Reba was thinking at times. It had all seemed so simple when he'd seen her sitting outside in the darkness—either continue on in an escalating round of arguments, or make their peace. He hadn't considered what a peace between him and Reba might look like.

She shook her head. 'I'm driving so I don't want too much. Maybe a glass at lunchtime.'

This was nerve-racking… And then Rosalie piped up. 'I'll show you the bathroom so you can wash your hands. It's next to *my* room.'

'Maybe later on, eh, Rosie…?' John fell silent as a lump formed in his throat, at the brilliance of Reba's sudden smile.

'That's very thoughtful of you, Rosalie. If it's okay…?' She flashed a querying look at John and he nodded. If Reba didn't mind, then Rosalie's decision to play the hostess was certainly taking the awkwardness out of the situation.

'This way.' Rosalie flounced out of the kitchen and Reba followed, turning to shoot him a smile as she went.

He could hear them upstairs. Rosalie had dropped another heavy hint that Reba might like to see her room, and the footsteps above his head and the sound of Rosalie's excited voice and Reba's laughter moved to the back of the house. If he'd stopped in his ever increasingly panicky trajectory and thought about it for a moment he might have realised that Rosalie would be an excellent partner in this enterprise. But then a five-year-old had a habit of going their own way, and John doubted he could have schooled Rosalie into doing anything better than this.

Maybe he should be *her* wingman. The lunch was taking care of itself for ten minutes and he took two glasses from the cupboard, making a pretend cocktail for Rosalie with orange juice and fizzy lemonade, and adding a paper umbrella and a cherry. For Reba, half a glass of wine.

He found them in Rosalie's room, sitting on the two wicker chairs by the window. Rosalie's stance mimicked Reba's, her legs crossed and one elbow leaning on the arm of the chair, and they were clearly discussing the bird feeder that hung outside the window. Reba caught sight of him and gave him the smile that always made his knees go weak.

'Drinks! How lovely… Thank you.'

Rosalie beamed at him as John set the drinks down on the small table between them. 'Lunch is in ten minutes.'

This was important to Rosalie—having a room of her own, somewhere that she felt was hers and where she could bring her friends. He was grateful to Reba for her obvious appreciation of Rosalie's wish to play hostess.

He turned, hiding his smile. Rosalie didn't need him here, in the best possible way.

CHAPTER SEVEN

THE BEST WAY that Reba could describe lunch was that it was civil. That in itself was an achievement, since every instinct seemed to cry out that the very last thing she wanted to be with John was civil. That was the problem—it meant that even the slightest spark between them had the potential to explode into flames.

But Rosalie's presence precluded any flames this afternoon. The little girl had been so eager to welcome Reba and show her room off to her, and that had set the tone. Bringing drinks upstairs, to give it all the feel of a girls' get-together, had been a nice touch on John's part and after he'd gone back downstairs Rosalie had taken Reba's lead and sipped her pretend cocktail instead of drinking it down all at once.

And John made a mean roast, with all the trimmings. They rounded it off with the trifle, and then Rosalie, who'd reached her limit in terms of sitting still for one day, ran to the mess of toys that had been hastily pushed into a pile in the corner of the lounge area of the long open-plan ground floor. John fetched the coffee and showed Reba through a set of glass doors which led to a conservatory. He could keep an eye on Rosalie, who seemed intent on taking up as much floor space as possible to sort her toys into some kind of order, but when he closed the connecting doors they were alone.

Somehow, the temperature seemed to rise a couple of degrees. Probably not the conservatory's fault—the space was shaded by a couple of huge ferns at either end, and was very clearly a place for plants with some seating added as an afterthought. But whenever she was alone with John the room became warmer…

'Rosalie's room is lovely. And such nice colours.' Maybe if they *talked* about her then it would be a good second best to having her presence.

He nodded, seeming to relax back into his chair in the dappled green of the space. This was clearly John's quiet place in the house.

'That was thanks to Cathy. I was busy painting it pink and she came round and gave me a lecture on how little girls don't always prefer pink. She told me to choose a few colours that I reckoned we could live with for more than ten minutes, and let Rosalie pick the one she liked.'

Reba couldn't help smiling. 'The more I hear about Cathy, the more I really like her. You were friends before you took the job at the hospital?'

Maybe she shouldn't question him. John's way of dealing with things was not to talk about them, and today was supposed to be all about making their peace.

But he nodded. 'Yes, Cathy split her time between four different units, and when I was just qualified and working in the paediatric A&E department of my previous hospital I met her there. We had a lot of kids coming in with injuries after a school bus collided with a lorry and turned over onto its side. That was an awful day, and I was just starting to wonder how any of us were ever going to get through it when I found Cathy, sitting with a little boy whose arm was broken, holding him and singing to him.'

Reba nodded. 'That's a nice memory to have of her.'

John smiled suddenly. Not the arm's length smile that he used to ward off any hint of real feeling, but one that ran the gamut of emotions between sadness and fond remembrance.

'She was one of the best. When I adopted Rosalie I reckoned I knew what I needed to do to look after her, because I'd known her ever since she was a baby. I learned pretty quickly that there's a difference between being an involved uncle and a father. Cathy had two girls of her own who are grown-up now, and she came to my rescue with a lot of good advice.'

'It's good that you had someone like her.'

He nodded. 'Are you about to tell me that it's good to talk about that?'

Something hovered in the still air between them. The possibility of Reba rushing in and speaking her mind. Rosalie was on the other side of the glazed doors but she was in sight, and while her presence meant that there wouldn't be raised voices, there was still the possibility of a vehemently whispered disagreement that would result in Reba bidding him a tight-lipped goodbye and going home.

She didn't want to set foot on that path. She wanted to stay.

'I'm not about to tell you anything. I came here to listen.'

That smile again. The one that told her that John was slowly letting his guard down.

'Yeah. I asked you here with the intention of listening too.'

They sat in silence for a few moments. It was hard, being here with John and feeling all that she felt for him but wouldn't recognise, without having the comforting disguise of conflict to pour her emotions into. Reba reminded herself that it wasn't her style to shrink from a challenge.

'I really love Rosalie's room. I didn't have a room to my-self when I was little.'

'You have brothers and sisters?'

She shook her head. 'No, but space wasn't the reason. We were always on the move, travelling with my father.'

'That sounds…different.' John seemed to be carefully avoiding making any value judgements, and Reba laughed. He was nothing if not true to his word.

'Most children think that normal is whatever *their* fam-ily does—I certainly did. It was a great way to grow up, we lived in so many beautiful cities and whichever house we were renting at the time was full of wonderful musi-cians whenever my parents threw a party. But I never had a room like Rosalie's, where I could keep all those things that kids keep. Name me one person you know who doesn't still have a pebble that they picked up when they were lit-tle, somewhere.'

He thought for a moment, and then got to his feet. 'You've got me wondering, now…'

John walked out into the main room, opening a drawer in the long, low sideboard in the dining area. Whatever he was looking for must be at the back and as he reached in Rosalie ran over to see what he was doing. They exchanged a few words then Rosalie raced away and Reba heard her thundering up the stairs.

She'd obviously started something. John clearly hadn't found what he was looking for here and he extended his search, moving to the kitchen. Reba followed him and found him emptying a drawer that seemed to be full of useful things—a light bulb, a screwdriver and several pieces of shaped plastic that didn't have any obvious use but must fit somewhere.

'Ah! Got it…' He grinned, reaching for the back of the

drawer, and Reba held out her hand. His fingers brushed her palm as he dropped something cool into it.

'That's lovely.' A piece of dark blue sea glass, frosted over by the water.

'I'd forgotten I even had it.' John leaned in, turning it over in her hand as if this was the first time he'd seen it.

The ever-present heat rose suddenly. His scent seemed to fill her senses, together with a sudden longing to feel his touch again. When she looked up at him, his gaze seemed to devour her.

And then he stepped back. Sensible. She should have done that a lot sooner. John reached into the drawer again, and took out two more pieces of sea glass and a round pebble with a hole in it.

'I used to have quite a collection. I reckoned that sea glass must be very old for it to have frosted over like that, and I imagined a Viking sailor dropping it over the side of his boat...'

Reba smiled. 'Did the Vikings make glass?'

'No idea. Don't spoil it for me.'

A little piece of his child's imagination that she could hold in her hand. This seemed so special.

'If you hold the stone up you can actually look through the hole. I had an evolving set of theories about that...'

Reba would have liked to know what happened when you looked through the hole in the stone, but it seemed that piece of magic wasn't to be. Rosalie's footsteps sounded on the stairs and she pushed between them, clutching a plastic box to her chest.

'I've got more than Dad...'

But nothing quite so special. Reba closed her fingers around John's treasures, feeling the powerful spell they cast. Then she tipped them back into his hand, his fingers closing around hers a little as she did so.

One exchanged glance of regret that told her he felt it too. That little piece of his past that had become all-important for being shared. Then Reba smiled down at Rosalie, who had planted the box on the kitchen counter now. John lifted her up, sitting her next to it, and Rosalie took the lid from the box. Reba caught her breath, her wonder not quite as keen as the one she'd felt when John had found his small treasures.

'You *have* got a lot. Would you like to show me…?'

The afternoon that had promised to contain everything that John feared the most had become golden. Maybe not quite *easy* because John was still on edge, still wondering if this was wise on so many levels. Allowing someone in again, after he'd sealed himself off from the people around him, maintaining his usual face with the world while constantly on the run from the things that hurt. Allowing *Reba* in, someone who he hardly knew but so badly wanted to touch. That had been just as terrifying as he'd anticipated, but he hadn't reckoned on it feeling right and natural as well, in a world where lately everything had been feeling wrong.

'I don't want to keep you—but you're welcome to stay for tea…'

It had been raining all afternoon, but the time had flown. The house had become a playground, sorting through Rosalie's box of stones, selecting books from the shelves and recommending things to read to each other… Everything that Reba touched seemed to gain a piece of her magic. Even the small plants in the conservatory, that he and Rosalie were nursing along, seemed to straighten and stand to attention when Reba gave them a laughing pep talk about how much more growing they had left to do.

'It's still tipping it down. I will stay for tea if that's all right...?'

The non sequitur was clearly an excuse. Rain wasn't going to stop Reba from going out to her car and going home now, pressing ahead from each completed task with the smiling determination that he'd seen at the hospital. But she wanted to stay, and he wanted her to stay.

'Nothing to do for the morning?' The question just slipped out before he could stop it. Apparently that urge to throw a spanner into the works, and see how she reacted, was still there...

For a moment he thought she was going to rise to the implied challenge and that he'd messed everything up. Then suddenly she laughed. 'What do you think, John? I've always got something to do for tomorrow morning at work. But a woman has to eat.'

There were a thousand answers to that. John swallowed them down because they all had an element of the judgemental, and turned his attention to settling Rosalie down in front of the TV with the favourite film she'd been clamouring to watch for the last ten minutes. Maybe Reba would sit down with her, when he walked back to the kitchen...

But he heard her footsteps behind him. She plumped herself down on the sofa at one end of the kitchen, shifting slightly to remove one of Rosalie's building bricks from the cushion and putting it onto the low table in front of her with the pile of other bricks.

'Sorry, they get everywhere.'

Reba shrugged, smiling. 'You're not going to ask...?'

'Ask what?' John decided that playing dumb was probably the more tactful option and Reba rolled her eyes.

'How much I have to do for tomorrow morning when I get home.'

John thought carefully about his answer. 'Today was meant to be all about not rising to the temptation of discussing what we each thought the other should be doing about their lives.'

'That's fair.' She leaned back into the sofa, crossing her legs.

'But you're still at liberty to tell me when I need to chase you away to get on with whatever it is you do have to do. I have a spare umbrella if keeping dry on the way to your car is a concern.' He looked out of the kitchen window. It had stopped raining now anyway, but the sky was still overcast and it could start again at any time.

Hearing Reba laugh seemed to satisfy his craving to prompt a reaction from her. 'I was up early this morning and I have everything I absolutely *need* to do for tomorrow finished.'

He was sure she could have found something else if she tried. John bit his tongue and nodded, reaching for the bread and a carving knife.

'I'm currently struggling with the things I don't need to do.' Reba supplied the answer, as if she knew that was going to be his next question. 'It's my hothouse mentality.'

Now she'd lost him completely. John felt that the comment begged his question. 'Hothouse? You want to revisit the conservatory?'

She laughed. 'Not *your* conservatory, no. I grew up in a different kind of hothouse, where music was everything. There was always more practice, always more to be achieved.'

'You didn't want that?' It was a new concept for John. Reba always seemed to take such joy from her music.

'I wanted it. I started learning the piano when I was four, and the violin when I was five. Our house always had musicians coming and going, and my favourite thing was being allowed to play with them.'

'Did you ever think of performing as a career?'

'At one point that was the only thing I thought about. I changed my mind, though. What would you say is the most important? Performing to a packed auditorium of people, or using music to heal sick kids?'

He laid down the carving knife, reckoning that was enough bread for sandwiches. 'Trick question. What do you expect me to say? Although I imagine that a lot of good things come out of performing to an auditorium as well.'

'Yes, that's good too. But I decided to go with the sick kids. When I finished my degree in music I pretended to do the rounds of auditions and performances, but instead I was taking an MA in Music Therapy. When Hans—my father—found out he was incandescent.'

'He didn't know?'

'He and my mother were in South America—he was playing a season of concerts there. My parents phoned me every week and asked me how I was doing, and I said *great* and that I was working hard. By the time they got back to London it was all a done deal, I'd already lost six months of knocking on every door in town looking for performance opportunities and was halfway through my MA. It was all a disaster of epic proportions in his eyes.'

'You're giving me chills. Is this what Rosalie and I have to look forward to?'

Reba chuckled. 'I very much doubt it. The trick is to ask her what she wants, instead of just assuming. And allowing her to say anything in reply, without exploding.'

'I'll bear that in mind.' Maybe it was a way forward with

Reba as well. No assuming and no exploding. 'I take it that your father did explode?'

'That wasn't such a big thing as it sounds. He's volatile at the best of times, and sometimes that's wonderful, but he has a habit of throwing things when he can't cope with his emotions.'

'Things that break?' John remembered the balled-up paper that Reba had thrown and realised the gesture was a little more than just the delightful expression of emotion that he'd taken it for.

'The more breakable the better. When it became impossible to hide the fact that I'd decided on a change of career, he was furious. He said that I was wasting all the opportunities I'd had, and he was never going to forgive me. It was a good six months before he'd even speak to me again.'

John wasn't sure what to say. Reba had described it as if it were almost a joke, but he saw real hurt in her face. She was sitting bolt upright now, as if still needing to defend herself. He forgot about the sandwiches, turning to lean against the kitchen counter, facing her.

'We got over it. Hans makes sure to throw a few comments about me wasting my talent whenever he sees me and I ask him when he last helped a child to recover from life-changing injuries. My mother generally gets in between us and...' Reba shrugged. 'I guess we love each other, even if we don't agree.'

And Reba had something to prove. Her dogged determination to be the best, making leaflets and staging concerts, wasn't just because she was committed to her work. She was driven by her childhood and her father's clear message that she'd settled for second best, which dismissed everything that she was achieving now.

'When I first adopted Rosalie I had to learn how to stop

being a favourite uncle, and start being a dad. Less of a friend, and more someone who'd always be there for her and accept her.' He shrugged. Maybe that wasn't relevant.

'That's exactly it. Hans gave me a wonderful childhood. He was my mentor and my friend. Somehow he seemed to lose the *dad* part.'

'But you didn't.'

'Does any child? His disappointment in me really hurt.'

'So what made you change your mind about your career?'

'I was part of a quartet that played in schools and homes for the elderly. Hospitals…anywhere that would have us, really. We started off thinking that this was a way to perform together in lots of different environments, and then suddenly the environment became a great deal more important to me than the performing. I talked to a therapist at one of the hospitals we visited and… I just knew that this was what I wanted to do.'

He nodded. 'I can identify with that. When I went to medical school, I had ideas of being at the cutting-edge of my chosen field, whatever that turned out to be. It wasn't until I rotated onto Paediatrics that I realised that the cutting-edge that I wanted to be on was a child's smile. It's all just a matter of priorities.'

Reba gave him a delicious grin. 'You'd be surprised how many people will tell me differently when they find out I had the opportunity to play professionally…'

She fell silent suddenly, listening. Rosalie was singing along to her film, and John imagined that she was also replicating the actions.

'She does that a lot—' He fell silent as Reba pressed her fingers across her lips in an urgent message to be quiet. She got to her feet, walking quietly to the kitchen door to listen. John couldn't resist joining her, wondering what had caught Reba's attention.

'Did you hear that?' She smiled up at him.

'She really likes the song.'

'And she hit every single note.' Reba was whispering vehemently, as if she were in a concert hall and someone was about to shush *her*.

'Yes, she does. When I try to sing along with her, she puts her hand over my mouth. She tells me that I don't do it right.' John was beginning to catch Reba's meaning and the familiar tension curled in his stomach. All the things that he might need to do to make Rosalie happy. All the mistakes that he could make...

'Are you telling me that Rosalie's musically gifted?'

'I'm saying that she has a good ear. She can hit a note and she can tell when you don't.' Reba looked up at him in surprise. 'Is that a problem?'

Maybe. John didn't know and that was what was killing him at the moment. He turned away from her, ignoring the half-made sandwiches and going to sit down on the sofa. He had to think about this.

Reba came to sit next to him. The temptation to reach for her, tell her that he wasn't sure how to keep Rosalie safe from all of the gazillion things that might be a problem and might not...

It was almost a surprise to find that he *hadn't* reached for her. It had seemed so clear in his mind that he could hardly tell the difference between that and the stunned silence that he'd maintained.

'John. Is it a problem?'

He could ask. Reba was a professional musician and it was natural to seek her opinion. That couldn't be construed as seeking comfort.

'I don't know… What do you do with a child who has a good ear?' Let alone one who was musically gifted—that was a scale of challenge he didn't dare contemplate.

She reached out, brushing the back of his hand with her fingers. Even that small contact made him shiver and she pulled her arm back as if she'd been stung, turning the corners of her mouth down.

'Look, I wouldn't presume to tell anyone how to raise their child. I'd find it terrifying to have that little life in my hands. But this I know about. Rosalie seems to have a good ear for music, and if that's the case then it might—just might—bring her as much joy as it has me over the years. That's all you need to know right now. My own experience tells me that if she wants to play you won't need to push her. Just don't have any expectations.'

Reba was speaking from the heart. Her passion showed through, but that just touched a place in his own heart, which allowed him to reach out a little.

'So what would you advise? Practically speaking.'

'Let her listen to music—local parks often do great concerts, which are good for kids because they're informal and she can stay as long as she likes, or go and do something else. Maybe put an instrument in her hand and see what she does with it. I have a glockenspiel at home that she can try. It has a nice tone.'

John couldn't help laughing. 'You make that sound as if it's every little girl's dream.'

'Some kids like dolls or train sets. I was pretty fond of the glockenspiel, until the piano took its place.' Reba gave a shrugging grin. 'I imagine there was a lot that was hard about adopting Rosalie. This isn't hard at all.'

It was an invitation to talk. One that John had extended to Reba but he now realised that it was a lot easier to listen than to talk. One day, maybe, he'd tell her about the tearing fears that could still leave him almost breathless.

'Thanks. And if Rosie could try your glockenspiel out I'd be very grateful. It sounds like a fun thing to do...'

CHAPTER EIGHT

REBA HAD STAYED at John's house for longer than she'd meant to. Rosalie's energy had started to flag suddenly, and she'd gone to her dad, getting up onto his lap. She'd followed the conversation for a while and then her eyelids began to droop.

'I'd better be getting her to bed.'

'Yes!' Reba shot to her feet. She'd got too comfortable here, and she did have a few things to be getting on with at home. 'I should be making a move.'

John left Rosalie curled up on the sofa, and walked with her into the hallway to see her out. This lone goodbye presented yet another challenge—to kiss or not to kiss? Reba decided to act as she would with any other friend, and stood on her toes to brush a kiss against his cheek.

She felt the light touch of his fingers on her shoulder, his hand suddenly snatched away. All the same it was all kinds of wonderful to be this close to him. As she stepped back, she realised that she was still holding on to his arm, and felt herself redden.

'I guess that needs a bit of work.' He smiled suddenly and everything seemed all right again.

'I reckon so. Thank you for a lovely afternoon, I really enjoyed myself.'

'My pleasure.' His hand found hers, his fingers cool

against her skin. A moment of slight pressure that told her he really meant what he'd said, and then he stepped away, opening the door for her.

And then she was outside in the cool evening air, making for her car. Feeling relief, because she *hadn't* done what she'd really wanted to do and kissed John's mouth. And he hadn't done what she'd really wanted him to do and responded. Because the only passion that she had room for in her life was music and the career that she was making for herself.

Driven to make for herself, in pursuit of Hans' forgiveness and his approval. In those quiet moments of conversation she'd seen that in a different light. She shrugged the thought off, getting into her car.

So much for good intentions. They'd lasted for nearly two days, although admittedly for one of those days Reba had been working with private patients and hadn't been anywhere near the hospital. If you counted it in terms of time spent within hailing distance of each other it came to around eight hours.

Reba had bumped into him on her way into work on Tuesday, and they'd exchanged a smiling hello. Then she'd retreated to the therapy room, and a full schedule of appointments with her patients.

The first note had been clipped to the front of one of the patient files.

Looking forward to seeing how Meera's sessions go. Please let me know.

The second was waiting for her in her pigeonhole at lunchtime.

The rounders team is a person down. Interested?

The third had been sent via Joanne, who happened to be

passing. Reba unfolded the sheet of paper and glanced at it. Apparently John had a sudden urge to know about current research on how music therapy could help autistic children. This one was signed with a single 'J' and that small intimacy made her shiver.

'Is Dr Thornton's email not working?'

Joanne shrugged. 'I should be so lucky. He's been emailing me about one thing or another all day.'

So John was clearly in a mood to say something, and Reba guessed it had very little to do with what was contained in his various notes. There was only one way to find out.

She had to wait because she had two more patients to see, but at five-thirty she made her way up to John's office. There was no need to knock, the door was wide open and he had obviously just returned from the wards, his sleeves rolled up from scrubbing his hands.

'Reba…' He turned, giving her that melting look that turned her legs to jelly. Reba reminded herself that jelly wouldn't get her anywhere in this situation. If her friendship with John was based on anything, it was based on honesty.

'I've got some answers for you…' She approached his desk and he perched himself on the near side of it, apparently unwilling to give her the advantage of something solid between them. Fair enough. Hand to hand combat, up close and personal.

'First…' She laid his first note on the desk. 'Yes, I'm looking forward to seeing how music therapy might help Meera. It's not always successful in helping with asthma, but if someone enjoys singing and making music then it may give specific benefits. I'll keep you informed.'

'Great. Thank you.'

She'd wanted to see that smile. The real smile that he

didn't take a moment to think about before he put it into effect. *Careful what you wish for, Reba*, because now it was playing havoc with her sense of purpose.

'Second… No, thanks, I'll give it a miss.'

'Really?' He raised an eyebrow. 'Your loss, the rounders matches are good fun.'

'Are you speaking from experience or is that just what you've heard?' Reba smiled sweetly at him.

'It's what I've heard. I was thinking it was about time I started supporting the team.'

'It probably is, but you're on your own with that. I don't do that kind of thing—smashed fingers or a sprained wrist could be a real problem for me.' She held up her hand, silencing him as he opened his mouth to speak. 'And before you say that I could be an idle spectator, remember who you're speaking with.'

'Good point. You *never* watch sports, then?'

'I don't watch. I might cheerlead, or organise the refreshments or even do a bit of coaching…' Reba smiled at him. 'Only you probably don't want to be on the other end of my coaching demands.'

'I'll bear that in mind.' He leaned forward, taking the second slip of paper from her grasp and putting it onto his desk. 'Next?'

'No answer. If you want to know about current research then do what everyone else does, and send me an email. I'll return it promptly with helpful links.'

He took the final piece of paper from her hand, screwing it up into a tight ball and throwing it in the direction of the wastepaper bin. It hit the wall and dropped onto the floor.

'You missed.' Suddenly her gaze was locked with his,

and Reba's heart began to beat faster. *Don't... Don't be excited by every little thing that contains some hint of passion.*

'Yeah. Not quite so satisfying when you don't hit the mark.'

'I wouldn't know. I always manage to hit the mark...' She grinned up at him. 'It's a matter of practice. I've never played rounders, but I've coached.'

A slow smile spread across his face. 'Yeah? I expect you could show me just how it's done, then.'

Oh, yes. She wanted to show him exactly how it was done. 'It's all in the balance. And the rhythm, of course.'

He nodded. 'I reckoned that rhythm would come into it somewhere. Any chance of a demonstration?'

Reba took a step closer, taking hold of his wrist. 'It's better if you stand up...'

He got to his feet, his bulk towering over her. Reba tried not to catch her breath. 'You have to get the angle just right...'

She manoeuvred his arm back, then started to move it slowly through a throwing arc. The higher his arm went, the closer she was drawn in, stretching to reach his wrist. She found herself pressing against him and when she tried to step back his other hand coiled around her waist.

'We should stop, John...' She felt him let go of her suddenly, stepping back. 'I meant... *I* should stop. Because...' Reba gestured over her shoulder at the half open door.

He nodded, grinning suddenly. 'You could always shut it. If you wanted.'

She walked back to the door, swinging it closed. When she turned, John was watching her thoughtfully. 'Now what? We argue?'

Suddenly, Reba knew what she wanted. With the kind of

absolute clarity that only seemed to hit after a whole succession of mistakes. 'I don't want to argue with you, John.'

She could see it in his eyes. He wanted exactly the same as she did, but they were both afraid to ask. Both far too wary of tipping their lives upside down. Since when had Reba been afraid of rash gestures and bold moves?

Ever since she had something to lose. Since she'd learned to pile all of her passion into ambition, and showing everyone that she was the best at what she did. Waiting...always waiting for Hans to recognise that.

She took a step towards him, laying her shaking fingers on his chest. Feeling his heart beat faster. John had a lot to lose too, the carefully constructed life that meant he could look after Rosalie and continue to steer the department into excellence. The life that was going to crumble if he didn't stop and give his own emotions a chance to make themselves heard.

'What *do* you want, Reba?'

Each one of her movements seemed mirrored in his. When she slowly reached up to lay her hand on the back of his collar she felt his arm circle her waist, barely touching her. As she stretched up, he bent his head. Lost in his gaze and the exquisite anticipation of the moments that seemed inevitable now, she brushed a kiss against his cheek.

The increasing pressure of his hand on her back allowed her to move closer. She spread her fingers across the back of his head, and suddenly he was kissing her. The passion that they'd both denied, because it was inconvenient in their lives, spilled over suddenly...

So much from one kiss. Passion, rage and vulnerability. Arousal that escalated out of control until it seemed that they were passing a point of no return. John held her close, his fingers exploring the sensitive skin behind her ear and moving further to tangle in her hair.

Then suddenly he moved back. Holding her, his fingers tender against the skin of her cheek.

'Not here…'

'Not ever?' Reba felt her lower lip quiver at the thought.

'I didn't say that…'

A knock sounded at the door. They had about two seconds to compose themselves before whoever it was would be on their way in, and Reba had just lost those seconds thinking about it. John had moved faster, and put three feet of empty space between them.

'Oh, sorry…' Joanne looked startled. 'Didn't realise you were in conference.'

'That's okay, Joanne, we were just about finished…' Thankfully John had decided not to look at her while he delivered the barefaced denial.

'It's just a quick question. I can come back.' Joanne turned to leave but John beckoned her into the office.

'Ask me now. You'll be downstairs, Reba?'

'Yes, I…think I left the leaflets you wanted in my car…' Oddly, her voice sounded relatively normal and her brain was functioning again, telling her that she and John needed to get away from the hospital and find some neutral ground somewhere.

'I'll see you there, then. Just for once, let's all get out of here at five-thirty…'

There was just one thing that John needed to say to Reba and then he would let things take their course, expecting nothing. All of his senses, every last instinct, wanted all that their kiss had promised and tonight he wasn't sure he could bear to let her go. But the one thing he knew for sure was that Reba had to be the one to make that decision.

'Rosalie's with my parents tonight.' There. He'd done it and Reba could make whatever she wanted of the information.

'My place, then?' She looked up at him, her hair glinting in the sunlight. 'Unless you have to be at home.'

'I have my phone.' All they needed were these blunt practicalities. Everything else was already there, all of the passion and all of the answers to his questions, flashing in her eyes.

Reba got into her car, winding down the window to tell him the address and ask if he knew how to get there.

'I'll follow you.' Wherever she went. Wherever *this* went. Despite all of his fears, and the sure knowledge that the kind of letting-go that he experienced with Reba could shake loose the anchors that kept his life on track.

But the fifteen minutes alone in his car couldn't make him change his mind. He and Reba were something he'd never encountered before, a relationship that just wouldn't stay where they'd both decided to put it. One that pushed way past his boundaries and yet still left him smiling to himself when no one was looking.

Her house was at the end of a quiet cul-de-sac, which led down to a footpath with a small urban waterway on the other side. The purple front door led into a narrow hallway, the afternoon sun slanting through the open door of the sitting room. John had thought a lot about what Reba's home might be like, but now he didn't even glance at his surroundings because she'd slammed the front door shut and taken him into her arms.

'You can't fix me. You know that…?' This didn't *feel* like

one of Reba's projects, it was too uncertain and had far too many loose ends to it. But he still had to ask.

'I know. I'll take you just as you are.' Reba kissed him and a sheer, brilliant feeling exploded deep in his chest.

'With nothing more to offer you than just this?'

'This is what I want, John. You can't fix me either, and I have a lot of things to do and places to be.'

'Not tonight, though.' He turned her round, backing her against the wall. When she flung her arms around his neck he lifted her, feeling their bodies lock together as she wrapped her legs around his hips.

'Not tonight…' Her dark eyes became even darker as he unzipped her jacket with an assertive confidence that surprised even him. Reba was clinging to him, her cheeks flushed and her lips parted, ready to welcome his kiss.

They'd gone from nought to a hundred in seconds flat, and he could hardly think straight. Then everything else fell away as he slipped his hand inside her jacket, feeling the heat of her body beneath the soft cotton of her shirt. He belonged to Reba now, and the only thing he had to do was to try and deserve that.

He kissed her and sheer happiness flooded through him. He knew they'd be lying down together before too long, but he wanted this to last just a little longer. And then his world tipped again as Reba nuzzled against his neck, whispering just two words into his ear.

'Upstairs. Now.'

CHAPTER NINE

REBA HAD THROWN the duvet hastily across the bed this morning, dressed in a hurry and not looked back before hurrying downstairs to grab toast and coffee. If she'd known, she would have tidied up a bit.

But there was no stopping this swelling tide of passion and Reba reckoned that John wasn't going to be inspecting for dust. She wriggled free of his embrace, hustling him up the stairs and into her bedroom.

The first time with anyone was always a matter of negotiation. And in the grip of this maelstrom of desire they tested each other. John's determination, his passion against hers. Her wins, when she found herself owning the moment and he gave himself up to her. Her delicious losses, when she lost all sense of time and space and felt only his caress.

'Condoms?' Even that slice of practicality held a promise that made her shiver.

'Top drawer of the dresser...' Reba changed her mind about letting him find them and broke free of him, opening and closing the drawer quickly so he couldn't see the jumbled contents. As he reached to take the condoms from her she snatched them away, hiding them behind her back.

'What would you have done if I hadn't had any?'

'Maybe I would have left you here and run all the way

to the nearest chemist.' He grinned when he saw her look of dismay at the thought. 'Or maybe resorted to creative improvisation.'

The feel of his lips against her neck, his hand on hers as he teased the packet from her fingers, left Reba in no doubt that his backup plan would have been wonderful too. 'There are only three in the packet.'

'Then we can find out what happens when we have to make do without.' He must have felt her shiver at the thought, because his voice took on a teasing note. 'Later...'

The smart answer wasn't going to wash. Three weren't going to be enough to quell the desire that was raging through her, filling her mind as well as her body. John was all action now, tossing the condoms onto the pillow and picking her up, laying her down on top of the rumpled duvet. When she reached to pull him down with her onto the bed he batted her hands away, bending to unzip her ankle boots and strip off her socks, tossing them onto the floor.

His shirt was already half undone, and he pulled it over his head. Marvellous. Reba could imagine her fingers playing a melody of desire across those taut muscles. John's grey-blue eyes taunted her as he took off the rest of his clothes, and then moved quickly on to hers.

And still he teased her. He put off that moment when his skin touched hers in an embrace, shifting her round and smoothing her hair out on the pillows. Kissing her, and murmuring how much he wanted her. Reba reached for the condoms and suddenly the balance between them tipped again. He was all hers...

She didn't waste these moments, because they were precious and she knew they wouldn't last for long. Pulling him down, feeling his weight on her and the touch of his skin. Feeling his reaction as she guided him, almost losing her mind as he hooked one hand beneath her knee and moved deeper inside her.

Reba didn't need to beg him not to wait—there was no way either of them could stop this now. They moved together and cried out together. When she miscalculated, pushing him too far and too soon into a shuddering climax, he somehow managed to keep hold of his senses long enough for his fingers to coax her own orgasm from her trembling body.

'That was…only slightly short of perfect.' John shot her an apologetic look and Reba kissed away his frown.

'Did I give you any choice on the timing?'

He chuckled quietly. 'Not that I'm aware of. Are you okay?'

'It *was* perfect, John. I loved every moment of it.' She nestled against him, whispering into his ear. *'Especially the last part.'*

That seemed to reassure him, and he pulled her close into his embrace. 'I'll remember my manners next time. Ladies first…'

John had wanted so badly to be inside her when she reached her climax, but it seemed he'd have to wait for that experience. It was a complete mystery to him how he'd managed to keep from falling exhausted on the bed for long enough to make sure that she came too.

He couldn't promise her that it wouldn't happen again, just as he could never predict the outcome of any of the things that seemed to explode without warning between them. But this was the epicentre of it all, the place they'd feared going but which everything else had relentlessly mimicked. The way her music seemed to ooze passion. The arguments. John's insatiable curiosity about everything in her life, and their shared drive to fix each other. It had all been about this.

She'd started to shift against him as if she had something on her mind, and John opened one eye. 'You're thinking of throwing something?'

'No.' Reba kissed his cheek. 'I could do, if that's what floats your boat...'

'Nah. You floated my boat far better, just now.' He felt as if he were floating still. Bathed in the warm light of the evening, and bereft of all the things that seemed to weigh him down.

Reba chuckled. 'We'll keep the throwing things for those times when this isn't possible then. I was just wishing I'd tidied up a bit this morning.'

John looked around the bedroom, seeing it for the first time. An assortment of diverse pieces of furniture that seemed to go together so much better than if they'd matched. Walls and fabrics were cream, providing a backdrop for a set of framed line drawings on the wall, which looked as if they were originals rather than prints, and an eclectic mix of ceramics that lined the deep windowsill.

'If you have the urge to tidy up, then put your clothes on and we'll go over to my place.'

She laughed. 'You have a five-year-old to contend with.'

'Rosalie appears to have a natural sense of order. Which isn't always quite the same as tidy.' John kept everything tidy, but there was a deep disorder about it all that always gave him the feeling of chaos. This room had a continuity of feeling about it that would make sense even if everything wasn't necessarily in its right place.

'And you?'

'I just put everything where it's supposed to be, so I know where to find things. This room's nicer than that.'

He meant the observation as a compliment and Reba

took it as one, smiling and snuggling against him. 'In that case, I think I'll just stay here.'

'I'm puzzled, though.' John looked around the room again. 'I thought you'd have at least one musical instrument in each room...'

'The back bedroom's my music room, they're all in there. Apart from the piano, that would have been very tricky to get upstairs. And a piano's more a living room kind of thing, don't you think?'

John had never really thought about it. 'See. Natural sense of order. What does that tell you about what we should do next?'

'I could take a shower... You could join me if you like. I'll show you my piano, and then make something to eat.' Reba seemed to be thinking of things in order of importance, and it was gratifying that she'd put showering with him ahead of the piano.

'No work to do...?' He'd been hoping that wouldn't feature in her to-do suggestions and made an insincere effort to make the comment sound like a joke.

'There's always work to do. Just not tonight.'

John couldn't help smirking in triumph at the thought that he'd managed to knock that entirely off the list. He must be doing something right.

'Then perhaps we should stay here a little longer before taking that shower. Just in case we're not quite done yet.'

She smiled, running her fingers across his chest. That warm, tingling feeling in the pit of his stomach and the way that she moved against him when his hand caressed her hip told him that they definitely weren't done with each other yet.

'Yes. It would be a pity to go to the trouble of putting our clothes back on, just to find we had to take them off again...'

* * *

They still weren't done with each other at ten o'clock, although it wouldn't have been humanly possible to act on that any further. John had succeeded in his resolution to show Reba he could hold out until she'd taken every moment of pleasure that she could, before he was shaken to the core by his own reaction. They'd slept a little and woken up hungry.

Watching her tie up her hair and walk naked to the bathroom was a whole new exercise in pleasure. Showering, dressing, walking downstairs even. Whatever she did fascinated him and he followed her in a kind of happy daze.

'Come and see my piano…' She almost danced into the sitting room and John felt himself running his hand across his creased shirt, as if he was about to be introduced to a member of the family.

The long room that stretched from the front of the house to the back was in much the same style as Reba's bedroom. An eclectic mix of furniture and fabrics which matched perfectly even though they shouldn't, set against plain cream walls. Everything seemed to be arranged around a gleaming upright piano, which seemed slightly deeper than others he'd seen and stood against the wall in the middle of the room, with the sitting area to one side of it and a dining table to the other.

Reba sat down on the long leather stool, beckoning for him to join her. 'It's the piano that my father used to take with him for practice when we travelled. It has a really good tone.'

The instrument oozed a quiet quality, and when Reba played a few notes the sound belied its size.

'He doesn't use it now?'

'No, now that he's a big star he has it written into his

contract that he's provided with a grand, on loan, when he travels. This is the piano I learned on, and he gave it to me.'

'It's a lovely thing…' John hesitantly reached out to touch the keys and Reba nodded him on. A note sounded, pure and clear in the quiet of the night.

'I'm lucky to have it. It's not something I could afford all that easily.' She started to play, a simple melody that John recognised without knowing the name of it, which seemed to reach straight into his heart.

'What's that?' He almost choked on the words.

'Clair de Lune, by Claude Debussy. You like it?'

He nodded. John had revelled in the feeling that he was floating earlier, but the weight that usually burdened his heart did have one advantage, in not allowing him to feel all that much. He was defenceless now, and the music brought tears to his eyes.

This wasn't the time. John steeled himself against the loss that the music seemed to represent, turning on the seat to look away from the piano. Reba seemed to sense that something was wrong, and stopped playing suddenly.

'Sorry, Claude.' She seemed to be addressing the empty air. 'I'm just not feeling it at the moment.'

She started playing again and this time he recognised the piece. A waltz by Shostakovich, that seemed to encompass all of the romance of the dance. Eroticism even, but maybe that was just the way that Reba chose to play it. The thought made him smile, this new emotion more welcome than the last.

'Food.' Reba ended the piece with a dramatic chord. 'I don't have much in the fridge at the moment, but I do a mean toasted cheese sandwich. Or will the cheese make you dream?'

He nudged her shoulder with his, chuckling. 'It would be a waste of tonight not to dream.'

Reba laughed, getting up from the piano stool, her light step seeming to reproduce the airy precision of a waltz. She didn't just play, the music ran through her like an ever-changing tide.

Maybe he was getting himself into something that he shouldn't. But John had no choice, he was already mesmerised by her. He was just going to have to learn to handle it.

Reba had set her alarm for six, which would give John the chance to get home and then into work on time. She'd woken in his arms at five, and they'd welcomed in the dawn together before John dressed and went downstairs, grabbing his car keys as Reba handed him a cup of coffee.

'Have a great day.' He kissed her, seeming suddenly more distant. Hurrying away maybe, from something that he'd decided couldn't happen again. Reba had had her share of short-lived romances, which had drifted into oblivion as a succession of partners had realised that her music and her career pushed them into third place on her list of priorities. But she'd never had a one-night stand before, and she wasn't sure how to behave. Wasn't sure how to even ask if this really *was* a one-night stand.

She'd never had sex like this before either. And this was something that she wanted to keep.

'You too.' She took the cup from his hand, sipping the coffee. As if that could keep him here for a moment longer. 'I guess…maybe we can manage not to argue when we see each other again at work?'

His eyes softened suddenly. 'Last night wasn't a mediation exercise. Not for me, anyway. It was something that I wanted very much, and loved every moment of.'

Good… Good. Maybe she could ask…

'I loved it too, John.'

He nodded, taking his coffee back. They were standing in the hall, staring at each other like a couple of awkward teenagers who hadn't yet learned how to ask whether a parting was a *goodbye* or a *see you later.* Last night, desire had seemed a wonderful and all-encompassing thing, but this morning it was confusing.

'I want to ask… But I don't want to make this all about when I'm free, that's not fair to you.'

Reba caught her breath. John felt the same way she did, and his hesitancy was a matter of respect, not taking it for granted that she'd be able to fit in with his responsibilities, or that she'd even want to.

'Ask. Please ask.'

He smiled. 'My parents have taken Rosalie on a midweek break in the Lake District, and they'll be back on Friday. I don't suppose you have tonight or tomorrow evening free?'

'I have a private client tonight, but I'm free on Thursday.'

'Yeah?' He smiled suddenly. 'If you'd like to come to my place, I can cook for you.'

'That would be nice, thank you. We can pretend it's not all about amazing sex…' Reba pressed her lips together. That hadn't been quite what she'd meant to say. 'I didn't mean to imply that last night was all about the sex.'

'I know. It wasn't for me either.' He put his coffee and keys down on the stairs, and took her in his arms. 'Although the sex was…*really* amazing.'

She could let him go now. They knew where they stood, even if it wasn't particularly easy ground for either of them. If they just kept talking, they could work it out.

CHAPTER TEN

REBA HAD MISSED JOHN. An ever-present thrill of longing had permeated the last two days, and she'd been less focused on her work. But no one had seemed to notice, and so far the sky hadn't fallen in on her head.

Maybe she'd be able to concentrate a little better when this wasn't all so new. And Reba had to admit that there had been a different joy in her sessions with her young clients. Not just in the music, although that remained, but in life itself.

John's front door opened before she got the chance to ring the bell. He was grinning, his phone held to his ear, and Reba walked quietly inside, putting her bag down in the hallway.

'No, sweetheart. Just because I'm having pizza tonight, it doesn't make it Pizza Night. It's not Pizza Night unless you're here.' Clearly he was talking to Rosalie.

'Okay. No, I won't enjoy it as much without you.' He flashed Reba a grin, beckoning her into the kitchen.

'Yes… I'm glad you had a nice day with Gramps and Grandma. Sleep tight and I'll see you tomorrow. Does Grandma want to talk to me…?' John raised his eyebrows, looked at the phone and then put it down on the kitchen counter.

'Rosalie hung up on you?'

'Yes, she'd said all she wanted to say. I dare say my mother will call back if she wants to tell me anything.' John reached for her, curling his arms around her shoulders. 'But how was *your* day?'

His kiss still had the same hunger that had shaken her world two days ago. But now they had the confidence of knowing that whatever came next didn't have to be crammed into the space of one night, for fear that otherwise it might be lost for ever.

'Getting better by the minute. Although I'm disappointed that we won't be having Pizza Night.' The two pizzas that lay half-finished on the counter looked nice.

'We're at liberty to have pizza. We just can't call it Pizza Night, but since I won't be arranging the toppings into smiley faces, I think the distinction's clear enough.'

'No smiley faces? I'm devastated.'

'You're welcome to come on Pizza Night.' He pressed his lips together in a frown. 'Although—'

Reba laid her finger across his lips. 'I know. No staying the night when Rosalie's here. That's okay.'

'Is it? I don't want to confuse Rosalie, not right now when she's just starting to settle again. But the more I think about it, the less fair it seems to you.'

'It's not fair to me if I become someone who's going to unsettle your daughter, John. I knew exactly what I was getting into, right from the start. And I've got my own things to do, you know.'

'You mean cutting a swathe of excellence in your chosen profession?'

'Yes, as it happens. I thought we weren't going to try to fix each other.'

He laughed, bending to kiss her. 'You're quite right. And I don't need to fix you, you're perfect as you are.'

'Don't give me the task of being perfect, John, it's too much for either of us to aspire to. Just take me for who I am.' She returned his kiss, making this one last longer than the first.

'I'll take as much as you want to give. All I have to give you in return is pizza.'

And a raging heart. The storm of feeling behind John's controlled façade, which both excited her and made her sad because he didn't express those feelings often enough. But she'd made a promise, and fixing him wasn't an option.

'I'll take pizza. For now…'

Pizza and a glass of wine. They sat in the leafy conservatory as the sky darkened, talking and touching. Kissing. Happy to let the anticipation build, until they couldn't bear it any longer and thundered up the stairs. Hit again by the lightning of John's passion, and watching as he was hit by hers, until finally they curled up together to sleep.

But when Reba woke in the night he wasn't there. She rolled into the warmth of his side of the bed, expecting that he'd got up for some reason and would be back again soon. But as she lay awake the bed grew cooler, leaving her shivering and alone.

The house was quiet and she got out of bed, pulling the emerald-green wrap she'd brought with her across her shoulders and tying it at the waist. The bathroom door was ajar, and he wasn't there. When she padded quietly down the stairs, the kitchen and sitting room were both in darkness, but she saw a figure sitting in the shadows of the conservatory.

'John…?' He seemed to be lost in thought, and jumped when she spoke.

'Uh… Sorry, did I wake you?'

'No.' Reba hesitated in the doorway, wondering if he wanted to be alone. 'You want some company?'

His lips formed a smile in the darkness. One of those smiles that he had to think about first... Something was wrong, and perhaps he'd decided that he didn't want to talk about it.

'Sure.'

It wasn't exactly an invitation, but she decided to make it one. When she sat down next to him on the large wicker sofa he didn't reach to touch her.

'What's up?'

Silence. That was okay, she could just keep him company. Reba leaned back into the cushions, tucking her legs up underneath her in a signal that she wasn't going anywhere.

'I...don't know if I can do this, Reba. I thought I could, but...it's just not fair on you.'

What? They'd discussed this, hadn't they? Maybe there was something more that he hadn't told her yet. The dead look in his eyes told her that this wasn't simple practicalities. Reba took a breath. Her first impulse was to demand to know what was going on, but that was spurred by the sinking feeling that John might be about to end their relationship before it had even started. If she wanted to fight him on that, she had to take a gentler approach.

'Didn't I already tell you? It suits me as well.'

He turned to look at her, and she saw regret in his face as he shook his head.

'John, you're frightening me.' Terror was more the word. Reba swallowed it down. 'If there's something else, please tell me.'

Something registered. 'I never want to frighten you, Reba. I don't mean to.'

'I'll reword it, then. *I'm frightened because I think I'm about to lose you.* That's how I feel and I have a right to it. It's not your responsibility.' She heard annoyance creep into her tone, and bit it back.

Too late. John had heard it too and the ghost of a real smile showed in his face. Maybe battling him was the right way to go.

'Okay. Point taken. Maybe you are about to lose me, but that's my fault not yours.'

'John! I've had it with tiptoeing around you, just spit it out. Because this hurts…'

This was what he understood. He knew all about passion, and he knew about hurt too.

'I can't let it go, Reba. I feel something with you, and that makes me afraid. As if everything's going to come crashing down around me. I can't let that happen, but I can't shut you out either.'

Reba thought for a moment. 'Is this about your sister's death? And Cathy's?'

She thought she saw tears in his eyes. Her instinct was to shy away from that, to do something to change his mood, but that wasn't going to help. If there were tears he needed to cry, then he should cry them.

'I have to care for Rosalie. I have a department to run.'

'Yes, you do. Neither of those job descriptions includes not allowing yourself to grieve.'

'I can't…' He shrugged. 'I can't make sense of that thought.'

'Why not?' She leaned forward, laying her finger on his cheek. 'Look me in the eye, John, and tell me why not.'

That seemed too much of a challenge. His fingers curled around hers, pushing her hand away. But even though he wouldn't look at her, he was still talking and that was something.

'My sister Cara left home when she was eighteen. Fell in with the wrong crowd, and there was quite a bit of drinking and drug-taking. Mum and Dad knew they couldn't compel her to come home but they let her know that they loved her and that they were there for her. No questions asked. Eventually she did come back. Six years ago.'

'She was pregnant?' It didn't take a mathematician…

'Yep. She'd stopped with the drinking and drug-taking as soon as she found out, but she didn't know how she was going to make that resolution stick. Mum got her into a rehab group and that helped a lot. I took a job in a local hospital because I wanted to be there for her too. I used to take her down to the coast and she'd practice screaming at the sea.'

A tear rolled down his cheek. John went to brush it away, and Reba caught his hand. 'Don't deny yourself these memories, just because they're hard. Did screaming at the sea help?'

John shrugged. 'I have no idea, I never tried it. Maybe. Something did because Cara turned her life around, she stayed clean and when Rosalie was born she was a healthy baby. Mum and Dad helped with a deposit on a flat, and we all babysat regularly to give Cara a break. When Rosalie was two, Cara asked me if she could nominate me as Rosalie's adoptive parent, in her will.'

'Was your sister ill?'

'Yes, she was. No one knew it at the time, but she had congestive heart disease, as a result of drug use. I asked her if everything was okay, and Cara said that she was just tying up loose ends and as a single parent she needed to make sure that Rosalie was provided for. The guy she was living with when she became pregnant threw her out as soon as he found out, and said he wanted nothing more to do with her or the baby. Rosalie's birth certificate doesn't name him, and so what she put in her will was legally binding.'

'And you said yes to it?'

'Of course. I'd been a very involved uncle and I loved Rosalie. It was my privilege to be chosen, then and now. I thought I knew all about bringing up a child, but of course I didn't really learn that until I adopted her. But learning's been my privilege as well.'

He fell silent. There was more. All of Reba's instincts told her that there was more.

'I'm so sorry, John. Your sister's loss must have been devastating for you and your parents, and for Rosalie. The way you all seem to support each other...'

'Mum and Dad have been amazing. They were heartbroken when we lost Cara, and no one ever really gets over the loss of a child. But they adore Rosalie.'

'Have you ever talked with them? About how you feel? I've never been in that situation but it might be a comfort to them to know that someone else is grieving too.'

He shook his head. 'I have to cope.'

That was the heart of it. No one could cope with something like this without talking about it, but John was trying and it was eating him up inside.

'It's a lot. Looking after Rosalie and running a department—'

Now he looked at her. And there was fury in his eyes. 'I can cope, Reba. I *have* to.'

She stared at him in shocked silence. Maybe he understood that there was more he had to say, because John's expression softened suddenly.

'I'm sorry. I didn't mean to snap.'

'It's okay. Snap all you like.'

'Okay. I didn't *want* to snap then. I was with someone when Cara died. Elaine had seemed as happy as I was to be involved with Rosalie while Cara was alive, and she knew all about my promise to her. I guess that, like me, she never thought it would happen because when Cara died she told me that I couldn't possibly adopt Rosalie. I'd just got the job as head of department and it was too much. Elaine said that Rosalie would be better off with my parents or another adoptive family.'

'Was that her decision to make?'

John shrugged. 'I didn't think so. The plan was always that we should do as we do now, I'd adopt Rosalie but my parents wanted to be there to help out. It would have affected Elaine, of course, but only because it affected me. I always planned to take full responsibility for Rosalie.'

Reba couldn't get into another person's head. But it didn't sound as if Rosalie's care was really the issue here. She shouldn't say so, bad-mouthing an ex wasn't a good look.

But John was ahead of her. 'I talked about giving up the new job, or going part-time even, but Elaine wouldn't have any of it. She said that if we were going to get married then she wanted to be able to give up work herself and have children.'

'Wait...you were going to get married?'

'Apparently so.' John twisted his mouth. 'That was news to me, although I suppose we might have done, if things had been different. But Elaine had decided what was going to happen next without asking me, and she gave me an ultimatum. It was Rosalie or her. When I told her that I couldn't give Rosalie up, and that I'd make it work somehow, she told me that I'd never cope and she left.'

Everything fell into place. John's assertion that he had

nothing to give. Shutting out everything else in his determination to not just cope, but be seen to cope. It was eating him up.

'And Cathy came to your rescue, and helped you become a father.'

'Yeah. My mother was hurting so badly and Cathy knew that and stepped in. She taught me how to make Rosalie happy and I think that in her way Rosalie's helping my mother learn how to be happy again.'

'But *you're* not happy. And you're not really coping either.' Reba wondered whether he would accept that truth from her.

'I don't have anything to give you, Reba. If you had an ounce of sense, you'd run.'

Oh, no. He wasn't going to get away with that.

'Look here, John. This is a devastatingly sad situation, and I don't blame you for feeling as you do. I don't know what I would have done, if I were in your shoes. You can shut me out if you want, but don't you dare tell me to run.'

Something stirred in his eyes. The same response he always gave when Reba resorted to passion. She held out her hand to him.

'You take it or you don't, John. Make your own decision, but be under no illusions that it *is* your decision, because I'm here for you.'

He stared at her. John knew what this meant, and she was asking no small thing of him.

Then suddenly, as if he had to do this before he thought better of it, he reached out to take her hand. 'I don't know what to do, Reba. Will you help me?'

'I don't really know what to do either. But I will help you and we'll muddle through together.' Reba flung herself into his arms, feeling his warmth as he held her close.

She needed that warmth, because even though she'd just climbed a mountain to get through to him, there was another, much steeper path to negotiate.

'Have you taken any time off since Cara died?'

She felt him shrug. 'A few days. Mostly things I needed to do with Rosalie's adoption. Mum and Dad took her away for two weeks at Easter.'

'Would you be able to take the day off tomorrow?'

He thought for a moment. 'Probably. What for?'

'Joanne told me that everyone in the department who was close to Cathy was offered grief counselling. I'm assuming you didn't take that offer up.'

'No, I didn't.'

'Then I'd like you to think about making that appointment. Tomorrow if you can.'

She felt his chest heave in a sigh. 'I guess… I don't need a day off to make the appointment, though.'

'No, but maybe you do need to stop for a moment and acknowledge your pain. Take a long walk, or whatever else it is you do to let off steam. Think about it, make the appointment. That's going to be hard if you're really serious about making it work, and not intent on going along and telling the counsellor that everything's all right and that you're coping.'

'Because that would be dishonest, wouldn't it?'

'Yes, it would.'

'Thought so. Would you like to come to bed now? We've only got a couple of hours before it's time to get back up again.'

'So you can forget all about this?'

John chuckled quietly. 'No, that would be dishonest as well. So I can hold you, and just summon up the courage to take you up on your suggestion.'

* * *

They'd stayed in bed, dozing in each other's arms, until the very last moment. John had called his line manager, who had reminded him that it was her suggestion that he take a few days off. Reba had seen him smile as he told her that she'd been right all along, and as soon as he ended the call she'd kissed him and raced for the door so that she wouldn't be late for work.

John had called mid-morning, saying that Rosalie wanted to come to the music evening, so Reba had suggested that she bring her home afterwards. Everything seemed to be slotting together nicely, to give John a little time alone. All she needed to know now was whether he'd made use of that time.

She clung to Rosalie's hand as they walked to the front door, only letting go when John opened the door, and Rosalie flew into his open arms.

'I missed you so much!' John looked tired, but he was smiling. He straightened up, taking Rosalie with him. 'Did you enjoy your holiday?'

'It was a mini-break, Dad,' Rosalie corrected him. 'Gramps said that it wasn't a proper holiday but that it felt like one.'

John smiled at Reba over Rosalie's shoulder. 'Okay then. Well, let's invite Reba in then, shall we? And you can tell me all about your mini-break.'

So much for finding out how John's day had gone. Reba had hoped they might get some time together to talk, but she'd have to wait. She stepped inside, shutting the door behind her, and John set Rosalie back onto her feet. The little girl raced after him, capering around his legs as he walked through to the kitchen.

A sandwich, along with a small tub of fruit and jelly

seemed to divert Rosalie's attention, and she decided that she wanted to eat in the conservatory, as she and her grandparents had done at the hotel. John fetched her a drink, and then he returned to the kitchen.

'So?'

He smiled. 'I had a good mini-break too. I drove out of London and took a long walk. I did think about shouting at a tree, but decided not to. Instead I found somewhere to sit, and made a list of the things that I definitely didn't want to talk about with the counsellor, since they were probably the things that I needed to talk about.'

'Okay. I would have shouted.'

'Yeah, I know. Then I called the hospital's bereavement counsellor. We actually had quite a long chat, which I probably couldn't have done if I'd been at work. I've got an appointment with her on Monday afternoon.'

'Wow. That's quick.'

'She had a cancellation, and she says that she thinks there's a lot to work through.' John turned the corners of his mouth down.

'Well…how do you feel about that?' Reba was trying hard not to put words into his mouth.

'Honestly? Not so good. One thing that today's shown me is that there *is* a lot to work through and… I have a suspicion that's not going to be easy.'

'Probably not. Are you going to stick with it?'

He leaned forward, stealing a kiss from her lips. 'Yeah. I've decided now, and I'll stick with it.'

However hard it was. However much he had to break down and in spite of how much that was going to hurt. John had made a decision and his relaxed air was because he knew he wouldn't go back on it.

'I've got something for you. For Rosalie, actually. I went

home and got my glockenspiel at lunchtime so she could have a try with it.'

'You took a whole hour for lunch?'

Yeah. Reba hadn't felt too good about that, the pile of things she had to do was growing larger by the minute. But this was more important. She held up her car keys.

'Will you carry it in for me? You can't miss it, it's the large black carry case in the boot. Rosalie's bag's in there as well, your mother gave it to me when she brought her along for the music evening.'

He grinned at her, taking the keys from her hand. John returned with Rosalie's pink backpack slung over his shoulder, labouring under the weight of the heavy carry case.

'Are you sure about this? It's heavy enough to be the real deal, not a child's toy.'

'I'm sure. She'll hear the difference, and I've brought a pair of rubber mallets for her so that she can't do any damage.'

'You're fully aware of the destructive capacity of a five-year-old?'

'The whole point of it is that it's a great way to introduce kids to music.' And it mattered that Rosalie had a well-tuned instrument, even if John couldn't hear the difference.

'Okay, if you say so. I'll make sure to keep an eye on her though. Where shall I put it?'

'It has a stand, so in front of the sofa will be just fine for the time being.' Reba moved the coffee table out of the way, and John put the glockenspiel down. She shushed him away and he retreated with Rosalie's bag, sorting through it and throwing clothes into the washing machine.

Reba unclipped the protective case, and extended the stand to what she reckoned would be about the right height for Rosalie. She put one pair of mallets on the coffee table and sat down on the sofa with the other pair in her hand.

John turned suddenly when she started to play. The Shostakovich waltz sounded eerily beautiful when played on the glockenspiel, even if Hans would have labelled the rendition sloppy in places. But John didn't hear that, he just heard the magic.

'That's exquisite.'

'I'm a little out of practice.' Reba skipped back, getting the phrasing right this time. Then she started again, using a little more force with the mallets so that the sound would reach out and find Rosalie.

John was standing quietly, leaning against the counter on the far side of the kitchen. Reba didn't turn when she heard a noise in the doorway, and kept playing. Then she felt Rosalie's hand on her knee.

'You like that?'

Rosalie nodded.

'Okay. Those are yours...' Reba indicated the second pair of mallets, and started to play again. Rosalie ducked quickly around the end of the glockenspiel to fetch the mallets, climbing up onto the sofa and leaning against Reba's arm so she could see what she was doing.

'That's no good, how are you going to reach from there?' Reba curled one arm around Rosalie and the little girl scrambled across her leg so she could stand in front of her.

'Look at how I strike the bars...' she played a few notes '...do you want to try it?'

CHAPTER ELEVEN

REBA WAS AMAZING. Okay, so he was biased, John would admit that. But the way she'd drawn Rosalie in, making her want to play and then helping her to hold the mallets correctly and strike a few notes was pure magic to watch. They'd played a couple of simple tunes together and then Reba had reached into her bag, producing a dog-eared book of tunes, with sticky notes on the ones that she thought Rosalie could manage.

'Here. You can help if Rosalie wants to do some more tomorrow.'

'Tomorrow?' Rosalie tugged at his arm. 'We can do it tomorrow, Dad?'

What was he supposed to do in the face of Rosalie's excitement but swallow his doubts about whether he was up to the task of helping with something he knew precisely nothing about?

'Yes, sweetheart. Reba's going to lend us her glockenspiel for a few days, so we can play tomorrow if you like.' John was about to remind Rosalie to say thank you, when the little girl turned and flung her arms around Reba's waist. Reba's smile was almost as excited as Rosalie's when she hugged her back.

He sent Rosalie upstairs to clean her teeth, reminding her that the sooner she got into bed the sooner tomorrow would come. Reba picked up her coat and bag, and he walked with her to the front door.

'Thank you.' He bent to brush his lips against hers, and couldn't resist a slightly deeper kiss.

'It's my pleasure.' She wrapped her arms around him in a tight hug. 'Are we all right, John?'

'Better than all right, I'd say. You're sure you don't want to come to lunch on Sunday?'

'I thought I'd pop into the hospital, and catch some of the parents who can't come during the week. But give me a call if you want some company.'

'You get on with what you have to do. It looks as if Rosalie and I will be busy too, we've both got something to learn.' John was beginning to wonder whether Reba hadn't lent the instrument for his benefit as well as Rosalie's. He was looking forward to spending some time helping her.

'I've written down the ABC notation for most of the tunes in the book. And there's a chart at the back that tells you which bar to hit for each note.'

'Thanks. I was wondering how I was going to work that out. I might give it a read-through tonight. I'll see you on Tuesday.'

Reba reached forward, squeezing his hand. The gesture somehow meant more than any of the words that could have passed between them, and he could let her go now. He watched as she made her way to her car, and then closed the front door.

John was tired. He'd woken at two in the morning for the last three nights, mired in the hollow sensation of loss that he couldn't admit to during the day. He'd come to the conclusion that maybe he should just go with the flow, and gone to bed an hour earlier, getting up when he woke and trying to walk off the feeling that Cara had been taken from his family too soon, by pacing the length of the sitting room, back and forth in an endless repetition of grief.

But the days had been fun. He'd decided to leave the mallets for the glockenspiel where Reba had put them, and let Rosalie pick them up whenever she wanted to, which turned out to be eight o'clock on Saturday morning. John had applied his concentration to which of the bars on the glockenspiel was associated with each note, and then it had become suddenly clear, and he and Rosalie had managed to play a tune together. They'd practised until Rosalie was happy that she'd hit all of the right notes and then John sent a sound file to Reba. Five minutes later he received a call from her, demanding to speak to Rosalie so that she could tell her how beautifully she'd played. Then, late that evening, another sound file appeared in his inbox, which turned out to be a piano accompaniment to Rosalie's tune, which she could play along with.

He sat in his office at eight in the morning on Tuesday, waiting for her. Reba flung open the door without knocking and flipped the switch on his desk that lit the *engaged* light outside.

'Good weekend?' John enquired mildly.

'Yes, actually.'

Reba plumped herself down in a chair. Her hair was done up in a mysterious arrangement which made it look as if it might fall free at any time. John wondered if she might be persuaded to replicate that when they were next truly alone, so that he could find the one pin that released it. He cleared his throat, trying to forget the fantasy of those shiny dark strands caressing her naked shoulders.

'I got quite a bit done on Sunday and I'm feeling pleased with everyone's progress.'

'You were here all day, then?' John felt a little guilty about having been home with Rosalie, making the most of the weekend sunshine.

Reba shrugged. 'Most of it.'

That probably meant from first thing in the morning until the evening. But Reba always looked more relaxed when she was happy with the way things were going with her work, and since he was beginning to understand the healing properties of music for himself he wasn't going to argue.

'So what do I owe the pleasure of this visit to?'

She smiled suddenly. That naked connection, which was overwhelming in their night-time embraces, was only slightly less so when just her gaze met his.

'I was wondering… Do you suppose we should tell anyone? About us…'

'Who were you thinking of telling?' John looked at her, mystified.

'I don't know. I've never had a…thing…with anyone I've worked with before. Do you think HR should know?'

John leant back in his seat, laughing. 'I very much doubt it. You could tell them if it makes you feel any better.' The idea that Reba thought that their relationship was significant enough to notify someone was surprisingly gratifying.

'I don't really *want* to tell them. You're a manager, don't you know what the correct procedure is?'

John applied his rational mind to the situation, remembering what he was supposed to say to anyone from the department who asked about this. 'Well…unless there's a close friendship, a family relationship or a romantic involvement between two people whose work roles are such that one is supervising the other…'

Reba rolled her eyes. 'You mean if I'm sleeping with my boss.'

'Yes. And since I'm not your boss and we each have a different line of senior management, the hospital policy is that it's none of their business. Unless we work closely together and allow personal issues to intrude into our work.' He grinned. 'So no arguing or kissing in the office.'

Reba grinned back. 'Well, strictly speaking that was before…'

'Yeah, well, I don't think they'll be looking for a blow-by-blow account and none of this is going to be a problem. The hospital's not looking to intrude on our personal lives, it's just a matter of making sure that our personal lives don't intrude on the people we work with. I'll mention it in passing to my boss and you can do the same with yours.'

'Yes, okay. That'll put everything straight.' Reba leaned forward, flipping the switch on his desk to extinguish the *engaged* light on the door.

She was a stickler for doing things right. It was all part of her ambition, Reba wouldn't allow anything to mar what John imagined was a perfect work record. He imagined that she'd be behaving with scrupulous propriety from now on, and that only made thoughts of their nights together more sweet.

'Anything else?'

'As a matter of fact, yes. I'd like to talk to you about Meera.'

The little girl who had been admitted to hospital for surgery on a compound fracture to her leg, and who had been having increasingly frequent asthma attacks. John was concerned about Meera as well.

'Yep. I was going to mention this to you. Before the injury to her leg her asthma was infrequent and under control, but we've had to put her on daily preventer medicine since she's been here.'

'She's under a lot of stress. Her mother said that her injury was a result of having been bullied in the playground and that she was pushed off a climbing frame.'

'Yes, that's right. I gather you've spoken to her counsellor.'

Reba nodded. 'She's happy for me to try and use music to make Meera feel more calm, and we're going to be working together on that. I'll make sure that I have a session with Meera every day I'm here, and on Sunday I gave her a file with some of the favourite songs that we'd played together when I first saw her. I've got this programme that creates little blobs in time to the music—it's a bit like a sound-sensitive lava lamp and she likes that.'

John chuckled. 'Right. Sounds interesting, I'll have to take a look at it. Meera can use it when you're not here?'

'Yes, she has a tablet that her parents brought in for her. The thing is, though, that I was discussing with her parents how techniques involving relaxation and breathing control can't replace the medicines that she takes for her asthma. They may help with her confidence and make her quality of life better, but if she has an asthma attack then she must use her inhaler. I stress that with all my asthma patients but maybe I didn't need to in this case...'

John nodded. 'I know what you're about to say. Her nurse told me yesterday that there have been a couple of occasions where her mother's called her over saying that Meera won't use her inhaler. It turned out that she wasn't having an asthma attack at all, she was just upset about something and she needed a cuddle.'

'Yes, her mother's very fearful. This isn't a case of an over-protective parent, she's been traumatised too, and she needs support. She was obviously very upset when she told me how Meera was injured, she said that the bullying came completely out of the blue and that the other girls involved were Meera's friends.'

'All right.' John wondered how Reba was going to like this idea. 'I think we need a very joined-up approach to this one. It may be best if you could be there when I visit Meera on my daily rounds, and if I come to a few of the sessions you have with her. Make it clear that we're addressing different aspects of her treatment in ways that are complementary. I know a few people from a local asthma group, so I might have a word and see if they can give Meera's mother some support.'

Reba shot him a suspicious look. 'It wouldn't need to be you, John.'

'No, it could be any one of the doctors on the unit. But I happen to be Meera's doctor, and I'm also taking an interest in how we handle this, because how the different aspects of our work fit together is part of my remit as departmental head.'

'But…we said that we weren't going to bring our relationship into the workplace.'

John sighed. 'I'm not aware that we are. Let's get down to the basics, shall we—is this the best solution for Meera?'

'Yes, I think so.'

'And…don't spare my feelings, here. Do you think that you'll be able to keep your obvious adoration for me under control if we're in the same room together?'

Reba dismissed the idea with a wave of her hand, clearly not in any mood to spare his feelings. 'I don't adore you at all at the moment. Will that do?'

'It'll do. I'm hiding my feeling of mortification very successfully, don't you think?'

That made her smile. Reba was new here, and she seemed to care a great deal about the assessments that other people made of her, always holding herself to a higher standard than she needed to. John guessed that her father's influence featured in that somewhere.

'All right. You're telling me that I can trust you, aren't you?'

If she could bring herself to do so, he'd like that very much. 'I know that your career's important to you. Mine's important to me, and whatever happens between us, stays between us. I'd never do anything to embarrass you or damage your reputation.'

'Thank you. Yours is safe with me, too.' She shot him an impish smile. 'At least during work hours.'

Reba had to admit that she *had* been worried. She knew in her heart that she could trust John, but growing up in a hothouse where the pursuit of excellence had been everything, she'd learned to be wary of anything that might blemish that excellence.

But she'd already learned a lot from John. He might be flawed and struggling, but he was one of the bravest people she'd ever met. When he'd reached out to her and asked for her help, she'd had to bite back her own tears because the gesture had touched her so deeply.

And today there was more to learn. He'd understood her fears and put them to rest with a liberal application of common sense. And when he ushered Reba and Meera's mother into the small private room where Meera was being cared for, the little girl smiled.

It was one thing to make a child smile when their favourite music was a tool of your trade. When you were the bringer of potentially uncomfortable procedures, needles and horrid-tasting medicine, it was quite another.

'How are you doing today, Meera?' He was quiet and

undemonstrative, but John's whole demeanour was one of kindness and understanding. Kids had a habit of knowing who was on their side, and Meera was no exception to that rule.

'Okay.'

John nodded sagely. 'I'd like to listen to your chest and take a look at your leg. Just to make sure there's nothing you're not telling me…'

Meera nodded, and John started to examine her. Her leg was *'coming along nicely'*, her heartbeat *'very strong'* and her breathing *'good'*. With each new pronouncement Meera visibly cheered up.

'I hear that Reba's given you some music to listen to.' He sat down on the plastic chair next to her bed, waiting while Meera reached for her tablet to show him. They both chuckled over the way the shapes on the screen moved in time to the music, and John seemed to have all the time in the world when he explained to Meera that the physiotherapist would be coming to see her, to help her get moving again.

'I'm going to have a chat with your mum now, and tell her how well you're doing.' John gave the little girl a parting smile of encouragement. 'Do you have any questions for me?'

Meera shook her head.

'Okay then. I'll be seeing you again this afternoon, so if you think of anything you want to ask me, you can save it up until then.'

'How is she *really*?' Meera's mother asked the question as soon as John closed the door behind them.

'Meera's leg seems to be progressing nicely, she's stable and her chest seems clear. We're monitoring her very regularly, and as you know she's being given medicine which we hope will prevent the asthma attacks.'

'But you won't release her yet, will you? I don't think I can cope with that...' Meera's mother was beginning to look a little tearful again.

'No, we won't be letting her go until we're sure she's stable. And we're doing all we can to achieve that medically and in terms of coping strategies. I'll be liaising closely with Reba and with Meera's counsellor and physiotherapist, so this is very much a joint effort.'

'Thank you, Doctor.'

'And how are you doing?'

Meera's mother brushed the question off with a shrug. 'I'm fine. I just want her to be better.'

John nodded. 'You're only ever as happy as your unhappiest child, eh?'

'Yes.'

'I want you to know that we're here for you, as well as Meera. If you have any questions you can always ask the ward manager to get hold of me. And maybe it would help to talk to a few other parents whose children have asthma?'

Meera's mother shrugged. 'Maybe. I don't know...'

John produced a business card from his pocket and gave it to her. 'This lady runs a group of mums who got together to support each other. You can call her any time, and she's willing to come along to the hospital and meet you. Sometimes it's good to talk with someone whose been in the same situation as you.'

Meera's mother nodded. Despite John's gentle, reassuring manner she looked unconvinced, but at least she put the card into her pocket.

'She's not going to call, is she?' Reba murmured the words as they walked out of the ward together.

'No. Not this time.' He shot her a pained look. 'I can understand that. I just hope she doesn't wait as long as I did...'

CHAPTER TWELVE

ALTHOUGH MEERA WAS everyone's first concern, no one was going to give up on her mother either. Sitting in the corner of the therapy room, John watched as Reba started to work, talking to them both and playing songs that they chose. It seemed light and easy, but beneath it all there was purpose. To find music that Meera and her mother could listen to together, and which might help Meera to breathe and relax.

Reba didn't push, but she was gently guiding the little girl towards finding a way to express her feelings. She invited her to select something from the range of colourful musical instruments that were laid out on a low table, and before long both Meera and her mother were adding their own sounds to the tunes that Reba played.

'That's all we have time for today. I'll see you again on Friday, but in the meantime I'll play some of the songs you've chosen and email the sound files to Dr Thornton.' Reba had been rolling a ball of paper in her hand and suddenly she turned, lobbing it in John's direction. 'Can you put them onto Meera's tablet for her?'

'I'll ask the ward manager, she's pretty good with that kind of thing.' He caught the missile, throwing it back. The sudden lightness in Reba's movements as she reached to catch it made Meera laugh.

'And don't you forget what we've been talking about.'

She threw the paper ball gently towards Meera, who batted it towards her mother.

It was a nice way to end a session. Reba's characteristic sense of fun made even Meera's mother smile and hug her daughter, looking suddenly like a different woman. As Reba bent to unlock the brakes on Meera's wheelchair she started to sing, the sound of her voice trailing joy as they walked back to the ward.

May I walk you to your car?

A seven-word text that made Reba thrill with excitement. She texted John, telling him that she had a few things to finish off for the day and she'd meet him in his office in half an hour.

He was sitting behind his desk, grinning. 'So how did your line manager take your revelations?'

Reba had delivered a carefully worded announcement of their new relationship, along with an assurance that it would be kept strictly separate from their work. 'He smiled politely and told me it wasn't an issue. Yours…?'

'She had a bit to say about it.' John chuckled as Reba's eyebrows shot up in panic. 'I got the whole story about how she'd met her husband at work twenty years ago, and how it's good to be with someone who understands the demands of the job.'

So no one considered this was a big deal. Apart from Reba, of course. And John. They both considered it a very big deal.

No one seemed to notice that they were walking in roughly the same direction, at more or less the same time, from John's office on the third floor. But when the distinctive sound of the pager app sounded on John's phone she still jumped guiltily.

'What is it?'

His face darkened. 'Meera.'

The words of annoyance about being pulled back to work just as they were leaving died on her lips. Reba followed John to the ward, where the quiet activity was about as close to panic as things ever got.

Meera's mother was crying as a nurse led her from the room, gently but very firmly. When they entered, the ward manager was with Meera, supporting her in a sitting position as the little girl gasped for breath.

'Inhaler?' John dropped his bag and jacket on the floor in the corner.

'Yes, two doses. It's not making any difference.'

'Do we know why this happened?'

'Apparently she got an email. Her mother was saying it was from someone at her school. Girls…' The ward manager nodded towards Meera's tablet, which was lying on the floor.

John's face darkened. For all the safety that the hospital provided, it hadn't shielded Meera from this. 'Take it away. Reba, over there…' He nodded towards the other side of the bed.

For all his apparent calm, it was clear from his quiet instructions that John was worried. The ward manager picked up the tablet and hurried away to get the drugs that John was now asking for, while Reba took her place at Meera's bedside. The medication was familiar to her and John must consider this a life-threatening situation.

And yet she could do nothing. A tiny part of the helpless anguish that Meera's mother must be feeling gripped at her heart. She sat down, taking hold of Meera's hand, determined that no one was going to have to lead her from the room. If she could bring one ounce of comfort to the little girl, she was staying.

Another doctor arrived, working together with John to administer drugs and oxygen. Meera's lips had taken on a bluish colour, and she was still labouring for breath. When the ward manager arrived, quietly putting a tray down which carried the instruments needed for intubation, a new realisation of the seriousness of this hit Reba hard in the chest. Intubating an asthmatic was a measure of last resort, used only when everything else had failed.

John didn't look round. They hadn't got to that point yet, and Reba didn't dare think about it. She raised Meera's hand to her lips, kissing her fingers, willing her to breathe and listening to John's calm, steady voice as he spoke to Meera, encouraging her.

Fight, darling girl. Breathe... Those words weren't for her to speak, but they sounded over and over again in Reba's head. Meera's small body was beginning to tire in the battle for survival, and her frightened eyes began to close.

'Meera.' John's voice had a slight edge of urgency, as if he were trying to wake her from her sleep. 'Meera...'

The other doctor turned to the tray that contained the instruments for intubation. John shook his head suddenly. 'Give her a minute.'

Just one? One minute before it got to the point where John considered that the drugs weren't working and that another intervention was needed to save her life. One minute before Meera would be intubated and taken down to the ICU, with all the trauma and uncertainty that brought with it, and Reba could do nothing to help stop this.

John was monitoring Meera carefully, ready to make his decision. And suddenly Reba heard her own voice, a little quavery and hoarse, following the notes of one of Meera's favourite songs. John's gaze met hers for a fraction of a second, and she saw him nod her on.

She sucked in a breath, and continued to sing. Surely the minute had passed by now, and John was still tending to Meera, glancing up at the screen which displayed her vital signs every few seconds. She put all of her hope into the song, wondering if Meera even heard it.

'She's responding.'

Maybe the drugs, or the oxygen. Maybe Meera *had* heard the song and kept fighting. Reba didn't care. She continued singing while John and the other doctor cautiously began to consolidate the work they'd already done.

By the time she'd moved on to the third song, John was keeping a watchful eye on Meera while the ward manager made her more comfortable, re-taping the hastily inserted cannula in her arm, humming along with the tune as she did so. A nurse appeared, taking the intubation tray away with her, before leading Meera's mother back into the room. She'd clearly been comforted and told to stay quiet, and Reba jumped from her seat and motioned for her to take her place at Meera's bedside.

'Does she hear us?' Meera's mother asked. An unanswerable question, but John nodded.

'I think she does.'

Meera's mother took a shaky breath and choked on the song that she started to try to sing. Reba put her arm around her and sang with her, seeing John and the ward manager exchanging brief smiles. Meera's eyes fluttered open at the sound of her mother's voice, and now it was Reba's turn to fight back the tears.

* * *

Meera's father had arrived, obviously straight from work as he was wearing a suit. John had judged Meera's condition stable enough to leave her with a nurse watching over her, while the worried parents sat by her bedside. He retreated to his office, and after sitting outside the ward for a while, watching the quiet comings and goings of the evening shift, she went to find him.

He laid his phone back down on the desk in front of him, clearly finished with the calls he'd been making. Reba sat down in the chair opposite him, leaving the door open, and he smiled.

'Good choice of song.' His smile broadened as Reba shot him a querying look. 'You don't even know what you were singing, do you? That's the song from Rosalie's favourite film where the prince, who's disguised as a shepherd, is trapped in a cave, and the princess is outside moving the rocks. I've heard it at least two hundred times…'

'Ah, yes. And she sings to him to let him know she's there. No, that didn't really register with me at the time. I just knew it was one of Meera's favourites.'

'Rosalie's too.' John pressed his lips together, a faraway look in his eyes.

Of course he wanted to hug Rosalie right now. Reba could have done with a hug from the little girl as well and she barely knew her.

'Can you call her?'

'I called my mother. She knows this feeling, and she gave me a blow-by-blow account of the football match that my father and Rosalie were having in the garden. Apparently it's looking as if it'll be down to penalties.'

'Why don't you go round there? I'm sure Rosalie could use you on her team.'

'No. She's all right and she can do without me traipsing in for no reason and interrupting her evening.' He flashed Reba a smile. 'And I could do with hugging you too.'

Those quiet moments, when John had waited just a little longer for the medicines to take effect, had brought them closer. If all that Reba had been able to do was to sing, at least she'd done something.

'I wish I could have done more for her.'

'Who knows what any of us did? Maybe it was the drugs and oxygen that pulled Meera through, and maybe she heard the song and knew that she had to fight. Medicine isn't always a science, there's something unknowable there too.'

'I know my limits—'

'Own it, Reba.' The quick exchange might at one time have turned into an argument. Now it was simply encouragement.

'I wouldn't have even thought to do it if you hadn't told me the story about when you met Cathy.' This wasn't all hers to own, it was Cathy's as well. John acknowledged the thought with a smile.

'I notice you haven't asked me about my first counselling session yesterday.' The mention of Cathy's name seemed to prompt John's observation.

'You got my text, didn't you?' Reba had texted him to wish him well and John had texted back after the session to let her know that he hadn't chickened out of it. That was all she'd really needed to know.

'Yes, and it was extremely tactful. I appreciate you not expecting me to say how it went at this stage. I prepared a whole list of things I reckoned I ought to say, and came out having half said a load of completely different things.'

'Sounds promising.' Reba reckoned her comment was

vague enough to be encouraging without having any specific expectations.

'I suppose so. You might be in the process of fixing me. I'm not sure yet.'

'I don't need to fix you. You need to fix yourself...' Reba broke off, turning as she heard a noise at the door. Had something happened with Meera...?

A middle-aged woman in jeans and a bright red jacket was standing in the doorway, and John greeted her, beckoning her in.

'Lila. Thanks so much for coming.'

'Much as I adore your company, I didn't come for you, John.' Lila walked into the office, sitting down in the other visitors' chair and flashing Reba a smile.

'This is Reba, our new music therapist. Reba, this is Lila, she runs the support group for parents of asthmatic kids that I was telling you about.'

'Ah, you've taken over from Cathy.' Lila smiled fondly when she mentioned her name. 'She was a good friend of ours, she came to speak with us a couple of times about how music therapy could help people with asthma...'

John leaned back in his seat, rolling his eyes. 'Which is a very thinly veiled hint—'

'Of course it is, John.' Lila interrupted him. 'We didn't grow the group without quite a number of thinly veiled hints, which I hasten to add come with no expectations.'

'Reba's only here two days a week—'

It was Reba's turn to interrupt. 'Thanks, I'd love to come along and chat to your group. Let's make a date.'

'Wonderful. I can promise you as much cake as you can eat. John has my number and we'll fit in with whatever's convenient for you.' Lila beamed at her, and Reba smiled back. She was starting to like Lila.

'Well, if that's all settled…' John paused, waiting for another interruption, and Lila obliged.

'Yes, of course. I gather you have a mum who was distressed when her daughter had an asthma attack this evening.' She turned to Reba. 'I know just how she feels, it happens to us all at one time or another.'

'I gave her your card earlier today, but she didn't say that she'd call you.' John finally managed to get a whole sentence out.

'I know that feeling too. Not easy to walk into a room full of people you don't know. I'll be very discreet, just introduce myself and give her my address, then leave. I'm only five minutes' walk away from the hospital, Reba, and my husband's a doctor here so we get people popping in all the time. Which is a thinly veiled hint to feel free to do the same. Henry makes a mean cup of Lapsang Souchong.'

'Thanks, I will.'

'So if you'll call the ward manager and tell her I'm on my way, and to let me in, John…' Lila got to her feet.

'Sure. Thanks Lila.' John picked up his phone and made the call, while Lila wished Reba a good evening and hurried away.

'So, what are the odds?' Reba smiled at him as he put the phone back onto his desk.

'Of Meera's mum just taking Lila's address and letting her go? Not great, I imagine. But Lila *is* very discreet and she won't intrude where she's not wanted.'

'She seems nice. Is the Henry who makes a mean cup of Lapsang Souchong the same Henry who's head of Orthopaedics here?'

'Yep. He and Lila are good people.' John pinched the bridge of his nose, stress and fatigue showing in the gesture. 'I'd like to stay for a little while longer, just to make sure that everything's okay with Meera and her parents. Would you like to give tonight a miss? Or I could come over to you when I'm finished here?'

Reba wanted to stay too, but she hadn't been sure how to ask. 'That fits in with me perfectly. I'll be here for at least another hour. I need to tidy my cupboard.'

'Ah. Urgent cupboard-tidying.' He grinned suddenly. 'If you're sure...'

'I'm sure. We can pick up a takeaway on the way home from the Chinese restaurant around the corner from me. Eat it at the kitchen table, and then you can sing me to sleep.'

'A takeaway sounds great. You don't want me to sing you to sleep though. The bad things that Rosalie says about my singing really aren't exaggerations...'

CHAPTER THIRTEEN

OUTWARDLY, EVERYTHING SEEMED to be falling into place. For the last three weeks, John had spent all of his free nights with Reba, and missed her during the weekends, which was okay because there were always texts, and calls that left him under no illusions that even though she was working she was also missing him. Rosalie had navigated the bumpy one-year anniversary of her mother's death, and seemed to be blossoming again. John was feeling much more equal to the demands of his job, and although his twice-a-week counselling sessions still perplexed the life out of him he still felt that he took something away from them every time.

Inside, the numbness that he'd felt for the last year seemed to be wearing off. That was good and bad. Anger, frustration and grief were difficult bedfellows, and John still woke in the night burning with helpless rage. But Reba... Who wouldn't want to feel every exquisite moment spent with her? To be able to react to her music, and match her passion.

He hadn't got around to telling his counsellor about his relationship with Reba yet, because he didn't consider it to be a problem. Which meant the question of whether and when he might ask if Reba would like to spend some time with him and Rosalie at the weekends had gone unanswered as well. But Rosalie had clearly been cooking up some ideas of her own.

'No! Don't record me, Dad!' Rosalie carefully put the mallets down on the glockenspiel and then flounced off into the sitting room. John switched his phone off and followed her.

'Okay. I'm sorry, I should have asked you first. Would it be okay to make a recording later to send to Reba?'

'No!' Rosalie sat down on the sofa, crossing her arms. 'I want Reba to come *here* to listen. I'll make pizza for her.'

'All right. So you'd like me to ask her over for pizza and you'll play the glockenspiel.'

'No, Dad.' Rosalie gave him a look that plainly said he was being a little slow. Sometimes she was so much like Cara, and John almost recoiled from the mixture of pleasure and pain. 'I can ask her for myself.'

John wondered how Reba might take that. Perhaps a quick phone call first to check... But Rosalie was already on her feet and on her way into the kitchen.

'Hold it right there, Rosie.' John managed to cut her off before she got to his phone.

'I can do it, Dad.'

Yeah, that was exactly what he was afraid of. He thumbed the shortcut to the text conversations between him and Reba, and started to type.

'I've just got a text from someone at the hospital and I need to answer that first.' John supposed that technically Reba was someone at the hospital, even if their text exchanges rarely had anything to do with work.

'All right.' Rosalie was used to the odd phone call from work over the weekends, and retreated back into the sitting room. John waited for a reply to his text, wondering whether he should close the door and call Reba instead, to explain a bit more fully.

It's okay. Let Rosalie call me.

The text was accompanied by three hearts, which quietened his mind a little. All the same he texted back.

Sure?

His phone rang. Reba plunged straight into the conversation, much as she usually did.

'Are you okay with this, John?'

'Yes. Absolutely.'

'She's within earshot, isn't she? On a scale of one to ten, ten being that you'd really like me to come and one—'

'Ten.' John didn't need to know what one was. He walked forward, closing the kitchen door. 'I'd love it if you came round for pizza with us, but only if you're ready. I know you've been here before, but this feels as if we're making things official.'

'I'm not even remotely ready.' Reba chuckled. 'But it's something you'd like to do and so would I, so let's just do it. We're both adults, and if Rosalie comes up with any surprises then we can deal with them.'

That was one of the many things he liked about Reba. She was unafraid, without the caution that loss had ingrained in him.

'All right. Don't say you didn't ask for this...' He walked into the sitting room, handing the phone to Rosalie.

'Will you come for pizza tomorrow? I'll play the glock... en...spiel for you.'

Reba seemed to be talking for a little longer than it would normally take to say yes. Rosalie was listening carefully.

'Can we go to the seaside as well?'

Another pause, and then Rosalie turned her head up towards him.

'Reba says I have to ask you, Dad. Can we go to the seaside?'

'That sounds nice. Did Reba say she'd come tomorrow?'

Rosalie nodded. John waited while she had a conversation about the glockenspiel, telling Reba all about how they practised at weekends, and then Rosalie ended the call and dropped the phone back into his hand, climbing up into his lap and giving him a hug. Clearly he'd done something right.

'What time is Reba coming?'

'Tomorrow.'

'Okay…' His phone buzzed and he opened the text from Reba, which contained the answer to his question. 'She'll be here at nine o'clock, so we'd better be ready to leave by then…'

Reba was less sure about this than she'd made out. She'd spent time with John and Rosalie before, but as their relationship had started to deepen there was an unspoken rule that it should be kept away from Rosalie, just as it was kept away from work. Something that was between themselves and didn't have to answer to the everyday.

And then there was the work that she'd intended to do this Sunday. She'd looked regretfully at the musical scores that she'd been planning to convert into child-friendly display boards so that the children under her care could play a short piece together. It didn't really matter if that waited a week, but somehow it felt that her purpose in life was slowly being diluted. As if she was moving away from everything that Hans had taught her.

But the excitement of arriving on a sunny Sunday morning for a trip to the seaside outweighed all of that. John had prepared a cool bag full of food, and they'd decided to head for Brighton and then along the coast to a beach where John had promised they could go fossicking for treasure.

The famous chalk cliffs undulated gently for miles to the east of Brighton. John seemed to know where he was going, and Rosalie was already excitedly clutching a small plastic bucket on her lap. He parked the car at the top of the cliffs and they looked down on a sand and pebble beach, strewn with white boulders that had been smoothed by the sea. Ahead of them, steps zigzagged their way down the cliff face.

'What do you think? Not quite the place for getting sand between your toes and drinking cocktails.' John grinned down at her. He was keeping a tight hold on Rosalie's hand, but she was jumping and hallooing with excitement.

'It's wonderful. Much more interesting than sand and cocktails.'

'I think so too.' He turned back to the car. 'Let's get you ready for an expedition, Rosie.'

Rosalie sat on the tailgate of the vehicle while John got her into a windcheater, waterproof trousers and a pair of non-slip neoprene-soled shoes. A magnifying glass was hung around her neck inside her jacket, and a notebook and pen tucked into her pocket. Finally a little sou'wester with flowers on it that matched her jacket was tied under her chin.

'You look so cute, Rosalie!' Reba squatted down on her heels in front of the little girl.

'Cute?' John feigned an expression of mild outrage, pulling on a windcheater and shouldering a small backpack. 'What are we, Rosie?'

'Explorers!' Rosalie raised her arms, shouting at the top of her voice.

John nodded, handing Reba her waterproof jacket and a large plastic bucket with a fitted lid. 'Are we ready to go?'

They walked down the steps and onto the beach, turning to look at the white cliff towering above them. Rosalie ran to the nearest outcrop of rocks, her head down, looking for treasure already.

'You're right, she does look unbearably cute, doesn't she?' John grinned down at Reba. 'As do you…'

They spent hours, sorting through shells and stones on the beach, bending over rock pools to catch sight of small crabs scuttling to and fro and digging holes in the sand. John's backpack had all kinds of useful items in it, a book to identify the wildlife they saw around them, a torch and an underwater viewer that allowed Rosalie and Reba to take turns in looking at the inhabitants of the rock pools without disturbing them.

It was hungry work. They found a smooth flat rock to sit on, and John went back to the car to fetch their lunch. Reba helped Rosalie untie the bow beneath her chin, putting the sou'wester into her pocket before it blew away down the beach.

'I came here before. With Mummy and Uncle John.' Rosalie was sorting through her bucket now, picking out stones and shells that caught her eye. 'It was a long, long time ago. Uncle John's my dad now.'

Reba looked up at John, who'd just reached the top of the cliff steps. Maybe she should put this conversation off until he returned, but Rosalie was looking at her, expecting an answer.

'Did you have fun?'

Rosalie nodded. 'We were explorers then too.'

'And are you having fun today?' Reba hardly dared ask. Rosalie's mother was no longer here, and perhaps the little girl didn't want her to be replaced by anyone else, even if it was just for a seaside outing.

'Yes. I'm bigger now, so I can climb up higher. Are you having fun?'

Reba smiled. 'Yes, I am. Thank you for letting me come with you.'

'That's all right. You can come again if you want to.' Rosalie picked a piece of sea glass from her bucket. 'I like this one. What is it?'

'It's called sea glass—it's ordinary glass that's been in the sea for a while, so that it's smooth and frosted over. It takes a long time for that to happen, but it's really pretty, isn't it?'

Rosalie nodded, looking up at the beach behind them. 'Dad! Look! I found a piece of sea glass.'

John was striding towards them, grinning. 'That's a great find, Rosie. You know that sea glass is magic, don't you?'

Rosalie frowned at him. 'It's just glass that's been in the sea for a very, very long time. Maybe a whole year, I don't really know.'

'Ah. Well, I stand corrected, then. Put it in your pocket and I'll zip it up so that you don't lose it, eh?' John put the bag down, pulling out a packet of wet wipes. 'Then we can clean our hands and have something to eat.'

John had prepared a stack of sandwiches, and they'd eaten nearly all of them. He and Reba sat together, sipping coffee from the vacuum flask, while Rosalie took the box of juice that John had given her and wandered towards a nearby collection of stones, looking for any that caught her eye.

'Rosalie told me that she remembers coming here before. With you and your sister Cara.'

'She remembers that?' John's eyebrows shot up in guilty surprise. 'We used to go out exploring a lot together. Cara loved the sea and we'd usually end up on a beach. We only came here once, though.'

Gently. Go gently.

Reba had a hundred questions, but they had to be asked one by one.

'She called you Uncle John.'

'Yeah, she does that sometimes. Particularly if she's talking about something that happened before Cara died. I suppose it's her way of distinguishing between then and now.'

'Rosalie said you're her dad now.'

John thought for a moment. 'That's a nice way of putting it. That's what I want to be to her.'

He was staring at Rosalie now. He'd been watchful all day, never letting her out of his sight and keeping her within his reach if they were climbing. But now he appeared to be trying to see inside the little girl's head, just by the force of his gaze. That wasn't going to work.

'She seemed to want to talk about it. She told me she'd been here before right out of the blue.'

A pulse began to beat at the side of John's brow. Maybe she'd gone too far.

'I find it hard to know what to say to her sometimes. I don't want to push her. My parents are a lot better at this than I am. Rosalie's always coming up with things that my mum or dad have told her about Cara. I guess they've had a bit more practice at being parents, I'm still learning.'

'I wonder if they'd say that they're still learning too?'

'Probably. What do *you* think?'

Reba puffed out a breath. 'I know even less about being

a parent than you do. But you're a doctor, and you deal with kids every day. How would you approach a child in your care?'

'I'd…make space for them to talk. Then leave the decision about whether they want to talk up to them.'

'Yes. That's what I'd do too. Only I'd probably put a percussion instrument into their hand at the same time, in case they wanted to make a noise.'

John thought for a moment and then emptied the dregs of his coffee onto the stones around their makeshift picnic area, dropping the cup back into the cool bag. 'Do you mind…?'

'Of course not. Go.'

She watched as John walked over to Rosalie, squatting down on his heels beside her. The little girl showed him her newest finds, and John patiently looked at each of them in turn. Then she saw him indicate the cliffs with his finger, asking a question. Rosalie's hand strayed to his knee as she moved a little closer to her dad.

John picked her up so that they could talk face to face as he strolled slowly down towards the sea. They seemed to be in their own world, Rosalie safe in his arms, her small hands clinging to John's shoulders. It was a picture so intimate that it seemed wrong to even look at them, and Reba started to gather the remains of the lunch things together, putting them back into the bag.

When she zipped the cool bag closed again, looking up, Rosalie was walking next to John, back up the beach towards her. John was smiling, and when Reba waved to them both, Rosalie waved back.

'We've decided we'd like to shout at the sea.' John's grin broadened when Reba raised her eyebrows.

'Dad says that you like to shout…'

'I didn't quite say *that*, Rosie…'

'So you have to come and help us.' Rosalie ignored John's protest.

'I'd love to come and help you. Your dad's right, I'm really good at shouting. If you shout at the sea you have to do it as loudly as you can.' Reba wondered if the shouting was really just for her and Rosalie, and John would just open his mouth, letting nothing out.

They walked back down to the shore together, and Rosalie chose their spot.

'Let's go then, Rosalie…' Reba grinned down at her. 'Three… Two… One!'

Reba shouted as loudly as she could and Rosalie jumped up and down, waving her arms and hallooing wildly. And then suddenly from behind them came a loud, deep bellow, shot through with strands of despair and pain. But as John's roar reached the open sea, the only thing that Reba could hear was hope…

They'd shouted, and John had skimmed stones into the sea, much to Rosalie's delight. Reba and Rosalie had sung in the car on the way home, and John had tapped his finger on the steering wheel. The plan for smiley-faced pizzas had been abandoned in favour of a huge takeaway pizza, and they sat on the sofa in the kitchen eating slices with Rosalie's haul of shells and stones scattered on the table in front of them.

When the little girl began to yawn, John waited while she kissed Reba goodnight and then lifted her up, taking her upstairs to bed, while Reba sorted through the pile of oddly shaped stones that Rosalie had declared were dinosaur bones, arranging them in a row on the table. John came back down the stairs ten minutes later.

'Out like a light. She barely managed to clean her teeth…'

He sat down next to Reba on the sofa. 'Thanks for coming today. I had a really good time.'

'Me too. Thanks for asking me.' Reba leaned forward, picking up the stone that she'd set to one side. 'I think Rosalie's managed to find a *real* fossil.'

'Really?' John took the stone from her hand, looking at it. There was the clear imprint of a tiny shell, half obscured by a thin slice of stone. 'I think you're right. I wonder if I could prise off that piece at the side to see all of it.'

'Looks as if it might come off. You'd have to be careful.'

'Yeah. On second thoughts, I wouldn't want to damage it. I'll make sure that Rosalie keeps that one, it's a real find.' He leaned back on the sofa, his arm resting on the cushions behind her. Reba shifted a little closer, leaning against his shoulder.

Just a few moments. Then she'd go home…

Reba drifted into wakefulness. She was lying on top of John, his arm curled around her shoulder. And there was light coming from somewhere… Had they slept through the alarm…?

She sat up suddenly, hearing him grunt softly as her elbow dug into his chest. The light was still on in the kitchen and she had her clothes on. She cursed under her breath as he began to move, opening his eyes in the same panicked process that she'd just been through.

'What time is it?' John shook his head, as if trying to gather his wits.

Reba focused on her watch. 'Two o'clock.'

'Okay. It's no problem. I'll get Rosie up and put her in the car, and take you home.'

'No, that's not going to work. You take me home and

come back here. So in the morning I'm stuck without a car, and I need my car because I'm doing some home visits.'

'Then…' John thought for a moment. 'You drive your car, I'll follow you and see you home. That'll be better, won't it.'

'No, it won't. Think about it for one minute and tell me how you get to be less vulnerable than I am when you have Rosalie sleeping in the back seat of your car.'

'Stay here, then. In the spare room.'

His brow was creased, and a pulse beat at the side of his temple. John didn't want that and Reba didn't need it. She was awake now, and the thought of spending the night here seemed suddenly far too complicated.

'I'll be perfectly all right. You can watch me to my car if you feel you must. I live alone, and it's been known for me to go out after dark and drive home in the early hours of the morning before now.'

'But…you don't need to. I know we'd decided not to tell Rosalie about us just yet, but she's got to know sooner or later.'

But his first reaction was all that Reba saw. He'd been afraid, and Reba had to admit that she had too. Not of telling Rosalie, because she was sure that could be managed. He was afraid of the same things that she was. That telling Rosalie meant a commitment to a relationship, when they both knew that they were only in the early stages of fixing the things that stood between them.

'Look, John. You're making a mountain out of a molehill. I'm going to do what I planned on doing all along, and go home. Just kiss me goodbye and let me go, will you.'

'Okay. I guess…' He drew her into his arms, hugging her. 'I don't mean to insinuate that you don't know how to look after yourself.'

'I know.' She snuggled against him, wondering if this

wasn't exactly where she wanted to be. Which was why she really had to go home…

He switched the light over the front door on, watching as she walked down the front path. Reba got into her car, locking the doors and flashing the headlights in a signal to him that he could go inside now. Fifteen minutes later, when she stepped inside her own front door, she called him and John answered on the first ring.

'All safe and sound. I'll see you on Tuesday.'

'Thanks, I appreciate you calling. Sorry if I came on too strong.'

'It's okay. We had such a nice day today, and I didn't want to end by rushing into anything before we'd decided it was the right thing for all of us. I came on too strong too.'

'First argument?'

'First of many, let's hope.' Reba made a stab at a joke, and heard John laugh quietly.

'I'll make it up to you when I see you. Goodnight, sweetheart.'

Reba ended the call, puffing out a breath. John had been her perfect man from the very start. A committed doctor, who understood why she'd made the choices she had for her own career. Perceptive, kind… She could spend all day writing a list of things she loved about him. All night with a list of things they got up to when the sun went down.

He'd been broken and he'd struggled against the immediate chemistry between them as hard as Reba had. But he was strong enough to mend, to try and put the past behind him and make a place in his heart where they could be together.

Reba had been trying too. She'd been driven to succeed by a childhood that had been moulded around the pursuit of excellence, and an adulthood that had been marked a disappointment by her own father. She was beginning to come to terms with that now.

But what if she couldn't change? What if she broke John's valiant heart? Or hurt Rosalie, who'd already been through so much? Reba had tried to balance her work with this new relationship and it had been a constant battle, one that she'd only won because John had commitments of his own. How would she manage if they took the next step and she found she wasn't as strong as John, and couldn't leave her past behind her?

She was too tired for this, too confused to think straight. Reba stumbled up the stairs, catching the scent of the sea in her clothes as she pulled them off. Maybe tomorrow would take care of itself, because suddenly Reba wasn't sure what to do.

John was coming slowly to the realisation that something was the matter. Their telephone conversation on Monday evening hadn't lasted as long as usual, but Reba obviously had a project of some sort on hand and he dismissed the thought. He was just being paranoid. On Tuesday she'd made her apologies and said she couldn't make their date that evening. That was okay, she had a life and it didn't always fit around his. Whatever she was doing was clearly consuming her attention because she apologised again on Wednesday, saying she couldn't make Thursday evening either.

It wasn't so much that he missed her. Or that he clearly wasn't going to be able to see her this week. But Reba *never* apologised for working, and she wasn't usually as vague about what was going on with her. He missed the Reba who might sometimes speak first and think later, but who always told him what was on her mind.

The days dragged by, punctuated by the regular evening calls, that seemed to have lost some of the ebullient sparkle that Reba brought to them. On Friday he abused his position as head of department, and asked Joanne if she had a copy of Reba's appointments diary for the day, since he wanted to know when she was free for lunch. She tutted and showed him how to look it up on the department's intranet, and then John had all the information he needed.

CHAPTER FOURTEEN

Car park. Now.

THERE WAS ONLY one reason why the head of the children's unit would want to meet with the music therapist in the hospital car park. Reba supposed that she deserved to be called to account for her actions.

She'd been working with the kind of focus that was unusual even for her. Guilt and uncertainty had spurred her on, and she'd been busy for every second of the time that she usually spent with John, telling herself that she wasn't really avoiding him but just giving herself some time to think things through.

And now it was all catching up with her. The worst of it was that she was no less confused than she'd been at the start of the week.

She could have texted back and told him no. But John deserved an explanation, even if she didn't have one to give. She opened the doors that led out of the therapy room and into the garden, cutting across the grass to the car park. She could see John standing by his car, watching as she approached.

'You have an hour for lunch?'

'Yes. But John, I'm not going to spend it arguing with you here.' It would have been better to meet in his office.

At least that wasn't a shortcut from one side of the hospital campus to the other, and overlooked by rows of windows on one side of the main building.

'No. We're not going to argue here.' He opened the passenger door of his car, walking round to get into the driver's seat. Fair enough. This had to happen.

He was quiet, but seemed almost relaxed as he drove out of the hospital gates. The fifteen-minute drive to his house was made in silence, as Reba tried to get her muddled thoughts in order.

No such luck. He parked on the hard standing outside his house, and Reba stayed resolutely in her seat. 'Why did we have to come all the way here?'

'Frank exchange of views.' He seemed really committed to the idea that this wasn't an argument. 'We can't do it at work, and so we'll have to do it here.'

'But John…' He'd got out of the car now and had unlocked the front door. Reba hurried after him. 'Listen, we've talked about all of this. You said that you didn't want it to be all about when you're free and that you respect that there'll be times when I'm not.'

'And that's still the case. But you're making excuses, and you've *never* made excuses for anything. It's one of the things I love about you.'

Love. That word. It had been intruding into her own thoughts for the last week, taunting her that it was way beyond her capability to love anyone as much as she loved her work. That was why she'd deliberately avoided John, because he was the answer to that question.

And John had gone and said it now. The man who kept his feelings under wraps, who pretended that everything was going smoothly while he raged inside… He'd said the word *love*. That was how far they'd come together, and Reba felt a sudden, unwelcome warmth for him in her heart.

'This is confusing me, John.' It was the one honest thing she'd said to him all week and he knew it. His lip curled in an expression of triumph.

'Great. Really, that's great. It's a place to start. Reba, I know that you're ambitious. I know that you care about your work and that you have something to prove. That doesn't mean that you have to shut me out—'

'Yes, it *does*.' A second piece of the truth flew from her lips. 'You're right, I do have something to prove, and I'm not particularly proud of that. You're the one person that makes me forget all about it.'

He stared at her. 'You mean…? Actually, Reba, I have no idea what you mean. You're telling me that our relationship is too good for its own good?'

'I don't want to hurt you, John. Our relationship meant change for both of us, and I'm fully aware that you've been a great deal better at that than I have. What if I don't have it in me to change?'

He flung up his hands in an expression of frustration. 'When was the last time you decided you wanted to do something, and then bottled out because you thought you couldn't?'

Reba thought for a moment, her mind suddenly a blank.

'I'm waiting…'

'Stop it, John. You're a normal person. You're kind and brave and you know how the world works. I didn't grow up like that. I was taught that the only thing that matters is achievement.'

John puffed out a breath, turning away from her. The light in his eyes was hidden now, and suddenly Reba felt cold.

'Did you honestly think…' He turned suddenly, his eyes

blazing. 'Did you think that I wouldn't be there for you, Reba? After you've been so present, so clear-sighted with me.'

'I'm afraid that I'll let you down and I won't be there for you. When we fell asleep at your house I saw you were worried that Rosalie might find out about us, but when you thought about it you were willing to take that step. When I thought about it, all that I could think of was that I wasn't ready and I was afraid.'

'But do you want to be?'

'Yes. That's never changed. It's not just the amazing sex...'

He smiled suddenly. 'Mind-blowing... Is that what it's really supposed to be like?'

'You're asking *me*?' Even when they argued, the honesty and the love was still there between them.

He held out his hand to her. 'Take it, Reba. I don't know what's going to happen next, and there are a lot of ways that we could both be hurt. I'm able to take that risk now and I want you to trust me and take it with me.'

Suddenly she was in his arms. They were both trembling, and this felt...so good. As if John really could protect her from an unknown future that might involve a little failure but might involve the biggest success of all.

A thud sounded from upstairs and they both jumped. John stepped away from her, quietly taking her arm and moving her towards the front door.

Did you leave a window open? Reba mouthed the words up at him and John shook his head.

Then footsteps. He opened the front door, clearly about to push her outside, and Reba wriggled against his grasp. If he thought he was going to face an intruder alone, then John had another think coming. Then a voice.

'John… Darling?'

John froze. 'Mum?'

Babs appeared at the top of the staircase, looking flustered. 'John, I'm so sorry. Did I give you a fright? The school called to say that Rosalie had left her workbook at home, so I thought I'd collect it and then drop it in for her. I was just looking for it when I heard you come in. You were obviously engaged in…something important…and I should have called out, but… I sat down on the bed and blocked my ears…'

John swallowed hard. To his credit, he made no attempt to run.

'It's okay, Mum. I should have realised it might be you.'

'I imagine you had other things on your mind…' Babs was walking down the stairs, clutching Rosalie's book. 'Hello Reba. So nice to see you again.'

Perhaps Babs hadn't heard the part about the mind-blowing sex. 'Lovely to see you too, Dr Thornton.'

'You can't be having amazing sex with my son and call me Dr Thornton. Babs, please.' Reba saw John close his eyes, probably trying to convince himself that this wasn't happening.

Reba stepped forward, her knees shaking. 'I'm really sorry, Babs. We've managed to get ourselves into an awkward situation, and I didn't mean to embarrass you.'

Babs seemed to be weighing the question up. 'I think it's for the best. You two clearly need some time together to sort things out between you and so I think that Rosalie should stay with us tonight. You can come and collect her tomorrow afternoon some time, John.'

'That's not necessary, Mum. You're supposed to be going out for the evening.' John was struggling to hide his embarrassment and not succeeding very well.

'That's all right, darling. Irene's already cried off and Maggie and Tim are on holiday in Paris, so we were talking about cancelling this week. And this is important. You don't take enough time for yourself.'

He could say no. John could insist that they didn't need to take Babs up on her offer and that would be an end to it. But she and John *did* have things to work out. One sentence had changed everything—*Did you think that I wouldn't be there for you?*

'Thanks, Mum. I really appreciate it.' He turned to Reba, his face full of warmth. 'What do you reckon, Reba?'

'I reckon that Friday evening and Saturday morning might be just what we need.' She saw a flash of knowing humour in Babs' eyes. 'To talk…'

'Right then.' Babs straightened. 'Well, I'll be off now. Don't talk too much, will you. In my experience, actions are far more reflective of your real feelings, and they speak a little louder sometimes.'

John ignored the comment. 'Thanks, Mum. I'll see you on Saturday.'

'Yes, and both of you come for a late lunch if you're free.' Babs hugged John and kissed him, then took hold of Reba's hand, kissing her cheek. And then she was gone, leaving both John and Reba staring after her.

John cleared his throat awkwardly. 'How much do you think she heard?'

Reba doubted that Babs really had had her hands pressed to her ears, but she reckoned that John needed that element of doubt.

'I don't think we should dwell on that.'

'No. Probably not.' He thought for a moment. 'Was my mother *really* telling us that she thought we should iron out our differences in bed?'

The words *amazing* and *mind-blowing* might have contributed to Babs' stance on that one.

'Yes. I think she was, but we probably shouldn't dwell on that too much either.'

'There's really only one thing I want to say to you, Reba. I know that we can't fix each other, we have to do that for ourselves. But you've already given me the space that I need, and it would be my privilege to give you the space that you need. If we can be honest and accept each other on those terms, I'd love to keep working and playing, arguing and loving with you.'

'I would too, John. I was frightened, but... I don't feel that way now.' Reba laid her hand on his arm, standing on her toes to plant a kiss on his cheek.

He returned the kiss, brushing his lips softly against hers. 'Until tonight, then.'

'Yes. Until tonight.'

They had to leave now if they were going to be back at work in time. As John turned the corner at the end of his road, looking out for the traffic, Reba saw Babs' car parked on the busier main road. She was about to wind down the window and wave when she realised that Babs had her phone pressed to her ear and was deep in conversation.

Probably cancelling her night out tonight. John didn't need to know about that, but Reba would remember to thank Babs with a bunch of flowers the next time she saw her.

John was a happy man. All of the women in his life appeared to be conspiring against him, but that did nothing to take the edge off his contentment.

Rosalie had informed him that Grandma was teaching her to knit, and that she needed to go and look at lengths of wood with Gramps because he was building a new shed.

This was all better done on Sunday mornings, and since they needed to get an early start it would be better if she spent Saturday night at Grandma's house. The words obviously came straight from his mother's mouth, with a few embellishments from Rosalie, and John gave his approval to the plan.

His mother and Reba seemed to be engaging in flower wars, each giving the other thoughtful little arrangements where points were scored for originality rather than size. They'd taken to laughing together in the kitchen, and John had decided that he was better off not knowing what the jokes were about.

And Reba. John had made it clear to her that he supported her ambition, and she'd clearly taken that on board. Their time together might be limited, because of his schedule as well as hers, but it was full of golden moments that reached out into his dealings during the rest of the week.

Last night they'd sprawled naked on her bed, and Reba had carefully set out carved chessmen on a board between them. If he'd wondered whether this might be an exercise in seeing how long they could concentrate before they were distracted, then he was wrong. Reba played to win, and since the unforced error which had sacrificed two of his men had been the result of John's preoccupation with the way her hair fell across her breasts, he'd demanded a rematch. This time he'd managed to capture her queen, but then Reba had won again with a beautifully executed pincer move that he hadn't seen coming. When she'd offered him the chance to make it the best of five he'd declined, carefully laying the board aside and lovingly executing a few moves of his own.

But he reckoned that today would be the biggest challenge for Reba. A whole Sunday afternoon spent with nothing to do.

The fete was an established feature in the life of the hospital, and much the same as it had been when John and Cara went with their parents as children. There was a large bookstall, a games tent for the kids, refreshments and a band, along with a few friendly sporting activities for those who wanted to take part. It all provided a framework for staff, patients and half the local community to turn up and spend an afternoon in the sun.

Reba had enquired tactfully what the provisions for music would be and when she was told that the brass band that was playing had been an essential part of the afternoon for the last twenty years she'd expressed her delight and backed off. John happened to know that it would have taken her a few phone calls to summon world class musicians, ready to take part in a Sunday afternoon jamming session for charity, but, however tempting that was, Reba didn't like to step on anyone else's toes. The Friends of the Hospital had the refreshments in hand, so it appeared that Reba would be consigned to a deckchair for the afternoon.

But she was nothing if not a team player. Reba donned a filmy feminine dress, perfect for a Sunday afternoon fete, inspected the contents of the bookstall with John's father and cheered Rosalie on in the games tent. This might not be the most sophisticated event in the world, but everyone made an effort and it was always a lot of fun.

'Can't *you* play?' They were sitting on the grass, watching the races, and Rosalie lolled to one side, leaning against Reba's arm.

'No, sweetie. There's a brass band.'

Rosalie frowned, clearly not impressed. 'They play the wrong notes.'

'Only one or two. That doesn't matter if you're playing with your heart, does it?'

Rosalie shrugged, jumping to her feet as the staff three-legged race was announced, which she'd already decided was her favourite race. 'Dad... Dad!'

'I'm just going to watch.' John leaned back on his elbows.

'But you could do it with Gramps...' Rosalie's face took on an imploring look and John shook his head. 'Or Reba.'

'No, Rosie, Reba doesn't want to get her dress dirty.' John remembered Reba telling him that contact sports weren't her thing when he'd suggested rounders to her.

'Reba...?' Rosalie turned her pleading look onto her. 'You'll only get dirty if you fall over, and my dad will hold you up.'

Reba grinned suddenly. 'Okay, why not? What do you reckon, John?'

'You're sure?'

'What's the worst that could happen?'

They took their places at the starting line, and Reba took off her shoes and knotted the hem of her dress so that it wouldn't get in the way. There was some delay as everyone tied the fabric bindings around their ankles, and John rolled up his trouser leg, taking off his own shoes so that he wouldn't be in danger of crushing Reba's toes.

'We can get into a rhythm. I'll call the steps, since my legs are shorter than yours.'

'Yeah, okay. Are we going to win this, then?'

Reba looked along the line of competitors. 'Of course we are.'

It looked as if they might for the first half of the course. And then Rosalie started to squeal with excitement from the side of the course and Reba looked round, momentarily losing her concentration. She reached for him as she lost her balance, but her fingers only grazed his arm and John couldn't stop her from falling. It was as much as he could do to stop himself from falling on top of her, and he landed on both hands, one on each side of her.

'Are you okay?' She'd fallen on her side, one arm beneath her body.

'Yes…' Reba grimaced as the other competitors thundered past them. 'We're not going to win now, are we.'

'That doesn't matter. Did you hurt yourself?'

'Couple of bruises, I expect, but I'm all right. No excuse for us to spend too long lying here like this.' She rolled onto her back, laughing, but as she pulled her right arm out from under her she yelped in pain.

John looked down and realised why. Her index and middle fingers were both at a sickening angle, obviously broken or dislocated. And Reba was beginning to cry…

The one thing about being injured at a hospital fete was that there were plenty of people on hand to help. He felt someone untying the fabric around his and Reba's ankles, and when he levered himself away from Reba an ambulance paramedic checked her over quickly and gently sat her up.

'John… John, my fingers.' She was reaching for him, and he caught hold of her left hand.

'Okay. You're okay. It looks worse than it is.'

The paramedic shot him a glance. It might not look worse than it was, but Reba was almost hysterical now, and he knew that she was seeing her music stripped away from her by one fall. Someone appeared with a wheelchair, but she wouldn't let go of him and so he lifted her gently in his arms, carrying her into the hospital.

Reba was trying to keep it all under control. Trying not to look at her fingers as John set her back onto her feet, walking her into the radiology department. Babs arrived with their shoes and, since there was no queue, John rapped briskly on the door to the X-ray room, which was opened by a technician.

'Dr John Thornton. I'll do the paperwork later. I need a lateral and posteroanterior hand view.'

'You can come straight through.'

In a daze, Reba sat down next to the X-ray machine. John was arranging her fingers carefully on the table, and the technician retreated into her cabin.

'I'll be gone for one minute. Just stay still.'

'I can't… I can't feel them, John. They don't even hurt.'

'You're in mild shock right now. They'll start to hurt later.' He tipped her face around. 'Don't look at them, just close your eyes. Trust me.'

Closing her eyes didn't help much, because all she could see were the grotesquely twisted fingers. Her bow hand. How was she going to play the violin now? Reba began to feel sick and opened her eyes, closing them again when she caught sight of her injured fingers. They actually did look worse when she looked at them.

Everything seemed to be going out of focus. She remembered John slipping her shoes onto her feet and replying that his parents were looking after Rosalie when she asked about her. The lift up to his office. People hovering around, and John firmly shepherding everyone away, apart from one man who sat down opposite her.

'I'm Henry. I believe you've met my wife, Lila.'

'Lila. Yes. Who are you?'

'Dr Henry Poste. Head of Orthopaedics.' Henry smiled at her.

'Good. That's good, thank you. Where's John?'

'Right here.' John closed the door behind the last of the

people who'd gathered to help, pulling a third chair over to sit next to her. 'Henry's the best.'

'Kind of you to say so.' Henry smiled, leaning towards Reba. 'I am, of course. Now, let's take a look at your hand, and hopefully we'll have the X-rays in a few minutes.'

John held one hand while Henry gently examined the other. There was a short pause while John opened his laptop and logged on to pick up the X-ray files, and Henry looked at them carefully while John stood behind him, looking at the screen.

'Well. Good news, I believe. Your fingers are dislocated, as we can all see, but there are no broken bones.' Henry peered at the screen. 'There's a very tiny chip of bone in your index finger. Right there, John, you see it?'

'Uh…no.' John leaned in, squinting at the screen. 'Ah, yes.'

'It's very small and that's not going to be a problem. The bone will heal naturally, and there are no fractures. We can reduce the dislocations, give you supports for your fingers, which you must wear for a while, and you'll be as right as rain.'

'Thank you.' Reba breathed a sigh of relief. 'They're starting to throb a bit now.'

'Yes, they will. That's all to be expected. Would you like to see the X-rays?'

'No. Thank you.' Looking at her fingers was hard enough, let alone X-rays. But Henry's reassurance had already made her feel a little better. 'I play the violin. And the piano…'

'Well, of course you'll have to take a break from both for a while, but once your fingers have healed you will be able to play the piano. And the violin, naturally.' Henry chortled at his own joke. 'I've been waiting to say that for many years.'

'Too soon, Henry,' John murmured and Reba managed to summon a smile.

'No, it's not too soon. Thank you.'

The process of setting her fingers straight again wasn't as painful as she'd expected. John had fetched a canister of gas and air and sat beside her, holding the mask in case she needed it. But Henry was swift and precise in his movements, and the pain didn't last long. He applied padded splints to both her fingers and suddenly Reba could look at her hand again and examine the bruises that were forming at the base of her fingers without feeling sick. A sling to immobilise the hand made it feel far more comfortable, and John proffered two paracetamol and a glass of water.

'You'll take Reba home, John?' Henry asked.

'Yes, and I'll stay with her to make sure she's all right.'

'Well, then, I won't need to go through the list of dos and don'ts, I'm sure John is perfectly capable of that.' Henry reached out, taking her left hand and giving it a reassuring squeeze. 'It's been a pleasure to meet you, Reba. I only wish it were in better circumstances.'

'Thank you.' Was that the hundredth or two hundredth time she'd thanked him? Reba wasn't sure but she meant every one of them. 'I really appreciate all you've done.'

'I'd better be off to see how Lila's doing. We have four grandchildren and it usually takes both of us to manage them all...'

Reba had put on a smile when John took her downstairs and out into the sunlight. Babs was sitting with Rosalie under a sunshade at the corner of the grassed area where the fete was still in full swing, and as soon as she caught sight of Reba and John she jumped up, running over to them.

'Are you all right?' Rosalie was leaning against her father's leg, looking at Reba uncertainly, and John put a comforting hand on her shoulder.

'Yes, thank you. I'm fine. No harm done.'

Rosalie craned up, trying to get a glimpse of her hand. 'Your fingers were crooked. I saw them.'

Rosalie must have run forward when she'd fallen. Reba felt herself redden with remorse. 'Well, they're not now. Your dad X-rayed them for me, and Dr Poste straightened them up. Look.'

Reba bent down so that Rosalie could see inside the sling, and wiggled her fingers as much as she could. The sudden throbbing was worth it, because Rosalie nodded in satisfaction.

'My dad will make you better.'

Reba swallowed down the lump in her throat. No one could make this better. She hadn't injured her hand too badly, but this was a sudden, bitter taste of what it would be like to lose everything she'd worked so hard to achieve. John was a good man, and he'd persuaded her that she could change. The panic and horror she'd felt when she'd thought she might lose her ability to work had brought the truth home to her. She couldn't change, and John deserved better than that.

'I'm going to take Reba home and look after her. Will you help by being a good girl for Grandma and Gramps tonight?'

'Yes, Dad.'

'Okay. Give me a hug…' John swept his daughter off her feet, kissing her, and Rosalie chuckled delightedly. Babs walked over, giving Reba a kiss and telling her to take care, and then John ushered her over to his car. Reba relaxed back into the front seat with a sigh of relief.

'I'm so sorry, Reba.' John didn't start the engine when he climbed into the car.

'Sorry? What for? You've been looking after me so well.'

'I should have stopped you.'

'What do you reckon the odds are of competing in a three-legged race and coming away with two dislocated fingers? And since when do you get to stop me from doing anything?'

'I still wish I'd tried.'

'You did try. You told Rosalie that I wasn't going to take part and then I said I would.' It had been that pleading look that Rosalie gave her. Wanting to do something to make her happy. To make John happy. When she'd looked at her fingers her first thought was to resent him for it, and Reba was thanking her lucky stars that she'd been too dazed to voice the undeserved sentiment.

She leaned across, laying her hand on his arm before he reached to start the car. 'Just take me home, I don't need you to stay. I'll be fine and you should be with Rosalie.'

John shook his head. 'No. You're not kicking me out to-night. This time I *do* get to stop you.'

A part of her wanted to be alone, but another part wanted him to stay. Just one last night sleeping next to him, in the hope that she might be able to persuade herself that she could deserve John.

'Okay. Thanks. I'll do as you say.'

He nodded, starting the car. 'Now I *know* you're not well enough to be left on your own.'

CHAPTER FIFTEEN

JOHN HAD LEFT Reba on Monday morning with strict instructions to call him if she needed anything. This fall, the injury, had shaken her badly. Anyone would be shaken by it, but for Reba it meant more than just the physical ramifications. It had threatened everything she'd worked so hard to be, and all that she was so driven to achieve.

He'd taken Rosalie to see her for an hour on Monday evening, and she'd seemed better. More settled, as if she'd made up her mind that this was just a temporary setback. Which was why it was such a shock when she answered the door to him on Tuesday evening.

She looked pale and drawn, as if she hadn't slept a wink last night. Reba walked into the sitting room and lowered herself into an armchair, unable to even raise a smile.

'What's the matter, Reba?'

'I've been thinking, John, and I have something to say to you.'

'Okay. Fire away.' The beginnings of dread curled around his heart. He knew how to meet Reba's passion, whether it took the form of anger or love. John had never seen her so devoid of any emotion, and she didn't seem to be the woman he knew any more.

'I'm going to leave my job at the hospital, John.'

'But… There's no need for that, is there? Henry said

that it's just a matter of keeping your fingers supported for a while, and they'll be fine. Has he been in touch and told you any different?'

'No. When I go back to work I'll be concentrating on my private practice for a while.'

It took a moment for what she was saying to sink in. 'I don't understand. Are you telling me that you're leaving *me*?'

'Yes. I'm sorry, but that's exactly what I'm telling you.'

Something cold settled around his heart. There had been passion right from the start in their relationship, but there was none here. He could hardly even bring himself to ask Reba why she was doing this, but he couldn't leave without knowing.

'Why, Reba?'

'You fixed yourself, John, and I can't. I've never had a relationship that's lasted longer than a few months, and it's because I can't focus on more than one thing at a time. That's the way I was taught to be, and I don't know anything else.'

'And we can't just love each other for what we are?' John could feel the world beginning to close in on him again. The numbness of loss, and the sure knowledge that he would carry that burden and keep going.

'I don't think we can. I've tried to do the work that I need to, so that we can both move on together, but I'm not sure that I know how to. This is my fault and I'm sorry for the pain it's causing, but carrying on is only going to make it hurt even more.'

Pain? He could hardly feel it. Maybe he'd start to feel the throb in time, but right now all he could feel was shock. Reba must know what that was like, she'd experienced much the same on a physical level when she'd fallen.

'I've made sure that the children's unit is covered for a music therapist. The colleague that I work with at my private practice, who filled in for me today, has experience at a number of different hospitals and she's willing to stay for as long as she's needed. She's very talented, and I've told her that she can call me at any time if she has any questions.'

'That's fine. I met her today and she seems very capable.'

They were down to this. Temporary cover for her job and handover periods. There really was nothing more. They'd had all of the highs and lows, Reba had helped John to fight for himself and then he'd fought to keep her, but every victory just seemed to make her less able to cope with their relationship.

And he'd failed her. He knew that Reba was vulnerable, but he hadn't been able to reach the part of her that constantly drove her on to succeed.

'I should go.'

Reba nodded. 'As you wish, John.'

No, he didn't wish this at all. But there was no point in telling Reba that because her mind was made up. His was too, now. Reba had paid a high price for loving him. Her injury would heal, but she would still be torn between spending time with him and working to appease the voices in her head that only accepted excellence as being good enough.

'I'll have the glockenspiel delivered back to you in the next few days.' One last end to tie up. He knew that Reba's musical instruments were precious.

He got to his feet and Reba sprang to hers. She followed him out into the hallway, seeming to lose her composure for a moment.

'If… Maybe she doesn't… Whatever you think's best. It's up to you…'

A glimpse of Reba's tendency to open her mouth before

she'd decided what to say. Suddenly he could feel again, and it hurt so badly he caught his breath.

'I mean…' Reba turned the corners of her mouth down. 'If Rosalie would like to keep the glockenspiel then it's hers. I'd really like her to have it. Tell her to keep playing with her heart.'

John didn't know what to say to that. It was a generous gesture, and it meant that he wouldn't have to explain to Rosalie why she had to lose the instrument that she loved. But he was done with generosity and love now.

'We'll see. I don't know.' He turned, opening the front door, and walked to his car. Nothing hurt any more.

John had taken to leaving his office door open. Every time someone knocked and opened the door a little too quickly he couldn't help remembering how Reba had always flown into his office with an armful of challenges for him. That constant reminder that she was no longer here was a pain that he could do without.

He'd discussed their parting with his counsellor—or rather talked about it while she nodded and asked a few questions. John supposed that was how non-directive counselling worked, but he wished she could come up with a formula to make it hurt a little less. Or maybe hurt a little more. There were times when he got through the day just by cultivating a feeling of numbness.

His mother had asked after Reba and he'd told her they were no longer together.

'I'm sorry to hear that. I like Reba very much.' His mother thought for a moment. 'Would you like us to take Rosalie for a couple of weeks?'

John shook his head. 'To be honest, Rosie's about the

only thing keeping me going at the moment. You can't mope around with a five-year-old in the house.'

'Exactly. You know that there were days when I couldn't get out of bed after Cara died, but you always coped. You looked after Rosalie so well.'

'It was different for me.'

'Maybe… But losing Cara was still hard for you. I never quite forgave Elaine for her attitude to it all.'

'I don't think about her all that much now.' Elaine was a pale shadow from the past, obscured by the vibrant colour that Reba had brought.

'I can't say I'm sorry to hear you say that…' His mother puffed out a sigh. 'Look, John, I don't want to meddle but I can see you're upset. I really think you should let your father and me take Rosalie for a little while. It's about time you stopped coping.'

Reba had said something of the same. Warmth and pain rushed into his heart at the thought, almost bringing tears to his eyes.

'I might take two weeks off work.'

'Do it. You've hardly had any time off in the last year, you must have plenty of leave saved up. Aren't you going to lose it if you don't take it?'

'Maybe. I hadn't really thought about it.'

'John! Am I going to have to nag you about this?'

The glimmer of something began to flutter in his heart. He'd been paralysed before he met Reba, and could do nothing to help himself. But she'd given him the tools to mend, and he knew how to do it now. It wouldn't be easy, but things that were really worth it never were.

John set out at six on a Saturday morning a week later. And just drove. That night he stayed in a pub just outside

Melton Mowbray, and the following night in a rather smart hotel in Yorkshire that happened to have a vacancy. He was a traveller, with no fixed abode for the week and no particular place to go.

On the fourth day he found himself in Scotland, and drove north past mountains and lochs. The wild countryside, and the fact that he'd hardly spoken to anyone in the last four days, hadn't provided him with any sudden revelations about the way that life worked, and John still didn't know what he was hoping for.

He found somewhere to stop for lunch, taking his sandwiches down to a deserted waterside and sitting down. It was breathtakingly beautiful here, and as he ate alone he seemed to find her again. Reba's smile in the rippling loch. Her dark hair in the shadows that moved across the sunlit hillside. Her sudden passion as birds rose in perfect synchronicity in response to a sound across the water.

Something brushed against his cheek, cool in the breeze. When he raised his hand to brush it away he felt tears.

'Reba. Reba.'

He murmured her name and then heard it echo back amongst the hillsides as he shouted across the water.

Reba!

Things were not going well. The first annoyance was that it took twice as long to do even simple tasks with two fingers in splints and when you were supposed to keep that hand immobilised as much as possible. Typing and keyboard work was awkward one-handed and, since she was right-handed, writing was impossible. Dressing was time-consuming and she was running out of easy-care clothes that didn't have buttons or need ironing.

Maybe it would have been better if Reba could have

worked her feelings out with a few exhaustingly angsty pieces of music, but playing either the violin or the piano was out of the question at the moment. And work was difficult. She could do many of the things that she usually did in her therapy sessions, but wasn't happy with giving her clients any less than a hundred percent. Her colleagues at the private practice had taken over most of her caseload, which left Reba trying to do as much as she could to help but at a loose end for most of the time.

These things would pass and they were just the tip of the iceberg. Everything else would have been bearable if she hadn't missed John so much. She was angry with herself for being the one who'd broken them apart, and she was angry with him... She didn't know why she was angry with John, he'd done nothing wrong. But sometimes being angry was a little less painful than just missing him. There was no going back because it was her own way of life that had come between them. And when she woke in the night, crying for him, it seemed that she would still be missing him on the day that she died.

This morning was going to be different. She said that to herself every morning and these days it never was. Reba tumbled out of bed, going through the annoying process of showering one-handed, fixing her hair and getting dressed. Today she would be recording the music of the river.

Saturday morning strollers were walking along the path that ran past the side of her house, and Reba tucked a note into her letterbox, in case the parcel she was expecting arrived this morning. She climbed carefully down the short sloping bank, staying within sight of her front door so that a courier would find her, and sat down in the grass. A startled duck flapped away across the water before she could get the microphone out of her pocket, and she cursed. That might have been a good one…

She sat for an hour in the sun, not getting a great deal done but it was slightly more constructive than moping inside the house. When she heard footsteps behind her, swishing through the long grass, she wondered whether she should record those…

'Reba?'

She froze. Didn't dare look around. Then John sat down beside her.

'What are you doing out here?'

'What sort of question's that?' she bit back at him automatically, already hurt by three weeks of having to do without his smile.

He looked great. His hair was a shade blonder, as if it had seen some sunshine recently, and it suited him. And here by the water his eyes seemed a little less grey and a little more blue.

'It's one of those throwaway opening questions. When you have no idea what to say to someone.'

Reba's heart started to beat faster. His relaxed air suited him a little better than the buttoned-up man she'd first met. She was beginning to feel frumpy, sitting here in an oversized sweatshirt, with rings under her eyes from too little sleep.

But she knew John. If he was here then he had a reason. It wasn't just curiosity or to throw something at her in revenge for all the hurt she'd caused. And, despite herself, despite knowing that there was no hope for their relationship, she wanted to hear what he had to say.

'I'm recording sounds. Maybe matching them up with music at some point, I'm not sure yet. I haven't thought it all through yet.'

He nodded. 'So you're bored.'

'Yeah. What are you doing here?' That was the zillion-dollar question.

'I didn't like the way we left things between us. I wanted to try and make that right.'

Closure, then. Maybe his counsellor had put John up to this, but Reba didn't imagine that it had been all her idea. John was more of a leader than a follower.

'I don't think we can make it right, can we?'

'I wouldn't be here if I believed that. Reba, there's something I want to say to you.'

'Would you like to come inside?' Reba instantly regretted the question. She'd been plumbing new depths of untidiness lately.

'Wherever you're most comfortable.'

'Here's nice.'

He nodded, looking at the gently flowing water in front of him. 'I've been thinking about that night, when you held out your hand and challenged me to reach out. I want to thank you for being there for me when I was in crisis. For telling me the hard truths that I didn't want to hear.'

Reba swallowed down the lump in her throat. 'You made it work, John. It was worth it.'

'I told you once that I wanted you just as you are. That was the truth, but I let you down by telling you that. You cared enough to see the man that I could be and not the one that I was, and to challenge me to change.'

'It was obvious…'

He nodded, shooting her a wry smile. 'Then I'll return the challenge. You have to stop seeing yourself through your father's eyes and value the things that make *you* happy.'

It was simpler and a lot more straightforward to just go on as she always had, putting everything else second to her work. But suddenly, faced with all that she'd lost, that hurt too much to even think about.

'So this breakup is going to be the most civilised ever? We'll be friends who can tell each other anything.' Reba hit back at him again. Trying to deny her own pain and the truth in his words.

'No. I can't be your friend because I'll always want more. I love you, but I have to learn to live without you. I don't know how I'm going to do that yet, but you've given me hope that I might just work it out.'

'John, just... I appreciate what you're saying but just go. Please, I can't take this.' Reba felt tears pricking at the corners of her eyes. She blinked them back and saw his beautiful eyes fill with tears. John *had* changed and at this moment all she wanted was to be able to do the same.

'Just one more thing?'

'One. No more.'

He felt in his pocket and then took her hand, dropping something into it. Keeping his fingers around hers so she couldn't look at what was there.

'I'll always love you and be there if you need me, and... you can throw this away if you want to. Just hold it in your hand and count to ten first, and know that you have a piece of my heart. You'll never be able to give that back because it's freely given, with no expectation of anything in return.'

They were both trembling. 'Go, John. Please.'

He got to his feet and walked away without looking back. Reba opened her hand and saw a piece of blue sea glass that she recognised as one of the treasures that John had shown her, kept from his childhood. Held in place by a tracery of silver wire, it hung from a silver chain.

She raised her hand, ready to throw it into the river.

Count to ten...

It felt as if it was burning a hole in her palm, but before she got to ten she found herself holding the sea glass to her heart, crying bittersweet tears.

'Are you all right, love?' A voice sounded from the path behind her and Reba turned, wiping her face with the sleeve of her sweatshirt.

'Yes. Thank you, I'm fine.'

And Reba had things to do. She stood up, putting the microphone and recorder back into her pocket, and made for her front door with all the purpose that had been missing from her life since she'd lost John.

The house in Berlin was beautiful, with soaring white-painted spaces and a grand piano which took up a whole section of the huge open-plan ground floor. Reba hugged her mother and father, ignoring Hans' dismay at the supports around her fingers.

'It's fine. It'll heal.'

'I'll make an appointment for you with my doctor in Harley Street.'

'No, you won't, Hans. I had the head of Orthopaedics at my hospital do the reductions and he's the best there is. And free.'

Hans shrugged. 'You should have only the *very* best, Rebekah.'

'That's what *best there is* means. The very best.' It appeared that Reba wasn't going to have to find a way to broach the subject that she'd come here to talk about. She'd been here for five minutes and Hans was already doing it for her.

It was good to see her parents, though. Hans was creative, funny and a great raconteur and her mother was the anchor of the family with an easy-going warmth that Reba had missed. They went out for dinner at one of the best restaurants in Berlin, strolling through the streets afterwards so that her parents could point out places of interest to her.

Her mother was an early riser, leaving Reba and Hans sunk in their armchairs talking while she took her book with her to bed. Reba had been afraid of this moment, knowing that it was coming, but somehow it didn't seem quite so confronting now that it was here. She laid her hand on the blue sea glass pendant around her neck, to remind herself of all the reasons she had for doing this.

'I've missed you, Reba. We used to be so close.'

'I've missed you too. It's one of the reasons I came.'

Hans regarded her thoughtfully. 'To clear the air?'

'Yes, actually. I didn't know that you were aware that the air needed clearing, though.'

'You think I didn't notice that I haven't seen you for two years.'

'I've been busy. And a little cross.' Rebecca took a sip of her nightcap. 'And I'm wondering why I don't call you Dad.'

'You've always been my equal, Reba, even when you were a little girl.'

'No. That's my point. I wasn't your equal. I was your child.'

Hans narrowed his eyes. 'You think I was a bad father? You may be right.'

'I think you were a great father. You showed me things and places that many people never get to see and you taught me how to make wonderful music. You loved me and I'm grateful to you for all that.'

'But…?'

Reba took a breath. 'Can you help a child who's had brain damage speak again? Or comfort a child in pain, or help them to express themselves? Because I can. That's my calling, my passion. It's not second best and I haven't sold anyone short—neither you or me.'

'And I mustn't say that. Is that what you mean?'

'No, you're at liberty to say whatever you want. But I want to ask something of you.'

'Anything, Reba.' Hans' face became grave. He knew that she was serious about this.

'I want you to support me in the career I've chosen for myself. Because it was a good choice and it makes me happy. I'm asking you to do it against all of your own inclinations and for just one reason. Because you're my father.'

'You never said this before.'

'No, I didn't. Because I'm your child, and your judgement matters to me.' Reba was quivering with anxiety. But Hans seemed perplexed rather than angry.

'Tomorrow I want you to tell me all about it. About the children whose lives you can change and about the music. And I promise I'll listen to you. But in the meantime… Can we play?'

Maybe he'd mellowed. Maybe Reba had grown up a bit. Or maybe stones drawn from the sea really did have magical properties. Reba wasn't sure, but her hand strayed again to the sea glass that hung around her neck, tucked into the neckline of her top.

'I'd really like that. I haven't played since…this.' She held up her fingers, turning the corners of her mouth down.

It was nice to sit on the long piano stool with him. Beethoven for three hands took a little improvisation, but Hans' choice was one of those little jokes that they both understood without explanations. Beethoven had been deaf and yet continued to compose despite it all, so two fingers that were sure to heal weren't such a hill to climb in comparison.

Reba led, and Hans fell into step alongside her. Effortless, if you didn't count the hours of practice that were a way of life for them both. Soaring in the cavernous space, and yet intensely personal. And she missed John so much…

'Dad…' She stopped playing, her shoulders shaking, tears running down her face. Her father's concentration broke suddenly and he put his arm around her shoulders, comforting her.

'What is it, Reba?'

'Dad, I've been a fool. And I think I've really messed up…'

CHAPTER SIXTEEN

SOME THINGS JUST HURT, whichever way you cut them. John had said what he'd wanted to say to Reba, done what he'd wanted to do. He felt a little more at peace with himself, as if he'd repaid some of the enormous debt that he owed her. But that didn't stop the pain or the grief at losing her. There was no getting around going through the hard stuff.

The worst parts of it were when he was alone at home. No longer on the open road, with the feeling of movement to lull him. Without Rosalie, or his parents or any of the people at the hospital whose company seemed to insulate him from what was going on in his heart. When he was alone he had to face it all.

He'd taken to sitting in the conservatory as the sky darkened, the doors into the garden slightly ajar so that he had the company of the noises of the night along with his thoughts. The strains of music drifting in the quiet air seemed a natural progression to loving Reba and for a moment he didn't move, simply enjoying the strains of Clair de Lune that were floating in his mind.

Clair de Lune…? It sounded a little different when Reba played it on the violin but the sadness remained. The longing that seemed to permeate every note. When he got to his feet, flinging open the doors, he saw her.

Dressed in black, as if she were playing to a full concert

hall, her face seeming to shine in the moonlight. A piece of blue sea glass suspended around her neck. The supports around two fingers of her right hand meant she was holding the bow a little awkwardly, but the music was still the same. She must have seen him, but she kept playing until he was close enough to reach out and touch her.

'You came.' Maybe she'd been summoned by his thoughts and it occurred to John that she might not be here at all.

Reba smiled up at him. No fantasy could have fabricated Reba's smile, or the effect that it had on him.

'I love you, John. I couldn't stay away.'

Her words gave him the courage to take the violin and the bow from her hands, the first time he'd dared touch either of them. But she didn't reach to retrieve them, back into the safety of her grasp. Reba followed him into the conservatory and he laid the instrument down carefully on the long sideboard.

'Am I too late?' She looked up at him.

'How could you be? Always is a very long time…' The shock of seeing Reba again was beginning to recede now, and John realised that he needed to say the words as much as she seemed to need to hear them. 'I love you, Reba. Now and for ever.'

She reached for him and he curled his arms around her, hearing her own trembling sigh mirror his own.

'I've been doing a lot of thinking. A lot of talking as well. I went to Berlin to see my father and I said some things that he needed to hear a long time ago.'

She could tell him about that later. There was only one more thing that John wanted to hear now. 'Will you stay?'

'Yes. You're my centre, John. The thing that holds everything else together and gives it meaning. I can't promise to always get it right, but I'm here for that as well.'

It was all he needed to know. Everything else would fall into place around that. They could talk later.

'May I kiss you?'

'I think you should. We've already had to wait too long.'

John held her close, kissing her, feeling the accompaniment of passion that always ran through their most tender embraces.

'This is everything, Reba. Your love is all that I want, and everything I need.'

Her lips curved against his. 'This is just the start, John. We have everything to look forward to.'

EPILOGUE

One year later

REBA HAD PLANNED everything down to the last detail.
She'd given John a printed spreadsheet detailing where everyone would be, and at what time, and there was one gap.
From nine until nine-thirty, after the hairdresser had left
and before her bridesmaids arrived, she'd be alone at home.

John slipped his door key into the lock, entering the quiet
house. It was different now. When Reba had sold her house
they'd stored all of her furniture in the garage and had taken
their time in integrating their households. Reba's eclectic
exuberance somehow blended perfectly with his fondness
for calm, natural surroundings and now their home seemed
a great deal more than the sum of its parts.

When he walked upstairs he saw a chair in the hallway,
outside their bedroom. Tapping gently on the door, he sat
down and heard Reba call his name.

'Not like you to leave a whole half hour unaccounted for.'
He grinned, leaning against the door that separated them.

'It isn't, is it. What must I have been thinking?'

She'd been thinking the same as he had. Reba wanted to
do things properly and John had stayed with Rosalie at his
parents' house last night. But if it was bad luck for him to
see his bride on the morning of their wedding, there was

nothing to prevent him from hearing her. Just as she did with everything else, Reba had turned the accepted way of doing things into something that was deliciously theirs alone.

'How's my dad doing?'

John chuckled. 'Surprisingly well. I think he took the lecture that you gave him about this being *our* day to heart.' The choice of music for the ceremony had been something of a sticking point between Reba and her father, but Reba had stood firm and Hans had capitulated. He still spoke his mind, but now that Reba had learned to expect him to accept her choices, he did so.

'You'll make sure he's here by eleven, won't you? I don't want him rushing in at the last moment.'

'He was already looking at his watch when I left.'

John heard Reba laugh. 'And you've got your buttonhole from the florist?'

'Yes. Mum cried when she saw her corsage. That was such a nice thing to do.'

Reba had asked John about Cara's favourite flowers, and John had told her that she loved the purple hues of violets and lilacs. So Reba had chosen lilacs for her own bouquet, and matching shades for the buttonholes and corsages. Rosalie loved her pale lilac bridesmaid's dress, and the fresh flowers that she would wear in a headband.

'Babs is okay, though?'

'Yes, she's a lot better than okay. I'm not sure she realised how much she'd love it, when we asked her about the idea.'

'I can't wait, John. I love you so much.' He heard the brush of her fingers against the other side of the door, and raised his own hand to touch it.

'Did you look? You can tell me…'

Reba laughed. For months John had been heading her

off when she tried to sneak to the end of the garden and see the inside of the large music room that he'd been building as a wedding present for her.

'No, I didn't look—where's the fun in that? Is it finished?'

'Yes, it's finished. So any time you like we can move your music room from the spare bedroom, and come up with some ideas about what we can do with an extra bedroom.'

'I could buy you a train set…' Reba's voice took on a teasing note.

'Nah. I like the colours you picked for a nursery.'

'Me too…' He heard Reba sigh. 'You're going to have to sneak out before long, if the bridesmaids aren't going to catch you here.'

'Yeah. Just a few moments more.' John pressed his hand against the door, knowing that Reba was doing the same…

It had been worth the wait. Reba appeared at the entrance to the church exactly on time, and Hans accompanied her proudly down the aisle. She looked so beautiful, in a simple white dress with flowers in her hair and a bouquet of exuberant colour.

Rosalie was the star of the show. Her bridesmaid's duties were carefully choreographed to fit in with a four-handed piano piece with Hans, who skilfully made her role shine while his supported it. When Hans nudged her into standing up and giving a bow, the wedding guests turned into an audience and applauded, led by the bride and groom.

'Thank you for making me so happy, John.' Reba danced in his arms in the huge marquee, to the music that was being played by an assortment of the guests. 'I love you always.'

'I love you too, Reba.' He twirled her round, accompanied by an impromptu swell in the melody. 'Always.'

'Sickness and health. Agreements and disagreements.' She kissed him.

'All of it. Especially the disagreements.'

* * * * *

FALLING AGAIN
FOR THE SURGEON

KARIN BAINE

MILLS & BOON

For Stella, Sam & Miriam. xx

CHAPTER ONE

'I'M NOT HIS MOTHER,' Jessie found herself repeating to the latest attending doctor, as she had to every other medical colleague she'd encountered earlier, on the way through the emergency department with the small child on the stretcher.

'What's his name?' the doctor asked, ignoring her protestations and continuing his examination of the boy's X-rays and CT scans.

She heaved out a sigh of frustration. 'Simon. I don't know his surname or anything else about him. I was simply there when the accident happened. The fire and rescue service are still on scene, trying to get his parents out of the car. He was catapulted through the window into the road. I was in the car behind—I was able to keep him talking for a while until he lost consciousness.' The paramedics had passed on their preliminary findings to the A&E staff but Jessie repeated it, trying to process what she'd witnessed. He'd been in a lot of pain and they'd suspected a spinal cord injury, which was why they'd ordered a battery of tests on his arrival.

'You shouldn't be in here if you're not family.' He

attempted to dismiss her but Jessie was reluctant to leave the boy alone when she'd seen how frightened he'd been. She'd stayed with him while he'd been examined and before they'd wheeled him in to X-ray. There should be at least one semi-familiar face when he woke up.

'No, but he was responding to me, and I do work at the hospital.' That info, along with the lanyard she flashed at him, at least made him pause for a second.

'You're a doctor?'

Jessie grimaced. Skating around the facts had got her this far with the busy paramedics but now she'd been rumbled. 'Not exactly. I'm a physiotherapist.'

As expected, that information drew an eyeroll in response. 'Thank you, Ms…Rea, but I think we can manage without you from here.'

'She can stay for now,' a voice announced as another doctor arrived with a swish of the cubicle curtain.

Jessie was about to thank the new arrival for his compassion when she saw who'd entered, and suddenly lost the power of speech.

'Good to see you, Jessie, though I wish it were in better circumstances.'

Taller than she remembered, his hair a deeper auburn than the red she recalled blazing in the summer sun the last time she'd seen him, Cameron Holmes was as handsome as ever.

'He's not my son,' she blurted, the shock of seeing him again as great as the emergency situation she'd been drawn into on her way home from work.

He paused his glance over his patient's chart to shoot her a smile. 'I gathered that. You can sit with him for now but he'll be going for surgery soon.'

'Surgery?' she repeated, blinking at the vision before her of her first love—the only man she'd ever loved—standing before her. Cameron wasn't so much the one that got away as the one she'd chucked back in the lake in an attempt to give him a second chance at life.

'Yes. The sooner he has surgery, the greater chance there is of him making a full recovery. I'm an orthopaedic surgeon. I specialise in spinal injuries, that's why they called me in. Usually I work in the Belfast Community Hospital.' That explained his somewhat casual attire of paint-splattered jeans and ragged T-shirt along with his sudden appearance at her place of work. If he was on call to cover the area he would've had to drop whatever he was doing and come straight here to the hospital in Innisheg village. She hadn't known he was still living in the country, never mind living less than an hour away from her.

The other attending medics seemed grateful to hand over Simon's care in the meantime so they could go and treat other patients waiting for their attention, leaving Jessie and Cameron alone in the cubicle with the boy.

He must have seen her assessment of his attire, following her gaze to the large hole at the seam of his tight black crew neck, exposing a tantalising patch of smooth taut skin. 'I was decorating. I'm not usually this unkempt but I didn't want to waste time when every second counts in cases like this.'

It was on the tip of her tongue to tell him he looked good to her when she realised how inappropriate it would seem, not only due to the current circumstances but also because they hadn't parted on the best of terms and hadn't seen each other in nearly fifteen years. She should be more impressed by his career status than how well he'd aged.

'I'm still trying to get my head around the fact that you're a surgeon. All of your hard work really paid off. Your family must be so proud.' It had been his dream to work in medicine, something which had seemed so far out of reach for someone who'd struggled with dyslexia. With hard work and the right support, he'd obviously shown everyone exactly what he was capable of.

Jessie had never doubted him. When she'd studied with him he'd been driven, his work ethic second to none. That was part of the reason she'd fallen for him. Despite the obstacles, how many people had disparaged him, he hadn't let that get in the way of his goal. It was a pity fate had prevented her from following her dreams too.

He raised an eyebrow at her. 'What do you think?'

It was a bucket of cold water over her initial enthusiasm at seeing him in his dream job to find his family were still treating him as abysmally as they always had. She wondered if that was why she hadn't seen him around their hometown since the day he'd left for medical school. Every Christmas or bank holiday weekend she'd wondered if she might run into him, but the dates always came and went without a single sighting. Now she knew why. He'd had nothing to come back for.

'I'm sorry. I thought perhaps, with time, they might have supported you better. You always deserved more. It shouldn't have mattered that you were the youngest of six siblings, they still should have taken care of you.'

'Yes, well, having parents who call you stupid even after it's discovered you have dyslexia teaches you not to have high expectations. Everything I achieved is down to you and to the support I finally received in high school.'

'I was merely your study buddy. It was you who put in the work. I'm not sure I can take any credit.' Especially when he'd completed his studies in a different part of the country, away from her.

'We both know you were a lot more than that.' He didn't have to say any more than that to stop her arguing, bringing back memories of their time together as teenagers. Before the heartache.

With Cameron's neglectful family and Jessie a young carer for her mother, they'd both been set apart from their classmates, loners who'd gravitated towards each other.

'It didn't take a lot of research to find out that visual stimulation helps dyslexics to retain information and having a good study schedule helped both of us.' She deliberately chose to ignore the reference to their past relationship. It wouldn't do either of them any good to revisit that. Especially when she'd worked so hard to make sure he moved on without her.

He took a moment before he responded, as though he'd toyed with the idea of saying more on the subject then changed his mind.

'I see you went into an area of medicine after all.' He pointed at her work pass, though she was sure he'd already heard what field she'd gone into.

'Yes, physiotherapy meant I could study at the local college instead of the city.'

It was a touchy subject when they'd planned to go to medical school together. The time she'd spent with Cameron had been the happiest of her life, but circumstances had brought that to a swift end.

'Listen, Jessie, I have to go and prep for surgery. It was nice to see you again.' His abrupt exit would suggest he looked back on their time together with less yearning than she did, but she had only herself to blame. She'd broken his heart and now, spying the wedding ring on his finger, she was breaking her own all over again too.

Cameron Holmes was a reminder of everything she'd lost, everything she could never have again. Worse than that, she suspected she was going to see even more of him in the future. As Simon's surgeon he would be overseeing his progress and Jessie would be tasked with helping the boy walk again. And she cared too much to abandon the child simply because of her own discomfort around her childhood sweetheart.

Although she was probably nothing but a footnote in Cameron's story now he appeared to be a successful married surgeon, her highlights reel had begun and ended with him. He was the only man she'd ever loved, ever dared to plan a future with. Now it seemed she was going to have to pay the price for her mistakes by seeing him on a regular basis.

Cameron had to take a moment outside the emergency department to compose himself. Being on call was always full of tension, not knowing what he'd be walking into when he came through the hospital doors. Emergencies he could deal with—his job was fraught with life-changing decisions and surgeries he was ultimately responsible for—but seeing Jessie again was something which had thrown him completely out of his comfort zone.

He clutched his hand to his chest, almost certain he could still feel that hole she'd torn in his heart when she'd dumped him before medical school. It would be much easier if he didn't remember, or if that pain had lessened over time, but neither had happened. He'd simply had to grow around the void she'd left inside him. It had always been there but now it had awakened like an angry volcano, Jessie's reappearance filling him full of anger and hurt. Except there was no room in his life to deal with it all now.

He had enough to keep him occupied, with Thomas

and work. Spending time looking back wasn't going to do him any favours now. Especially wondering why he hadn't been enough for her, and if she'd met someone who could give her everything he'd apparently been lacking.

But it wouldn't do anyone any good for him to start soul-searching now. Fifteen years apart was a long time. They were adults who'd gone on to have lives apart from one another, even though there'd been a time when he'd thought he wouldn't survive without her.

Jessie had been the first person who'd ever shown him love and kindness. Perhaps that was what had kept her alive in his heart for so long. He'd put her on a pedestal that not even his wife had been able to reach. Whatever it was about seeing her again that got under his skin, he hoped it was short-lived. Along with their reacquaintance.

He was here to do a job and he'd do it much better without his brown-haired, green-eyed first love monopolising his thoughts.

'Hey, Mum, I'm going to be late tonight so don't wait up for me. There was an accident on the way home. I'm fine, but there was a young boy hurt so I'm staying with him for a while.' While she was waiting for Simon to come out of surgery Jessie phoned home so her mother wouldn't be sitting up worrying about what was keeping her.

Jessie's father had left before she'd been born and

her mother had suffered a blood clot during her pregnancy, which had subsequently caused a stroke and left her partially paralysed.

Ever since then Jessie had been burdened with the guilt of thinking she was to blame for her mother's physical decline and she'd spent her life in penance, trying to make up for it. As a result, she still lived at home, taking care of her mother when she wasn't at work.

'Oh, Jessie. Are you sure you're all right?'

'I'm fine. I came along after the accident but this boy's parents were hurt. I thought someone should stay with him until his family can get here.'

'Of course. Is he going to be okay?'

'He had some spinal damage and he's in surgery at the minute.' She hesitated before telling her the rest, unsure if she should mention Cameron when that period of their lives had been a difficult time for both of them. In the end she knew she had to confide in someone when her emotions were in such turmoil and her mother was the only one who could possibly understand.

'Mum, the surgeon is Cameron Holmes,' she finally said, and it seemed an age before her mother responded.

'Did you tell him?'

Jessie sighed. They'd had this conversation fifteen years ago, before he'd left for medical school, and they still had differing views on the subject. 'No. It wasn't the time or the place.'

'Jessie, he had a right to know then, and he has a right to know now. It would give you both some closure to finally tell him what happened. I know you never got over it, or him, and you've been pushing people away ever since.'

'I don't want to get into this right now, Mum. You know why I didn't tell him what happened. We were eighteen, we weren't ready for a baby, and I didn't want to ruin his future. He would have insisted on dropping out of medical school to take care of us and it didn't seem fair on him to keep him trapped here after he'd worked so hard.'

Even the mention of their baby was enough to make her feel as though her insides were being squeezed until she could barely breathe. She'd been young and foolish, and so carried away with the passion and love she felt for Cameron she'd taken stupid risks. The result being an unplanned pregnancy that threatened both of their futures. She hadn't wanted to lose Cameron but she didn't want to be responsible for ruining someone else's life when she was still burdened with guilt over her mother's ill health. Cameron, being the man he was, would have insisted on staying if he'd known there was a baby on the way, so she hadn't told him, instead simply insisting it was over and that she didn't want to be with him any more. What might have seemed cruel at the time was actually an act of love, setting him free instead of holding him back, the way his own family had done. Though he would never know it.

'You had plenty of time to tell him after you lost the baby. I'm sure Cameron would have understood why you acted the way you did. You could have tried to make a go of things.' Her mother's voice was soft, touching gently on the subject Jessie never wanted to talk about.

The miscarriage had felt like a double loss, as though she was losing Cameron all over again. The one consolation she'd had after their break-up was the knowledge she was carrying a part of him with her. She'd imagined raising a mini-Cameron, all red hair and long legs, pouring all of her love into their son when she couldn't be with his father. To lose the baby so soon after the love of her life had caused her such physical and emotional pain she'd thought she wouldn't survive it. It was as though she'd lost her breath and hadn't been able to catch it again.

If not for her mother's support, Jessie wasn't sure she'd have made it through her grief. Since then she'd put all of her energy into work and looking after her mother so she didn't have time to wallow, mourning everything she'd lost fifteen years ago.

'No, I couldn't. What sort of future would we have had if I couldn't give him children?' It was ironically cruel that the pregnancy she'd been afraid to tell him about had ended in her finding out she had the same health issues as her mother. Antiphospholipid syndrome, a disorder of the immune system, meant she was at great risk of developing blood clots. It also meant a higher risk of miscarriage, and although she now regularly took a small dose of aspirin to thin her blood there were no guarantees she wouldn't miscarry again.

When she and Cameron had talked about their future together he'd made it clear that he wanted a family some day, but only when he had a successful career with the money and time to devote himself to his children. His own upbringing, where he was neglected by his parents, had left a lasting impact on him and he didn't want to inflict that on another generation.

Perhaps if they'd still been together they could've weathered it all, looked into alternatives like adoption, but there wouldn't have been anything to gain by telling him she'd lost his baby and could never give him another one. It had been best to let him live his life and find happiness with someone who could give him a family.

'I still think you should have let him make that decision.'

She could almost see her mother shrugging her shoulders.

'It's in the past, Mum. There's no point in dragging it up again. He's married, probably with a family. He's moved on. Maybe that's all I need to know so I can do the same.' There'd been many reasons why none of her relationships had worked out over the years—the time she spent looking after her mother, the knowledge that she probably wouldn't have children—but at the heart of it she knew it was because she'd never loved anyone the way she'd loved Cameron.

Now she'd seen for herself the same wasn't true for him, perhaps she could stop comparing everyone else to her first and only love.

'I'm sure you know best.' Her mother's tone, sounding much like the one she'd used when Jessie had sent him off to medical school without telling him about the baby, suggested different.

'I didn't phone to discuss the past and the what-might-have-beens. I just wanted you to know I'll be late home tonight.' Jessie put an end to the subject, refusing to venture down that road when she'd spent too long wondering if she'd made the right decision at the time. Now she knew he was a successful married surgeon, it appeared she had. All she had to do was reconcile herself with the past and her own actions and maybe she'd find someone else too.

'Okay. I'll say a prayer for you all before I go to sleep. 'Night, Jessie.'

''Night, Mum.' Jessie ended the call, her burden a little lighter after sharing the evening's events with the only other person who knew the real history she had with Cameron.

It was going to be a long night, not only waiting for news on Simon's surgery but also because she'd likely spend the time revisiting the past in her head. Seeing Cameron again was making her confront the decisions she'd made and she was afraid that, under such scrutiny, she might realise that not all of them had been for the best.

CHAPTER TWO

'IT'S NEVER EASY when it's a child,' Bobby, the anaesthetist, commented as they waited for the anaesthetic to kick in.

'No. I mean, surgery is never routine when you have someone's life in your hands, but one mistake or complication and this is a child that might never walk again.' Cameron was performing spinal fusion surgery to join the damaged vertebrae the boy had sustained in the accident, to provide stability and relieve pressure on the spinal cord. If left untreated there could be permanent damage but, hopefully, operating so soon after the accident would preserve a healthy blood flow to the spinal cord after the trauma suffered.

'No pressure then.'

He could see the smile in Bobby's eyes, even though his mouth was hidden behind his surgical mask. Although they were a team in the operating theatre, Cameron took personal responsibility for his patients. Simon, who couldn't be much younger than his own son, Thomas, had his whole life in front of him if he did his job well.

He thought of his ten-year-old son and the lengths

he'd gone to so he could lead a normal life. Although it had likely caused the breakdown of his marriage, he'd fought until they'd got Thomas's ADHD diagnosis so they could give him the support he needed. Ciara hadn't understood his fixation on giving their son 'a label', nor had she been able to cope with their son's extra needs. But Cameron had been there and knew how important it was to get Thomas the right help in order for him to have all the same opportunities available to his peers. He was determined to do the same for Simon with this operation.

Once they were satisfied that Simon was completely under the anaesthetic, Cameron made the first incision along his back. The procedure meant painstakingly removing debris from the injury site so he could then pack bone in and around the metal screws needed for extra support, and to promote further healing in the damaged vertebrae.

'Clamps, please.'

It was a surgery he'd undertaken many times before but he was feeling under more pressure than usual, having seen Jessie Rea again, and by the time he'd finished stabilising the damaged bone, sweat was forming on his brow.

Both he and Jessie wanted this boy to recover from his ordeal and he knew her kind heart would deny her the chance to walk away. She was a physiotherapist, exactly who Simon would need to help him back to full mobility. It was guaranteed she would be first in line to offer the boy her professional assistance and with a shared patient they were fated to work together—the very sort of distraction he did not need in his life.

He closed up the vertical incision he'd made at the injury site, knowing he'd done everything in his power to prevent this from being a life-changing injury. As long as there were no unforeseen complications, Simon would be able to start his rehabilitation and get back to some semblance of normality. The same might not be said for him now Jessie was back on the scene.

He'd never believed the spiel she'd given him at the time of their split because of the love they'd shared, the plans they'd made. Jessie was not the kind of cold-hearted woman to walk away from anyone without a good explanation. Yet he'd let her, figuring if she really didn't want to be with him there was no point sticking around to debate the matter. He'd wanted to get away from his family and he'd believed the same to be true about Jessie with her mother. So he'd gone on without her, never looking back because it was too painful. Jessie had become just another person to disregard his feelings, to cast him aside as though he were nothing and remind him he was unworthy of love.

Before he'd had the opportunity to change out of his scrubs he was seeking her out. He found her in the canteen. It had long since stopped serving hot food but it was well lit, comfortable and kitted out with vending machines packed with snacks and hot drinks.

He hadn't planned to stay any longer than it took to give her an update on Simon's progress but the sight of tears streaking down her face was sufficient to make him pull up a chair at her table. 'What's wrong? What happened?'

'Simon's parents didn't make it. That poor boy.' She burst into loud hiccupping sobs, prompting Cameron to take her hands in his.

'I'm so sorry, Jessie.' Offering condolences to anyone else in this situation might have seemed absurd. By all accounts she didn't know anything about the family beyond witnessing what had befallen them tonight. But, unless she'd changed dramatically in the fifteen years since he'd seen her, he knew Jessie would take the news badly. She cared as deeply and completely for strangers as she did for loved ones.

It was the very reason he'd fallen for her in the first place and the reason he found it difficult to reconcile this version of her with the Jessie who'd coldly told him she no longer wanted a future with him.

'I am sorry to hear about young Simon's parents.' Cameron directed the conversation back to the reason they were both here.

'How did his surgery go? Will he recover?'

'It went as well as could be expected. I don't foresee any problems with his recovery, at least nothing physical.'

'I know, the poor mite. Social services will have to get involved now to try and find family willing to take him in.' Her heart broke for the child whose life had changed in an instant. His future was uncertain and now he would have to learn to walk all over again. It was a lot for someone of that age to face all at once.

'I know I'm being ridiculous.' She sniffed. 'I don't know the family at all but I can't help feeling sorry for poor Simon.'

She lapsed back into tears, her compassion manifesting in liquid form.

'Hey, you've been through a lot tonight too. It's only natural for you to be emotional. Have you had a check-up yourself?' Shock after a traumatic event like a crash was real and, though not physically injured, Jessie had nonetheless experienced emotional trauma. Processing what had happened, including the deaths of people involved, could have a definite impact on her mental health.

'I'll be fine. I'm not the one who was hurt.' She pulled her hand away from his to wipe her eyes. She was the same Jessie who had always put everyone else's needs before her own. Not for the first time he wondered if she'd had a more altruistic motive for ending their relationship. He had no clue what that could have been but it made more sense that she'd been trying to protect him from something rather than suddenly deciding a life together was something she no longer wanted.

'You should go home and rest. Do you have someone who could come and get you, and look after you?' It was likely she would suffer flashbacks and a sleepless night replaying the horrific details of the car accident. She should have someone to comfort her, to support her in her time of need, the way she had done for him when they were younger.

Cameron was no longer part of her life, or someone she cared for, and he found he was envious of the man who got to do that for her. To hold her in his arms and kiss her was a privilege not to be taken for granted, as he'd learned too late.

'No, I… There's only Mum.'

'You're still living at home? What about all those plans you had to travel?' That was the main excuse she'd given to end their best-laid plans. A sudden need for space so she could explore the big wide world instead of being trapped in a relationship at too young an age.

What a kick in the teeth it was to find she had stayed and never spread her wings. It was a disservice to both of them that she hadn't gone on some epic soul-searching, life-changing adventure after all.

'I never left.' Jessie hung her head, knowing her mother was right. He did deserve to know and have some closure on that shock break-up she'd sprung on him.

'Why do I think there's more about that time that I don't know?'

'Because there is.'

'Okay…' He folded his arms and waited for her to fill in the blanks in their history, a task both daunting and long overdue, yet she knew they wouldn't be able to move on if she wasn't completely honest with him.

She was also aware it wasn't going to be easy, either for her to say or for Cameron to hear.

'I was never going to go travelling.'

'Apparently not, but why did you feel you had to lie to me, Jessie? If you didn't want to be with me you could have just been honest with me.' There was tension already in his voice, anger and frustration at her lies building in him. If he was ticked off now she couldn't imagine how he'd react when he heard the full story.

Jessie gulped, hoping that his past feelings for her meant that eventually he would forgive her.

'I wanted to be with you more than anything but—'

Cameron opened his mouth as though he was about to interrupt her, but she had to get this all out now.

'I was pregnant.'

'What?' He seemed to slump in his chair, that apparent rage extinguished by his shock. Jessie could not have felt more guilty about being responsible for that look of anguish on his face.

'I didn't want to stop you achieving your dream of being a doctor because of one stupid mistake. I thought by telling you a white lie, by ending things between us, you would move on and forget about me.'

'You were wrong.'

'Was I? You're married, I'm not.' It was a low blow considering that was her motivation to act the way she had. The whole idea had been for him to move on and live his life, yet the fact he had done so without her still ate away at her. Because they should have been together, raising their child.

'What was I supposed to do, Jessie? You told me you didn't want to be with me. I believed it. Should

I have spent the last fifteen years alone, mourning the loss of our relationship? The one you told me you didn't want?'

She couldn't answer when that was exactly what she had done.

'If I'd known there was a baby involved I would have stayed and looked after you both.' Cameron's head was buzzing with memories of that time, of how things could have been so different. It felt like a betrayal for Jessie to have lied to him about how she felt, making decisions about his life without even consulting him. She'd broken his heart for no reason when he would easily have chosen her and their baby over his career. He would have made it work if it meant being with her and having a family of his own.

'That's exactly why I didn't tell you. You'd worked so hard—I didn't want to be the one to take that away from you.'

'Yet you took everything else away from me. The chance to be part of the decision-making or to have a family with you. I would have chosen you, Jessie. Every single time.' Despite the urge to shout and scream over the injustice of it all, his voice was barely more than a whisper, so filled with emotion it was beginning to crack. It didn't help seeing tears glistening in Jessie's eyes at his reaction.

She'd denied him this information for fifteen years. They could've had a teenager by now, saved two people from an unhappy marriage. He wasn't sure he could ever forgive her for keeping such a huge, life-altering secret.

'I just wanted you to be happy,' she said, reaching out for him.

He shrugged her hand off his arm, unable to bear her touch when he was struggling to process what she'd done to him. 'Yeah? How's that going for you?'

'I'm sorry, Cameron. I know I should've been honest with you at the time but I thought it was for the best. No one in your life had ever put you first and I thought I was doing the right thing for you.'

'How admirable.' He knew he was being facetious but he couldn't see past his own pain at present. No, he couldn't remember the last time anyone had done that for him but he wasn't convinced it had been the right call for either of them.

It shouldn't surprise him that Jessie had carried it all on her shoulders when she'd always been mature beyond her years, taking on more responsibility than any young girl should ever have endured on her own because of her situation at home. But it didn't make it the right decision. It said a lot about their relationship then if she'd felt she couldn't talk to him about such an important subject, just as Ciara had been unable to discuss her feelings with him during their marriage. Perhaps he'd been the problem, not approachable or compassionate enough for the women in his life to feel safe including him in huge decisions affecting their lives.

'Was I really so unapproachable?'

'Not at all. Please don't think that. I guess I was simply trying to protect you. You'd been through so much at home and at school, I didn't want to give you more problems.'

It went some way to easing his conscience to find out he hadn't been some sort of monster to his exes but it didn't ease the hurt of not knowing the full circumstances of their break-up until now. When it was too late to do anything about it.

'And the baby? Why didn't you tell me about it later on?' He swallowed down the sudden swell of nausea accompanying the thought of what had happened. If she'd got rid of their baby, or had it adopted, without his say in the matter, it would be a betrayal he could never come back from. The child had two parents, even if one of them hadn't known about its existence.

He could see the pain surrounding that time there on her face even before she spoke.

'I had a miscarriage before the end of my first trimester. I didn't even get to see it on a scan.'

'I'm sorry. I wish I could have been there for you both. I wish you would have let me.' Learning about the baby they might have had together, then finding out it had died, was too much to take in in the space of one short conversation. It changed their whole history, the life he should have had. With Jessie. They should have mourned their baby together but she'd done it alone. As he would now have to do.

'I'm sorry, Cameron. There didn't seem any point in

upsetting you…' Her voice trailed off, as though she knew it was a lame excuse.

The whole time he'd been studying and beginning his new independent life, Jessie had been left behind, dealing with the aftermath of their relationship—a pregnancy and a loss. He hadn't been there to console her or say goodbye to their baby. Though that wasn't his fault, it would stay with him for ever.

'I… I gotta go, Jessie.'

'Are we okay? I mean, I know this was a lot to drop on you.'

'I just need some time.'

'Of course.'

He heard the disappointment and regret in her voice but he needed to focus on his own feelings right now and work through them before he could even look at Jessie again.

'I'll liaise with social services every step of the way where Simon is concerned. It's important if anyone does come forward that they know exactly what they're dealing with. It won't be easy to take on a grieving child, and one who's suffered a debilitating injury at that. I can't do anything to improve his family circum- stances, but I will be there to provide any advice or assistance required for his recovery.' He was clearly setting boundaries between them. It was no wonder that he wanted some distance after everything she'd hit him with tonight, but she would have preferred it if he'd stay to talk through his feelings.

Although that was something he'd never been particularly good at. She'd always had to guess what was bothering him and gradually coax the information out of him. That was likely due to his upbringing when his family had never validated his feelings, or even acknowledged them. Still, he was an adult now and she would have thought if he was married he would've learned how to communicate better.

The idea that he might be going home to discuss the intimate details of their personal relationship with his wife made her stomach lurch. She'd kept their baby to herself for all this time and it seemed a betrayal for him to share it with another woman, even though he hadn't been hers in a long time.

'You're staying on?' That information eventually penetrated through the fog of grief to reach her brain.

It was one thing running into Cameron unexpectedly, dealing with the feelings suddenly thrust forward in the highly emotive circumstances. However, it would be entirely different if she were to be working alongside him on a more regular basis.

'I would like to continue monitoring my patient's progress, yes. Why, would you have a problem with that?' Cameron held her gaze, challenging her to be brave and admit it would be difficult for her to be reminded every day of the love she'd thrown away.

It crossed her mind to do so, but she was already too invested in Simon to simply walk away and leave him.

'No. Not at all. We've both moved on and the past should stay there. It's Simon's needs that matter. I'm sure we can work together to give him the best pos-sible chance of recovery without our personal history getting in the way.'

Jessie rose from her chair and on slightly unsteady legs tossed her empty cup into the bin as she made her exit.

She wasn't sure if she imagined the voice behind her saying, 'Let's hope so.'

CHAPTER THREE

'Now, Simon, you know we have to do these exercises to keep your muscles working.' Jessie attempted again to pull back the covers on the hospital bed in order to start his physiotherapy.

They had established a few things in the few days since he'd had his surgery—Simon was seven years old, his surname was Armstrong, he didn't have any siblings or other immediate family, and he was stubborn as a mule when he wanted to be.

'Go away,' Simon cried, bunching the sheet tighter in his fists.

'That's not very nice, Simon. Ms Rea is only trying to help you.' Trust Cameron to walk in when their patient was being combative and making her look incompetent. Yesterday Simon had been as meek as a lamb, complying with her every instruction, but, as all young children, his mood was as changeable as the weather.

The boy huffed out a breath and relinquished his hold of the bedcovers on the doctor's command. She'd almost have preferred Simon to maintain his resistance and see Cameron sweat for a bit. They had to make allowances for the boy's age and circumstances, but on days like this it didn't make dealing with him any less problematic. Especially when the prospect of Cameron popping up like this at any time added to the pressure. Any attempt to portray herself as the capable, independent woman she wanted him to see her as was thwarted in the opposition of her patient. It was important Cameron should see her in a positive light to make her sacrifice seem worthwhile, even if the truth differed.

He would probably never forgive her for what she'd done when he'd been so distant around her since she'd told him about the baby. It wasn't surprising, she supposed, but it was hard when they used to be so close.

All she could do was get on with her job and try to make a positive difference in her patients' lives. Even if she'd messed up her own.

'I know the exercises aren't fun for you, Simon, but I promise they will help you get better.'

He relented with a huff and with no further resistance she was able to peel away the sheet and begin to manipulate his limbs. Getting him mobile again as soon as possible was important but he was still in pain after the surgery. For now it would be one less hurdle to get over if she maintained the strength in those limbs in the meantime. It was necessary to keep the muscles and joints moving so they didn't atrophy.

'I'm bored. When can I play football?'

Jessie glanced at Cameron for guidance on the matter. It was he who would have the final say on their patient's capabilities. When Simon was ready Jessie would take over his recovery, working to get him back to full strength in terms of his mobility.

Cameron perched on the side of the bed and faced Simon directly. 'Do you remember how we talked about how sometimes we have to do something we don't really like before we get to do the good stuff?'

'Like having to eat broccoli before I can have my jelly and ice cream?'

'Exactly.' Cameron ruffled his hair affectionately. They seemed to have formed quite a bond and Jessie didn't think it was merely because he was Cameron's patient. He was a father, he knew how to talk to and interact with a young boy. More than that, he cared. Cameron had taken it upon himself to break the news about his parents, once they'd established a rapport and got social services' approval. Jessie, as a familiar face in the absence of any family members to be found, had been in attendance for the heart-wrenching moment. Cameron had been compassionate and sympathetic, holding the boy tightly in his arms while he sobbed. He'd offered the love and support she doubted he'd had himself growing up. She imagined the relationship he would have had with their child and it made her yearn even more for the family she would never have.

Social services were doing their best to place Simon with family and keep track of his progress, but with their other caseloads to keep track of, and different care workers visiting, they hadn't completely gained his trust. He often grew upset at the notion that they were going to take him away, not an unjustified fear, given the circumstances, but their involvement wasn't helping aid his recovery.

She and Cameron were his only constants at present and sometimes it felt as though they were a little dysfunctional family of their own. They'd assumed the interim role as his guardians, coaxing him to heed their instructions for his own benefit, taking turns playing good cop and bad cop, and whatever else it took to get him back on his feet.

Jessie let herself indulge in a moment of folly, daydreaming of just such a scenario. If she'd told him about the pregnancy, if she'd been able to carry to full term, they might've had a family of their own and enjoyed a love she'd failed to find with any other.

But, given the chance to do things over, she knew even now, if their baby had lived, she still would have chosen Cameron's future happiness over her own. It was a futile exercise anyway, looking back and wondering what if, knowing she would never get to experience the joy of having a husband or family, the things most people took for granted.

'Jessie and I are working together to get you back on your feet as soon as possible, but if we rush things it might exacerbate your injury.'

'That would mean it takes longer for you to heal and have more physiotherapy. Extra stretches,' she added, bending and straightening Simon's legs, flexing them to keep him supple.

'Yuck!' He rolled his eyes.

'Exactly, so be patient,' she reminded him as she finished rubbing down his legs with soothing lotion.

'I could do with some of that myself,' Cameron said, stretching out his back as he stood up.

Jessie arched an eyebrow at him.

'I mean a massage in general. I'm getting old. Some of us have to pay for that sort of thing.'

She couldn't help but snort as he dug himself deeper into a hole. He flashed her a scowl, suggesting her laughter wasn't appropriate, but she was enjoying seeing him on the back foot for once. It was nice to know Cameron was human and he was capable of making a fool of himself too.

In the old days he would have laughed at himself but after opening up old wounds and rubbing salt in them with the news about their baby he'd been cool towards her. It made her almost want to volunteer to help him with whatever ailed him, to try and mend some bridges. However, she managed to catch herself in time, knowing that having her hands on his body was never going to help her get over him. He was still an attractive man and her memories and vivid imagination wouldn't do anything to help her move on if he was stripped to the waist for her.

Thankfully he made to leave so she didn't feel obliged to offer her healing services after all.

'I have to go, Simon, but make sure you do everything Jessie tells you. I'll see you both again in the morning.'

'Okay.' Simon gave Cameron a fist bump, followed

by some convoluted handshake they'd made up as though they were members of some secret society she wasn't party to.

'I'll walk out with you. Simon, get some rest for now, but make sure you practise those exercises I gave you before I see you tomorrow.'

'Okay.' Simon sounded miserable.

He obviously didn't anticipate her next visit with as much excitement as Dr Holmes', but she didn't take it personally as they left the ward. She was just glad Simon was responding so well after his surgery. Some children might have shut down completely after the trauma of the crash and losing two parents but, even though he was a bit resistant to his physical rehabilitation, the presence of that feisty spirit was a good sign. He would need it to get him through this ordeal.

Cameron was flicking through his notes as they walked down the corridor, paying little attention to Jessie. It would be difficult to tell they'd ever been in a relationship, had talked about living together and getting married one day, when he treated her like every other member of staff. He was courteous and co-operative but didn't go beyond a respectful profes-sional discourse with her.

Whereas over the course of the last few days she'd been increasingly curious about the life and times of Dr Cameron Holmes, keen to find out if he was the same man she'd known way back before she'd broken both of their hearts. He didn't give much away, seemingly more guarded and private than the quiet teen she'd befriended and fallen in love with.

Extra guilt piled onto her shoulders at the thought that she'd caused him to increase his defences. But, then again, perhaps this armour he wore was something he donned only when in contact with her, reserved for someone who'd let him down more than once.

Jessie was determined not to do it again.

Someone let the double doors on a side ward swing behind them, causing a gust of air to catch Cameron's notes out of his hands. The pages blew halfway down the corridor, falling at different intervals like drifting autumn leaves.

'Let me help you get those.' Jessie began snatching up the escaped notes, trying to make amends with every small gesture she could manage.

'I've got it,' he insisted, a muscle in his jaw twitching with irritation. It wasn't that he was rude to her, but she still knew him well enough to see he was ill at ease around her. Despite the life he'd gone on to have without her, he clearly hadn't forgiven her for the way they'd parted. And now he'd been apprised of the reasons she'd done so his behaviour was justified. For Jessie, it was too late for recriminations and regret. She'd done all that a long time ago.

The past was the past and it was clear he wanted it to stay there.

He gathered the pages and hurried on without looking back. Just as he'd apparently done fifteen years ago.

* * *

Cameron knew he'd have to stop spending so much time with Jessie. Of course he was overseeing Simon's recovery but the visits during his physiotherapy sessions were proving challenging. It had been clear since their unexpected reunion that there was going to be a problem. They had unfinished business and his feelings for her had sprung back to life the moment he'd set eyes on her again.

Yet nothing could have prepared him for what she'd told him. A baby. It was difficult to come to terms with the idea that she'd been carrying his child at that time, when she'd told him she no longer wanted to be with him. Everything could have been so different and it was difficult to forgive her for keeping it all from him, even the miscarriage. They should have grieved the loss together.

His emotions were complicated and fragile like a gossamer web. It would be easier if he only thought badly of her, but at the same time he was still attracted to her and the person she was now. Time hadn't made her any less compassionate or patient—the qualities which had made him fall for her in the first place. He was doing his best not to think that way, but it was proving to be a task beyond his capabilities.

Never mind that he hadn't been with a woman at all in the years since Ciara left. This was Jessie, the woman he'd never stopped loving. It wasn't easy to simply forget someone he'd thought he'd be with for ever.

He also had questions that he wasn't sure he wanted

to know the answers to. Did she have a husband and family of her own? Why hadn't she loved him enough?

But he wouldn't ask. He shouldn't care and he'd been hurt too much by those he'd loved to add to those scars.

As soon as Simon was able to be discharged Cameron would sever all ties to Jessie and go back to the life he'd been leading without her. Until then he'd do his best to remain level-headed and focus on his patient, not his personal issues.

Although he was a few feet ahead of her, trying not to engage, he could hear her quick steps trying to catch up with him. It was only when he was faced with the sight of his tearful son and the childminder that he came to a standstill.

'Thomas? What's wrong?' He was accustomed to his son's emotional outbursts but he looked genuinely upset by something and it wasn't like Maggie to bring him to Cameron's place of work. Usually she was able to pacify him until Cameron got home.

When his son didn't answer but continued to weep uncontrollably he looked to the older woman holding him by the hand.

'I'm sorry, Doctor, but he was so upset I was worried he'd hurt himself.'

His red-faced son's wailing was now drawing attention from passing patients and though Cameron tried not to be embarrassed by his son's displays of frustration he was aware it was becoming distressing for those on their way to the children's ward.

Even Jessie had caught up with them now and he

knew he'd have to explain what was going on. So far he'd managed to avoid sharing anything of his private life, ashamed at the failure of his marriage, and wanting to protect Thomas. Being divorced reaffirmed the idea that no one loved him enough to stay with him. He didn't want Jessie to pity him or even get close enough to know he had a son, but it was too late now.

'There's an empty office down here if you want some privacy,' Jessie said, immediately making him feel churlish about letting her in on his life when he was aware how sensitive and caring she was with everyone—exactly what he and Thomas needed right now.

'Thanks.' He waited until they were behind closed doors before he made introductions. 'This is my son, Thomas, and Maggie, my childminder.'

'Nice to meet you.' Jessie acknowledged the older woman before she bent down to speak to Thomas. 'And you're the spitting image of your daddy when he was younger. We used to be friends a long time ago and now we work together.'

It seemed so simple when she said it. As though there was nothing for him to be afraid of as his past and present collided in front of his eyes. Though 'friends' or 'colleagues' could never hope to adequately convey the relationship they had back then or now. It was difficult to work alongside someone and not show any emotion. Even though he'd once loved this woman she'd broken his heart and only decided to tell him fifteen years later it had been because she'd been pregnant with, and later lost, his baby. He defied anyone to stay neutral in those circumstances.

Thomas momentarily stopped sobbing to stare at Jessie, wiping the tears away with the back of his hand to leave a grimy smear of dirt on his cheek, seemingly already captivated by her.

'Do you want me to go and give you some privacy?' Jessie asked.

'No. It's fine.' Now that she'd met his son there seemed no point in sending her away, especially when she'd managed to calm Thomas down so that Cameron could find out what had happened.

Cameron pulled over a chair and sat down so he was at eye level with his son, doing his best not to intimidate or frighten him and simply let him explain.

'Teacher…said… I…can't…do…it.' He hiccupped before breaking down into loud messy tears again.

Cameron looked to Maggie for some sort of explanation.

'The class are doing a home project on the subject of their choice. There's a prize for the best one but his teacher thought that, under the circumstances, Thomas might want to sit it out.'

With the suggestion that his son was being prevented from participating in something which was upsetting him to this degree, Cameron's body was already tensing up, preparing for a fight. He'd been doing that almost from the moment Thomas had been born, challenging the system to take care of his son better than they had him.

'Thomas has someone in the classroom to help him with his learning difficulties,' he explained to Jessie. 'Unfortunately, it's not so easy to get the work done at home when I'm working a lot, but we'll figure something out, won't we, buddy?' He gave Thomas a fist bump because a hug wasn't always welcome. Even when he wanted to gather his son up and squeeze him tight, protect him from the outside world.

'I'm sorry, Dr Holmes, but I can't help with his homework either. All this modern technology is beyond me, unfortunately.' Even Maggie was beginning to get upset about the situation, which might have been avoidable if the school had consulted him before dropping this bombshell on Thomas. He knew the teachers were over-stretched and most likely thought they were doing a good thing by excusing Thomas from taking part, but excluding him from activities was exactly what Cameron had fought against.

'I know, Maggie. You're a great help picking Thomas up from school and looking after him until I finish work. This isn't your problem and you did the right thing by bringing him here. I'll have a word with the school and see if we can work something out.'

'He needs a mother. It's not healthy for either of you to be cooped up in that house together all the time.' Maggie, as usual, overstepped the mark in discussing his personal business, but since she was the only help he had in looking after Thomas he couldn't very well disagree with her. It didn't help that she was partly correct. Thomas did need someone in his life, someone who could devote the time and love his mother hadn't managed to give him.

Jessie was watching the exchange, taking everything in, and thanks to Maggie's oversharing he was going to have to admit to the failure of his marriage too.

'His mother left three years ago.' He kept it blunt and to the point. Jessie didn't need to know the painful details, and he certainly didn't want to go into them with an audience which included the son who could barely remember her. It wasn't going to do anything other than embarrass them both and upset Thomas to tell Jessie that Ciara hadn't loved him enough, or that he hadn't considered his wife's feelings as much as his son's. That she hadn't felt as though she could talk to him and tell him she was unhappy, or that he hadn't seen it. Either way, he hadn't been a good husband and it wasn't something he was proud of.

'Oh. I'm sorry.' She already looked uncomfortable with that small snippet of information, glancing back at the closed door, probably preparing her escape from the awkward position she was in.

'It just means we're a little short on babysitters. I have another appointment, Maggie. Can you look after him here until I've finished? I can give you some money to take him to the canteen, or I think there's a play park—'

'I can't stay, Dr Holmes. It will take me another hour to get home on the bus and my granddaughter is coming to stay. I'm sorry.' Maggie was twisting the handle of her bag in her hands, clearly worried about adding to his burden, but Cameron couldn't think badly of her because she had a life and family of her own.

'It's fine, Maggie. You go on home. Thomas can stay with me. Thanks for bringing him over.'

She made sure Thomas had all of his school belongings before she left and Cameron gave her a hug to show there weren't any hard feelings on his part. It wasn't her fault that the school had messed up, that Thomas had had a meltdown, or that he had no one else in his life who could step in to help in a crisis.

'I can take him with me if it would help?' Jessie, who'd been standing quietly since the revelation about his absent wife, stepped forward.

'I'm sure you're busy.' It was one thing seeing her every day and attempting to keep a lid on his emotions, but they'd be moving into dangerous territory if he let her get close to Thomas. He was trying to keep her out of his life, not bring her further into it. If Thomas hadn't been so upset and needing a safe space, she wouldn't even be in here, intruding in his family business.

'I've finished for the day and was just about to head home.'

'But you've got your mother to look after.' If it wasn't for their personal history and his wounded heart he would've jumped at the chance for such help. He probably would have accepted it from anyone other than her, but he was still reeling from the revelation of what she'd done a decade and a half ago. There was no way he wanted a second round, to find out what else she was capable of inflicting upon him.

'Cameron, you need someone to keep an eye on him and I'm volunteering an hour of my time. I can stay here or I can take him home. If that's okay with you, Thomas?' She included Thomas in the conversation, displaying some understanding of what she was dealing with here. Being in the medical profession, they were both used to dealing with children, often with special needs requiring that little bit more attention and sensitivity.

'Here,' Cameron spat out quickly. The last thing he needed was to set foot back in his home town, and into Jessie's house, when he was already struggling to cope with simply seeing her at work. It would be too much seeing the people and places which had hurt him so deeply, not only crossing that line between their working and professional relationship but entangling their lives again, when he should be doing everything he could to protect himself, and Thomas, from any further pain. Getting involved, in any capacity, with the woman who had taken his heart and stomped it casually into the ground was only ever going to be trouble. Even if it only destroyed his peace of mind.

However, the fact that he had no one else to turn to, and that Thomas had stopped crying since Jessie started talking, was the clincher.

'Good. You go and see your patient and Thomas and I will keep ourselves occupied.' She tried to usher him out but Cameron was still reluctant to leave his son, even with a qualified medical professional whom he'd known for a long time.

The original vetting process to find a suitable child-minder had been rigorous, but he'd needed someone he could trust completely to deal with Thomas's physical and emotional needs. His son had been through enough upheaval with Ciara abandoning him and the challenges he was facing at school and with his peers. It wouldn't have been fair to inflict a series of unsuitable carers upon him too, and so Cameron was a touch overprotective.

'Just go, Dad.' It was Thomas in the end who finally persuaded him to go, clearly embarrassed by this display from his helicopter parent.

'I'll be back in an hour. Here's my number in case you need me.'

'We'll be fine,' Jessie insisted, but she put his mind at ease by taking it anyway.

CHAPTER FOUR

JESSIE WAS STILL in a state of shock as Cameron left the room, leaving her with his son. His son. It was going to take a while for that to sink in. Looking at Thomas was like glimpsing back in history, and not all of it was to her liking. It was a reminder that Cameron had moved on quite quickly.

Although the end of their relationship had been at her behest, it was a blow to come face to face with the child he'd had with another woman. He hadn't known about their baby, or the loss she'd suffered, until recently, so he wouldn't have understood how meeting Thomas cut her so deep. Perhaps later when he'd had time to think about it he would realise how big a moment it was to her. It was telling, however, that he hadn't mentioned the end of his marriage, or the existence of his son, until he'd been forced to, making it clear he didn't want her to know anything about his personal life.

She probably deserved that. In his eyes she'd abandoned him as much as his wife had, and his family was none of her business. In other circumstances she would have left it at that and backed away, aware that he had no desire to let her anywhere near his son or his life. Except she could see how upset Thomas was and what a bind they'd been left in. Neither of them should get worked up over a spot of babysitting. She was just a colleague doing him a favour. He wouldn't be indebted to her, she wouldn't expect anything from him in return. And once Cameron had finished work and collected Thomas, that would be the end of their association, outside of the workplace. It appeared that neither of them wanted to revisit their past and they were begrudgingly putting up with each other for the sake of their young patient in the children's ward.

For now she simply had to keep Thomas calm and busy enough to take his mind off his school problems until Cameron collected him.

'I don't think there's much for you to do in here. Would you like to come with me to the children's ward and we'll see if we can pick up some games for you to play?' It was really the only child-friendly part of the hospital and they usually kept a cupboard full of toys and books to stimulate the children who were bed-bound due to their health problems. She was sure the ward sister wouldn't mind if she borrowed a few things for a while, but she didn't want to leave Thomas unsupervised and risk Cameron's wrath.

It was clear he was protective of his son and she could understand that when his family had failed to look after him. He was over-compensating for the rough time he'd had growing up, but she knew Thomas would benefit from his father's harrowing experience.

His mother and father had shown him how *not* to parent and Jessie knew he would give his own child all the attention and support he'd never had. Especially since his wife was apparently out of the picture too. She might never be party to the details of the breakup but she was sure Cameron loved him enough for two parents.

'Will there be art stuff?' Thomas asked, wiping his nose on his sleeve, his problems temporarily forgotten with the novelty of his new surroundings.

'Sure. Do you like drawing?' If she could find something he was interested in it could make this afternoon easier. They were strangers to one another and she didn't know how Thomas would react to being around her any more than she knew what it would do to her to spend time with Cameron's son. The child they should have had together.

He rummaged in his school backpack and pulled out a sketchpad, foisting it on her without a word.

Dutifully perusing the contents, she braced herself to face the childish scrawls of the average school kid, ready to feign admiration to keep his spirits high. As it turned out, she didn't need to.

'Thomas, these are amazing.' She turned the pages quickly, greedily taking in the pencil-drawn images with splashes of watercolour highlighting the details of the scenes he'd captured.

He shrugged. 'Can we go now?'

'Yes. I'll just send your dad a text so he knows where we are.' He hadn't said she couldn't leave the room with his son but she wanted to keep on the right side of him. She also didn't want him to worry unnecessarily if he came back and found them missing.

Jessie led Thomas to the ward and got permission from the ward sister before bringing him in. Ordinarily she wasn't sure if she would be permitted but mentioning he was a surgeon's son apparently opened doors. Namely the one to the toy cupboard.

She rifled through the stacks of board games and mentally did a fist pump when she found a stack of paper. Her euphoria was short-lived when she realised it was pages of crude outlines for the younger children to colour.

'I suppose we could turn them over and use the back. There must be some paint or pens in here somewhere.' She reached further back but, aside from a few broken chubby crayons, there wasn't much that would pass for art supplies.

'I'll go and ask one of the nurses—' When Jessie turned around to find Thomas was no longer there her heart just about stopped.

She quickly got to her feet, scanning the corridor for her charge, her mouth suddenly dry when she couldn't see him. 'Thomas? Where are you?'

It wasn't in her nature to panic but Cameron had been so concerned about leaving his son in the first place and now he was missing within minutes. The more she looked for him and called his name, the harder her heart pounded. Her concern for Thomas was as great as the worry about how Cameron would kill her for letting him leave her sight for even a second.

'Have you seen Dr Holmes' son? He was here just a second ago.' Jessie went back to the ward sister in case he'd retraced their steps.

'I think he's making friends.' She nodded towards the beds across the hall, sending Jessie running to find him.

'Thomas? What are you doing in here? You shouldn't have run away like that. What on earth would I have told your father if I hadn't found you?' The relief of seeing him was manifested in her rambling to the be-mused ten-year-old who was sitting at Simon's bedside.

'I wanted to paint,' he said, with no indication he understood the distress he'd caused in the short time since he'd left her sight.

'Okay, but I need you to tell me if you want to go somewhere.' Jessie couldn't be too hard on him when she was the one who'd offered to look after him and should have done a better job of it. It was good to see he was not only safe but also providing Simon with some company.

Seeing him sharing the paints and paper with the boy who didn't have anyone else in the world choked her up. Simon was propped up, the table over his bed covered in art supplies, happily drawing away with his new friend sitting beside him.

'Simon, this is Thomas, Dr Holmes' son.' It might be a bit unorthodox to have him in the ward but since they'd already met she thought she should make some introductions. She didn't think Cameron would mind when he was very fond of this particular patient and had become an important male figure in his life.

All the other children on the ward had their parents and other relatives visiting, it would do Simon good to have some company and Thomas seemed to be happy. She pulled up a chair beside him, content to simply watch over him until his father returned.

The three of them sat in companionable silence and Jessie watched as the boys daubed poster paints on sheets of paper. Simon had drawn himself playing football, no doubt something he was desperately wanting to do once he was back on his feet. Thomas had begun painting a woodland scene, outlining the silhouette of a magnificent tree with branches reaching up towards a starry night sky. He really was talented.

'Jessie? What the hell is going on?' Cameron appeared, looking a little flushed.

Even though she hadn't done anything wrong she immediately felt guilty about sitting here with Thomas and Simon. 'Didn't you get my text? I told you we were heading to the children's ward. Thomas wanted to paint.'

'I didn't get any text. I finished up early and I've been searching the whole hospital looking for you.' He pulled his phone out of his pocket and checked it.

Jessie could see the moment he realised he was in the wrong, red blotches breaking out on his cheeks. 'Sorry. I didn't hear it.'

'It's fine. I wouldn't have taken Thomas anywhere

without telling you. We just came to get some art supplies but it seems he's found a friend too.'

'I'm not sure crossing professional boundaries will endear me to the staff here. Thomas, let's go,' he said gruffly, grabbing his son's belongings and making Jessie believe she'd really stuffed things up, even though she'd done everything she could to keep Thomas happy.

'I got the sister's permission and he was quite content.' Unlike now, when he seemed agitated at being forced to leave. She knew why Cameron was uncomfortable about her being around his son but it didn't seem fair for their troubled history to impact on those around them.

'Can I do the project now, Dad?' Now that his distraction was being packed away it seemed Thomas's attention was back on the problem which had brought him here in the first place.

'No, sorry, son. I haven't had time to speak to your teacher and I doubt there will be anyone in at this time. I'll phone first thing tomorrow, okay?'

'I want to do the project. It's not fair if I can't win a prize too.' It was clear that Thomas's frustration was beginning to build again. He'd abandoned the picture and the paints he'd been so engrossed in until his father had arrived, his attention totally focused on the project he wasn't being allowed to participate in.

'I know, son. I told you we'll try and sort something out.'

'But you're never at home.' Thomas was in tears again and Jessie felt bad for everyone involved, including Simon, who was quietly watching on. She knew Cameron was devoted to his son, but as a single parent who was also a surgeon he probably couldn't be at home as much as he wanted to be. It was clear Thomas needed extra care and attention but it was equally obvious that it wasn't something easily acquired.

Jessie wanted to help but she was acutely aware that Cameron wasn't completely over their historic breakup. Or, if he was, he simply didn't want to spend any more time around her than was necessary. She was finding their reacquaintance difficult for different reasons and, though they would likely never be as close as they once had been, she could do without seeing that look of betrayal in his eyes every time he spoke to her. Perhaps if she could help him with his current crisis he would see that she wasn't the enemy. That she'd only ever wanted what was for the best.

As they left the ward, Thomas walking ahead, arms folded and doing his best to ignore his father, Jessie ventured to express an idea.

'Tell me to mind my own business if you wish, but what if you incorporated his love of art into his school project?'

'What do you mean?' Cameron's scowl made her swallow hard, concerned that she was stepping over the line which he had clearly drawn from the moment he'd set eyes on her again.

'The project can be on any subject of his choice, right? Perhaps he could do a study of wildlife or nature using his artistic skills. With such a broad spectrum for the basis of the project, I don't see why he couldn't showcase his talents in such a manner. I'm sure the school would be pleased that he'd be able to participate with the rest of his classmates and hopefully Thomas would enjoy it too. He showed me his sketchbook and he's really good.'

'He doesn't usually share that with anyone,' Cameron confided, letting her know this was a privilege she shouldn't take lightly, something which had obviously taken him by surprise.

'I take after my mum, Dad says,' Thomas interrupted without a trace of arrogance or yearning for the mother missing from his life, evidently forgetting his vow of silence upon leaving the ward.

Jessie glanced at Cameron for confirmation.

'It's true, Ciara is an artist too. She preferred sitting in her studio alone to spending quality time with her family.' It was clearly a sore point. Perhaps Cameron hadn't mentioned where his son's interest and talent lay because it reminded him of his wife and the end of their relationship.

'Well, I think if you base the project on Thomas's artwork, and add some text on the subject he likes to accompany the illustrations, it could work.' The idea certainly had Cameron thinking, his haste to get away from her now slowing so he could consider the suggestion. Thomas too was listening intently.

'I like birds. Can I do my project on birds, Dad?'

'We'll see, Thomas. I would still have to find someone who could help you. You know there are some nights and weekends when I'll have to come to work and I don't want you to start something if you're not going to be able to finish it.'

'What about Jessie? She could help me.' Thomas looked at them both with such hope and faith that she would be the one to fix this problem that Jessie was rendered speechless, knowing that whatever response she gave would upset one of the Holmes men.

Thankfully, Cameron answered for her. 'Jessie has her own work and family to take care of. I'm sure she doesn't have time to supervise your homework too. I'll see if I can persuade Maggie to help you with it.'

It wasn't surprising that he didn't want her venturing any further into his private life when he'd barely given his consent for her to mind Thomas for that short time this afternoon. Jessie wasn't part of his world any more, apart from the time they were forced to spend together at work, and it seemed as though that was the way he'd prefer to keep it.

'Maggie doesn't like it when I make a mess with the paint and she's no good with homework. I want Jessie.'

It would be difficult to explain to him that the reason she couldn't help him was because they'd been together once and his father couldn't stand to be near her after the way she'd treated him.

'Listen, Cameron, I could maybe spend an hour or two a week helping him. It would solve the problem, and keep him happy.' She knew the last thing either of them wanted was to be forced together for any longer than necessary, but this would be about her helping

Thomas. Other than giving his permission, Cameron wouldn't have to get involved.

'I can't ask you to do that,' he said, his forehead furrowed in a frown.

'You didn't. Thomas did.' He was the reason she was even contemplating it, and trying to avoid another meltdown. Along with her need to make amends for all the hurt she'd caused Cameron fifteen years ago, and more recently.

His decision now would tell her once and for all how desperate he was to have her out of his life for good. Only now was she realising that she wasn't ready to lose him again.

He was stuck. Caught between his son's educational needs and his own wish to keep an emotional distance from Jessie. It had been a tough call even to leave him with her in this afternoon's emergency but doing it on a regular basis seemed like madness. Yes, Jessie's help would solve a lot of problems, but at what cost? Having her around could cause him even more.

He'd been in a real bind today, with no other option but to leave Thomas with her after his upset. However, when he'd come back to find the room empty he'd gone into a tailspin. He didn't know what he'd imagined Jessie had done with his son, only that he didn't want her to hurt Thomas the way she'd hurt him. It was a ridiculous thought, of course. Jessie would never have done anything to put Thomas in any danger, but it was a knee-jerk reaction.

The reason he was trying not to get involved with her again was to avoid that pain she'd managed to inflict on him before. But it wasn't fair to deny his son an opportunity like this when he'd fought so hard for Thomas to be treated the same as his classmates. Besides, he remembered how much it had helped him to have Jessie as a study buddy and perhaps it would have the same positive effect on Thomas's work too.

'Well, if you're both sure…' He supposed it wouldn't be for ever, probably only as long as he'd be here for Simon's recovery. Neither was going to be a permanent arrangement, and it would at least help them over this one hurdle for now. He had to look to the future instead of back at the past. Jessie certainly didn't seem to be too concerned about what had gone on between them before. He knew he hadn't wanted to revisit that time with her, but so far there had been no apology or real explanation for what had happened. It was about time he followed her lead and moved on.

CHAPTER FIVE

THIS WAS ASKING for trouble. Cameron knew it and yet he was still walking headlong into the disaster he knew would surely follow.

When the doorbell rang he felt that first date excitement, regardless that this was anything but a romantic liaison. It was home schooling for his son that, despite his complicated history with the person who'd come to assist him, he'd been compelled to accept because he knew she had the patience Thomas required.

'Hi. Where do you want me?' It was such a loaded question from the woman standing on his doorstep.

The answer uppermost in his mind was *As far away as possible*, as he knew being this close to her again had the potential to break his heart all over again. Despite everything she'd put him through, Cameron knew he still had feelings for her. Otherwise it wouldn't be so hard for him to be near her.

After a pause that was slightly too long he said, 'Thomas is in the kitchen at the table.'

Jessie flashed him a smile as he stood aside to let her in.

It was a big deal for Cameron to let someone into his

life again, on any basis. Especially someone who'd hurt him and let him down the way Jessie had. He was trusting her not to betray him again, by inviting her into his home and into his son's life too. Although they hadn't had much choice. Jessie couldn't invite him to her home with her ailing mother in residence and a coffee shop or library would have been too distracting for Thomas.

'Hi, Thomas.' Jessie waved and unhooked the backpack she was wearing over her shoulder.

'Thomas, this is Jessie. You remember? From the hospital.'

'Hi, Jessie,' Thomas dutifully acknowledged as he reluctantly set his game console down on the table. They'd had a conversation earlier where Cameron had laid down some ground rules—no games, full concentration, and to be polite to Jessie. All of which were easier said than done with a ten-year-old.

Jessie plonked herself in the seat next to him and began unpacking notebooks and pens onto the table. 'So, Thomas, is there any particular subject you'd like to do your project on?'

'I want to do mine on birds,' Thomas said.

With Jessie's support, Thomas had a fighting chance along with everyone else. Cameron knew from experience. When they'd been revising for exams and he'd struggled to remember details, Jessie had covered the place in brightly coloured notes because she'd read that visual stimulation helped dyslexia sufferers retain information. It was something, along with her tips on mind-mapping, that he'd continued utilising in his medical school studies too.

'There should be some reference books over here you could use.' Glad to be of use in some capacity, Cameron went in search of some bird-related tomes from the shelves in the living room. He gathered as many wildlife books and encyclopaedias as he could carry.

'That's a good start. I'll print out a few things from the Internet for next time.'

'I'm really grateful to you for doing this, Jessie. Thanks again.' Cameron walked away, afraid that he might say or do something he'd come to regret.

It had been a long time since anyone had done something thoughtful for them and it said a lot that it was Jessie who'd come to the rescue. He couldn't help but think there was a reason she'd come back into his and Thomas's lives now. But it was too frightening to dwell on why that might be.

Would it be nice to have a loving, caring partner, someone who would be there for Thomas too? Yes, and yes. The risks involved in thinking that Jessie could be that person, however, were too great to let his imagination run too far ahead of a nice gesture.

He closed the door between the living room and the kitchen, between him and Jessie. Keeping temptation at bay for a little longer and letting her do the job she'd come here to do.

Jessie took a moment to take in her surroundings, the house Cameron had shared with his wife and son. His family home. One which didn't include her.

The house was more than big enough for the two of them, and she wondered if Cameron had planned to have more children. Maybe his wife's reaction to their son's extra needs had ended those plans. She knew he wouldn't have wanted a large family when he'd been lost among his siblings, but he was obviously such a great dad it was a pity he hadn't been given the chance to expand his young family.

If things had been different he would have had two children now. She would never know if they would have eventually worked something out, had she told him about the baby and if it had survived. Now children were no longer an option for Jessie.

She would've loved children, a family of her own, and a husband who would've supported her. Circumstances had made that impossible for her. So, instead, she tried to keep busy at work and looking after her mother at home. Helping Thomas with this project was something different for her to focus on.

It was difficult not to be bitter at times, especially when Cameron had gone on to have that life with someone else. Perhaps if she'd been honest with him instead of trying to fix things the way she'd always done they might have had some sort of relationship, but there was no going back and they had to live with the decision she'd made.

She was being punished for it now, sitting in her ex's stylish home, helping the son he'd been given by another woman with his homework and knowing Cameron didn't want her there.

'We could start with a list of garden birds and write a description of what they look like. What's your favourite?'

'Robins, I guess.' Thomas was swinging his legs and flicking idly through the stack of books Cameron had provided before disappearing.

She knew he was invested in his son's education so she had to put his vanishing act down to having her in the house. It wasn't ideal for either of them, but she was sure it was best for Thomas to meet her in a safe, familiar environment.

So far he didn't seem to have any problems with her but he was having trouble focusing. She supposed, faced with a stack of books and little stimulation, she might have trouble maintaining interest too.

'We could just print out some pictures, but it might be nice for you to do your own illustrations.' It was important to make a connection, to discover his interests and use them to keep him engaged. Sometimes half of the battle when dealing with children this age was keeping their interest and preventing them from becoming bored. She wasn't an expert by any means, but she'd dealt with a lot of paediatric patients and practising physiotherapy on children required a lot of patience and understanding. To get the best results for her and her patients she needed their co-operation, so she always went the extra mile to get it. Whether that included playing their favourite music or watching TV while she worked with them, she did whatever it took to improve their circumstances.

Thomas clearly wanted to participate in the project, so all she had to do was find the best way to channel his concentration. That might not be through copying from a stack of dusty old books.

'Sometimes we go to the beach or to the park and I like to draw there.'

'That sounds lovely.'

His artistic talent was something his parents should have been proudly showing off, but she noticed that none of Thomas's pictures had been displayed on the fridge or anywhere else. If this was her child's amazing artwork she'd have decorated the entire house with it.

She reminded herself that Cameron's personal issues were not her business and focused her attention back on the matter of the school project she was here to assist with.

'I don't want to copy from boring books. Can we go to the park, Dad? Please?' Thomas called to his father, sounding desperate for an escape from the house.

It was entirely Cameron's decision whether or not they went exploring elsewhere, although when he came to the doorway and flicked a glance at her she was compelled to add her opinion.

'It might help Thomas to have first-hand experience rather than simply copying information and illustrations already available. He could put his own spin on things.'

In fact, it could benefit them all if they weren't confined to this house full of memories which didn't include her.

* * **

Being a part of Jessie's study session hadn't been in Cameron's plans. He wasn't always going to be around to help with the homework so he'd thought it more prudent to let her get on with it without him. Driving his son to a park wasn't a hardship. It was something he enjoyed, spending time together feeding the ducks and watching the world go by. Today, having Jessie join them, was simply an added dimension to their quality time together—an air of jeopardy. But he knew it would be worth giving up his time and peace of mind to make a start on Thomas's project.

'Do you want me to wait here until you've finished?' It was a last attempt to separate himself from Jessie, to let her get on with the job she'd come to do without him being involved. Even as he asked the question he knew he wouldn't get away scot-free.

'No, Dad, you come too. You can take some photographs.' Thomas immediately found him a job to keep him occupied and be a part of their expedition team.

'I doubt Thomas will be able to sketch everything in real time. We'll have to document his surroundings for future reference. If it seals the deal, I'll buy the hot drinks.' Jessie's bribery tactics worked as he undid his seatbelt and resigned himself to spending the afternoon with his son and his ex-love. Though the promise of an afternoon together only put him on edge. He didn't want a reason to have Jessie go up in his estimation. He wanted to hold on to his anger surrounding the pregnancy he hadn't known about. But that was proving difficult when he was witnessing the lengths she was willing to go to in order to assist his son.

She'd already gained Thomas's trust and found a way to integrate his interests into this school project to make it more fun for him. Not to mention this outing away from the kitchen table to keep Thomas excited about this take on his homework. It had been the right decision, but he'd do well not to let these positive feelings edge out the older negative ones. It was important not to forget how devastated he'd been by her rejection and the pain which had all but ripped his heart in two. He couldn't afford to let history repeat itself when his son was involved now too.

It would be so easy to let her slot into their little family and fill that void Ciara had left, but he'd learned his lesson about getting close too quickly. In his experience it wasn't better to have loved and lost, when he'd been hurt twice over by the women he'd loved.

Both he and Thomas had been rejected and abandoned enough and that was why he donned his armadillo shell when it came to love and relationships now. Not even Jessie could penetrate that armour and cause more internal damage.

'Can I go to the lake and draw the ducks, Dad?' Thomas was bouncing on the balls of his feet, his sketchbook and pencils clutched in his hands, raring to go.

Cameron had never seen him so eager to do any work and it was entirely down to Jessie. She had that knack of engaging others. Though she hadn't had to try that hard with him in their schooldays. He'd been gone since the second she'd asked him if he wanted some help, the only person then who'd ever taken the time to notice him. It helped that she'd been, and still was, gorgeous.

He watched her now as she walked back from the coffee van, the sun shining on her chestnut curls, picking out the reds and golds in her hair like burnished autumn leaves. She turned and smiled at him, her big green eyes shining on him so he felt as though he was the only person in the world, making him forget his son, who was pulling on his shirt reminding him he was there.

Focus, Cameron.

'Uh…just don't go too close to the edge. Stay where I can see you.'

Remind me why I'm here.

Thomas ran off as Jessie carried over the paper cups. 'I treated you to a latte instead of that muddy water they pass as coffee at the hospital.'

'Thanks. Thomas has gone on ahead. I booked us a seat under the tree out of the sun.' It wasn't overly hot, but warm enough that he'd made Thomas put on sunscreen and a hat before they'd left.

'How thoughtful of you to make a reservation. It's definitely a step up from the hospital canteen.'

They both sat down and Cameron tried not to look when her olive-green shirt dress fell open at the knee when she crossed her legs. He didn't need to be reminded of all the times those slender legs had been wrapped around him.

'Simon seems to be doing well.' Desperate to divert his thoughts from places they really shouldn't be going, he chugged back the milky coffee and burned his tongue.

'Yeah. Kids bounce back. I just hope social services can locate some family for him. He's been through enough without ending up in the care system at the end of it all.'

Cameron opened his mouth wide and stuck out his tongue, letting the cool air soothe his scorched tongue. 'He'th a good boy,' he lisped.

Jessie faced him with a frown etched on her forehead. 'Are you okay?'

'I burned my tongue.'

'Idiot—' she laughed '—you never did have any patience.'

For a split second they just stared at each other, the laughter dying away, and he knew she was also thinking of all the good times they'd once had together. If only the moment wasn't spoiled by the reality of how that time had ended, he might have managed to hold his scalded tongue.

'Not when it comes to food or drink. I would've waited for you, though, if I'd been given the chance.' Despite all the promises to himself not to go there, a couple of minutes alone with Jessie and he was spilling his guts.

She looked away. 'Please don't do this, Cameron.'

'Sorry. I just can't help thinking about what could have been.'

Every time I'm with you.

'It's all in the past. Besides, you wouldn't have Thomas if you hadn't gone on without me.'

'I know, but sometimes I think Ciara was simply my rebound. We got married too young, too quickly. I shouldn't blame her for things going wrong. You were a hard act to follow.' He smiled, trying not to make her feel bad, but she refused to look at him.

'Something else I should feel guilty about, I suppose.' She took a sip of coffee, though he suspected she'd rather throw it at him.

He was trying, and failing, to explain why he'd married someone who wasn't her. Even though it was Jessie who'd broken things off, and nothing could come of it anyway, he wanted her to know that he hadn't simply stopped loving her. He hadn't gone off to uni and forgotten about her. Far from it.

'Definitely not. It was entirely my doing. I guess we'd made all those plans together and I carried them with me. I still wanted those things, but it wasn't what other eighteen-year-old students were looking for in a boyfriend. Then I met Ciara after graduation and I thought we were on the same page.' Until the reality proved too challenging for one half of their partnership.

'At least you found someone, even for a while. You have Thomas and a life together. I'm still living at home with my mother, so who's the loser here?'

'Okay, you win.' He toasted her victory with his cup, attempting some levity so he wouldn't wander too far down that road which only led to heartache over everything he'd unknowingly lost.

Jessie rewarded him with that sceptical side eye.

'Seriously, though, you could still get married and have children of your own. You can make the break from the past if that's what's been holding you back. Unfortunately, no one else can do that for you.'

Now his initial anger was beginning to fade, it finally occurred to him that she'd been holding on to this secret, and guilt, all this time. Although he disagreed with the decision she'd made, he didn't believe she should punish herself for it. Jessie deserved to be with someone who loved her unconditionally, who could give her the family they had missed out on together.

Ultimately, though, she would put others first and continue to deny herself the same love and support she gave to everyone else in her life. That was just who she was.

Neither this conversation, nor the day itself, had gone where Jessie had expected and she wasn't comfortable with the new direction. She kept telling herself that everything they were doing was for Thomas but she was enjoying being out here, sharing the day with his father too. It wasn't her place, she wasn't part of their family and never would be, as this conversation was proving.

'Of course I wanted a family of my own. There's nothing I would have loved more than to get married and have a baby.' She choked down the tears of grief already bubbling up at the thought of the child they should have had together, and for the ones she would never get to have.

'You could walk away from your mother, you know, or at least entrust her care to someone else. No one would blame you for wanting a life of your own.' Cameron misunderstood the reason why she couldn't do all the things he'd been able to do, but correcting him meant telling him the whole truth. She wasn't sure either of them were ready for that yet.

'I look after Mum because she's the only family I have, the only family I'll ever have. It turns out I have the same condition she does—antiphospholipid syndrome. The autoimmune disorder caused the stroke which left her paralysed, and it's the reason I lost our baby.'

'I'm so sorry, Jessie. I didn't give you the chance to explain what had happened before. But you can still have children, right?'

'There's a high chance of miscarriage and I know I can't put myself through that again. Anyway, I've come to terms with it so there's no point in getting maudlin over things we can't change.' She got up and brushed the grass from her dress before walking down to the water's edge to check on Thomas's progress, and put some distance between her and Cameron. And the pity emanating from him.

That was why she hadn't told him before. It was one thing dealing with his anger at her but sympathy would only make her want to cry. She didn't need him to be nice to her when it made things easier if he remained mad at her.

There was nothing she wanted more than a family. It had been a dream, a possibility, once upon a time. Then fate had stepped in and Cameron had gone on to have that family with someone else. It was futile to convince herself otherwise. He wasn't her husband, Thomas wasn't her son and this wasn't her life.

Trying to avoid opening up any more old wounds, she redirected her attention away from Cameron, peering over Thomas's shoulder to see what he'd been working on. There in the middle of the page he'd captured a mother duck and her ducklings cruising along the water.

'Thomas, that's wonderful,' she said, kneeling down so she could see the drawing in detail.

He'd managed to capture the downy fur of the baby ducks with the soft strokes of his pencil, as well as the small concentric circles emanating around them.

'I still have to add some colour,' he said, batting away her compliment as he wet his paintbrush.

Her enthusiasm drew Cameron down to join them.

'Well done, son. Your mother would be proud of you.' He kissed the top of his son's head and the display of fatherly pride choked Jessie up until her throat was raw and her eyes stung with the effort of not crying.

Witnessing the beautiful moment and seeing what a great father he'd become was a privilege, especially knowing what Cameron had gone through. Thomas's mother should have been proud of both of them and Jessie realised the woman had sacrificed just as much as she had. Whether she'd had the best of intentions by leaving them Jessie couldn't say, but Cameron's ex was missing out on a hell of a lot by not being part of this family.

They fell into silence, watching in amazement as Thomas worked quickly, adding splodges of colour here and there to pick out the features. Later they could add some information about the species and their characteristics to make his study as informative as it was aesthetically pleasing.

A group of rambunctious teenage boys suddenly burst through the quiet, kicking a football between them and occupying the space Jessie and Cameron had just vacated. One of the older, taller lads booted the football high, lodging it in the branches of the tree.

'Forbesy, climb up and get that, will you?'

'Why me?' a smaller, curly-haired teen asked, even as he began to traverse the lower branches.

'Because you're more agile, like a cat.'

'Or more obedient and stupid, like a dog,' the nominated ball retriever grumbled.

It was difficult to ignore what was going on when they were being so loud and disruptive during what had been a peaceful interlude. Jessie had one eye on Thomas and one on the teen antics beside them, so she saw the fall before she heard the shout.

'Forbesy' had slipped on the branch he'd been balancing on when he'd thrown the ball down. Time seemed to stand still as she helplessly watched the boy bounce off the bottom branches before landing flat on his back at the base of the tree.

It took a few moments before it registered with him what had happened, not least because he'd clearly been winded by the fall. By the time he cried out in pain his mates were shouting and rushing to his aid, as Jessie alerted Cameron, 'That looks like a really bad fall.'

Telling Thomas to stay put, they rushed over to offer medical help. Several of the footballers were watching, hands behind their heads in disbelief and looking pale, not knowing what to do. The older boy who'd urged him to climb the tree in the first place was trying to get him into a sitting position.

'Come on, mate. I'll help you up.'

'Do not move him!' Cameron yelled, stopping them all in their tracks. 'I need you to take a step back and give him some air.'

'He's a doctor. Your friend's in good hands,' Jessie explained as Cameron knelt down to check on the boy.

'We just have to make sure he hasn't injured his neck or spine in the fall before he's moved.'

'Should…should we call an ambulance?'

Jessie took up a position on the other side of the injured boy, noticing his arm was bent at an odd angle. 'I think that would be best, yes.'

Now the pain was really beginning to kick in, the boy's face was contorted and he was wiggling around, using his feet to try and lever himself up.

'What's your name? I'm Cameron and I'm a surgeon over at the hospital.'

'Jamie. Jamie Forbes.'

'Well, Jamie Forbes, we need you to stay as still as possible until the paramedics get here. I want to stabilise that neck in case of any spinal injuries. I'm sure you'll be fine, but in my job it's important to take precautions.' He was smiling, his voice calm and steady, and Jessie saw first-hand that he was every bit as patient, caring and understanding with his patients as he was with his own son. She'd seen him with Simon but this was further proof that his nurturing nature wasn't limited to within the hospital walls.

Not that she'd doubted him. The years might have passed, circumstances had changed, but he was still the good man he'd always been.

He bundled up his jacket and used it as a makeshift support for Jamie's neck before moving to look at the teen's arm. Jamie was pale as Cameron located the fracture area just below his elbow and checked his pulse, comparing it to the one in the uninjured arm.

'You're going to be okay, Jamie, but I think you've fractured your arm. Are your parents here?'

'No.'

'Okay. I need you to tell me if you can feel this.' Cameron touched his arm gently but Jamie shook his head.

'Can you open and close this hand for me?'

The boy complied with a yelp of pain.

'The paramedics will be able to give you some pain

relief when they get here, and they'll need to put a cast on that arm. Your pulse in that arm is weak, suggesting your fracture might be putting pressure on the artery. I'm afraid I'm going to need to straighten it out and immobilise it. Bear with me.'

Cameron rolled his sleeves up and took a strong grip of the arm. 'I need you to brace yourself. Scream and shout all you want, but please try not to struggle. We need to get this bone back in place. It'll be over really quickly, I promise, Jamie.' He gently applied traction in order to align the limb again.

The teeth-grinding sound of the bone being forced back into place was accompanied by Jamie's short, sharp scream. Most of his friends had to turn away, probably glad they weren't the one in his position. Cameron then gathered some nearby fallen branches to improvise a splint and checked his pulse again.

'Good man. The pulse is sounding better, which means there's no disruption to the blood supply going to the limb.'

'You can use this to immobilise the arm.' Jessie pulled off the blue chiffon dragonfly print scarf she'd been wearing from around her neck.

'Thanks.' Cameron met her gaze and she could feel the warmth of his gratitude radiating from his entire being.

She was sure fixing a broken arm was nothing compared to the life-changing operations he performed daily and she'd played a minor role in it. Yet he was looking at her as though she'd been the hero of the day, simply for being there. It made her wonder how long it had been since he'd had anyone's real support.

By all accounts his wife hadn't been there for him, and she knew his family had never been supportive. Cameron deserved so much more. For a man who gave so much, he didn't seem to receive anything in return. With no significant other in her life, she knew a little about that herself. They were two peas in a pod, caring too much for others and getting little in return. She suspected that the only time they'd both felt loved and cherished was when they'd been together.

Okay, he'd had it briefly with his wife, but ultimately she'd betrayed him. Jessie had too, but she'd never stopped loving him. She doubted she ever would.

CHAPTER SIX

'COME ON, SIMON, I know you can do this.' Jessie was urging him alongside the walking frame, willing him with every cell in her body to take those steps.

His face was scrunched up with the effort of concentration in putting those limbs to work again, but this was a huge milestone for him. The more progress he made, the better the outcome and future prognosis. If he gave up now and accepted his limitations it was doubtful he would ever be fully mobile again and at such a young age that would be a tragedy. Especially when he'd had these early years with full use of his limbs, leading a full life. If he had to go into the care system as well she wasn't sure if he would ever get the same support for a full recovery as he was receiving now with her and Cameron as his cheerleaders. He was here with her in his free time, urging on their patient who was so much more to both of them.

'I want my mummy and daddy,' Simon cried as he struggled to put one foot in front of the other, and Jessie almost joined him. Life had been so unfair to all of them in this small room, but they were doing their best now. She and Cameron wanted to get Simon back on his feet so he could live as full a life as possible. Cameron, although he'd turned her world on its axis once more, had given her something to look forward to every day. Finally sharing all of those secrets which had burdened her for years had made her soul lighter. Seeing him might have made her think too much about the past, about what she'd lost or would never have, but he was undoubtedly the highlight of her day. In between her duties to her patients and her mother, there was always that anticipation of seeing Cameron to fuel her through her day. He was beginning to thaw towards her, perhaps even learning to trust her again, and Jessie wasn't taking it for granted.

Seeing his wariness around her had almost broken her. Now, getting to see him, working with him reminded her every day why she'd fallen in love with him first time around. She'd forgotten what it was to feel alive, her blood pumping so hard through her body she thought her heart would actually explode at the sight of him. Her existence was no longer simply moving from one task to the other, her emotions completely dependent on the mood and circumstances of those she cared for. She had feelings of her own, regardless that she could do nothing about them, pining for a love that she'd thrown away and a family which would never be hers.

Some day, when it came to an end, when Simon moved on and Thomas had completed his project, she would have to come to terms with never seeing him again and return to her lonely life.

From the second he'd appeared back in her world she'd had cause to be concerned, but spending time with him and Thomas, seeing how he'd treated that boy in the park, had confirmed what she already knew to be true. She still had feelings for Cameron.

He was a great father, a compassionate doctor and a great man. His only fault had been loving her. It had hurt them both when they'd parted, but she was sure he wouldn't be ready to make the same mistake again even if she was.

'I know, buddy, but Jessie and I are here for you as long as you need us.' Cameron wrapped his hand around one of Simon's as he slid the frame along the floor, willing his legs to follow.

Jessie loved that he was as sincerely invested as she was in the boy's progress. Simon looked up at Cameron, his respect and admiration for the man who'd given him this chance to even try and walk again shining in his young eyes. He pursed his lips and braced himself on the frame, a renewed determination on his face because of Cameron's support. She had got him this far with his physical rehabilitation, building his strength and confidence along with the means to recover, but motivation and support were equally important.

Having Cameron working alongside her was an extra source of assistance for both her and Simon. If she had this level of teamwork with every specialist for her patients she would see quicker progress and improved recovery rates overall.

'Just a couple of steps, Simon...' she urged.

Simon moved forward, slowly dragging one foot in front of the other.

'That's it. The first steps are the hardest, now we need you to get to the end. You're doing so well.' She was clapping him on, hoping the momentum would carry him along the length of the hallway. It would do so much towards his mental recovery as well as his physical progress, knowing he could walk through the pain if he really set his mind to it.

'When can I sit down?' Simon asked, breathing heavily with the effort.

'As soon as you get to the wheelchair.' Jessie manoeuvred the wheelchair they'd used to transport him from the children's ward to Rehab.

They couldn't push him too hard in case his body failed him and damaged his morale. He needed to go out on a high.

Simon grunted and propelled himself the last few steps. His face lit up as they smiled and clapped his efforts.

'I did it.'

'You did.' She had to turn away before she made a fool of herself crying over his success, and busied herself getting the wheelchair into place.

Simon all but fell into it, exhausted, red in the face but clearly delighted with himself, and rightly so. It would've been easy to give up after everything he'd been through and had still to face. The exercise and physiotherapy, though necessary to get him walking again, was nevertheless hard work and painful at times. Her adult patients struggled to get motivated and here was a seven-year-old boy who'd just lost his parents pushing himself to the limit. Jessie was proud of him, and Cameron, and herself.

'Good job.' Cameron congratulated him with a high-five.

'We'll take you back to the ward so you can get some rest now, but tomorrow we'll be doing it all over again. The more you practise, the better and easier your steps will become.' Despite her euphoria she needed to warn him that this was the beginning of his journey, not the end. They couldn't get too complacent about his progress and had to keep pushing him further if he was going to gain full mobility.

Cameron helped her to get Simon back into bed and poured him a glass of orange squash. 'Get some sleep, buddy, and we'll be back to see you tomorrow.'

It was such a sweet moment. Jessie almost expected him to kiss the boy on the head the way he did with Thomas when showing affection. That was how caring he came across and how much of a father-figure he was to this orphaned child who had no one in his life.

'Bye, Simon,' she said, voice raspy with emotion.

'I'll see you tomorrow.' He waved. 'Can't wait to walk again,' he said with the biggest grin on his face she'd seen since his admission to the hospital.

That alone made her job, her dedication and lack of a private life worth it.

As they left the ward she could see Cameron's smile

growing wider by the second until they were in the corridor and he seemed unable to control his excitement. She mirrored his happy expression.

'Can you believe that just happened?'

Jessie knew he was talking about Simon taking his first steps, but she was equally buoyed at his enthusiasm to try again tomorrow. It meant they hadn't pushed him too far, too quickly, and his enthusiasm to carry on could be the motivation to get him walking unassisted in no time.

'It's amazing how resilient they are at that age.'

'I think you had a lot to do with young Simon finding his feet again, Ms Rea.'

'That wouldn't have been possible without your surgical skills, Dr Holmes.'

'We make a great team.' He high-fived her then pulled her into a hug with a burst of vocal glee.

Jessie's laugh as he wrapped his arms around her to share the excitement turned into a contented sigh as his body enveloped her. That familiar heat and security of his hard chest and strong arms was something she'd missed for so long.

The colleagues celebrating a patient's progress hug soon turned into something else. A longing for the past, a reconnection they'd been dancing around since they'd found each other again, and a yearning for more. Instead of coming to her senses and pulling away, for once Jessie just wanted something for herself—Cameron holding her and pretending that they'd never parted. He didn't attempt to extricate himself either but rested his chin on the top of her head and squeezed her tighter. The confirmation that he might just miss her was sufficient to undo her. They were a good team, they always had been. It was other circumstances which had been the problem. Now those secrets which had ruined their relationship the first time around made being together more impossible than ever. Even if there was any sign that he had any interest in her.

Cameron now knew about the baby, and the syndrome she'd inherited, but that didn't change anything. It only explained her reason for letting him walk out of her life. She wanted the best for him and that still wasn't her, someone who could never give him a family.

Eventually Cameron's grip on her loosened and they took a step away from each other. He didn't let go of her arms though and when she looked up at him his eyes were staring at her mouth. She watched him dip his head in slow motion to claim her lips with his. It was a mistake, a stupid move which would only serve to make things more awkward and complicated between them.

Yet she didn't try to stop it happening. Her eyes fluttered shut and she gave herself over to that feather touch of his lips brushing hers. How she'd missed this, missed him, missed being loved. Later she could blame her loneliness, her nostalgia and regret, for letting her defences down. She purposely avoided relationships to dodge family complications and guilt, and Cameron embodied everything she should be resisting instead of embracing, but it had been too long and this felt so good.

This kiss was not the hard passion of infatuated teens but a tender longing for one another which brought tears to her eyes. She was almost thankful when they heard chatter coming from around the corner, causing them to break apart and end the beautiful, painful moment.

As tears fell silently down her cheeks, washing away her initial happiness, Jessie turned on her heel and ran from him. It was too heartbreaking, too unfair to be continually reminded of the life, the love, the man she could've had if she'd been braver.

Cameron was pacing the kitchen floor like a first-time expectant father, not sure what to do with himself. Jessie was due to come and help Thomas tonight but, after what had happened between them at work, he couldn't be sure she'd turn up, much less talk to him.

He'd messed up, given in to that temptation to hold her, kiss her, and pretend everything was okay. After hearing about her health issues he'd stopped blaming her for everything that had gone wrong. She hadn't asked for it any more than he had. In true Jessie fashion she'd been trying to take care of him, protect him from potential harm. Of course she'd been wrong and he would remain devastated that she'd locked him out of that difficult time, but he'd forgiven her.

It was hard to stay angry at her when she proved

every day how kind and caring she was. And he'd begun to realise those strong feelings he'd had weren't just about the past. He was still attracted to her and he'd foolishly acted on it. Sure, she'd folded right into his arms and appeared content to be there, but crying and running away after he'd kissed her was not the sign of a good time.

He brushed his hand through his hair for the thousandth time, resisting the urge to pull it out, or do damage to the nearest inanimate object instead. He needed his hands in one piece to do his job and he'd let enough people down for one lifetime. Namely, Jessie.

She'd been honest about steering clear of relationships, and the reason why—the same explanation she'd given for breaking things off with him. Yet sharing the achievement of Simon's first steps with her had given him a false sense of intimacy with her. Why else would he have kissed her in their place of work, not only crossing the line in their friendship but potentially endangering their jobs too?

He swore loud enough for Thomas to pull his headphones off and look up at him from the table.

'It's fine. I stubbed my toe, that's all.' He could add lying to his son to the list of his recent misdemeanours.

Whether Jessie had wanted him to kiss her or not, and despite his longing for her, he shouldn't have done it. His action had jeopardised not only Simon's recovery at the hospital if she decided she could no longer work with him, but also his son's progress. If she didn't feel safe around him there was no way she would come to his house.

He checked his phone. There were no missed calls or new messages and she should've been here fifteen minutes ago. He walked out of the back door to mutter another expletive out of earshot of his impressionable offspring. If he'd ruined all the hard work they'd done to improve the lives of the two boys he'd never forgive himself.

It was only when he heard the knock at the front door he was able to stop beating himself up, though he knew he had some grovelling to do before she'd forgive him.

He hot-footed it back through the house, only to be overtaken by his eager son, clutching his sketchpad. Thomas yanked the front door open and immediately shoved the picture of the park swans he'd been working on in her face.

'Hello to you too, Thomas. Glad to see you've been working away on your own. May I come in?'

Thankfully, Cameron could hear the smile in Jessie's voice, even if he couldn't see it with a drawing pad obscuring her from view. She didn't sound as though she'd come here to slap him with a lawsuit or a restraining order.

'Let Ms Rea in, Thomas.' Cameron rested his hands on his son's shoulders and gently ushered him aside to allow Jessie access to his home.

'Ms Rea, is it now?' She cocked an eyebrow at him, one corner of her mouth curved upward in the tease.

Relief flowed out of him in one short heavy breath. 'I wasn't sure if you'd even come tonight after…you know…' He squirmed, facing her like that awkward teenage boy who'd kissed her when they were supposed to be revising—moving in, caught up in how close she was sitting next to him, only to plant his lips on the end of her nose instead of her mouth. They'd laughed about it then before he'd made a successful second attempt, which was imprinted on his brain and his lips for ever.

'I did think about it. Not showing up, I mean, but that wouldn't have been fair on Thomas.'

'I know. I'm so sorry. Please forgive me.'

'What for?' She was going to make him spell out his transgression in minute detail to make sure he'd never do it again.

'For kissing you without permission. I'm truly sorry. I don't want to ruin things for Simon and Thomas because of my foolish, selfish actions.'

Now it was her turn to look puzzled, evidently confused by the words.

'What made you think I wasn't a willing partner? Was it the snuggling into your chest or the kissing you back?'

'No, it was the crying and running away.'

'Oh. Oh! You saw that, huh?'

'Yes, and I've been kicking myself ever since. Are you telling me I got it wrong?' He was struggling to comprehend an alternative explanation for the abrupt departure.

Jessie pressed a hand to his chest and sighed. 'I

missed this, Cameron. I miss you, but we both know it would only end in tears again. As proven today.'

'Wow. So let me get this straight… You wanted me to kiss you?' That made him see the incident in an altogether different light. It hadn't been the disastrous act of a desperate man crossing the line but the culmination of a mutual attraction and want for one another.

Jessie bunched his shirt in her hand and pulled him down so his face was a breath away from hers. 'I wanted you to kiss me, I liked it, and I'd love to do it over and over again.'

To illustrate her point, she pressed her lips against his and lingered there for a brief moment before he could fully enjoy the sensation.

'But neither of us are in a situation to take this any further, so I suggest we put it behind us and concentrate on the boys' needs rather than our own.'

She let go of him and sauntered past towards the kitchen, leaving Cameron reeling from another all too brief intimacy. In the three years since Ciara had left he hadn't even looked at another woman. Now, with Jessie on the scene, he seemed to have become some sort of sex maniac because being with her was all he could think of, wanting what they used to have together before complications beyond his control got in the way.

Far from putting his mind at ease, the knowledge that Jessie wanted him too was only going to make things even more unbearable. Look but don't touch had always seemed a particularly cruel rule to him.

* * *

Jessie was flushed with her bravado and the feel of having Cameron pressed against her again, if only for one more precious second. She'd agonised over coming tonight, knowing it was leading her straight into the path of temptation—a dangerous journey she apparently couldn't resist.

In the end she'd thought of Thomas's little face and the prospect of having to disappoint him. If left to finish the project alone, he might never find the motivation. Just like Simon, he needed her support and his needs had to come before hers.

She'd convinced herself that coming to Cameron's house was the right thing to do for his son, the selfless path. Except within a heartbeat of seeing Cameron again she was mauling him and trying to snog him senseless. Thank goodness for a ten-year-old distraction.

'Hey, Thomas, how's the project looking?' She sat down and sorted through the loose sheets of paper currently covering the table.

'Okay, I guess. It's not the same working from photographs. I can't get the stupid colours right.' He didn't sound as bright as he had been since they'd started working the art angle on the project.

'I'm sorry, Thomas, but I can't take you to the park every day. I have work and by the time I get home sometimes it's too dark.' Cameron joined them at the table. Even when he could be taking a time out with Jessie there to take the reins for a while, he still wanted to be a part of everything. He was a much better parent than his own had been.

Jessie guessed the photographs that Thomas was working from had been printed out from Cameron's phone. He'd made the effort to snap the birds at some point during his working day as he couldn't spend the whole afternoon there with his son. She understood Thomas's frustration but she could also see how much he was loved by his father, who was doing his best in difficult circumstances.

'You're always at stupid work. It's not fair,' Thomas lashed out, swiping the jar of water containing his dirty brushes over the table.

Jessie gasped as a river of muddy water sloshed across his sketches and the printed photographs. She grabbed the pictures closest to her while Cameron's quick reflexes managed to rescue the rest. However, the torrent of water had cascaded over the sides of the table into Jessie's lap.

'Thomas, look at the mess you've made,' Cameron chastised. It was the first time Jessie had ever heard him raise his voice, but he was crouching at eye level, trying to get Thomas to understand that his behaviour was unacceptable without being intimidating or threatening.

'I think we've saved most of it,' she said, standing up to show them the drawings she'd salvaged, water dripping down her legs.

'But you're soaked through.'

'I'll live.'

'Sorry, Jessie.' Thomas hung his head and it was obvious he regretted his outburst so she saw no need to make him feel worse.

'No harm done. My clothes will dry out, but I think we should set your drawings somewhere to do the same while we clean this mess up.'

Between them they set to work mopping up the spilled water and setting aside Thomas's completed pictures. His work in progress had suffered the most damage, but Jessie hoped that once it dried out he would still be able to use it.

It had been an unexpected outburst but thankfully they had managed to defuse it quickly. They both had some experience dealing with such behaviour but she could see why some people found it too challenging to be around. She'd had patients throw furniture at her, directing their fear at her. It took strength and patience to deal with incidents like this. It was a shame that Thomas's mother hadn't been able to.

'I think perhaps we'll set the drawings aside for a while and concentrate on the text. It'll be better for you to put the information down in your own words, so I thought you could read some relevant articles and watch some documentary clips.'

She'd loaded her digital tablet with some videos since he seemed to enjoy his screen time. A now calm Thomas plugged in his earphones and Jessie set a notepad and a pencil beside him so he could take notes.

'That should keep him occupied for a while,' she told

Cameron, who was washing the paintbrushes and the jar at the kitchen sink.

'You're so good with him. He listens to you. Sometimes tempers flare and the whole thing escalates, but you handle him better than some of his teachers. And his mother.'

It was a compliment of sorts, but it couldn't lift the sadness around the family circumstances here. Jessie wasn't going to be around for long and they would all do well to remember that.

'He's a good boy, you know that, and it just takes a bit of time for others to see that. This was nothing. Just the average pre-teen having a tantrum.' She gestured towards her stained shirt and jeans.

He looked sheepishly at her. 'I'm so sorry. You're soaked. I should've offered you a change of clothes.'

'Honestly, it's not necessary—'

'I can't let you sit in wet clothes. I'm sure there's something you could change into.'

She followed him to the main bedroom, which was odd on so many levels when they'd agreed not to blur those lines again.

The décor had clearly been his wife's choice, with a cherry blossom and hummingbird theme decorating the pale blue walls. He opened one side of the wardrobe and Jessie was confronted with rails of shirts and suits. When he opened the other door, however, it was empty save for the coat hangers.

She'd half expected to find evidence of his wife still there, the bottom of the wardrobe filled with shoes, perhaps the top shelf loaded with handbags. As though he was waiting for her to come back and pick up where she'd left off with her family.

'She went to work one day and just never came home. All I got was a text message to say she'd left us and wouldn't be coming back, that our marriage was over, followed by a voice message saying that she wanted a divorce. No discussion, no mention of our son, she simply abandoned us and her life here,' Cameron confided, as though picking up on her train of thought.

There'd been times in the past when she'd wished she could do the same, walk away from everything to reinvent herself somewhere else. The difference was that she'd never had the courage to act. She had some appreciation for what Ciara must have been going through to have taken such drastic action, but would never understand her walking away from her family in such a brutal fashion.

Even breaking things off with Cameron all those years ago had eaten away at her conscience, guilt and regret shadowing her every decision since. She wondered if Ciara ever doubted the decisions she'd made, or ever thought about coming back.

Jessie shivered, the ghost of Cameron's ex haunting her even though she hadn't been a fixture in his life for years. Although Cameron had been hurt she couldn't be certain he wouldn't welcome Ciara's return if faced with the opportunity.

'I'll see if I can find something less formal and more

comfortable for you to wear.' He left her in the room, closing the door behind him.

Jessie began to strip off the wet clothes sticking to her skin. She tossed her shirt on the bed and was wriggling out of her jeans when Cameron burst back into the room.

'I found these in the spare room. They still have the tags on so I don't think they've been worn...' He came to a halt, the armful of clothes now falling onto the floor as he found her half undressed in his bedroom.

'Sorry, I should've knocked,' he said without taking his eyes off her, standing in nothing but her underwear.

He'd seen her in a lot less, but she liked seeing this look of desire darkening his eyes, letting her know he still wanted her even if circumstances forbade it.

'It's your house.' She shrugged and closed the distance between them to retrieve the clothes he'd brought, though she made no move to put them on.

Cameron bent down to pick up the T-shirt and tracksuit bottoms he'd brought and she saw the stiff way he lowered himself to the ground and the hand which flew to the small of his back when he tried to stand again.

'You were serious about getting that back massage?' she said as she pulled on the oversized leisurewear he'd provided.

'I'm fine. Being on your feet for hours of surgery can play havoc sometimes, that's all.'

'You need to get that seen to. It's only going to get more painful otherwise.'

'I don't have time. I'm sure it'll work itself out.'

Men, and particularly doctors, made the worst patients as they were too stubborn to acknowledge they had a problem and seek help.

Jessie rolled her eyes. Uncooperative patients were a daily hazard of her job, until they realised that her 'stupid exercises' and 'intrusion' into their personal space improved their physical ailments.

'Back pain never "works itself out". It's a sign there's something wrong, or that you simply need to improve your posture. Bad habits can have a detrimental effect on your physical wellbeing. It's down to me to retrain people's way of thinking or, in your case, standing.'

His look told her all she needed to know about how much she was annoying him because she was right and all the more determined to prove her worth as a fellow medical professional. She might have gone down a different route, wasn't perhaps regarded as highly as her more qualified peers, but it didn't make her role any less important.

The patients needing the most hospital care often had a multi-disciplinary team of experts working together to get them back to the best health possible. She was a part of that team and needed as much as the doctors, surgeons, counsellors or dietitians. When the injuries had been operated on, when people were working on getting their physical strength back, she was the one there pushing and cheering them on to recovery. She never let something as minor as a disagreeable personality get in the way.

Cameron seemed so determined to keep her at arm's

length she thought he'd rather crawl into work on hands and knees than ask for her help.

As he turned to leave, the awkward angle he'd twisted his body into clearly exacerbated whatever was already ailing him as he cried out.

'Cameron?' Jessie rushed to him as he muttered an expletive.

'I can't straighten up.' His face was contorted in pain, his breathing shallow, as he fought through the pain.

'Take deep breaths while we get you over to the bed.' In different circumstances she wouldn't have been so bold, might even have blushed at the unintentional innuendo, but she was more concerned with Cameron's back spasm. If he was out of action he wouldn't be able to keep seeing Simon, and as a result would be missing from her working days—his presence was the one thing she had to look forward to between her responsibilities. In short, she had to help Cameron so she could continue to get her regular fix of grumpy ex-boyfriend who only tolerated her because he had to.

She was beginning to suspect she had issues of her own.

'I don't want to hear *I told you so* either,' he grumbled as she helped him over to the bed.

'As if I would.' She feigned innocence when they both knew that was exactly what she wanted to say. Her competitive nature was what had got them both through their exams. They'd each challenged the other to be the best, comparing scores and teasing the loser, when in reality she'd been secretly pleased when his grades had surpassed hers. There had been something about seeing a happy Cameron that she'd found addictive. That was why it would've proved soul-destroying to ruin his life by tying it to hers for ever. It had been hard enough seeing him upset when she'd ended their relationship. She'd had to console herself with the thought that he would smile again once he'd achieved his dream, even if she'd cried herself to sleep more times than she cared to remember.

'Ouch,' he complained as she helped him into a sitting position on the edge of the bed.

'You were never a good patient.'

'You made an excellent nurse, as I recall.' Despite his obvious pain, Cameron managed to give her that dangerous *I remember what we got up to the last time we played doctors and nurses* look.

'Yes, well, we were young and stupid,' she said.

As nice as it sometimes was to remember being curled up in his bed together, blocking out the rest of the world from their little love nest, it wasn't going to do her any favours now.

Cameron was divorced, a father, a surgeon, and they had nothing in common except the pain of their past and the children they were helping. It would be foolish to wish for anything more when her circumstances hadn't changed.

Yet his blue eyes were still watching her with something more than interest in what she was doing. If she wasn't imagining it there was a longing there. Whether it was for something more now or for back then she couldn't tell.

'Shirt. Off. Now.' Her voice was so thick with that same yearning she could barely get the words out, never mind arrange them into a coherent sentence.

He started to unbutton, his eyes never leaving hers as he did so. Mouth dry, she wet her lips with a sweep of her tongue and saw the brilliant blue bloom of his irises darken to midnight.

Jessie positioned herself between his legs in order to help him out of his shirt. It was something she'd done countless times for her patients but never had it felt so intimate.

'You're very authoritative when you want to be.' The corners of his mouth tilted up into a smile as he watched her up close. Too close, she realised too late. When she'd pushed the shirt over his shoulders it left her nowhere to go but closer, until she managed to clear it from his muscular torso. By which point she was practically pushing her chest into his face while having a good feel of his biceps as she undressed him.

'I'd never get anything done otherwise,' she countered in an attempt to disguise the lust currently doing the fandango through her entire being.

In his late teens Cameron had been wiry and lean, limbs strong and long enough to wrap around her and make her feel safe. Now Cameron had filled out in all the right places until muscles visibly popped and chest hair comprised of more than a few straggly follicles.

'I need you face down. So I can work on your back,' she explained, to cover her wandering mind.

He smirked before gingerly turning over on to the bed to let her breathe a sigh of relief. Perhaps she could do her job more efficiently and professionally if he wasn't scrutinising her every move, looking at her the way he used to do when she was trying to study, until she'd been able to resist no longer, forced to admit to the chemistry between them when they were together in a room.

With a deep breath she rubbed her hands together before laying them on Cameron for the first time in years.

His skin was warm, his muscles rigid, as she moved her way deftly down his torso.

'Try and relax. I'm not going to hurt you. Much.' She attempted to bring some levity to the situation, to break the tension she felt under her fingers and in the air.

'It's the "much" I'm worried about,' he grumbled into the duvet cover.

Doing her best to focus on where she was needed, on treating him as a patient rather than an ex-boyfriend, Jessie kneaded and manipulated the tight knots she found under his skin, praying they'd both come out of this unscathed, maybe even recovered.

This was torture. It felt good, too good in fact, to have Jessie's hands on him again, but torturous all the same.

The way Jessie was working her magic on his back felt like an intimate, sensual act they'd participated in when they'd been lovers, making him feel things other than muscular relief. He hadn't helped himself by bringing up memories of the time when she'd nursed him through a nasty flu. With his family oblivious, calling him a drama queen, she'd been the one cooling his brow and bringing him soup. Okay, he might have prolonged his illness for that very reason, enjoying the attention, but they'd both benefitted in the end. He'd repaid Jessie's kindness over and over again when he'd recovered.

Given the chance to do things over again, he would have fought harder to keep her in his life all those years ago. He would rather have had her in his life above all else and it would have saved him the heartache of trying to replicate their relationship with someone who clearly wasn't Jessie.

'Are you okay? I don't think I've ever had such a quiet patient.' Jessie stopped the massage to check on him.

He couldn't tell her he was focusing hard on not enjoying her touch too much. Groans of appreciation would not have been appropriate in the circumstances. Regardless that her technique was primarily stretching out knots and not for pleasure, he was enjoying the pounding she was giving him.

'Sorry, I was just thinking about my surgery tomorrow.'

Liar.

Jessie tutted. 'You need to take better care of yourself. I'm going to work on some exercises for you to stretch out that back and improve your posture in the meantime. Do you think you can sit up again?'

Cameron tested his neck muscles, first turning his head so he could look at her. 'So far, so good.'

She took a step back, giving him some room to push himself back up into a sitting position. 'Good. You look a bit more flexible.'

He slipped his shirt back on and stood to stretch out his back a bit more. 'That seems much better. Thank you.'

'No problem.'

Having Jessie back in his life was confusing and disruptive. It was also playing havoc with his schedule when he was putting in more hours at her hospital currently than anywhere else in the hope of seeing more of her.

In a parallel universe they might have rekindled that teenage love. He'd realised that he still harboured wants and needs involving Jessie during their impromptu physio session. It didn't help when he'd caught her staring at him half naked, that lingering look telling him she was still interested.

If there was one thing he didn't need it was knowing that Jessie might be having regrets about ever ending things between them.

'Is this another one of those moments where I want to kiss you as much as you want me to?' he asked with a grin, pulling her towards him, finally giving in to those urges.

* * *

'You know, waiting for me to give you verbal consent really takes all the spontaneity out of it. I was half naked in your bedroom after all.' Jessie knew this was what she'd wanted from the second she'd decided to come over this evening.

'It's been a while. Sometimes I miss the signals.' He grinned as he swooped in to kiss her, an intensely passionate assault on her lips she hadn't expected but which made her body go languorous in his arms. This was how she remembered it with Cameron. It hadn't been the misremembered fantasy of a broken-hearted teen after all.

If their earlier encounter had been a gentle reintroduction to one another, this was fifth date, let's get it on unbridled wanting. They never could get enough of one another. After that first fumbled kiss things between them had quickly heated up. They'd been each other's first and only until she'd messed things up and sent him into the arms of another woman. Now she realised why no one else had ever come close to Cameron Holmes. No other man had been so demonstrative in their want for her, unafraid to give themselves completely to her the way Cameron did. The way he was doing now.

His warm hands on her back drew her towards him so that her breasts were pushed torturously close against his chest, the thin fabric between them too much to bear.

It was Cameron who called a halt this time, breaking off the kiss to rest his forehead against hers, his short breaths warming her lips where his had been only seconds before.

'I thought we couldn't do this again?'

'We can't,' she replied, her own breath as shaky as the rest of her body at this unexpected display of passion.

'Why is that again?'

'History, your ex-wife, my mother, your son...'

'Ah, yes.' It took the mention of Thomas for him to back away. 'I should go and check on him and leave you alone.'

He began to walk away but Jessie couldn't resist one last tease. 'If you insist.'

A growl and a stride later he'd taken her back in his embrace for a last lingering smooch. Then he took off again, leaving Jessie a quivering wreck, her body aching for more of him while her brain was yelling at her to run away.

As she pressed her fingers to her kiss-swollen lips she was beginning to think that playing it safe wasn't as much fun as the alternative.

CHAPTER SEVEN

'THANKS FOR COMING.' Cameron hadn't been sure whether to give Jessie a hug or a kiss and ended up settling on an awkward handshake. Things between them had been odd to say the least since they'd kissed—something which had been happening too often, yet somehow not often enough.

He wanted to kiss her every time he laid eyes on her, which was virtually all the time when he was seeing her at work in the hospital and at home when she was helping Thomas. He must have the patience of a saint not to have made another move that evening when he'd found her undressed in his bedroom, when she'd looked at him with the same hunger he was afraid would destroy their common sense again.

It was obvious that neither the chemistry nor the attraction had dissipated between them but, unfortunately, the timing still wasn't right. If it would ever be. Every time he touched her the world around them disappeared so all that was left was that longing for one another. A dangerous, selfish desire which would impact their real lives so much they shouldn't be playing with fire this way. It would be too risky to put his trust in her when there was every possibility that she could leave him again. He'd been through that too many times to put his faith in another relationship. But that tangible energy between them bubbled and hissed whenever they were in the same room, like water boiling in a pot that was going to spill over at some point and cause a hell of a mess.

With Thomas's project complete it should've been the time to walk away, especially when Simon was improving every day too. He couldn't really justify the amount of time he was spending with one patient any more and it was a good thing that the boy's recovery had gone so well after surgery. But Cameron was afraid if they lost that connection through the boys they would never see each other again and he wasn't ready to say goodbye.

That was why he'd extended an invitation to her tonight.

'I couldn't miss it, could I? Not when our little artist has worked so hard to be part of this.' Jessie put an arm around Thomas as they made their way into the school assembly hall, looking every inch the proud parent as Cameron was.

They'd pulled together as a team to get the school project completed. In order to avoid temptation he'd taken Thomas on more field trips without his tutor but she'd certainly been a big part of helping him finish the work. The result was a beautifully illustrated study of birds in their natural habitats, which would've been at home on any coffee table.

What they'd achieved together made Cameron wonder what their lives would've been like if Jessie had come into it sooner. If she'd never left his life. Jessie's return had filled that hole in his heart which had been there from the day he'd left for medical school without her, but the longing for the life they could've had together remained. When they were together they were like a little family. If they weren't careful, they could all start to believe that was what they were. But, just as had happened in the past, one day the bubble could burst. It wasn't just his heart on the line any more.

'Dad, are you listening? I said this is the work my class did.' Thomas took him by the hand and led him around the perimeter of the room. The sound of squeaky rubber soles echoed around the walls as his classmates trailed their parents to see the products of their work but Cameron was sure no other child had had the same input from the adults in their lives. He and Jessie had willed him to succeed just as much as they had Simon. Thomas had given them reason to work together, and now it was over they were going to have to make a decision. Did they go back to their separate lives, forever mourning their lost love, or for once in their lives do something for themselves and act on their feelings?

'These are all really good,' Jessie praised as they stopped briefly to glance at the competition, then bent down to whisper in Thomas's ear, 'But they don't come anywhere close to how brilliant yours is.'

Cameron wasn't really paying attention to the others when there was only one project he was interested in. 'Where's yours, Thomas?'

After all the time and effort put into it, and the fact that he hadn't expected to even participate, he expected his son's work to be front and centre of the exhibited work.

'Mine's in the corner, Dad, over there.'

'Look at this one, Cameron—someone's done their project on eighties and nineties cartoons.' Jessie paused by one table sporting a display of badly drawn animations, but he grabbed her by the arm and pulled her towards Thomas's project instead.

'We don't want to show too much interest in his competitors' stuff. Is there anything we can do to draw more attention here?' On Jessie's advice, Thomas had decorated his table with some extra sketches he hadn't used. Cameron made a promise to himself that once they were returned he'd have them framed and proudly displayed around the house.

The sound of Jessie's laugh drew him back to the present.

'What's so funny?'

'You. You've turned into a competitive dad all of a sudden.'

Thomas and Jessie were both grinning at him, but he knew how it felt to put your work out there and not have support. Even when people had stopped laughing and calling him stupid, he'd never had his parents there to share any of his achievements or support him. He wouldn't apologise for being invested in his son's work because when Jessie was gone he would be the only one left to champion him.

'I'm proud, that's all. Now, let's get some photographs. Thomas, you stand there with your project book open so I can see your paintings. Jessie, could you stand next to him?'

'You don't need me ruining your pictures,' she protested, but Cameron wanted a record of her involvement too, in case he never got to see her again.

'If it wasn't for you we would never have got this finished, so no more pretending otherwise.'

'It was Thomas who did all the work. All I did was give him a nudge in the right direction.' She slowly inched herself closer to Thomas until she was in the frame and Cameron snapped the shot.

'Well, we're very grateful for all your nudging, aren't we, Thomas?'

'Yeah. Let me take a photograph of you and Jessie, Dad.'

'I don't think…'

'Please. I know how to do it.'

He couldn't say no to his son after all the hard work he'd done. It was only one quick photograph to keep him happy. So he handed his phone over and took his place beside Jessie in front of the display table. He put his arm around her and he heard the change in her breathing at the same time his pulse seemed to skip a beat. They smiled for the camera and leaned closer than they needed to, held on to one another longer than strictly necessary.

That was when Cameron knew he didn't want this to be goodbye. She was part of their lives, and they owed it to one another to at least give this a chance. He wanted to kiss her right now and tell her he was willing to bury the past and try again, but now wasn't the time. Not in front of Thomas. It was too early for him to think they were in a relationship, even if that was exactly what Cameron was hoping for.

'Ladies and gentlemen, could you please take your seats.' During their little photo op the headmaster had taken to the stage to speak.

'I guess we should go and get a good viewing spot. Good luck, buddy.' Cameron slapped his son on the back and he and Jessie hurried to get a seat near the front of the audience. Thomas and the rest of his classmates walked up on the stage and waited to hear the results of the prize-giving.

'I know I'm biased but I think he's got a really good chance of winning something.' Excitement was emanating from Jessie. Cameron was trying to keep a lid on his own in case they were all disappointed, but as she clutched on to his arm he could feel that positive energy and couldn't fail to be infected by it.

'As long as it's not something patronising like a participation award, I'll be happy,' he said, having not entirely given up his err on the side of caution stance.

Jessie nudged him, forcing him to smile back, and they both sat on the edges of their seats, waiting for the results to be announced.

'A warm welcome to all parents, children and

friends of the school to our very special prize-giving ceremony. Our senior school have been working very hard on their individual projects and I'm blown away by the level of creativity and talent we've seen here tonight.' He turned and began a round of applause for the beaming students sitting behind him, which the audience continued.

'We're going to start with our year eights…'

Cameron and Jessie clapped and congratulated the winners along with the other parents until they reached Thomas's group.

Eyes trained on the stage, Jessie reached for his hand and clutched it tight. Whether she knew it or not, her love for his son was there in her worried expression and need to be held. They could keep pretending they were protecting themselves by not acknowledging their true feelings for one another but the damage had already been done.

'In third place… Max Shriver's *History of the British Royal Family.*'

Another anxious round of applause.

'In second place…' Jessie squeezed his hand tighter '…Angela Robinson's project on *The Ocean Around Us.*'

This time Jessie let go of his hand, clearly feeling as deflated as he was, realising the odds weren't in Thomas's favour.

'There's always next time,' he said, only to be met with a sad puppy look. They both knew there wasn't going to be a next time unless one of them was brave enough to take the next step beyond guilty snatched kisses.

'Jessie, I think we should talk…'

'And first prize goes to *A Study of Birds* by Thomas Holmes.'

Jessie's yelp as she leapt off her seat alerted him to the news before the announcement actually sank in. Thomas had won. Cameron was on his feet too, clapping and hollering at his beaming son as he accepted his first prize trophy.

'He won. I don't believe it.' Cameron thought his heart would burst, it was stuffed so full of pride and love at watching his son's achievement. All of the hard work and perseverance had paid off. He knew Thomas could do everything his classmates could, it just took a little more support to get him there—something which would never be in short supply as long as Cameron had breath in his body.

'He's amazing. You did a good job raising him, Cameron.' Another female voice to the right of him drew his attention. When he saw who it was speaking, clapping Thomas's success as though she deserved to be part of it, the world beneath Cameron's feet seemed to crumble to dust.

'Ciara? What are you doing here?' His head was spinning as that painful part of his life where his wife had left him to bring up their son alone collided with the present, just as he was making progress.

Jessie snapped her head around too at the mention

of his ex's name and he saw the euphoria of the moment die on her face. Ciara had spoiled everything.

Coming face to face with Cameron's ex-wife was everything Jessie had dreaded. Ciara was everything she wasn't—supermodel tall, slim and elegant. It was difficult not to compare her fun rainbow-print dress, bright pink tights and sneakers to the cream tailored dress and heels the woman on the other side of Cameron was wearing. If she'd known there was a remote possibility of running into her, Jessie would've spent longer getting ready. She might have gone to a hairstylist so there wasn't a stray lock out of place instead of simply bunching it up in an unruly ponytail. It was silly to view this woman as competition when she wasn't with Cameron, and Ciara had more right to be here than Jessie, but that didn't mean she wasn't envious. She'd had the years with Cameron that Jessie should've had, been married to him and had a child with him. Cameron had chosen her and he hadn't been the one to end the marriage.

The odds were not in her favour.

'You sent me a text, remember? I'm sorry I didn't reply, but I wasn't sure if I'd be welcome or not. I'm glad I made it on time.' Ciara's explanation for her sudden appearance didn't do anything to make Jessie feel any less of an intruder. Cameron had invited her. Even after years apart and a divorce, he had wanted her to be a part of this. Jessie's fragile heart broke a little more.

'Thomas asked me to send you a message. You're still his mother.'

With the prize-giving over and the other parents and guests beginning to make their way out, the mini drama was beginning to look a tad conspicuous, with Jessie hovering on the periphery. It wasn't as though he'd introduced her as anyone significant and she didn't think he'd even notice if she left.

'Jessie? Where are you going?'

She was wrong.

'You have family stuff to sort out. Congratulate Thomas for me.' Head down so he wouldn't see the devastation on her face, knowing she didn't stand a chance with him after all, Jessie left the hall.

She'd convinced herself lately that it was only a matter of time before they caved and gave in to that crazy chemistry she'd believed had grown stronger by the day. Their time together, no matter how short, was always full of that good sort of tension. The kind that could only be relieved when they got to rip each other's clothes off. She should've known when she'd been standing almost naked in his bedroom and it had only prompted a kiss that they weren't going to embark on the raging love affair she'd imagined on lonely nights. It was for the best, she supposed, when she had her mother to look after, and he had his family.

'Jessie, wait.'

She ignored his half-hearted plea, glad she'd come in her own car tonight so she could make a quick getaway. Though he hadn't tried too hard to get her back, staying to talk to Ciara rather than chase after her.

As she stood in the car park she could see the family reunion taking place in real time. An elated Thomas clutching his shiny silver prize was proudly leading his mother over to see his award-winning work, with Cameron following closely behind. She wasn't even an afterthought now the real matriarch was back on the scene. As Jessie watched the happy trio through the window she realised she'd merely been a stand-in until Ciara came to her senses and claimed her rightful place.

It was too late now for Jessie to admit she'd wanted more with Cameron than unbearable sexual tension. Despite her loyalty to her mother, she'd still found the time to be with Thomas, and Cameron, so she'd begun to wonder if maybe they could have tried to make things work. Yes, they still had issues and responsibilities making things difficult for them, but their feelings for one another had been just as strong. Or so she'd thought. One appearance from his ex and she was watching from the outside like a poor kid staring in at a candy store, looking at all the goodies she couldn't have.

Cameron said something that made Ciara laugh and a stabbing pain almost doubled Jessie in two at the sight. When he placed his hand in the small of her back, the way he did with Jessie, she had to look away. It felt so much like a betrayal when that small gesture to her always meant a reassurance that he was there with her. Until now.

She got into the car knowing she would be driving away from Cameron and Thomas for the last time. There were no more excuses to keep seeing them, and he hadn't come and begged her to stay in his life. She'd done her job and she wasn't needed any more.

As she pulled away it occurred to her she really needed to wash her windscreen. She could hardly see where she was going when her vision was so misted up.

'Tell me why you're really here, Ciara.' Cameron waited until Thomas had gone to collect his things before he asked the question which had been burning inside him since her unexpected reappearance in their lives tonight.

'Er...you invited me.' She still had the same smile plastered on her face as she had when she'd first come in. As though it was perfectly normal for her to swan in after three years away and pretend to be part of this family.

'Thomas invited you, but I didn't think you'd actually show up. It's not as if you've responded to any of my other texts over the past three years. I didn't even know if you'd changed your number.' In those first months after she'd gone he'd sent a flurry of texts asking if she was all right, what he'd done wrong, and if she'd give him a chance to fix things. When her only reply had been a voice message to tell him she was serving him divorce papers, he'd subsequently only contacted her to notify her of Thomas's milestones—photographs of his first day of school every term, losing his first tooth, and the time he'd won a medal on sports day. None of them had prompted her to show any interest in their son's progress so he'd stopped. Until Thomas had asked him to show her the project he'd done. It had meant a lot to him that he shared some of his mother's qualities and Cameron hadn't had the heart to refuse. He was simply surprised it had brought her here tonight.

The smile faltered. 'I needed time... I needed space... I...'

'Did it ever occur to you that Thomas needed you?' He hated that she'd shown up like this without a word. At least if she'd let him know she was coming he could've prepared Thomas, and himself, for seeing her again. This wasn't the ideal place to have this conversation and as much as he wanted to run after Jessie, it wouldn't look good to leave now. He was angry with Ciara, but if there was a chance for her to reconnect with Thomas he had to let it happen. There might never be another opportunity to discuss what had happened and, as with Jessie, he knew there was stuff they hadn't dealt with. If they were ever to have closure they needed to actually talk about what had gone wrong between them.

One thing he'd learned from Jessie was the importance of communication. If he'd been better at it he might never have lost her, and though there was no chance of a reconciliation with Ciara he wanted to understand why she'd left. It might help Thomas if he was able to explain, without guilt or recriminations, what had ended their relationship. He didn't want him going through life the way his father had done, convinced he was the reason loved ones didn't stick around.

Cameron understood it was better for his son to have two parents in his life who would support him. If that was why Ciara was here. He also had to be certain she wasn't going to get their hopes up, only to walk away again when things got too tough.

'Stop with the guilt trip, Cameron. This isn't all on me, you know. Where were you when I needed you? I was depressed and anxious all the time but you were so focused on Thomas you didn't see it.'

'I… I…' He had to think hard about her behaviour before she'd left them. He'd assumed she was being distant because she couldn't cope with Thomas's behaviour, or his diagnosis. It hadn't occurred to him that she was suffering herself, that she might have been ill too. 'I'm sorry, Ciara. I let you down.'

'We both made mistakes, Cameron. If I'd been honest with you about how I was feeling, maybe things wouldn't have got on top of me. I should have got help.'

'I'm a doctor, I should've realised…' Looking back, he knew she had struggled after Thomas's birth but he'd done everything he could to share the childcare and be there for his family. He'd thought it was motherhood in general that she had a problem with, not that she might have had postnatal depression. He should've known better, looked for the signs. It was a wonder they'd lasted as long as they had if she'd been suffering for seven years before she'd had enough. He'd failed her, and Thomas, by projecting his experiences onto his son.

After his upbringing, neglected and emotionally abused by his parents, ignored by the education system, he was afraid of getting it wrong with his child too. He'd put all of his energy into being a good father and in the process hadn't been the best husband. Ciara had suffered the consequences and it was time he stopped solely blaming her for the end of their marriage.

'I didn't even realise. I couldn't figure out why I was so unhappy. I thought if I left and started again I could be the person I used to be. It didn't work out like that.'

'So where have you been all this time?'

'I used up a lot of favours with old friends and family, drifted from one menial job to another, and I'm ashamed to say got into some relationships that weren't good for my mental health either.'

The information should have been a dagger to his heart, not least because he'd been so wounded he hadn't even looked at another woman until Jessie came back into his life. Except the only emotion he felt was sadness, for Ciara, and for him, that these past years had been so difficult.

'And now you're back.' He was sure there was a point to all of this, to her turning up out of the blue after three years of silence, and he'd prefer to get to the bottom of it now. If he was ever going to move on, if there was a chance he and Jessie could be together, he needed to know the mistakes he'd made in the past. Not just so he could make amends to Ciara and Thomas, but also so he could be the man Jessie needed him to be. He didn't want to mess up again.

'It's not like I haven't thought about him, or you, over the years. I just thought it would be better to let you get on with things. You were always better with him than I was.'

'That's not…' He let the words trail off because it was true and there was no point in pretending otherwise. That didn't mean she shouldn't be in Thomas's life. 'There's still time, you know, to be a mother to him.'

'You…you'd let me do that?' The confident Ciara who'd breezed in had been replaced with the uncertain woman she'd been the last time he'd seen her. When Thomas had come along it had seemed as though she'd lost her sense of self. His bubbly, creative wife had taken to shutting herself away, emotionally and physically. As if she'd been trying to block Cameron and Thomas out of her life. Then one day she'd made it permanent.

'It's not about me letting you do it. I would like Thomas to have his mother back in his life, but only if I know you're not going to walk out on him again. We both have to learn to trust you again and that starts with telling me why you're here now.'

He'd been resisting a relationship with Jessie, who he still had feelings for, because he was afraid of him and Thomas getting hurt. It was only natural he'd apply the same rules to another woman who'd abandoned him. That said, if he was thinking about giving Ciara a second chance, he needed to consider extending Jessie the same courtesy. If she would even talk to him again. He had a lot to say to her, some things to explain, and questions to ask. Having Ciara turn up had proved a couple of things to him—that his marriage was definitely over, and he didn't want to lose Jessie.

'I got help. I'm seeing a doctor and a counsellor regularly. It took me a while to settle, to figure out what I wanted in life. I know that came too late after getting married and starting a family, but I didn't realise I'd feel so overwhelmed by it all. Anyway, I've got a good job as a graphic designer in the area, I've got my own apartment, and I've had time to think about things. About how I treated you and Thomas. I was wondering how I could get to know him again when you texted me and I thought this might be the time to get reacquainted with my son.'

Cameron immediately folded his arms, a defence mechanism as he recalled those desolate feelings of rejection and confusion surrounding her sudden abandonment. 'I'm not going to lie, I was devastated when you walked out. It could've been handled differently, but we both made mistakes. I probably should've taken some time to talk things out, to see how Thomas's issues were affecting you too.'

She gave him a watery, grateful smile. 'Thank you for that. In hindsight, I think we got married too young. We should have been mature enough to talk all of this out back then, but we weren't big on communication, were we?'

'I guess not.' He'd never really learned to communicate his feelings well when his parents never wanted to hear anything he had to say. It was easier to keep everything to himself, or so he'd thought. Now he realised it had cost him his marriage. He didn't want to make the same mistakes with Jessie.

'Part of the reason I delayed getting in touch was because I was worried you would hate me. Then you sent me that message and I saw Thomas's work and I just knew I had to see him. I want to be his mother again. I know I'm ready and now I've moved back to the area I can see him all the time.'

'Whoa. Yes, he's doing well, and tonight is a big achievement, but he still has the same struggles with school and expressing himself. Even if you think you're up to dealing with that it's going to take time for him to get to know you again.' He was always going to put Thomas's feelings first and his own weren't as complicated as he'd imagined upon the first meeting with his ex-wife since she'd left him.

At intervals over the years he'd imagined this scenario and how he would react. It varied between begging her to come back in those early days, to a need to vent his hurt and anger at the way she'd simply vanished and left him to pick up the pieces. Seeing her now though, tentatively reaching out to her son and admitting to her mistakes in the past, had given him a certain closure. He wasn't wistful or nostalgic about the life they'd once had together, the way he had been about Jessie, and he certainly didn't feel the need to play the blame game, or to call her out for everything he and Thomas had been through since. It was surprising to find he no longer had strong feelings of any kind towards her. They were reserved for another woman he needed to see before he blew that relationship too.

'I'll have some leave from work soon. I thought perhaps Thomas could stay with me, or we could have a little trip together somewhere. You could come too, if you'd like, and be a proper family again.' She tilted her head to one side and batted her eyelashes at him, but that no longer had the same effect on him it used to. He didn't know exactly what she was hoping to come from this meeting tonight, but he had to make it clear he wasn't part of the deal.

With a shake of his head, he shot down the possibility that they could be together again before it grew out of control. 'That's never going to happen, Ciara. I'm a different person too and, if I'm honest, there's someone else in my life now. I think it's too early for Thomas to stay away overnight, but if he wants to see you and spend time with you, I have no problem with that. We can take things from there.'

'It was worth a try. For us, I mean. But I'm more than happy if I can spend some time with my son again.'

If she was disappointed or relieved that Cameron wasn't going to be part of the new version of Ciara she didn't show it as Thomas came bounding back.

'Can we go and get milkshakes now?'

'Sure. I think you've earned it.'

'Can Mum come too?'

Two sets of eager eyes landed on him, waiting for an answer.

'If that's what you want, son, Mum can come too.' That would be a good ice-breaker, a short reintroduction which would be easier for Thomas to digest than diving straight into living with a relative stranger. Ciara too would have to get used to being around Thomas. They'd have to take one step at a time and hope for the best.

'What about Jessie? Is she coming?' He peered behind Cameron, apparently expecting to see her in the background. Of course he knew why she'd felt she had to leave, even if she was wrong, but it wouldn't have been fair to deny Thomas this chance with his mother in case it had been lost for ever. He had to hope she would understand.

'Not this time, buddy.'

'Where is she?'

'I...er...she had to go. Something came up but she said to tell you well done.' He cleared his throat to dislodge the lie, not enjoying the crestfallen look he'd put on his son's face.

'Jessie? Is this your "someone else"?' Ciara quizzed, putting him on the spot, and he was grateful when Thomas butted in to save him from trying to explain she was the woman he'd never stopped loving.

'She's a friend of Dad's and mine. It was Jessie's idea

to paint for my project. I thought she'd want to go for milkshakes with us.' Thomas pouted.

'Maybe next time.' If she ever agreed to see him again outside of work.

'Uh-huh. She sounds great. Maybe you should see if she wants to join us?' Ciara was reaching out, telling Cameron that she wanted to be part of his and Thomas's life, even if that included befriending a new woman in his life. She wasn't to know he'd been so scarred by their past he'd barely let a potential partner breach his defences. That it had taken his first love reappearing in his life for him to realise he'd never got over losing her.

However, if he didn't act now, tell Jessie how he felt about her, what he wanted for them, he could lose her for ever.

CHAPTER EIGHT

'YOU'RE LATE TONIGHT.'

'I told you I had that school thing with Cameron and his son tonight, Mum. Thomas did really well, he won this awesome cup—' She ended the story there before she came to the part where Cameron's ex turned up and she was suddenly on the outside looking in.

'It's nice that you're spending time together again. Do you think you'll make another go of it?'

'No.' Although she was firm in her denial with her mother, Jessie was still conflicted over the matter. It was clear to her that while she still had feelings for Cameron, and perhaps harboured a fantasy of them being together again, it wasn't going to happen.

With Ciara back on the scene she knew her time was up. Not only had Thomas wanted her there but also Cameron had invited her, and never said a word, leaving Jessie as the intruder in what was clearly a family moment, celebrating their son's achievement. She was nothing more than an assistant who'd pointed him in the right direction and was now in danger of outstaying her usefulness, along with her welcome.

'That's a shame,' her mother said, eating the pieces

of roast chicken and broccoli Jessie had cooked for her earlier.

The doorbell rang, likely one of her mother's carers to help get her into bed. At least with company in the house she mightn't be tempted to wallow too much in her self-pity.

'I'll get it. You finish your dinner.' Jessie sighed out her misfortune in a deep, long breath as she opened the door. Only to forget how to breathe altogether when she saw who was standing on her doorstep.

'Cameron? What are you doing here? Where's Thomas?' She glanced behind him, but there didn't appear to be anyone else with him.

'He's with his mother, having a milkshake. I don't want to leave him for too long, but I needed to see you. To explain.'

'You don't need to explain anything. Ciara's back. It's what you all want—need. Thomas's project is finished so there's no reason for me to keep tagging along.' She was clutching the door, keeping it as a barrier between her and Cameron in an effort to protect what was left of her shattered heart.

'Ciara might be back but we're not together, and we're not going to be. There's only one woman I'm interested in.' He took a step through the door, forcing Jessie to let him inside, her heart hammering with the anticipation of what he was going to say.

'Oh?' She didn't dare to believe he was talking about her until he actually said the words.

'You,' he said without further hesitation, gathering

her in his arms for a swoon-worthy kiss, sealing how he felt about her once and for all.

'But…but what about Ciara and Thomas? How are we going to do this without upsetting anyone?' There was no question that she wanted to be with him, and pretending otherwise hadn't worked out, but those obstacles preventing their happy ending were still there on the horizon, casting a shadow over her potential jubilation.

'I've made it clear to Ciara that we aren't getting back together, but she's welcome to see Thomas. Although I think she'd already figured out my heart was with someone else.' He was looking down at her, his eyes filled with so much love for her, Jessie was afraid to leave his embrace to join the real world and have this moment of feeling wanted and loved completely disappear.

'I'm scared, Cameron.' Of getting hurt, of him not loving her as much as she loved him, but most of all of losing him again.

'Me too.' He grinned. 'But Ciara coming back has made me take a good hard look at myself. I wasn't there for her and our marriage ended because we weren't honest with each other about our feelings. I lost you for the same reason. So I'm putting it all out there now. I still love you and it frightens the life out of me, but it's clear I can't be without you any more.'

'Jessie, who's at the door?' Right on cue, her mother hollered from the living room and ruined the moment. Just when all of her dreams were coming true she was reminded that she had responsibilities to keep her from floating away on the fantasy.

'It's me, Mrs Rea, Cameron Holmes,' he yelled back, and Jessie found herself giggling at the untimely interruption.

'Come in so I can see you,' she demanded.

Jessie reluctantly let go of him and led him into the lounge, standing awkwardly as though she was introducing her first boyfriend. Which, she supposed, he still was.

'Hmm, you've filled out a bit from the last time I saw you. Good, that means you can help this one get me to bed.'

'Mum! Cameron hasn't come here to nursemaid you.'

'He's a doctor, isn't he? I'm sure he can help me get to my feet at least.' Ignoring Jessie's protests, her mother pushed her half-eaten dinner aside and beckoned Cameron.

'It's good to see you, Mrs Rea.' Ever the gentleman, Cameron offered her his arm so she could lever herself out of the armchair.

'You too. I always thought you two made a good couple.'

'Mum.' Exasperated by her mother's matchmaking, Jessie took her other arm so they could get her to bed in double-quick time.

Her mother's makeshift bedroom was in the former dining room, a change they'd made when she could no longer manage the stairs. Now it was filled with her mother's personal possessions and a mechanical bed.

Her mother stopped to peer closely into Cameron's face. 'She always loved you, you know. That's why she sent you away. She didn't want to hurt you.'

'Cameron has to go and pick his son up now, and I'm sure you're very tired, Mother.' Jessie glared at her, silently begging her not to say anything else. They were only just getting to know one another again and she didn't want to ruin things by raking up the past again.

Thankfully, her mother said nothing more on the subject and let them help her into bed.

'I'm so sorry about Mum. She shouldn't have said anything.' Jessie waited until she was seeing Cameron out at the door before she said anything more.

'It's all right. I'm glad you had someone to talk to and didn't go through it alone. How is she these days?'

'She has carers who come in three times a day to help her get washed and make her meals, but it's not unheard-of for her to send them away, insisting she can manage herself. She can't, of course. The stroke made an independent life impossible.'

Cameron opened the front door but turned around to face her before he set foot outside again, as though he'd been thinking about every word she'd uttered.

'So she relies on you to pick up the slack. That doesn't seem very fair on you.'

'She doesn't have anyone else. Neither do I.'

Cameron took her face in his hands and held her so close she could feel his breath on her skin. 'You have me. I want to be with you, Jessie. I don't know how we're going to manage it, or what will happen, but I'm sure of that.'

When he said it like that she was convinced every word was true. They'd take things one step at a time and, for now, being with him was enough.

'You should get back to Thomas. Thanks for coming to see me.' She appreciated that he'd left his family to come and clarify things with her but she didn't want it to come at the expense of Thomas's welfare. They were both going to have to learn to give and take when it came to each other's time and loyalties so they could be together.

'You're important to me. Remember that.' He dropped a kiss on her lips, so sweet and tender she could still feel it even after he'd got into his car.

'I hope you're not having second thoughts.' Cameron was waiting for her outside the main entrance to the hospital, their agreed meeting place for their first date since she couldn't face having to deal with her mother's input on the matter.

'Of course not. I was just checking on Simon. He was having some pain in his knees during our session so I thought I'd give him a joint rub to try and ease things for a bit.'

'Is there anything I can do?' The joyful smile he'd been wearing to greet her crinkled into a frown at the prospect of their favourite patient suffering any more than he already had.

'I think it's just from exercising the joints again. He's working hard and making great progress. If it gets any worse I'll let you know.' She didn't think it was anything more serious than overuse of the limbs that had been immobile for a while and were now getting used to being put through their paces again. If it didn't improve, Cameron would be her first port of call to investigate in case there were any complications they hadn't foreseen.

'Good. I know I'm not here as much as usual but you know I'll do whatever I can for him. Any progress on the search for family?'

'Not yet. Once he's well enough to leave the ward he'll have to go into foster care. Not a great incentive for him to get better but there doesn't seem to be an alternative.'

Now that Simon was well on his way to recovery there was no reason for Cameron to be here all the time any more, other than for the odd check-up. He still quizzed Jessie after her physiotherapy sessions with him but their time together was limited these days. They'd managed to snatch the odd kiss when they'd crossed paths but it hadn't been enough for either of them so they'd agreed to make time for a proper date, a big step for both of them.

He kissed her on the cheek before opening the car door for her. That graze of his skin against hers, the feel of him, was enough to give her pulse, and her mood, a lovely lift. She'd been looking forward to seeing him all day and this was her reward after dealing with difficult poorly patients.

'So, where are we going?' she asked, little bubbles of excitement fizzing in her veins for the night ahead when he'd kept it all secret from her this far.

'I'm not telling you until we get there,' he teased. 'You look beautiful, by the way.'

The unexpected compliment made her sit taller in the passenger seat, pleased with herself for making an effort even though he'd told her just to wear something casual. A date with Cameron was never going to be something she took for granted so she'd taken some time after her shift to do her make-up and shake her hair loose from its ponytail confines. One quick change from her uniform into some silky black trousers and a dusky rose wrap-over blouse and she was date-ready. She could get used to this double life, swapping wheelchairs and ice packs for mystery dates with a handsome man every night.

'Thank you. You're not so bad yourself.' She winked at him in the rear-view mirror, delighted by his bashful blush at the returned compliment. Even if he didn't realise, he was a very attractive man. Tonight he'd dressed in black jeans and a mossy green T-shirt, an outfit which usually wouldn't draw attention, except on him the slim fit emphasised the lean body barely contained within. Casual but still gorgeous.

'Ciara's taking Thomas for something to eat then on to the cinema, so we're not in any rush to get back,' he said, as though trying to deflect her obvious ogling.

'It's good they're getting on.' Although she would probably always hold some residual resentment, along with some envy, of the woman who'd given Cameron a family, Jessie admired her for having the courage to come back and build some bridges. It was better for a child to have two parents who loved him and wanted the best for him. And having someone else to share the childcare with would hopefully give them some quality time together in the future.

'Ciara's eager to catch up on everything Thomas is doing and so far he's enjoying sharing his sketches and getting to know her again. I think it's been good for all of us to have her back and work through our family issues. They're planning a trip to an art museum soon so we could maybe earmark that for our second official date.'

'I'd like that.' Although it was strange for her to think Cameron's ex was on the scene, Jessie knew it was helping him and Thomas deal with the past. He was much more open about his feelings now and she was doing her best to do the same to avoid making the same mistakes as before.

They were all entering into these newly forged relationships with caution in an effort to prevent anyone from getting hurt, and with good reason. All of them were nursing old war wounds but were determined to move on to a happier shared future.

Cameron reached across and squeezed her hand, holding it until they came to their final destination.

'I thought it was about time you experienced your first funfair.'

It didn't matter that it wasn't the place the cool kids once hung out, or that she was older than the teens rushing through the turnstile, eager to get right into the middle of the fun, Jessie was elated as Cameron made her dreams come true. It was so thoughtful of him to bring her somewhere she'd never got to experience as a child because she'd had to look after her mother. It was such a considerate place to take her on their first date that she couldn't stop herself flinging her arms around his waist and hugging him so hard she'd probably left an imprint of her face on his chest.

'Thank you.'

'If I'd known I'd get this reaction I would have brought you here a long time ago.'

'I wish you had.' Regardless of her high spirits, a dagger of regret would remain embedded in her heart for ever that they'd spent all of these years apart, hurting.

Cameron squeezed her back. 'Hey, no looking back, okay? Only forward from now on.'

He was right. The past held only painful memories of struggle and loss, when the future currently seemed as bright as the flashing neon lights beckoning them deeper into the carnival atmosphere. Here, now, with Cameron and the night ahead, she had so much to look forward to.

'I want to do everything, okay?' She took in the rides, the food stalls, the games, and she wanted to be part of it all. Reliving the childhood she'd never got to have, with Cameron, the only man she'd ever wanted to experience it with.

'Fine by me.' He paid for armbands which gave them unlimited access to the rides, but Jessie's first stop was at the concession stand.

'A candyfloss, please.'

Cameron insisted on paying, even though he didn't get himself anything. Jessie pulled off a chunk of fluffy spun sugar from the stick and let it settle on her tongue, coating it in sticky sweet joy.

'This is so good,' she said, sticking her face into the pink cloud to bite off another chunk.

'You're enjoying that, huh?' Cameron picked tufts of excess candyfloss from her hair and her cheek with a grin.

'You need to taste this.' She plucked a piece off and shoved it into his mouth.

'It's very sweet.' He laughed, licking the sugary substance from his lips.

Jessie was overcome with the need to kiss him, so she did, revelling in the sweet, warm, moreish taste of him on her tongue.

'Let's start with those spinning things.' She pointed to what looked like a giant mechanical spider with cars attached to each leg.

'Are you sure?' Cameron grimaced as they watched it in action, the cars spinning around as the mechanical legs shot in and out at high speed.

'Chicken?'

'No, too old to get spun around like a whirling dervish.'

'Nonsense, we're still young at heart.' She refused to believe that it was too late to recapture everything she'd missed out on when she was younger, including the relationship she'd hoped to have with Cameron. Life might have passed her by while she'd been busy caring for her mum, but she was seizing it now with both hands.

Cameron followed her over to the ride, protesting all the way. 'I'm serious. I think your centre of gravity changes as you get older and makes you less able to handle things like this.'

They got into the car and clicked the safety bar into place. 'If this is your way of telling me you'll be screaming like a terrified five-year-old I won't think any less of you.'

Cameron didn't get the chance to deny the charges set against him as the ride set in motion, the music and flashing lights increasing in tempo along with the momentum of the machine. It wasn't long before Jessie was the one doing the screaming, the motion and speed taking her breath away with excitement. The twirling, spinning movement of their carriage had her sliding along the double seat until Cameron put his arm around her to anchor her in one place. She was grateful for his steadying hand on her waist, knowing he would keep her safe no matter what.

'I might need some time out before we attempt another one of those,' Cameron joked as he helped her out of her seat. Jessie's legs were wibbly-wobbly as she attempted to step back onto solid ground so she was glad when he took her over towards the carnival stalls instead of veering towards the nosebleed-inducing vertical drop ride nearby.

'At least I can tick that off my list.' She wasn't sure she would do it again but she was over the moon to have experienced her first fairground ride with the boy of her dreams.

The night got even better as he tested his skill at the shooting range, his steady hands and sharp eye earning him enough points for the large stuffed unicorn toy she'd had her eye on.

'Am I getting Brownie points for my first date originality? It's been a while since I had to impress a lady. Although it's made easier by the fact you're that lady, and I know you so well.' His eagerness to please her was just as endearing as him holding her hand as they strolled through the fair like any other young lovers.

For once, Jessie didn't feel the stress of her responsibilities haunting her every move, enjoying living in the moment, free to express her emotions instead of pretending she didn't have them. Of course all their problems weren't solved by one carefree date, but it was a step closer to the life she wanted, the one she should have had all along with Cameron in it.

'It's been a dream come true, thank you,' she said, clutching him with one hand and her cuddly unicorn in the other. 'But yeah, let's take a break before our next bone-shaking ride.'

Soaking up the excitable atmosphere, they made their way around the fair until they ended up at the hot food wagon.

'Do you fancy sharing some French fries? I suppose as it's a date I should have bought you dinner but I was worried about the effect of going on to a rollercoaster afterwards.'

'I am hungry, and I suppose some fries would be nice…' She was wondering how to break it to him she'd already had her fill of fairground rides without losing face. There was much more fun to be had simply by being in Cameron's company without worrying about anyone else for a little while.

They ordered their food and ate it standing at a nearby upturned beer barrel which had been repurposed into a table. It was such a simple unpretentious meal in less than salubrious surroundings but Jessie knew she would always remember it as one of the best dinner dates she'd ever had.

As Cameron tossed their wrapper into the bin he sniffed the air. 'Can you smell something burning?'

The moment he said it there was a loud bang and she felt an intense heat filling the air. Before she could even figure out what was happening, Cameron had grabbed her arm and pulled her away from the source. When she glanced over her shoulder she saw flames blazing in the hot food van they'd just left, screams emanating from within and the woman who'd served them falling out of the door onto the ground, her clothes and hair on fire.

While other fair-goers looked on in horror, frozen by fear, Jessie and Cameron swung into action. She rolled the woman on the ground, attempting to put out the flames, then was straight onto her phone calling the emergency services as he grabbed the fire extinguisher propped up against the door of the food van. He blasted the extinguisher on to the fire blazing away in the fryer. In a cloud of smoke and steam, he fought until the flames were out and returned to tend to the injured woman outside. He was a real-life action hero, but she was relieved when he emerged again, covered in soot and sweat.

'The paramedics are on their way. So are the fire brigade. I didn't know you were a part-time fire-fighter too.' While Cameron had been battling the source of the blaze, Jessie had loosened the top buttons on the woman's shirt so she could breathe a little easier.

'When you have a ten-year-old son, you're prepared for almost anything,' he countered before coming to rejoin them on the ground.

'My name is Cameron and I'm a doctor. I know you've had a big shock and you're probably in a lot of pain…' he checked the name on her badge '…Debbie, but we need to move quickly to prevent the burn from getting any more serious.'

It was Debbie's right arm and hand that had been badly burned, the remains of her charred sleeve clinging to her reddening skin.

'Jessie is going to remove your jewellery in case there's any swelling, and give it to the paramedics when they get here for safe-keeping.' He gave Jessie the nod to gently slip off the bracelets from her arm, which she did, trying her best not to press against her burned skin. It was necessary to do it now before her injuries became swollen, preventing removal and potentially affecting her circulation.

Someone—likely a carnival worker—had set a first aid box and a blanket beside them. Cameron covered the injured woman with the blanket, careful to avoid the burned areas.

'We need to keep you warm and raise your legs to prevent shock setting in.' He grabbed Jessie's unicorn and used it as a makeshift platform to rest Debbie's feet on.

Debbie was sobbing now, the pain and shock of what had happened beginning to set in.

'The ambulance will be here soon,' Jessie assured her. 'They'll be able to give you something for the pain.'

'Debbie, I'm going to wrap your fingers individually to stop them fusing together. I'll be as gentle as I can.' Using the sterile bandages, he carefully dressed each finger before doing the same for the rest of her arm, covering the area with a loose sterile bandage.

She felt for Debbie, enduring that contact on her burned skin, but she also admired Cameron's sensitive treatment of her wounds. He was good in a crisis and, yet again, she was reminded that he would have been there for her during her struggles for all this time if she'd let him. She just wished she hadn't wasted so much time apart from him.

CHAPTER NINE

'IT'S NOT QUITE how I saw our date going…' Cameron pulled up outside his house, aware that they hadn't spoken since they'd called an end to the night once the ambulance had taken Debbie to the hospital. He was worried that all of the drama had proved too much during what was supposed to have been their carefree evening recapturing their youth. If anything, his job meant he had more responsibility than ever, and not just to his patients, as events had proved. He hoped it wouldn't spoil what they were just beginning.

Having Jessie back in his life enriched it on so many levels. Far beyond how good she was with Thomas, how extraordinarily patient and loyal she was to her mother, she was simply the part of him which had been missing for all of these years.

They'd been having fun up until the fire, and when they'd been treating the injured woman Jessie had jumped right in there with him. He'd been on his own for so long, doing everything himself, he'd forgotten what it was like to have someone there by his side. It would be devastating to have to go back to that lonely life when he was just realising how much he'd been missing the company, the fun and the love that Jessie brought with her.

They'd been dancing around each other for too long, trying to pretend they didn't need one another, but now he wasn't sure he knew how to be without her. And if he was being honest, he didn't want to be.

'I know, but I enjoyed it. It's a pity it has to end.' Jessie echoed his thoughts and he was reinvigorated at the thought of being given a second chance.

'We still have some time before Thomas gets back. Let me get showered and changed and maybe we can go for a drink or something.' Eager to get the night back on track, he bounded out of the car and let them into the house.

'We don't have to go out. You know, we could totally just veg out here on the couch. I don't mind where we are, Cameron, as long as I'm with you.' Jessie was standing toe to toe with him in the hallway, making it clear to him she wasn't going anywhere. It was sufficient to cause the last vestiges of his restraint to turn to dust.

All night he'd been entranced by her excitement and the way she'd thrown herself into everything, seizing the moment. Now it was his turn.

He caught her around the waist and pulled her towards him, claiming her mouth with his. She tasted sweet and salty, of candyfloss and fries, and everything he craved. Tonight, free from the worries of their everyday lives, they'd been free to be themselves, to be the couple they'd never got to be. He wasn't ready for it to be over yet either.

'Let me go get cleaned up, then I'm all yours.' He wanted to wash off the drama and responsibility again and be the fun person she'd started the night with, to be the best version of him for Jessie.

'You know, I could do with a shower myself…' Her eyes, full of mischief and desire, never left his as she began to strip off her blouse, sending a direct message to his groin.

'Are you sure?' He watched her undress, growing increasingly uncomfortable in the confines of his own clothes, but he didn't want to rush her into anything. They'd been taking things slowly and, as much as he wanted to take it to the next level with Jessie, he didn't want her to regret anything when she was still wary about getting into anything serious. She was always conscious of her mother's needs before her own, but he was doing his best to accommodate her duty as a carer along with them having some quality time together.

She let her blouse fall to the floor and undid her bra, exposing her full creamy-white breasts to his gaze and making his mouth water. 'I'm sure.'

Her determination to show him she was ready was a strong aphrodisiac, not that he needed one. When he saw her confidence waver as she bit her lip, waiting for him to respond, he went to her quickly. He cupped her breast, lifted it to his mouth and sucked on the rosy peak until she gasped. One of the good things about knowing her so well was that he was aware of what she liked, what turned her on, and what drove her crazy.

He flicked the pert tip with his tongue, at the same time caressing her other breast and tugging the nipple between his fingers, revelling in her breathy moans of delight, all the time making himself harder than granite. Jessie still made him feel like that horny teenage boy who couldn't get enough of her.

When she felt his erection through his jeans he damn near finished it all too soon. They needed to slow things down, take the time they'd never really had to enjoy one another.

With her face cradled in his hands now he kissed her on the lips, their bodies pressed tantalisingly close, but still not close enough.

'Let's go upstairs,' he whispered into her ear and watched the goosebumps appear on her skin, reflecting his own anticipation for the rest of their evening together.

She took his hand and they moved quickly up the stairs, Cameron shedding his clothes as they went, making Jessie giggle. When they reached the bathroom they were both wearing only their underwear, a problem he solved quickly, divesting Jessie of hers before removing his own.

He reached in to turn on the shower and pulled Jessie into the cubicle with him as he shut the door. Cameron watched the water cascade down the slope of her breasts, her nipples still standing proud and begging for attention. He caught them between his fingers and thumbs, pinching until they were bullet-hard, just like him.

Jessie wound her arms around his neck and pulled him under the stream of water with her as she latched her mouth to his. Her demanding kiss and her need to have him was sexy, intoxicating. He lifted her leg and positioned himself between her thighs, pressing his hardness against her soft mound. She groaned and pushed her body closer until her breasts were squashed against his chest.

He laughed, her sense of urgency a boost to his ego and his libido. After the last three years of thinking only about his son's wellbeing and locking his own needs away in that empty half of his closet, it felt good to be wanted. Jessie had opened up that part of his life again, that part of being a man, and reminded him that he deserved to be loved too.

'I think we've wasted too much time already. I've decided we need to live in the moment.'

'Uh-huh? You've decided?' he teased, though he loved the sentiment, knowing they were both thinking along the same lines.

'Yeah,' Jessie countered, chin tilted up into the air.

'As sexy as you are wet, I want to wait to take this to the bedroom. I don't want our first time to be over too quick, or end up in the emergency department at the hospital. It's not easy getting purchase on a wet floor in my bare feet and I want to give you one hundred per cent.' He set to work with the shower gel, lathering it over himself first to wash away the remnants of their earlier drama, then taking his time with

Jessie. Her breasts were slick beneath his hands, full and heavy in his palms.

'I will take you any way I can have you,' she teased, nibbling on his earlobe and almost convincing him to stay put.

With an amazing amount of effort he let her go and focused on washing her hair, letting the suds cascade down her delectable body. It was only when she began to return the favour that Cameron's resolve faltered. Her fingers massaging his scalp felt so good, calling to other parts of his body to stand to attention, want ing the same treatment.

He took her by the hand and led her into his bedroom. Standing there naked, her wet hair clinging to her now make-up-free face, she'd never looked so beautiful. She was softer, curvier and sexier than he remembered and he was going to enjoy getting to know her all over again.

The sexiness of their tryst was making Jessie's skin tingle with excitement. Especially when he seemed eager to make it so incredible. He slowed things right down, pulling her back into his arms to kiss her, taking a leisurely possession of her lips that made her weak at the knees. She was thankful when he backed her over to the bed and laid her down. Instead of joining her, he knelt on the floor, moving between her legs so they were resting over his shoulders. When he grinned at her and she realised his intention her eyes just about rolled back in her head in anticipation of the pleasure she knew was coming.

He kissed his way along her inner thigh, the touch of his lips burning her skin, followed by the soothing lap of his tongue. She lay back as arousal took control of her body, giving herself over to Cameron when he parted her with the tip of his tongue. That full feeling of having him inside her was nearly matched by the sensation of him circling that sensitive nub he found easily.

She drifted off on a cloud of bliss, her worries and responsibilities tiny specks in the distance. Only Cameron had the ability to take her mind off every little thing constantly taking up space in her brain, leaving her free to enjoy all the things he was doing to her, making her feel.

When Cameron sucked on that sensitive part of her which seemed to be totally controlling her whole body at present, that floating sensation suddenly changed to something more intense as she spiralled back down to earth, her complete focus on her impending climax at the tip of Cameron's tongue.

She bucked off the bed as her orgasm hit, yet he didn't relent in his pursuit. Jessie called out again and again as he brought her to that peak repeatedly, until she had nothing left to give.

Satiated, content, her body limp after her exertions, she could barely lift her head when he did finally join her on the bed, a condom at the ready.

'Okay?' he asked, dropping a tender kiss onto her mouth.

'More than okay.' She stretched and purred, well and truly satisfied by his attentions.

'I aim to please.' He grinned against her lips, making her smile even more.

'You definitely did that, but what can I say, I'm greedy for more.' With their wet bodies pressed so close together she was already aching for him again.

She reached down and took hold of him, revelling in his breathy gasp. With slow, deliberate movements she moved her hand up and down his shaft, driving them both crazy with desire.

Sex hadn't been a big deal in her life since he'd gone. It had been something she could take or leave with little time to explore a physical or emotional relationship. But she couldn't get enough of Cameron. The first time they'd slept together as naïve teens had lit that spark, that sensation of their bodies joining together quickly becoming addictive. Over the years she'd blamed that sexual awakening for convincing her she was in love, and that a husband and family could be in her future. Now she understood it was only Cameron who elicited those feelings because he was the only man she'd ever truly loved. Making love to him was just that because she'd never stopped loving him. She was afraid to look too far into the future in case her perfect world crumbled down around her again, but for now she was more than happy to live in the moment with him.

He covered her body with his, kissing her neck and beyond until he came to that erogenous zone right behind her ear. As she gasped, shivers tracing his path along her skin where he'd touched her, Cameron thrust inside her. It took a moment for her to adjust, to accept him again after so long. He hesitated too, resting his forehead against hers for a few seconds, his breath unsteady.

'It's been a while,' he confessed, seemingly fighting for control over his impulses.

Jessie stroked the side of his face. 'I know. For me too. There's no pressure. I just want to be with you.'

'Me too. I love you, Jessie. I always have.'

'I love you too.'

The admission of their feelings for one another after so long trying to hide them seemed to break the last of their defences, leaving the way clear for them to fully embrace this time they had together. Jessie opened up to him, taking everything he had to offer as he plunged deep inside her, determined to show the strength of his devotion.

Cameron's panting breath in her ear became a victorious roar drowning out her cry of ecstasy as they rode to that ultimate release together. Their bodies continued to rock, chest to chest, hips to hips, groin to groin, the ripples of their climax reverberating.

'Did you mean what you said?' Jessie asked once she was capable of speech again. She wanted to be sure that his declaration wasn't a crumb tossed her way when he was carried away at the height of their passion. Now that she'd opened her heart for him again she was vulnerable, and afraid another blow would prove fatal.

'I meant every word. I love you, Jessie. I'll get it tattooed if that's what it takes for you to believe me.'

He disposed of the condom and came back to lie beside her again, his eyes locked onto hers, beseeching her to believe him.

'I don't think we need to go that far but, you know, maybe a full-page ad in the newspaper would suffice.'

It was easy to joke about it when she believed him, but she was worried that the day would come when it wouldn't be enough. At some point the world outside was waiting to gatecrash their party for two and force them apart.

'I'll book a plane to sky-write it too, just to be sure.'

She felt his chest rise and fall beneath her head as he laughed at his own joke. They were so comfortable together she wished they could stay here for ever, but all too soon the spectre of their responsibilities haunted the perfect moment.

'I should really get back to Mum, and I'm sure Thomas will be on his way soon.'

Cameron groaned. 'I love my son but I wish we could freeze time for a little while longer.'

'I know.' She traced her finger around his nipple, watching with interest as it puckered beneath her touch.

Cameron grabbed her hand. 'If you keep doing that we're going to get in real trouble,' he growled.

Undeterred, Jessie continued her perusal, only for Cameron to flip her over on to her back and straddle her.

'You're such a bad influence,' he said, pinning her hands above her head so she was fully exposed to him.

He copied her actions, only this time using his tongue to tease her nipples into the same hard peaks as his.

She bit her lip, trying to resist giving him the satisfaction of hearing her excited moans. When she didn't respond he sucked her nipple hard enough it grazed the roof of his mouth, watching her all the while for a response. She tilted her chin up in silent defiance, only for him to dip a hand between her legs and feel her arousal for himself. He couldn't keep the grin from his face as he reached for another condom from the drawer. And when he forged their bodies together again with a thrust of his hips there was no point in trying to pretend she wasn't in raptures when her body betrayed her so easily.

She clung to him now, the bedroom echoing her cries of ecstasy as Cameron rushed her quick return to oblivion. If only she had him permanently in her life she might never have to think about anything beyond the bedroom ever again.

Their lovemaking this time was frantic, pure lust and the knowledge that their time together was coming to an end driving the need for one last release. Cameron pounded against her until they were both satisfied and exhausted, their bodies slick with sweat.

'I think I'm gonna need another shower,' he gasped between his ragged breaths.

'I'll let you have that one alone or else we'll never get out of here.' Jessie got up, leaving him to recover on top of the bed.

'Sounds good to me,' he said and smacked her backside with his hand.

That kind of sexual possessiveness on her anatomy from a man would usually earn him a slap back, but she liked that he couldn't get enough of her, that he was claiming her as his. She wanted to belong to Cameron as much as she wanted him to be exclusively hers. In her past relationships she'd always remained wary, her fear usually coming true that her partner would grow tired of her commitments elsewhere. With Cameron, she'd gone all in, giving him her body and soul, trusting him not to abuse either. She'd had a wobble in confidence with Ciara back on the scene, but he'd proved to her tonight it was her he would rather be with. Her heart should remain intact for as long as that remained true.

'You need to get dressed too.' She tossed his clothes at him once she'd located hers and put them on.

'Spoilsport.'

'I think I've been sporting enough. Now we need to get back to adulting.' More was the pity.

They drove back to her house in silence, but every now and then Cameron took her hand and placed it on his leg so he could feel her there. She leaned her head against his arm, the occasional sigh of contentment slipping out making him smile.

When they reached their destination, and the end of their wonderful night, Cameron walked her to the front door.

'Thank you for a most enjoyable date,' he said, lifting her hand to his mouth for a kiss, that twinkle in his eye as glittery as Jessie's whole body felt where he'd touched her.

'I don't usually put out on a first date. You're the exception.'

'Very privileged, although I think you'll find it's our second first date so your reputation is still intact.'

'I think my reputation is in tatters after what we've just done, but it was worth it.' She stood up on her tiptoes to give him a peck on the lips but Cameron had other ideas, wrapping his arm around her and pulling her flush to him. His mouth was crushed against hers, his tongue urgently seeking hers out, as though they were never going to see one another again and this was to be their final kiss. It was hot and intense, full of everything they'd done and wanted to do to each other again in the bedroom.

'Jessie! I need help!' Her mother's urgent cries ripped them apart.

'Mum? What's wrong? I'm coming!' She abandoned Cameron on the doorstep to run towards the bedroom, but she heard his footsteps following her down the hallway and was grateful she'd have him with her to face whatever was behind the door.

When she found her mother lying on the floor, blood pouring from the gash on her forehead, Jessie was overwhelmed by a sense of guilt.

'How long have you been lying here?'

'I don't know,' her mother said weakly. She was

very pale, making the scarlet stain spreading over the floor and her white nightgown all the more alarming.

'What happened?' She grabbed a handful of tissues from the box on the nightstand and attempted to stem the bleeding.

'I don't know. I think I got up to make myself a cup of tea and I must have fallen over.'

'I think you must have banged your head on the chest of drawers when you fell, Mrs Rea.' Cameron pointed out the blood staining the white melamine furniture.

'Oh, Mum, I'm sorry I wasn't here for you.' She just about managed to hold back the tears, but she was plagued by images of her and Cameron enjoying their time together as though they didn't have a care in the world.

'I called you,' her mother said, her eyes fluttering shut.

'I'm sorry I didn't answer. Please stay awake.' If anything happened she would never forgive herself.

'The ambulance is on its way,' Cameron told her as he hung up the phone.

Jessie couldn't help but wonder if this would be her some day. If her condition would leave her helpless, dependent on him, when he had his own responsibilities to think about. It didn't matter how much Jessie loved him, she'd been selfish. Fifteen years ago she'd made the most difficult decision of her life because she hadn't wanted to trap him. Yet that was exactly what she was doing now.

Her APS could lead to the same health issues her mother had—strokes, paralysis and a lifelong fear for those around her. It wouldn't be fair on Cameron or Thomas to put them through this in another few years down the line. Her condition had an increased risk of blood clots. That meant a higher chance of developing deep vein thrombosis, strokes, heart attacks or bleeds on the brain. It was one thing asking Cameron to come to terms with not having any more children if he wanted a future with her, but expecting him to give up his life to care for her was selfish. Why would she set him free as a teenager, only to trap him now, except to make herself happy?

She'd spent a life burdened by the guilt of causing her mother pain, she couldn't do it again with Cameron.

'You can go. I'm sure Thomas will be on his way home by now.' She pulled her mother's quilt off the bed and covered her in an effort to keep her body temperature raised.

'I'm not going to leave you—'

'Mum, open your eyes for me, please. You need to stay awake.' With a head injury she needed to keep her mum conscious.

'Please let me help, Jessie,' he pleaded, but she had to do this on her own. If she'd remembered that she might not have been in this position and her mother might not have been hurt in her absence.

'Just go, Cameron.' She sighed, the fight dying inside, along with all of those hopes and plans she'd made with him for a second time. This was exactly why she'd sent him away the first time around; he made her forget the reality of her situation and what it could mean for him. She wasn't a carefree thirty-something who could spend an evening at the funfair or fooling around in bed without consequences. She was a time bomb.

CHAPTER TEN

CAMERON WAS DETERMINED not to let Jessie push him away again but he had to go back to collect Thomas before he tried to make another stand. If it hadn't been such early days for Ciara back in their lives he would've asked her to mind him overnight so he could be with Jessie but he couldn't rush Thomas. It would take time for his son to build trust with his mother and he couldn't take advantage of that simply so he could pursue a romantic relationship.

But he knew it had frightened Jessie to see all that blood. She was close to her mum and it was natural for her to feel guilty about being out tonight, missing when she needed Jessie's help. Even though the same accident could've happened when she'd been at work or in the house. He felt the same when it came to Thomas but he knew he had to move past that guilt because he wanted to be with Jessie. She would have to do the same if they were ever going to have a chance of being together.

Hopefully, she would realise she didn't have to do everything on her own, that he would be there for her.

If she'd let him, he could share the responsibility and help carve out some time for them.

Looking to the future, he hoped it would make things easier for him and Jessie to spend time together now Ciara was there to share the childcare. He was sure Thomas would enjoy visiting museums and art galleries with his mother, exploring their common passions and getting to know one another again. It would also take time for Ciara to get used to his idiosyncrasies, and learn how to deal with them. Forcing them to spend time together too soon could have repercussions and set back their blossoming relationship if they didn't tread carefully.

Managed carefully, he hoped they could all benefit from Ciara being back, including Jessie.

'Is Jessie's mum going to be all right?' Thomas cut through his introspection as they hurried through the hospital corridor to find the pair Cameron had left behind to get his son.

'I hope so. She had a nasty fall but the paramedics would have taken care of her. I just want to make sure she and Jessie are okay.'

'It's nice to have a mum again. I'd hate it for anything to happen to mine. Jessie must be very upset.'

Cameron ruffled Thomas's hair. He was glad his evening with his mother had gone so well and would hopefully lay the groundwork for future interactions. His son deserved to have two loving parents in his life.

'She is, that's why I want to pop in and see her. Now, you sit here, you can play with my phone, and here's some money for the vending machine if you need something to eat or drink. I'll just be in that cubicle so shout if you need me, I won't be long.' He deposited Thomas in the seat outside the bay he'd been directed to by the receptionist and emptied his pockets to keep his son content while he tried to rescue his burgeoning relationship with the woman he loved.

'Okay, Dad,' Thomas mumbled, his attention already taken by the small screen in his hand.

Cameron walked over to the cubicle, where the curtain was partially opened. Jessie was sitting at her mother's bedside, head hung as though she'd been caught doing something wrong.

'Is it all right if I come in?'

'Cameron? What are you doing here?'

He watched as her emotions crossed her face—initial surprise followed by a smile, which eventually gave way to a frown.

'I wanted to make sure you were both all right. If it hadn't been for Thomas I would've stayed.' He wanted her to know he wasn't going to give up so easily this time and it had simply been circumstances which had got in the way as usual.

'She has a mild concussion so they're keeping her overnight for observation. How did Thomas get on with Ciara?' She was still holding her mother's hand even though the older woman appeared fast asleep and would have no concept of her being there. It wouldn't surprise him if Jessie slept in the seat all night to assuage some of the guilt eating her up over the fact she hadn't been there when her mother had hurt herself.

'Good. I think they're bonding. I'm glad your mother wasn't seriously hurt.' He hovered at the edge of the cubicle, knowing he wasn't welcome but also aware he hadn't done anything wrong except love Jessie.

There was an uneasy atmosphere, a heavy silence between them which seemed to go on for ever, punctuated only by the sound of the medical equipment monitoring her mother's progress.

'Jessie, I—'

'Cameron—'

They spoke over one another then laughed like awkward teenagers.

'You go first,' he insisted.

She glanced down at her clasped hands in her lap before she lifted her eyes to meet his and he knew she was gearing herself up to end things again. Knowing what was coming didn't make it any easier to stomach.

'I'm sorry for the way I spoke to you back there, but after what's happened tonight it's made it clear we can't keep seeing each other.'

'I don't understand. I know you've had a shock and you feel bad about not being there for your mother, but we were having a good time up until then, weren't we? Don't be hasty about this, Jessie.' He wanted her to think back beyond finding her mother, to the fun they'd had together at the funfair, and later, in bed. It was too special to throw away after one hiccup, which shouldn't even have affected them as a couple.

He couldn't wait another fifteen years to be with her because she felt guilty about leaving her mother when the accident could've happened at any time.

Her blush put some much-needed colour in her cheeks again.

'I'm not denying that, but can't you see, this could be me?' She indicated her mother lying helpless on the hospital bed. 'I have nothing to offer but an uncertain future. I've spent my life as a carer, I don't want the same for you. Being with me would be a life sentence for you and Thomas and reliving my childhood or wanting to be with a man isn't going to change that.'

'I'm not just any man, Jessie. I love you, and I know you love me. We can work this out. There's no guarantee your condition will worsen.'

'There's no guarantee it won't.'

Having done his homework on APS, he ignored her stubborn retort. 'You're already taking a low dose of aspirin to lower the chances of blood clots, right? Most people with your condition can lead normal healthy lives, and you've been doing okay so far. I mean, I know you lost the baby but there's still an eighty per cent chance you could carry full-term.'

'I told you I don't want to go through that again. See, you'd be better off with someone else if you are thinking about having more children.'

'I'm not. I just want you to realise your life doesn't have to stop. Don't do this to me—to us—again. You gave up medical school and a future together, making decisions on my behalf. For once, let me have a say in what happens next. There's no reason you can't live a normal life and I want to be part of it.' He moved towards her but Jessie didn't let go of her mother's hand to meet him halfway.

'I'm sorry, Cameron. I've made up my mind. There was a reason I ended things before. I don't want to be the one holding you back. Tonight was fun, a fantasy, but we both know it's not real and it's naïve and selfish to pretend otherwise. Where's Thomas now?'

'He's out in the corridor, why?'

'Because until I came along you would never have dreamed of leaving him out there. By being together we're only neglecting the other people we love. Let's quit before anyone else gets hurt. I need to look after my mother and you should do the same for Thomas. If something happened to him when we were out galivanting I'm sure you'd feel the same.'

He must have hesitated too long, considering that scenario but certain there would always be room for Jessie in his life.

'Anyway, Ciara's back now. I'm sure she would happily jump in to fill that space in the family. You don't need me.' She turned away from him so easily he wondered if she was simply using her mother as an excuse to get rid of him after all.

The thought made his stomach plummet as though he'd been on that dead drop ride they'd seen at the funfair. Cameron had gone against all of his self-preservation instincts to open his heart to Jessie and welcome her into his family, his bed, his life, only for her to drop him again as if none of it mattered.

'I love you, Jessie,' he said softly, not sure she'd even heard when she didn't look at him.

'Dad? I got my hand stuck in the drawer of the vending machine. It really hurts.' Thomas appeared next to him, clutching his red fingers, making Cameron feel like the worst dad in the world for leaving him, just as Jessie had predicted.

'Let's get that under the cold tap. Hopefully it won't need to be X-rayed.' He put an arm around Thomas's shoulder and guided him out of the cubicle, but not before he'd spoken to Jessie.

'Sorry about your mum, Jessie. I hope everything's okay. Mums are the best.'

'Thanks, Thomas,' she said, offering a smile which apparently Cameron didn't deserve.

If her mother and his son weren't here this would've been a very different scene indeed. Instead he had to swallow his emotions, hold back from kissing her senseless and reminding her how good they were together, because it wouldn't have been appropriate in front of their audience. It didn't mean he was giving up on them, even if she was.

Jessie was tempted to hook herself up to her mother's heart monitor to make sure hers was still beating. When Cameron finally turned around and walked away, admitting defeat, she sucked in a long shaky breath, desperate to get some air back in her lungs. She didn't want him to go, to walk out of her life for ever, but she knew it had to be done. They were addicted to one another, to the point of excluding reality. She knew how it was to be a carer, to lose her identity and a life of her own, and would never inflict that on him or Thomas.

It looked as though Ciara was slotting nicely back into the family and he hadn't argued when Jessie had suggested her as a possible replacement. She was Thomas's mother after all and she and Cameron had a longer relationship than they had ever managed. It made sense for them to get back together, even if the thought of it made her want to retch. He was right about one thing, though—she loved him. So much it felt as if part of her was dying by sending him away again, pushing him towards another woman who could give him a future and make him happy.

Cameron shouldn't be punished for loving her— he'd opened up his heart, and his life, to share it with someone again. If it couldn't be her it should be someone else he had a history with, whom he probably still loved deep down.

She would never have a husband or family when no one would live up to Cameron. If she couldn't have a life with him, she didn't want it with anyone.

'Thanks for being here. I just wanted to update you on Simon's situation.' The social worker who had been in charge of the case had asked Cameron for a meeting and he'd courteously invited Jessie to attend.

'Without strings,' he'd assured her over the phone.

She'd been in two minds whether to even answer his call in case it sent her right back into that dark place she'd been trying to crawl out of since they'd broken up, only a week ago. This time around, losing him seemed to hurt so much more. Perhaps it was because they were adults now, with stronger emotions, or maybe it was the sense that time was running out for her to have a life of her own, but Jessie had struggled to move on from him this time. When they'd been teenagers she'd been heartbroken but she'd managed to lock away memories of him along with her feelings in order to move on. It wasn't so easy to do this time around. She still wanted him and that life he represented and seeing him again was killing her, but they both wanted what was best for Simon.

'Have any of his family come forward?' she asked, hoping some good news would take her mind off the man sitting across the table from her, who was sporting a few days' beard growth. Despite her attempt to do the right thing by him, the thought that he perhaps hadn't bounced straight back to his ex, and might also be having some problems getting over her, did give her a fluttery feeling in the pit of her stomach.

'I'm afraid not. Unfortunately, his parents don't seem to have had any surviving family members. That's what brings me here today. I can see from the medical reports that Simon is due to be released from hospital soon and he's expected to make a full recovery.'

The social worker's pursed lips suggested this wasn't the happy news it seemed.

'So what happens to him now?' Cameron was frowning as he got to the crux of their concerns.

'Simon is going to have to go into the care system. We'll do our best to place him with a suitable foster family as soon as possible.' She shuffled through her case notes as Jessie stared at Cameron in distress. For someone who had already been through so much, putting the boy into care seemed to be merely adding to his woes.

'And this foster family, will there be other children there?' Cameron asked. She knew he was concerned that Simon would get overlooked in a houseful of other troubled children.

'Most likely. Our experienced foster parents usually take on a few of our children in need. We wouldn't want to put him with anyone just new to fostering when he's going to have ongoing needs.'

'Yes, Simon is going to require a lot more hospital visits to complete his rehabilitation. It's important the family understands that.' Jessie too was worried that a family with so much responsibility would find it difficult to find the time for his extra appointments for physiotherapy and check-ups. It wouldn't be the first time she'd had a young patient disappear off the radar when the parents struggled to find the time, or transport, to make their appointments, often considering their child 'cured' once they were back on their feet.

In this case, both she and Cameron knew it would be some time before the boy was fully recovered.

'Our foster carers will have all relevant notes on Simon and we will still be checking in on him, don't worry.'

Easier said than done.

'Will the family be local? I hope he won't lose the connections he's made here since he lost his parents. I don't want him to feel alone in the world.' Cameron was unsurprisingly emotional on the matter, no doubt including himself and Jessie on that list of friends Simon had made during his time at the hospital. He was a wonderfully compassionate man. But she knew that, and that was why she loved him. Why she'd had to let him go. He already had his hands full with Thomas and work, he didn't need to take on her and her mother too. Jessie never wanted to inflict extra pressure on Cameron. Even though it hurt like hell.

Seeing him again had simply opened up that raw wound where her heart had once resided. Especially in these circumstances where he'd proved once again what a kind, caring person he was to be so concerned with one patient's welfare. He was a great doctor and father, and she knew he would've been a fantastic partner if they'd ever stood a real chance of being together long-term.

'We'll do our best to house him in the same area, and I promise that we'll look out for him.' She began to pack her files away, although they'd had less than satisfactory answers to their concerns.

'And wherever he goes won't be permanent, I assume?' Jessie had visions of him being transferred from one house to the next, having to adapt to new families and schools with every move.

Agnes, the social worker, stood, her hands braced on the desk, clearly exasperated by their inquisition. 'Look, we want Simon to have a permanent loving family as much as you do and we'll do what we can to ensure that happens.'

'I understand.' Jessie knew it was out of their hands and Cameron would be every bit as upset as she was that it had come to this for Simon. He was just a little boy grieving for his parents and he needed love and stability. It didn't seem a lot to ask for but it was a case of circumstance. Simon didn't get a say in what happened to him.

She was the kind of person always pre-empting the worst in an effort to protect those around her. Her whole childhood had centred around taking care of her mother and making sure she was all right. So her life had been stagnant and unfulfilling through her own choices. The illness she lived with had cost her her baby, but it had been her decision to send Cameron away when the only happiness she'd truly known was with him. If only it had been as simple as loving each other, wanting to be there for one another, she knew nothing would have kept them apart.

'I just thought I should let you know what's happening. I'll keep in touch,' Agnes said before leaving the room.

'We'll still see him at his appointments.' Cameron moved around the table to be with her, offering her some comfort at a time when she was overwhelmed by melancholy for both Simon and herself.

'I suppose... Will you still be working here then?' When she'd called things off she hadn't factored in that she might have to keep seeing him at work, making it harder than ever to live without him.

'I would like to continue monitoring Simon's recovery, yes. Although if you didn't want our paths to cross I'm sure we could arrange to see him at different times.'

'I'm not sure that's necessary. It wouldn't be very professional.'

'Perhaps not, but you know I would do anything for you, Jessie. If I thought you didn't love me I would walk away and never bother you again. You know I would rather have a future with you, come what may, than be without you. It's you who insists on making the sacrifice.'

He walked out of the office and Jessie was glad he didn't resort to desperate tactics to get her back, like kissing her one last time to show her what she was missing. Because she wasn't sure she would put up a fight.

'I've left you something to eat and drink by the side of your bed here, so there's no need for you to try and get up. I'm just going to pop to the shops to get a few things. I won't be long, then I'll come back and we can watch TV together.' Jessie tucked her mum in bed, making sure she had everything she could possibly need beside her for the few minutes while she was out of the house. The fall had knocked their confidence, showing them how frail and vulnerable she had become lately. She was more dependent on Jessie than ever, leaving no room for any wistful thoughts about the life she could have had with Cameron.

'You really do need to get a life, Jessie.'

'Pardon me?' For the life of her, Jessie couldn't understand why helping her into bed and giving her everything she needed would have prompted that particular comment.

'You're young. You should have more to look forward to after work than getting an old woman into bed or going to the store for groceries.'

Jessie continued plumping her pillows for her. 'I'm looking after you, Mum.'

'But you love *Cameron*.'

The reminder caused a small, sharp stabbing pain in her gut but she powered on through it. 'It doesn't matter. He has his family to look after and I have mine.'

'I heard you, you know. At the hospital. I know he loves you too.'

'Oh, well, that's all in the past now anyway. Do you need anything from the shop?' She fixed the bedcovers again, even though they were perfectly fine, needing something to keep her thoughts occupied lest they strayed too far back towards Cameron.

Unfortunately her mother wasn't ready to let the matter drop. 'He wants to be with you.'

Jessie sighed. 'I told you, it's over. It doesn't matter what either of us wants.'

'You should be with him instead of wasting your life here with me.'

'Mum, he has Thomas, he doesn't need me to look after too.'

Her mother frowned. 'What are you talking about?'

'APS. No offence, but I don't want to ruin his life if I get sick too.'

'But you're fine, you're taking medication. I had the stroke because I was undiagnosed. Yes, I know you missed out on your childhood to take care of me, but this is different. If it came to it, you would have support. Stop using me and APS as an excuse. Cameron wants to be there for you, and you have a chance of happiness together.'

'What about you?' Jessie plonked down on the end of the bed, her legs no longer able to support her as her mother acknowledged the sacrifices she had made to take care of her.

'I want you to look into assisted living facilities for me—'

'No. I won't do that.' It was everything she'd been trying to avoid over the years, devoting her time to her mother's care so she could stay in her own house.

'It's not up to you, Jessie. I've made my decision. There are people who can look after me twenty-four hours a day if I need them. I'll expect you to come and visit, of course, but you need time and space to carve out a life of your own. I've been selfish for too long.' She patted the back of Jessie's hand with her own, the display of warmth and selflessness finally calling those tears forward.

'What will I do without you?' After so many years being a carer, Jessie didn't know who she was supposed to be, away from these four walls.

'I'm not dead, I'll just be moving away. You seemed to be enjoying a certain doctor's company until I had my little accident anyway. He's waited this long for you, I'm sure he'll take you back in a heartbeat.'

'I don't know, Mum...' As much as she would've loved to run off into the sunset with Cameron, she didn't want to have to give it all up again if circumstances changed.

'I let your father go and never fought for him—for us. That's how I ended up on my own. You lost Cameron once, don't make the same mistake again. Go tell him how you really feel, and make the decision about your future together.'

Jessie thought about what he'd said to her earlier about insisting on making sacrifices, which apparently he didn't think necessary. The last time she'd made decisions for him, with the best of intentions, had taken him out of her life for a long time. If she did the same this time it could be for ever. A life without Cameron now seemed unbearable and it was foolish to punish herself that way when he'd offered her one, even knowing the full circumstances surrounding her health.

She kissed her mother on the cheek. It was true, she had been finding excuses to keep him at a distance because she was afraid of loving and losing him. Her whole life had been shaped around the possibility of her mother dying, and protecting her. Even though he'd never asked her to, she realised she'd been doing the same for him, forcing them apart in a vain effort to save them from getting hurt, only to cause them more pain in the process. They loved each other and that was all that should have mattered.

Suddenly she was excited by the possibilities opening up before her. She could only pray it wasn't too late and Cameron still wanted her to be part of his family.

'Thomas, could we have a chat, buddy?' Cameron patted the seat next to him and beckoned his son over from the table where he'd been painting.

'Sure.' He set down his paintbrush and bounded over, landing on the sofa with a thump. 'Is this about Mum?'

'No. Why would you ask that?'

'I just thought she mightn't want to see me any more or something.' Thomas hung his head, obviously still harbouring some abandonment issues from his younger years.

'Not at all. She loves you. I hope you know that.' He waited for Thomas's nod before he continued. 'No, I wanted to talk to you about Jessie.'

'Is she moving in with us? I know you and Mum

aren't getting back together so I thought maybe Jessie would be your new girlfriend.'

It broke Cameron's heart that this new family they were hoping to have wasn't going to include Jessie when Thomas liked her so much. He loved her and if it had been down to him she would be moving in and taking her place in the family portrait, but her stubborn sense of duty had won out over love again for her.

'Sorry, bud, I don't think that's going to happen. Jessie has to stay and take care of her mum.'

He understood his son's pouty response when it was exactly how he felt about the situation—petulant and hard done by—not that it would change things. He had to keep going for Thomas, who would always be his priority, and he doubted he'd find another woman who could replace her anyway. Any thoughts of another relationship would be dead in the water the moment he thought of Jessie and what they could have had together.

The doorbell sounded and put an end to the heart-to-heart with his son.

'Thanks for the chat. You can get back to whatever you were painting.'

'I was sketching a picture of next door's dog for Mum. She likes dogs.' Thomas jumped up and ran off to get his box of craft and Cameron loved that he was so accepting about having his mother back in his life. He only wished Jessie was here to see it.

The bell buzzed again.

'I'm coming,' he yelled, wondering who was being so impatient at this time of night.

When he wrenched the door open he felt as though he'd been punched in the gut. 'Jessie?'

'Hey,' she said with a watery smile that completely undid him.

'Come in. Is everything all right? Is your mum okay?'

'Yes, and yes. I just wanted to see you.'

'Why? I thought you'd made your mind up.' Now that he had time to really look at her he could see she'd come out without a coat in the middle of a cold night, and something didn't seem right about the visit.

Without saying another word, Jessie stood up on her tiptoes, wound her arms around his neck and pulled him down for a kiss. He was too gaga over her to resist, taking the opportunity to indulge in the taste of her once more in case it was the last time. Eventually he knew he had to break it off before he lost himself in her again and forgot they were never going to be together.

'You didn't answer my question,' he said when he got his breath back from the passionate lip lock she'd engaged him in.

'I'm here because I love you, Cameron, and Thomas. I don't want to lose either one of you.'

A flicker of hope sparked to life in Cameron's chest that he could have it all, including Jessie, but it seemed too good to be true. 'What about your mother? Your illness? What's changed?'

There was little point getting his hopes up, for the same issues to still interfere in the future they wanted together. Her mother's fall proved it could all be taken away in an instant if Jessie's conscience got the better of her and she decided her fears should come before everyone else's needs. He couldn't let her do that to Thomas when he was still reeling from the consequences of her last freak-out.

It was understandable that she wanted to take care of everyone, but she took it to extremes. Making decisions on his behalf that only made them both miserable. That rollercoaster of absolute joy and utter devastation was not something he wanted to ride any more. As he'd told her before, he was too old for those games. All he wanted now was a happy settled life with the people he loved.

'We had a chat tonight. She wants to go into assisted living. I realised the unnecessary sacrifices I've made were because I'm afraid I'll make you miserable, that you'll resent me for inhibiting you. The way I've sometimes felt as a carer.'

The news was everything he wanted to hear but it was tinged with the hurt of knowing that Jessie hadn't come to the decision herself. 'That's great, but why are you here? What has that got to do with me?'

He saw the smile fall from her lips and took a step back to put some distance between them so he could think clearly. When he was near her, when she was touching him, he couldn't think of anything except being with her, and circumstances now meant he had more than himself to consider.

'I love you, Cameron.'

'Yet that has never been enough for you to be with me.'

'That's not fair.'

He shrugged. 'It's the truth.'

'I've been in a horrible situation my whole life. Only you ever made it bearable. I've only ever wanted what was best for the people I love. I'm probably never going to change.'

Cameron mulled over what she was saying to him and he realised that the selfless decisions she'd made over the years, though not always warranted or wanted, still made her the woman he loved. To ask her to change was impossible. If she'd been the kind of person who would've put her wants ahead of his, or her sick mother's, needs he probably wouldn't love her half as much as he did.

'I know,' he said softly, gathering her back in his arms. 'So, what are we going to do?'

'Well, I hadn't thought beyond apologising to the man I love and hoping he'd take me back.' She was looking up at him with such expectation and faith he was powerless to resist another second.

'Hmm, well, he might need a few more dates for you to convince him…and to let him have a say in things every once in a while,' he teased, only to earn himself a playful slap on the arm. 'But there's always a place for you in his heart.'

He kissed her again, a slow, leisurely display of his love, because now they had all the time in the world.

EPILOGUE

'THOMAS… SIMON…CAN you put the football away before you get your clothes dirty? Thank you.' Jessie folded her arms and waited for the boys to finish playing. Goodness knew how they'd managed to find a football at the register office, but they'd managed it.

She couldn't be angry with them when they were so good together, as though they were blood. Thomas had accepted Simon into the family just as easily as he'd accepted her. It had been a whirlwind year, her life, and theirs, changing beyond all recognition—for the better.

Her mother had made the transition into a care facility and seemed all the happier for it. She had friends and hobbies which filled her time and she had a new spark about her. It might have something to do with a certain Richard who resided there too and was never too far from her side when Jessie and Cameron visited. She was glad her mother had found someone too, they both deserved some happiness.

Once her mother had sold the house to pay for her care it was only natural for Jessie to move in with Cameron and Thomas. He'd asked her long before then, but she'd waited until her mother was settled before taking the next step herself. Cameron had been incredibly patient although, left up to him, they would have married last year, when he'd first proposed. He didn't want to waste any more time but Jessie had insisted they try living together first to make sure everyone was okay with the situation, including Thomas. She needn't have worried. Although there were moments when he found things difficult to handle, they managed, just like any other family.

With a stable home on offer for Simon, who had been living with a temporary foster family, it had been easier to get the green light on the adoption, although there had been endless paperwork and interviews to ensure it was the best environment for him. Thankfully, social services could see how much they could do for him too. He was now recovering well and attending the same school as Thomas. Both she and Cameron made sure to take time off so they could attend his follow-up appointments at the hospital, even though he had a different doctor now overseeing his progress.

Of course there were times when the loss of his parents became too much for him. But Jessie and Cameron made sure to talk about them often and kept their memory alive as much as possible for Simon so he wouldn't forget them.

Today, exchanging vows with Cameron was the last piece of the family jigsaw slotting into place.

'Can we go in now?' Thomas asked, pulling at his sapphire-blue tie, which matched his and his father's eyes.

'Yes, let's do this, boys.' With Thomas taking one arm and Simon taking the other, they made their way into the building and down the aisle to where her handsome husband-to-be was waiting for them.

They passed Ciara, Agnes, the social worker, and Jessie's mother, who were all smiling at the wedding party, enjoying the moment with them.

The registrar greeted everyone, then asked, 'Who here gives this woman away?'

The boys chorused, 'We do,' to a delighted audience before taking their seats in the front row.

Jessie faced Cameron, who was wearing a tailored navy suit and a smile as big as hers. Although they hadn't gone for a big church wedding, she'd still opted to wear a traditional white wedding dress, a thirties-style maxi with a fake fur wrap, and gypsophila in her hair. She wanted to look special for her husband as they embarked on their new life together.

'You look beautiful,' he whispered, taking her hand as she joined him, sending that familiar jolt of arousal she still felt whenever he touched her. She knew then that their love for one another would never die.

Whatever happened next, as they said their vows Jessie knew she was pledging herself not just to Cameron but to Thomas and Simon, and their future together. Every decision from now on would be a family affair. She would never be lonely again.

* * * * *

COMING SOON!

We really hope you enjoyed reading this book. If you're looking for more romance be sure to head to the shops when new books are available on

Thursday 11th May

To see which titles are coming soon, please visit

millsandboon.co.uk/nextmonth

MILLS & BOON

MILLS & BOON®

Coming next month

THE BROODING DOC AND THE SINGLE MUM
Louisa Heaton

Daniel couldn't stand still. He tried to. But his mind wouldn't let him settle. He felt as if his body was flooded with adrenaline and this was either a fight, flight or freeze response.

Most likely flight.

I thought about kissing her.

That was what he couldn't get out of his head. He'd been having such a fun time. A relaxing time. Playing football with Jack. He'd used to play football with Mason all the time, so the opportunity to play with Jack and remember what it had been like had been awesome! In a way, it had been almost as if Jack was his son. He'd been helping to guide him. Showing the little boy that he was interested in him. That he wanted to spend time with him. That he was important.

And then Stacey had joined them.

Penny had never joined in their football games. She'd always watched, or used the time that Daniel was with their son to get a few jobs done around the house. Daniel hadn't minded that. It had given them a little father-son bonding moment.

So when Stacey had joined in he'd been amazed, and then delighted. They'd had a fun time. It had been relaxing, the three of them together. Nice. Easy. So easy! He'd almost not been able to believe how easy it was for him to be with them.

And then the tackle.

They'd all gone for the ball at once and somehow tumbled into a tangle of arms and legs. And he'd landed on top of Stacey. Not fully. His hands had broken the fall, and he'd tried to avoid squashing her. But she'd been lying beneath him, red hair splayed out against the green grass. Her laughter-filled eyes had looked up at him, there'd been a smile on her face and he'd been so close to her!

He'd felt her breathing, her chest rising and falling. Her softness. Her legs entwined with his. Their faces had been so close. Mere inches away from each other! And the thought had risen unbidden to his mind.

What would it be like to kiss her?

Continue reading
THE BROODING DOC AND THE SINGLE MUM
Louisa Heaton

Available next month
www.millsandboon.co.uk

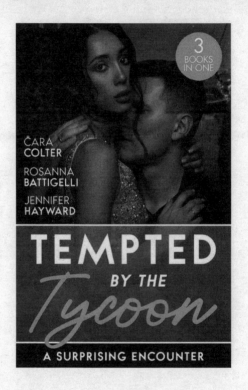

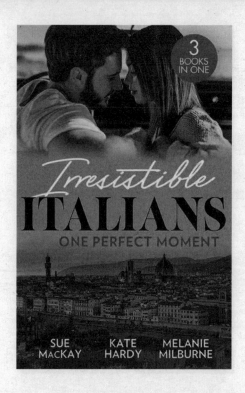

LET'S TALK

Romance

For exclusive extracts, competitions
and special offers, find us online:

f facebook.com/millsandboon

𝕐 @MillsandBoon

◉ @MillsandBoonUK

♪ @MillsandBoonUK

Get in touch on 01413 063 232

For all the latest titles coming soon, visit
millsandboon.co.uk/nextmonth

MILLS & BOON

THE HEART OF ROMANCE

A ROMANCE FOR EVERY READER

MODERN

Prepare to be swept off your feet by sophisticated, sexy and seductive heroes, in some of the world's most glamourous and romantic locations, where power and passion collide.

HISTORICAL

Escape with historical heroes from time gone by. Whether your passion is for wicked Regency Rakes, muscled Vikings or rugged Highlanders, awaken the romance of the past.

MEDICAL

Set your pulse racing with dedicated, delectable doctors in the high-pressure world of medicine, where emotions run high and passion, comfort and love are the best medicine.

True Love

Celebrate true love with tender stories of heartfelt romance, from the rush of falling in love to the joy a new baby can bring, and a focus on the emotional heart of a relationship.

Desire

Indulge in secrets and scandal, intense drama and sizzling hot action with heroes who have it all: wealth, status, good looks…everything but the right woman.

HEROES

The excitement of a gripping thriller, with intense romance at its heart. Resourceful, true-to-life women and strong, fearless men face danger and desire - a killer combination!

To see which titles are coming soon, please visit

millsandboon.co.uk/nextmonth

JOIN US ON SOCIAL MEDIA!

Stay up to date with our latest releases, author news and gossip, special offers and discounts, and all the behind-the-scenes action from Mills & Boon...

 @millsandboon

 @millsandboonuk

 facebook.com/millsandboon

 @millsandboonuk

It might just be true love...

GET YOUR ROMANCE FIX!

Get the latest romance news, exclusive author interviews, story extracts and much more!

blog.millsandboon.co.uk